BEAUTY AND DECEIT

A BEAUTY AND THE BEAST FAERIE TALE RETELLING

CAROL BETH ANDERSON

Elixa PRESS

Beauty and Deceit: A Beauty and the Beast Faerie Tale Retelling
by Carol Beth Anderson

Published by
Eliana Press
P.O. Box 2452
Cedar Park, TX 78630

www.carolbethanderson.com

Cover Design:
Christian Bentulan

Originally published as *Beauty and Deceit: A Faerie Tale Retelling* on Kindle Vella.

Paperback ISBN: 978-1-949384-19-2

First Edition

LISTEN TO THE STORY

Immerse yourself in the story by listening to the audiobook of *Beauty and Deceit*, narrated by the author.

Get it from Amazon, Audible, or Apple.

To Amy D.

And to every one-of-a-kind person who's underestimated by the world.

You are strong, worthy, and courageous.

To Jason.

"Because I love you."

"*H*ello there, handsome. You look particularly dashing today."

It was his morning ritual—standing naked in front of a full-length mirror, speaking affirmations.

"That skin. So striking. And were there ever shoulders so broad? There's strength in that body. Strength and beauty." He used to choke on that last word, but he'd learned to say it like he meant it.

The affirmations weren't for his ears. He said them for Cerise, the female who'd cursed him nearly ten years ago and now spied on him through all the mirrors in this castle. Every morning, he hoped she was indeed watching him as he claimed to love what she'd turned him into.

It was petty. But it was all he had left.

After winking one red eye, he turned, giving the mirror a dashing wave with his hairless, rat-like tail. He imagined Cerise's face, screwed up in disgust.

He dressed, and his broad, bare feet slapped on the marble floors as he made his way to the kitchen. He was just digging into a large plate of scrambled eggs when a tap sounded on the door that led outside. He jumped at the noise. No one had visited him in nearly ten years.

"Who is it?" His voice, rich and regal, was the one part of him the curse hadn't changed.

"Jacqueline," came the reply.

His old governess. He would've flushed with excitement if his skin, cursed to retain a stark-white pallor, were capable of it. He rushed to the door and threw it open.

Hovering there was a pixie, her purple butterfly wings beating rapidly. A hesitant smile split the pale-orange skin of her face. A breeze ruffled her hair, which was colored with the reds, oranges, and yellows of a flame. The tip of her head would be barely above his knees were she standing, but she packed a lot of beauty and energy into that little form. Like all faeries, she appeared young, and in her case, it was true. Jacqueline—Jackie for short—was only sixty-five. She'd barely begun her immortal life.

She threw tiny arms around his neck, and it was all he could do not to crush her with his too-powerful muscles. He gave her the tightest hug he dared before stepping back. "Jackie, how did you get here? Why did it take so long? What—"

"Hush, sweetie."

They were the words she'd said thousands of times in the first twenty years of his life. They were as effective now as they'd been when he was wailing in his cradle. His mouth closed.

"I was here the day Cerise cursed you," she said. "I fled before she saw me."

He sucked in a sharp breath. "You were there? Thank the gods you didn't come to the front door today."

"Why?"

"Cerise knew someone escaped that day. She felt it. She cursed you too. If she sees you through any of the mirrors in this house, you'll experience the same fate as my servants. There's a large mirror in the entry hall." He shuddered, then leapt up, eyes wild. "Hide in the pantry. Just for a minute."

As Jackie obeyed, he grabbed the steel soup pot from the stove and shoved it in a cabinet, then did the same with a ladle and several pieces of silver. He didn't know if Cerise could spy through other reflective items as she could with mirrors, but he wasn't taking any chances. Breathing heavily, he said, "Come on out. You can't stay long. It's not safe."

"What did she do to your servants?" she whispered.

"Turned them to stone."

Jackie covered her little mouth with a hand. But she'd always been levelheaded in a crisis. She pointed at a chair. "Sit." When he obeyed, she sat on the table, cross-legged. "I'll update you on all the things you've missed while trapped in this big house, and we'll talk about breaking your curse."

"All right."

"Everyone thinks you died of a fever," she said. "Cerise told them a mysterious beast swept in afterward and took over your estate. I know the truth, of course, but I can't seem to correct others when they spread her lies."

"That's part of the curse. We can't discuss it with anyone who doesn't already know about it. Not that I've had a chance to try."

She nodded. "You may not realize that Cerise cursed your estate too, moving it out of Faerie. It's on Earth now, protected from mortal detection."

He gaped at her. The thick fog Cerise had put on his land's borders had kept him from seeing the truth.

"It took me almost two years to find the estate," Jackie continued, "and eight more to discover a weakness in the border barrier."

All he could do was shake his head.

Jackie darted close to his face, jolting him to attention. "I don't care why she cursed you. All I care about is how to break it. What were the terms?"

"I have to get someone to agree to marry me. For love."

"Deadline?"

"Ten years."

The pixie drew in a sharp gasp. "You have less than two months to find a wife?"

His shoulders drooped. "Or be stuck in this form forever."

"There's more at stake than your looks and your servants," Jackie said. "Cerise did such a good job creating the border barrier that even she can't penetrate it. Months ago, she sent dozens of armed faeries to find a way through. As soon as they succeed, she'll steal your estate, bring it back to Faerie, and declare herself queen over all your lands and people."

His heart stuttered. Cerise would never get away with such an action if her fellow Fae knew he was still alive. Stuck in this beastly form, however, he could never prove who he was. His kingdom was small . . . but it was his. It had been ruled by his family since before the Fae had a written language. He pulled in a lungful of air. "I have to find a wife. One who will actually love this." He gestured to his beastly body. "It's impossible."

Jackie floated in front of him again, her green eyes sparkling with mischief. "It's not, now that I know how to get through the barrier. I'll bring faeries here—females who want to marry."

"They'll never come. Not for a beast."

Her high voice trilled with laughter. "Cerise's lies backfired. They think you're a beast who was strong enough to take over an estate and move it out of Faerie. You may not be pretty, but in their minds, you're intriguing, powerful . . . and wealthy. They'll come."

"How am I supposed to make one of them love me in a matter of weeks?"

Jackie fluttered about the room, her small forehead wrinkled in deep thought. Several minutes passed before she landed on the kitchen table and looked up into his red eyes. "It will be challenging. That's why we need to create an atmosphere that heightens their emotions and gives them a reason to fight for you."

His hairless brow furrowed. "How?"

Her bright smile made her whole face shine. "We'll have a forty-day competition. The winner gets your heart."

"A competition." He let out a low laugh. "It just might work. I wish you could be here for it. I could use your guidance."

She placed her small, soft hands on his pale-as-death cheeks. "I'll bring the females here and get them inside the barrier. If there's a way for me to help you further, I'll find it."

YOU'VE HEARD THE STORIES OF FAERIES IN THIS FOREST

I'm holding the most beautiful hat I've ever made—thick wool, flawlessly knitted. It's mostly cream colored, but I used a little of my precious green-dyed yarn for a single row of pines around the middle, like the trees in the forest near our village.

This hat will keep someone else's head very warm. The money it brings in will get me closer to patching our roof, so my own head can stay dry.

I'm considering whether there's an easier way to shape the hat's crown when my sister's voice breaks into my reverie. "Aeryn," Yvonne says, "the sun is setting!"

I gasp and stand, still holding the hat. The ball of cream yarn drops from my lap, turning brown as it rolls along the dirt that serves as a floor in this house. A yelp leaves my mouth as I grab it and brush it off, before shoving it and the hat into my work basket. "Why didn't you tell me how late it was?"

Yvonne's curly blonde hair quivers as she shakes her head. "Don't blame me! I was busy darning socks for Mrs. What's-Her-Name."

As I pull on my cloak, boots, and an old hat, I snap, "There are four of us. Someone should be able to keep track of the time."

"Brigitte is trying to put together something for dinner."

"And Marc?"

"Sleeping."

I huff. My brother Marc is twenty-one, a year younger than me. You'd think by now, he would have a job, but he always has some excuse. I grab a lantern and sling an empty bag on my shoulder, suspecting I'll need it. "I don't know why I'm always the one who has to do this," I say as I leave our little house.

"Yes, you do know." Yvonne's voice follows me through the closed door.

She's right, I do. I'm the oldest of four siblings, and our father is more likely to listen to me than anyone else. When he gets paid every other Friday, I rush to the mine to convince him to hand over his coins so I can buy food for the family.

Unless I forget. Like today. He left the mine at least half an hour ago, and it only takes fifteen minutes to walk home. That means he took a detour.

And I'm sure I know where he is.

I jog along the dirt road into town, every little stone making its presence known through the thin soles of my old boots. I shouldn't have brought the cloak and hat. The early-spring air still holds winter's chill, but running makes me warm. Within five minutes, I've shoved the hat in my pocket.

When the tavern comes into sight, I slow to a walk, catching my breath. I know I'm a mess, my pale skin bright red from exertion and strands of strawberry-blonde hair sticking to my sweaty face. Oh, well. My days of impressing people with my looks are long gone.

As I enter, my father's laugh fills the room. I spy him sitting on a barstool, handing coins to the busy bartender. Everyone around him is patting his bony back, thanking him. A big smile splits his scruffy blond-and-silver beard.

"Damn it," I mutter. Swearing is the single satisfaction poverty has afforded me. I wasn't allowed to do it when I was considered a lady, but when we sold our possessions, we let go of a lot of silly rules too. I need such words at a moment like this, when I realize my father isn't just buying booze for himself, but for those around him too. If he's spent all his coin, we won't have any food for the next two weeks.

I weave through tables. When I pass well-heeled patrons, my heart aches for the security of a past I can't return to. For the first twenty years of my life, I took our large house, full of luxuries and servants, for granted. Then pirates took Father's merchant ship, and he had to sell everything to pay his debts.

That was two years ago. I can't hold the pirate attack against him. It wasn't his fault. Now, however, he barely makes anything at the copper mine. When he spends his limited income on drink . . . well, there was a time when I forgave him freely, but that's gotten harder and harder the more often my stomach is aching and empty.

"Father," I say breathlessly when I reach the bar, "let's go home."

He gives me a grin turned slightly wobbly from alcohol, and God help me, I want to slap his flushed cheeks. I'd never do it—I love the man—but how could he betray us again?

"Aeryn," he says, "I'd offer you a drink, but I'm sorry to say . . ." He pats his pockets, which I'm certain are empty. He turns to the men around him and speaks in the booming voice that served him well when he was a merchant, making deals on the goods he traded. "Do you all know Aeryn? My eldest, the pride of my heart. She's turned into such a beauty!" He lifts a hand to pat my cheek, and when he lowers it, his elbow knocks over a mug of beer.

My whole body is now warm with embarrassment. "Let's go. Now."

Father doesn't argue. He's reasonably alert and steady on his feet, thank heaven. I hold his hand, not letting go even when we're out of the tavern and have turned onto the road.

"You're going the wrong way," he says, trying to pull me in the opposite direction.

I tighten my grip and keep walking. "We're heading into the forest to forage for food for the next two weeks. All we have left at home is half a loaf of stale bread and a small cheese rind."

He pulls me to a stop. "That can't be right! We have mushrooms and salted fish, and I think even a few apples—"

"We *had* all that. It's gone." I don't tell him I caught Marc feasting on the rest of the fish when he thought we were all in bed last night. My father doesn't need his heart broken yet again by his wastrel of a son.

Father's face drops. "But the money from your knitting . . . ?"

"We use it for rent and home repairs." Of course, it seems there's never any left for the repairs the landlord refuses to do.

He blinks. "I know nothing about foraging."

"I'll show you what to do. I've gotten good at it." I pull him along, increasing my pace. It's nearly dark out, and my lantern oil is almost gone.

We enter the trees together and soon find a patch of dandelions—weeds to some, but salvation for a hungry family. Even the roots are edible. I curse when I realize I forgot to bring a spade. "We'll dig with our hands," I say. "Go deep; get as much of the roots as you can."

We set to work. Before long, I have to use one of my precious matches to light the lantern. "Hurry!" I say.

We dig up all the plants and shove them in my bag before moving on. Father tries to make conversation, but the same anger that quickened my steps has also closed my mouth.

I head for an area where I recently saw some kudzu, another plant with edible roots. When we arrive, I shine my lantern over the entire area and let out a long sigh. The soil is overturned, and the pretty, purple flowers are all gone, along with the green plants they were attached to. Someone else got here first.

"It's dark, Aeryn," my father says, "and I just felt a drop of rain. We should go home. You can come back tomorrow, with your sisters."

"No!" I shout. "We're not leaving until I fill this bag! I've covered for your mistakes enough times!"

"You've heard the stories of faeries in this forest. They're dangerous!"

For a moment, my body aches for the days when he'd pull us kids close—two of us on his lap, two sitting at his feet—to read us faerie tales. He didn't stop when we outgrew both his lap and the fantastical stories. He just switched to more grown-up books, reading them in his warm voice. My favorites were the true ones, books about nature, history, design, and far-away cultures.

The people who bought our house worked his books into the deal. We left every single volume behind.

I swallow the memories down. "You don't believe those faerie tales any more than I do, Father. Now come on!"

I push forward, fury filling my head until it aches from the pressure. Tears blur my vision, and I barely even see the path in front of me as my feet move ever faster. I forget what I'm here for, too distracted by the pain in my head and my heart.

A few drops of rain plop on my cheeks and hands. Then, it's like someone took a sickle to the clouds. Cold sheets of water drench us in seconds.

"We have to go home," my father says.

In the dim lantern light, I scan the area. It's blurred by rain. But even if the sun were shining, nothing around me would be familiar.

We're lost in a frigid forest.

"Do you know which direction home is?" I ask my father.

As he shakes his head, the lantern flame goes out, the oil spent. Darkness envelops us.

I set down the useless lantern—I'll have to come back for it later. "Give me your hand!" I shout. Father and I grope around until our cold, slick palms are smashed together, our fingers intertwined so we don't lose each other. Then I run, pulling him behind me.

"Stop!" he cries. "You don't know where you're going!"

I barely hear him. All I can think is that this feels more like winter rain than spring rain, and we may freeze to death, and my siblings at home need food, and they'll wonder where we are, and it's my fault we're lost, but it's my father's fault this happened at all, and . . . and the only option is to keep running, my free hand extended in front of me.

The trees in this part of the forest aren't too close together, but my fingers still frequently scrape against bark and branches. We change direction countless times. A branch finds my face, scratching my cheek. I wince and keep running.

Soon, the forest grows thicker, and we have no choice but to walk.

"Darling," my father says, "the trees are blocking a lot of the rain here. Let's stop. We're lost. We need to wait out the storm."

I hate the thought of spending the night here, but I don't have a better idea. I sit against a tree trunk, wrapping my soaking-wet cloak tight around me. As soon as I'm settled, I begin trembling. My teeth are chattering, and I've never been so miserable.

This is my fault. I'm the one who makes plans for our family, ensuring we have food and can pay the rent. Tonight, I let my emotions get the best of me. If only I'd put more thought into this, we would've never gotten lost. A little moan exits my throat.

"Oh, Aeryn." My father sits next to me and pulls me close to his side, like he did when I was little. "We'll be all right, darling. As soon as it gets light and the clouds disappear, the sun will tell us what direction to go. We'll be all right."

His warmth seeps into me, despite how wet we both are. My breathing slows. At this moment, he's not the man who lost his fortune and started drinking to forget his troubles. He's just my daddy, holding me tight.

I'm about to fall asleep when I hear something that makes me sit up, every muscle on alert, ears straining.

Snort. Snort.

It's a wild hog. And where there's one hog, there are more. Good meat, if you've got something to kill them with. We don't . . . which means we're the meat. Hog attacks are common around here.

They'll dig their tusks into us. Take great, ripping bites.

My heart threatens to punch through my chest as I picture it.

Our screams will fill the forest, unheard by any but our attackers.

We'll at last go silent. They'll continue feasting. When they finish, only our bones will be left behind, to grow brittle on the forest floor.

I can't bring myself to breathe. I'm frozen in place . . . until my father whispers in my ear. "Run."

We leap to our feet and, hand in hand, rush through the thick trees.

The rain and our footsteps are so loud, I can't tell if we've left the hogs behind. And we certainly can't stop to listen. We run and run and run. My skin is icy, but there's fire in my lungs and legs. I keep expecting to collapse.

But it's my father who falls, crying out, his fingers releasing mine.

I fall to my knees next to him. "Father!"

Between moans, he manages to speak. "I tripped. I think—" He lets out a groan full of agony. "Oh hell, I feel something poking through—the bones—"

"Bones?" I gasp.

"My leg—it's broken."

2

MEDICINAL MUSHROOMS

"Oh, Daddy, no—what can I—I don't know what to do!" I'm kneeling next to my injured father, panting as if I were still running.

He releases an agonized moan, a sound I've never heard come from his mouth.

I stand. "Daddy! I'm getting help!"

"No!" There's still strength in his voice. "You'll never find me again. Stay. Until it's light."

He's right. I can't see a thing. If I leave now, I'll just get more lost.

It's still terribly cold, the rain refusing to let up. I grope around and find a spot beneath some closely spaced trees. "I have to get you somewhere a little more dry," I say. "I'll pull you. It's not far." I grab him underneath his arms. He cries and curses, but he helps me too, using his good leg to push himself along. Soon, we're under the trees.

"What can I do?" I force the words past the frightened knot in my throat.

"Try to set it," he says. "And wrap it. I'm bleeding. A lot."

I've never been the one to handle injuries in our home. Brigitte, who at nineteen is three years younger than me, doesn't flinch at the sight of blood. I can barely bandage a needle-pricked finger without getting nauseated.

I swallow my bile-tinged hesitation and ask him where the injury is. He guides me with pained words, and my fingers easily find the broken shin bone that's pressing against his right pant leg. I haven't eaten more than a few bites of bread today, but my belly lurches, threatening to expel it all.

I ask my father how to proceed, but I can't understand his words through his groans. His pain must be worsening. So I do what seems right. First, I tear his pants. His cuffs are so frayed that the fabric rips easily, all the way up to the knee, where there's a hole. I tear off two strips of fabric.

The injury is exposed now, and I'm oddly thankful my fingers are numb. It's making this job harder, but the splintered bone and sticky blood don't bother me as much with my sense of touch stifled by cold.

I don't warn him before I grab his leg and do a terrible mixture of pressing and pulling, attempting to set the bone. The roar of pain that leaves his chest is so forceful, I fear he's damaged his throat permanently. Then he goes silent and stops replying to my questions.

"Daddy!" I scream, my bloodied hands finding his neck. There's still a pulse. I hold my hand over his mouth and sigh in relief when a soft puff of air hits my palm. He just passed out, then. Probably a blessing.

I work as quickly as my cold hands and lack of knowledge allow, numbness spreading even to my turbulent gut. The bone feels like it's set, though I doubt I did it properly. I use the strips of dirty fabric from his pants to wrap the whole thing, hoping I'm doing more good than harm.

Then I lay in the crook of his shoulder, my arm around his thin waist, trying to keep us both warm. I begin shivering again. He wakes, moaning and pulling me closer.

We spend the night like that. My mind swings between wordless anxiety and wild flights of imagination, in which I picture the worst ways this could turn out. I doze off once and have the strangest dream of faeries at a castle in this very forest. They have wings and pointed ears and skin in shades I've never seen on a human. Purple rose petals float in the air, filling it with a sweet scent. It's all beautiful until I glimpse a beastly male faerie with bright white skin, red eyes, and a thick, hairless tail.

Then I wake, gasping. Wondering if maybe the faerie stories that float around my village are true. If perhaps the Fae are near here, making merry in their castle, unaware of the frozen woman and her injured father huddled on the forest floor.

The rain finally stops just before the sky turns gray with pre-dawn light. I hug my father tighter, sure of one thing: as infuriating as he can be, I'll do anything to save him.

When there's enough light for me to see where I'm going, I kiss his cheek and tell him I'm headed off to find help. He mutters an indecipherable response and appears to be asleep again by the time I'm sitting up.

In the faint light, I check his leg. The bone is no longer sticking out, and the makeshift bandages are tight. The skin around the injury, however, is swollen and bright red, and when I touch it, heat sears my cold fingers. I look closer and see yellow pus at the edges of the torn skin.

"No," I whisper. I know how quickly infections can turn deadly. "Love you, Daddy," I say as I push myself to my feet.

I note the sun's position. Sure enough, we ran in the wrong direction last night. Who knows how far into the forest we ventured? I run again, but this time, I pay close attention to tree stumps and broken branches and stones—the forest's natural landmarks. Once I fetch the midwife (the closest thing our village has to a doctor), I need to be able to guide her to my father.

I've been running for a few minutes when I encounter a creek, roaring with water from the torrential rain. I don't think I need to cross it to get home, so I nearly ignore it . . . until my eyes spot something on the opposite side. Bluish-brown mushrooms, speckled with black spots.

I know those mushrooms. They fight infection better than anything else. They could save my father's life. I have no idea how far away our village is. I can fetch this medicine and be back at his side in a quarter-hour. The delay will be worth it.

There's only one problem. The swollen creek is too wide to jump across.

I run along the bank and find a place where several stones protrude from the water, creating a precarious natural bridge. Not giving myself time to reconsider, I step on the first one.

It's jagged and more slippery than I expected. The next rock is worse—its top sits just underneath the surface, and when I put weight on it, it tilts back and forth. Holding my breath, I keep going. The third rock isn't too slippery, and my confidence grows. With my left foot, I step on the fourth rock. It's wide and mostly flat. The sturdiest yet.

Or at least I think it is. Until I lift my right foot, and the worn leather sole of my left boot slips off the flat rock. I tumble into the icy water.

Screaming, I grasp for something—a rock, a branch, anything. The only thing my fingers clutch is the madly rushing water that carries my body farther into the forest.

I tumble over sharp rocks that claw at my skin. My shoulder slams into a boulder. I try to lift myself onto it, but the strong current continues to pull me along. Water splashes over my nose and mouth, and I'm coughing wildly when my whole head dips beneath the surface. I emerge and cough up cold water, then gasp for air.

I grasp for a tree branch overhead, but my fingers barely graze it.

Then I look up and see a huge rock just ahead. I try to push myself out of its path, but I'm helpless against this creek that has turned into a powerful river.

The water spins me around. My head slams against the rock.

The frigid, wet world turns black.

3

A PATH OF PURPLE ROSE PETALS

My return to awareness is unpleasant, to say the least. I'm coughing violently, again spewing water from my lungs. I'm on my back, so I turn to my side, propping myself on an elbow.

My coughing slows at last. Spent, I pass out again.

When I wake, I take stock of myself and my surroundings. I'm still in the creek, which has turned wide, shallow, and slow moving. I'm shivering uncontrollably. My head aches terribly, and my whole body feels both bruised and numb … an odd combination. The sun is high overhead, and it's so bright, my brain feels like it's burning. I've been out for hours.

I should be dead, but I guess I survived, because I'm in way too much pain to be in Heaven, and I refuse to consider the possibility of ending up somewhere else for eternity. I let out a weary laugh.

Then I remember my father. Despite the pain, I stand. Dizziness nearly sends me to my knees. I will myself to stay upright and look around.

Nothing is familiar. I have no idea how far I traveled in the creek.

Regardless of distance, I must go back to fetch those medicinal mushrooms for my father. Then I'll have to cross the creek, which might require me to walk all the way back here, where it's shallow. I certainly won't brave the slippery rocks again.

I trudge through the murky water, then step onto the soggy bank. Mud squishes around my feet with every step. The sole of my right boot is detached at the back now, and there's a hole in the toe of the left one. But I have bigger things to worry about than dirty, damaged boots. Eyes locked on the ground to prevent me from stumbling, I take one painfully slow step after another.

Something colorful catches my attention. A few inches from my right foot is a purple rose petal.

Purple? I've never seen a purple rose. There are plenty of wild roses in this area, but they're all red or pink. And they're tiny, the thorns sometimes bigger than the blooms. This single petal is almost as big as my palm.

Someone must have cultivated it. And that means a talented gardener likely lives nearby. Such a person would probably have knowledge of the herbs and medicinal fungi in the area.

I bend down. Gritting my teeth against the pain, I pick up the petal. A sweet fragrance hits me. I blink, and my mind fills with a vision of rose petals floating in the air. I have this strange feeling it's not the first time I've seen such a thing. I shake my aching head to clear it.

Then I notice another petal. And another. A deeper chill comes over me as I realize they're lying in a perfect line, creating a winding path through the trees.

Could these unnatural petals be a product of my imagination? I almost convince myself they are, but they don't disappear or move as I stare at them, and the one in my hand is velvety soft, as real as the mud in my toes.

Oddest of all, they almost seem to be calling to me, begging me to follow them. For a moment, I think there's music emanating from the purple path, but when I stop breathing and put all my focus into listening, I hear nothing but the creek and distant birds.

I stand for several long moments, weighing my options. Try to get back to my father, all alone? Or seek help from the gardener who cultivates purple roses—and perhaps grows more useful plants too?

My mind is too fuzzy to think for long, and I'm too cold to keep standing still. For a second, I again think I hear music. My numb, dirty feet make my decision for me, trudging along the rose-petal path.

The petals lead me into the trees, which soon swallow me up. It's darker than it was out in the open, which helps my head a little. The lack of light should make it harder to see the petals. They, however, seem to glow a bit, remaining bright and vibrant on the shadowy forest floor.

I'm still dizzy, and every step is a chore. After a couple of painful minutes, I spy something strange up ahead through the trees. I frown. It's almost like I'm looking at a pure-white blizzard, but that can't be right, because it's a sunny spring day. I get closer and realize it's not snow. It's fog. It shifts with the breeze as I'd expect it to, but it's so thick, I'm pretty sure my hand would disappear if it entered the strange whiteness.

Once I have that thought, I don't have a choice but to try it. I've always been the curious sort, the one in the family who has to investigate everything. I approach the fog, my headache and shivers almost forgotten for the moment. I lift my hand and thrust it forward.

My fingertips hit the white substance but don't penetrate it. When I pull my hand back, I leave little divots on the surface. The impressions quickly refill with white. I try again, then again. It's impenetrable. I look up. The wall of white rises unthinkably high, filling my line of sight, disappearing into the sky itself.

My father's face enters my mind, along with his groans from last night. "What am I doing?" I say aloud. It doesn't matter how fascinating this strange white stuff is. My father has been lying on the forest floor for hours, fighting infection. Maybe fighting for his life. And I'm here investigating a strange wall of fog?

I spin around. I have no choice but to follow the petals back to the creek, then gather mushrooms for my father. I made it this far—maybe I can make it farther, despite my pounding head, dizziness, and persistent shivers. A master gardener is of no use to me if their garden is inaccessible beyond a solid cloud of white.

When I look down, I gasp. There are no petals. I stopped following them to investigate the fog. I do my best to go back in the direction I came, and when I see the petals again, I whisper, "Oh, thank God."

The petal path, it turns out, doesn't go all the way to the foggy wall. Instead, it veers off in a new direction, winding through the trees.

Maybe it will lead to a gardener after all.

My mind spins in circles. Mushrooms or petals? My father or a gardener? The very act of thinking sends a new wave of exhaustion through my body. *Just stick with the plan,* I tell myself. *Petals. Gardener.*

Once again, I follow the path. The fragrant petals lead me back to the solid, cloud-like substance. On the ground in front of the barrier, something reflects a ray of sunlight that's made its way through the trees.

It's a mirror, half buried in dirt. Drawn to it like iron to a lode-stone, I fall to my knees. I pick up the mirror and realize it wasn't buried—it's broken. It's half of a round mirror, one side sharp and jagged.

When I hold it up, my face isn't looking back at me. Instead, I see a smiling woman with pointed ears, pale-orange skin, and hair that's a riot of colors—red, orange, and yellow.

I drop the mirror and scramble backward, letting out the strangest sound—something between a gasp and a moan. It would be a scream if I weren't so tired.

But once again, curiosity triumphs over my uncertainty. A mirror

. . . with someone else's face in it? I can't just leave it there without investigating.

I crawl forward cautiously and pick up the mirror again.

The colorful woman is still there.

"Can you see me?" she asks in a high-pitched voice. When my eyes widen, she lets out a musical laugh. "Oh, you can—of course you can!"

4

FAE BARGAIN

The mirror begins to shake, and it takes me a moment to realize my hands are trembling. What exactly is happening here? All I can think of is how Father used to read us tales of faeries using mirrors to communicate. Magical faeries . . . who only exist on the pages of storybooks.

Right?

"What is this?" I murmur.

"It's okay." The woman in the mirror's voice instantly soothes me. "You've had quite a day, haven't you? I was flying about in your forest, and I saw you hit your head on that rock in the water. You're too big for me to carry, but I tried to keep your mouth and nose above the surface. I would've talked to you, if only you'd stayed awake for more than a few seconds. So I left the rose petals and the mirror. How's your head feeling, sweetie?"

I blink at her. "It hurts. A lot. And I'm so cold."

"Past the barrier, healing and warmth await you. I just finished up my task—I'm coming your way. I'll bring you to the castle."

Just as when I picked up the first rose petal, images assault me—

ones I seem to have seen before, of a beautiful castle and strangely colorful beings, some of them flying.

Faeries.

It was a dream, I think. And the woman in the mirror . . . she'd fit perfectly in it.

My breaths come faster. "You're a faerie."

She nods briskly. "First you've met, I presume?"

"Faeries don't exist," I whisper.

She laughs. "I beg to differ. I'm proof of it, as are you. You see— are you clearheaded enough to listen to me, dear?"

"I think so."

"Very well. I know this will be hard to hear, but if you were entirely human, this barrier's magic would look like nothing more than forest trees to you. Before reaching it, you'd have felt an urge to turn around and go the other way. You also wouldn't be able to see me through the mirror if you didn't have some Fae blood. It's why I rescued you—I sensed your heritage as soon as I saw you."

Fae blood? It can't be true. I'm human—wonderfully, imperfectly human. I can't have any connection to a race of beings I didn't even believe in until now.

More questions than I can count flood my mind, but I focus on what's truly important. "You said I can be healed. But I'm not the one who really needs help. My father broke his leg, and it's infected." I point behind me. "He's back there—I was trying to get medicinal mushrooms for him when I fell in the creek. Please tell me you can help him. My head will heal on its own. His leg could kill him."

Her pretty lips purse, and her forehead creases in concern. Sympathy fills her eyes. Which is why her next words surprise me. "I'll help him for a price."

"A price?" All at once, I remember the faerie tales Father used to read me about ignorant humans who made bargains with faeries. Mortals never got the better end of those deals. They always ended up imprisoned, dead, or somehow cursed. My heart pounds against my ribs.

"Not a bad price," she says. "There's a faerie in the castle inside this barrier who needs a wife. I've gathered nine Fae females to spend forty days here, competing for his heart. I wanted ten—and when I saw you, I knew you were meant to be the last. Join the contest, and not only will I help your father, but your whole family will also have all the provisions they need for as long as you're here."

I can't say yes to a Fae bargain. The risk is too high when I have a family counting on me to keep them fed and clothed, not just for the next forty days, but for the foreseeable future. If I go into this castle, I may never come out. "No," I say. "I can't do it."

"You don't want provision for your family?" the faerie asks.

"My family is fine. I just want medicine for my father—please—"

"I saw your clothes and boots," the flame-haired faerie says gently. "I don't think your family is fine."

"But . . . I'm human. Or at least mostly human, I guess?" I don't know why I'm arguing the logistics of this, why I'm arguing at all with a faerie. But the words keep tumbling out. "The Fae are immortal, so I can't marry one—I would—"

"Let's solve that problem if it becomes one, child. I'm not asking you to marry him today—just to compete."

"Against full-blooded Fae. I'll never win." I shouldn't be speculating about the results of a contest I've refused to enter, but I'm too cold and in too much pain to be logical.

She gives me a gentle smile. "I think he may like you. I just brought all those other faeries to the castle, and you're so different from them. He's . . . he's different too."

"Different how?"

"You'll see." This time, her voice comes from two places: the mirror I'm holding, plus a spot in the air several feet away from me.

I turn that direction and jump to my feet when I see her—a winged faerie, small enough for me to carry in my arms. My mouth drops open. "Is he tiny like you?"

Her delighted laugh fills the space around me. "He's not tiny." She reaches out a hand. "I'd like the other half of my mirror, please.

It's my favorite one—and I broke it just so I could talk to you. I knew I should've brought a spare with me." She shakes her head, clearly disappointed in herself for the terrible error of not carrying multiple mirrors.

Faeries, I'm beginning to think, are very odd.

I hand her the mirror. "I can't leave my family. I definitely can't leave my father." A high-pitched, pleading tone has taken over my words.

All at once, she flinches, her eyes widening. "Hush!" Her voice is soft but full of command. "There are Fae soldiers outside this barrier, looking for a way in. You're speaking too loudly, and I don't know what they'll do to you if they discover you." She's talking so fast, I can barely keep up. "I swear to you, if you join this competition, I'll do all I can to ensure your father and family are fine. If you don't win, you can go home, with your family a little better off than before you left. Please, child. Come."

Tears spring to my eyes. I need more information—I don't make decisions without plenty of time to analyze the options, unless I'm panicked like I was during our foraging trip. That experience went badly enough to convince me to never act without thinking again.

The faerie flutters in front of me, her green eyes fixing on my pale blue ones. "This is the only sure way to save your father. But we must go now, before the soldiers get here."

I look all around us. All I see are trees, underbrush, and the white barrier. I hear nothing but the breeze and birds. I don't even know if she's telling the truth about the soldiers. I swallow and speak, the words strained and quiet as they exit my tight throat. "How do I know you'll save him?"

With a reluctant sigh, she hands me back my half of the mirror. "After I reach him, I'll show him to you in the mirror. I'll help him however I can."

"Wait—you're going to him personally? Aren't you taking me inside?"

She gives me a sad smile. "I'll get you through the barrier, but I won't stay inside. The castle is a dangerous place for me. However, I'll tell you what I told the male whose heart you'll be competing for. If I can find a way to help you during the competition, I will."

"Okay." I can't believe the word is leaving my throat. But how else am I supposed to save my father? My legs are trembling with cold, weariness, and pain. I've never felt this weak. If I try to save my father myself, he and I may both die in this forest, never to be found. "Show me how to get in."

"We must hurry."

She takes my hand and ushers me along the strange, foggy barrier. My head pounds with every step, and I'm relieved when she halts. We're standing at a place that, to me, looks exactly like the one we just left. Brow furrowed in concentration, the flying faerie brings her hand to a spot in the barrier, a few feet off the ground. Unlike me, her fingers go through. She twists her wrist several times, as if she's unlocking something.

Then she grins and lets out a soft laugh. Still holding my hand, she pulls me forward. This time, the fog allows me to enter.

5

HE LOOKS LIKE A MONSTER

Inside the foggy barrier, I'm hit with a slew of sensations. The mist is surprisingly dry and powdery, and it exerts a strange pressure on me, like it wants to break through my skin. My heart pounds so hard, I fear I'll break a rib. Then the pressure lessens. I'm warm all over, my shivers gone. My head still aches, and the dizziness is worse in this world of white, but the heat of the barrier makes me feel better than I have in hours.

I can't see anything except the white fog. Even my body is lost to it. The faerie continues to pull me. We walk for perhaps half a minute, then emerge from the barrier into an environment I can only call *perfect*.

While the barrier's heat would've quickly grown uncomfortable, the temperature in this new location is ideal—warm but not hot, with a breeze that dances over my skin. I'm standing on bright green grass that's thick and lush. We're near the top of a series of gentle hills. The largest features a big garden leading to a castle.

Many of the faerie tales my father read to us were illustrated, but I never saw a castle so beautiful on those pages. As best as I can tell, it's made of white marble. Where the sun hits it just right, little rainbows dance on the surface. The structure is large, with five levels and more windows than I care to count. All four corners feature beautiful round towers that slope gently inward until they form sharp points. They're so high that my breath catches just looking at them.

The faerie flies right in front of my face and hovers there, her wings a blur. "Where is your father?"

As best as I can, I tell her how to find him and the medicinal mushrooms.

She nods. "I'll go to him. You're in bad shape too. I can touch you and give you enough strength to reach the castle. But it will be your host who heals you fully."

"He can do that?"

"All the Fae have at least some healing power." She holds out two tiny hands. "May I?"

I nod. She rests her hands atop my head, and my headache and dizziness lessen as some of my strength returns.

"Go ahead, dear," she says, pulling her hands away. "Tell him Jackie sent you. Please whisper it softly in his ear—don't say my name aloud." She points to the mirror in my hand. "Put that in your pocket. You can call to me any time. But do so outside the castle. If you must speak to me inside, ensure you are in a room without any mirrors."

I put the mirror in my pocket, thankful that the fabric of my skirt is too thick for the broken edges to poke through. A dozen questions fill my mind, but she's already turned back toward the barrier.

I walk across the hills. The mist dried my boots and clothing, and now I'm shedding clumps of crusty, dehydrated mud with every step. My strength is almost gone when I reach the large, unwalled garden.

I see several rose bushes featuring every bright color I could imagine, including a familiar purple shade. Other plants fill my sight— ferns and trees, hedges and herbs. Dozens of realistic statues, clearly created by a master sculptor, stand all over the area. There are males and females and even a few children, all with pointed ears. *Faeries.* They're facing an open circle of grass in the center of the garden.

I slow my pace to admire it all, but I don't stop walking until I reach a set of large, golden double doors. I knock, and a minute or two later, they open.

If the male faerie at the door is the host of the competition, I can see why Jackie called him *different*. He's tall, with muscles so large, they're grotesque. His skin is unnaturally white. A tailored navy-blue suit covers his body, but his wide, flat feet are bare. Wickedly sharp, red claws protrude from his fingers. He's bald, and from what I can tell, he doesn't have hair anywhere else either.

And his face—it's *wrong*. His cheekbones and brow bones are too prominent, his red eyes and pointed ears too large. While his mouth is quite normal, his nose is most certainly not. It's like someone made a nose of white clay, then cut it down the center and pasted it on his face. There's half an inch of skin between the two halves.

He looks like a monster, a beast, bred to frighten with his face and kill with his claws. Something about him looks vaguely familiar. Perhaps he featured in one of my dreams—or rather, one of my nightmares.

Just when I think I've seen enough to scar me for life, I glimpse a rat-like tail swishing behind him. I suppress a shudder. Did he have to have a *tail*?

"Hello." His voice is low and rich, surprisingly beautiful for that body of his. "Are you the tenth contestant?"

I try to form words, but I can't. What the hell have I gotten myself into?

The beast's red eyes rove over my face, then widen. "You're human. How did you get past the barrier? Is it down? Are they invading?" He's breathing heavily, clearly panicked. He rushes to the door, ushers me in, and shuts and bolts it.

His terrified reaction somehow gives me the courage to speak. "No one is invading. I . . . um . . . apparently I'm part Fae?" More than anything else, that statement makes me feel like I've entered a storybook. The beast and I stare at each other for a few seconds, until I suddenly remember what Jackie asked me to do. I stand on my tiptoes and, trying to ignore the pounding of my heart, beckon the creature to come close.

He glances at a large mirror on the wall, then brings a pointed white ear to my mouth.

I whisper, "Jackie found me and got me through the barrier. She said I'm your final contestant."

When he pulls back, there's a little smile on his pale pink lips. It transforms his face into something almost bearable. "Then you're welcome here. We'll have drinks at six and dinner at seven. In the meantime—"

I interrupt him. "Can you heal me? I spent the night in the cold forest, and a creek swept me away. I hit my head on a rock and almost drowned . . ." I smile ruefully. "It was a rough night."

"Of course." He lifts his hands, and when I stiffen at the glint of his razor-sharp claws, he flinches too. "I won't hurt you, I promise."

His voice is warm and soothing. I let him rest his large hands on either side of my face. I hold my breath, anticipating the moment his claws slip and slash my skin. Instead, strength and warmth and sweet, sweet relief rush into me. As the pain and dizziness flee, I nearly weep with joy.

"Are you injured anywhere else?"

"My lungs. From the water."

He touches my upper chest, and when healing warmth fills me, I draw a deep, pain-free breath. Eager for more relief, I point out a scratch on my face and several other scratches and bruises. He heals them with gentle hands, then steps back, watching me. His eyes are bright with fascination. "You look young."

"I'm twenty-two."

"The youngest female here."

A sense of dread bubbles in my chest. He could be thousands of years old for all I know. He might've spent entire eras trying to find a wife before arranging this odd competition. I can't help but ask, "What about you?"

"I'm thirty."

"Years?"

He laughs, and I love the rich fullness of the sound. "Yes, years. Not decades or centuries."

I can't help but join in his laughter.

"I would love to talk with you more," he says. "May I take you on a tour of the castle?"

I freeze. I should say yes. The longer I'm in this competition, the longer Jackie will provide for my family. But the mirror in my pocket is heavy, begging me to find a quiet place outside to talk to Jackie and make sure my father is safe.

The beastly faerie before me clears his throat. "I understand your hesitation. This is all so new, and I doubt I'm what you expected."

"That's not it—"

"It's fine." His smile is strained. Then he whistles, and the trilling sound brings three small, bright-blue birds into the entryway. "They're enchanted," he says. "Tell them what you'd like to see, and they'll take you there. The castle is yours to explore. When you're ready to go to your quarters, the birds will guide you." He turns to leave.

"Wait!" I call. "What's your name?"

His head turns my way. The smile is back, but it's sad. "You can call me Tor."

Then he's gone.

I botched our first meeting, I'm sure of it. But I have to check on my father before I can focus on romancing a frightening, magical male with a nice laugh.

I look up at the birds. "Can you lead me to a quiet spot outside? Maybe behind the castle?"

They twitter and fly ahead. I follow. Upon entering the castle, I was distracted by Tor, but as I walk, I at last pay attention to my surroundings.

The floors are all the same marble as the outside—glossy white, with thin, gold veins. There are plants everywhere. Vines climb the surfaces, rooted in cunning little vases carved into the walls. Large pots hold dwarf trees, and magnificent blooms spill out of smaller vessels.

There's art throughout—sculptures and painted canvases, plus murals on the ceilings and some of the walls, depicting all manner of faeries celebrating and fighting and wooing.

As we walk through the sprawling castle, open doors draw my attention. I see a magnificent ballroom with powder-blue walls and floors, a bathroom larger than the house I live in, and a library with multiple levels of colorful books.

I've never been anywhere so beautiful, even when my family had money.

At last, we reach the back door. "I'd like some time alone," I tell the blue birds. "Can I whistle for you when I need you?"

They chirp a few notes, and I hope that means *yes*, because they then fly away.

I exit onto a large, stone patio. A dried-up fountain featuring two merfolk sits in the middle, surrounded by stone tables and chairs. It's quiet out here.

Beyond the patio are more hills covered in beautiful, thick grass. There are trees here and there, and in the far distance sits the white barrier, disappearing into the sky.

There's a white gazebo on a nearby hill. The perfect place to get a little privacy and check on my father. Since being touched by Tor, I have more energy than usual, so I run to it, not even caring that my broken boot makes a slapping sound with every step. When I arrive, I enter, sit on one of the little stone benches, and pull out the mirror.

All I see in the glass is blue sky and leafy tree branches. But I hear a high-pitched voice too.

"That's right. Good for you!"

"Jackie!" I say.

Her smiling, pale-orange face flits into view. "He's eating the mushrooms."

"Can you touch him like you did with me? Heal him faster that way?"

"I would if he had Fae blood, dear. He doesn't."

My heart drops. My Fae ancestry must be on my mother's side. "Is he going to be okay?"

"You can look for yourself."

My view shifts rapidly, and then I'm looking at my father's leg. It's still red and seeping, but it's less swollen than it was when I left him. His body, it seems, had enough strength to start fighting the infection on its own.

Jackie moves the mirror again. My father's face, pale but smiling, fills my vision. "Aeryn," he says weakly, "I think I'm hallucinating. I've been talking to a faerie."

It isn't until I laugh that I realize I'm also crying. "She's real, Daddy. She's going to help you. And I'll be gone a while, but she'll make sure our family is cared for."

"Gone? Why? Where?"

I want to answer but find I physically can't speak of it. The magic in this place must be keeping me from forming the words. I settle for, "Trust me. I'll be okay. I may be gone for weeks, but I'm safe, and I will come home."

He nods weakly. His mouth opens a few times, like he wants to ask questions but doesn't have the strength. At last, he settles for, "Take care of yourself, love."

Then I'm looking at Jackie again. I wipe tears from my eyes as she says, "I need to go to your village and get the midwife. I'm sure she'll find someone to help her retrieve your father. He'll be fine."

"Will the midwife even listen to you?" I ask. "She probably doesn't believe in faeries."

Jackie releases a lighthearted laugh. "Human midwives are kindred spirits to the Fae. They have an instinctive understanding of the magic of life. I left Faerie for Earth eight years ago, and your village midwife is the first human I befriended. In fact, I've helped her with a few difficult births."

Relief fills me. "Can I talk with my father while you're gone?"

"The mirror's magic is tied to me alone. It wouldn't work if I left it with him. And—Aeryn, is it?"

"Yes."

"Aeryn, you're there for a reason. You must play your role. If you'd like an update on your father, come outside with the mirror late tonight. When you look in it, your half will connect to mine, and I'll hear you call me."

I tell her and my father goodbye and put the mirror back in my pocket. Then I trudge toward the castle.

Only . . . I'm not ready to go in. Inside that castle is beauty, yes, but I also may encounter a beast in want of a wife, plus a group of Fae females competing with me for his heart. I need a little time to clear my head before I can brave all that.

I wander the spacious, beautiful grounds, soon finding myself in the front garden again. The only sounds are the breeze and some unseen birds. I crouch before one of the purple rose bushes and draw the incredible scent deep into my lungs. Then I start examining the detailed statues.

They're made of gray stone. I stop at one that depicts a female faerie. She's facing the center of the garden like the others, but her eyes aren't looking that direction. Instead, she's turned her head to gaze at the grinning little boy on her hip. He can't be more than a year old. One of his pudgy hands has gripped her braid, and she's poking his nose playfully with her finger.

"That one's my favorite."

I jump and spin around. Right behind me is a gardener holding pruning shears. His smooth skin is grayish blue, and there's a barely discernible pattern of slightly darker splotches all over it, similar to leopard spots. His ears, of course, are pointed. His eyes are the same color as his skin, and his short hair is straight and black. He's reasonably handsome, though far from stunning.

Most importantly, he appears friendly, his mouth curved into a smile.

I KNOW WHAT IT IS TO BE AN OUTSIDER

The male faerie holds out a blue hand. "I'm Wyatt. The gardener. I'm the only other permanent resident here, besides your host."

I shake his hand. "I'm Aeryn. Apparently I'm the final, um . . . contestant."

"Jackie got you through the barrier, so I take it you have Fae ancestry?"

"So I've been told." I step closer. "She told me to whisper her name," I breathe. "Should we be talking about her?"

His eyes go serious. "Not inside. But out here, it's safe."

"Why?"

He smiles, but sadness pulls his brows together. "I can't say."

"That's what Jackie said too."

"There are a lot of things that can't be talked about when it comes to this place. And don't ask me to explain why, because . . ." He trails off.

"Because you can't. I get it." I sigh and turn away, wandering the garden again. But I can't focus on the gorgeous plants or fantastic statues. I approach Wyatt, who's leaning down, polishing a stone child's nose with a white cloth. "I have more questions."

He straightens and turns to me, tucking the cloth in his pocket. "I'm just a gardener. How much use could I really be?" There's a slight twinkle in his eye and a little twitch at the corner of his mouth.

"There was a time when the servants in my father's household far outnumbered the family members," I say. When his eyes widen, I laugh. "I know you wouldn't guess it from my clothes and shoes. But it's true. And if you're anything like our gardener and our cook and the woman who kept the fire going in my room, you know things."

He laughs softly, but like his smile, there's sadness in it. How old is he? A hundred years? A thousand? What's he seen in his lifetime?

"Care to sit?" Wyatt asks, gesturing to a nearby stone bench. Every surface of it is carved with intricate, gorgeous flowers.

I follow him, sit, and jump right in with my inquiries. "Why is there a barrier around this place? Why does Tor look different from other Fae? Why haven't I seen any servants besides you?"

"I'm impressed," he replies.

My brows lift.

He says, "You're remarkably talented at asking questions I can't answer."

"Won't or can't?"

"Literally can't. I'm sorry."

I examine his face—those wide, blue eyes and that somber mouth. "I believe you. So, Wyatt the gardener, what *can* you tell me?"

He grins—a big smile as bright as today's bold sun. It's an expression that looks great on him, and I find myself hoping I can get him to do it again later. "Finally, a good question!" He turns and props both elbows on his knees, leaning toward me. Instead of giving me information, he asks, "Do you want to win this contest?"

I hesitate, then decide honesty won't hurt. "I don't think so. But I want to stay awhile. Jackie promised to take care of my family while I'm here, and . . . they need it."

Wyatt nods slowly. "Fair enough. I know Tor isn't exactly beautiful. But if you want to stick around, you'll need to look past that. I —I think you'll find goodness in him, if you search for it. This contest, it's more important to him than you know. I—please, Aeryn." His eyes are locked on mine, pleading. "Please give him a chance."

I want to say yes, not just for Tor's sake, but for Wyatt's. For some reason, this is important to him too. "I will."

The big smile is back. "Good. Then let's strategize."

Those words are always music to my ears. Leaning toward Wyatt, I say, "The events that led me here were rather . . . distracting. I didn't talk to Tor much, and I barely paid attention to the castle as I walked through. But I'm ready to focus on the competition now."

"Yes, focus." His voice is quiet but intense. "But not on the castle. Focus on the *people*—your fellow contestants. This isn't just about Tor. If you're going to stand out, you'll need to get to know the females you're competing against."

My gut transforms into an acidic knot. "You mean the group of beautiful, magical faeries I'm supposed to compare favorably to? Even though I'm a mortal who didn't even know magic existed until today?"

My self-deprecation doesn't phase him. "Your apparent mortality is what makes you stand out—to Tor and the others. Some of those faeries are powerful, cunning creatures. They'll take you out of this competition in an instant if you let them."

I swallow and whisper, "Damn."

"But you, Aeryn—the one Jackie handpicked as the final contestant?" His blue eyes seem to peer into my soul. "I know you won't let those faeries take you down. Keep your eyes open and your guard up. Be yourself, and be confident that you're enough. *That* should be your strategy."

I gape at him. "Why are you giving me this advice? Is this what you told the other contestants too?"

"You really think any of them stooped so low as to ask a gardener for advice?" When I don't respond, he smiles. This time, it's full of

Fae mischief. "Oh, and go check out your room. You'll find a few more tools there that might strengthen your strategy."

I have no idea what he means, but I can't wait to find out. I thank him and take my leave.

The three blue birds are waiting at the door into the castle. "Care to escort me to my bedroom?" I ask.

They twitter, and when I open the door, they fly just ahead of me.

We go up a gorgeous, wide staircase carpeted in plush purple. I'm panting by the time we reach the fourth floor. The birds lead me down a long hallway. Its floors are the creamy, gold-veined marble I've gotten used to seeing. Every door is painted with a different flower, matching those I saw in the garden.

I hear talking and laughter behind one of the doors. Some of the contestants must already be friends. My chest aches at that thought. I used to be at the center of any social event, thanks to my father's name. After the pirate attack, our family's so-called friends disappeared as fast as our wealth.

I know what it is to be an outsider, how impossible it is to break past people's judgmental perceptions. If these faeries already know each other, do I have any chance of even making it through the first night?

We stop at a door on which a purple rose is painted. I thank the birds and ask if they'll come back later to lead me to the proper place for drinks. Hopefully, their brief, melodic response means *yes*.

I open the door . . . and stop in my tracks. The large room is stunningly beautiful. On one wall is a bed covered in fluffy blankets and way more pillows than one person would ever need. There's a desk with a chair, a bureau, and two wardrobes. All the furniture is made of inlaid wood, displaying finer craftsmanship than I've ever seen. In one corner of the room stands a full-length mirror. A window overlooks the garden. The walls feature works of brightly colored, whimsical abstract art. They lift my soul, sending joy through my entire body. To the side is a bathroom, and if I'm not mistaken, those are pipes for both cold and hot water. I rush to the doorway and grin in delight when I spot a massive tub.

A few steps bring me to a countertop containing a selection of fine cosmetics. I used to love wearing kohl on my eyes and color on my lips and cheeks. I can hardly wait to try out what's been left for me . . . and suddenly, I laugh.

This makeup—it's the tool Wyatt mentioned that will strengthen my gameplay, isn't it? I have no idea what Tor thinks is beautiful. But the better I feel about myself, the more likely I am to walk into that room with confidence tonight. Cosmetics as strategy. I like it.

Right now, however, I'm still wearing a peasant dress and boots that are falling apart. And while I've learned to hold my head high in the village wearing such things, if I'm to woo a faerie, even a beastly one, I'd like to have an unstained dress and shoes that tap the floor instead of slapping it.

I return to the room, heart pounding with hope. When I open the first wardrobe, I stifle a delighted shriek against my palm.

Dresses of all colors and fabrics greet my eyes. The other wardrobe contains more of the same, and one of them has at least ten pairs of shoes in it. When I pull open the bureau's drawers, I find silky underthings and soft sleepwear.

What should I wear for my first night here?

I return to the thought I had when I saw the cosmetics. I can't dress for Tor; I don't know his taste. And to be honest, I don't want to dress for anyone else. I'd rather attire myself in a way that pleases me. With a laugh of pure delight, I rush back to the first wardrobe and pull out a turquoise dress I know will look amazing with my strawberry-blonde hair, pale skin, and light blue eyes. It laces up in the back and has a square neckline, along with cap sleeves and a shimmery, flowing skirt.

There are only two problems. It looks far too big. Plus, even if it were the right size, I wouldn't have anyone to tighten and tie the laces. I sigh and replace it. But as I pull out one dress after another, I realize they're all too big, and they all need to be laced from the back.

Wonderful. I'll be self-conscious all night, swimming in a too-large dress with sloppy lacing. Oh, well. At least I can get cleaned up.

The bath is even more perfect than I expected, with plenty of hot water and Fae-made soaps and oils that are far finer than any I've ever used. When I'm done, I wrap up in a soft robe and set to work on my hair. It's wet, which isn't what I'd prefer, but I'll try to pin it up and make the best of it.

When I put a comb in my hair, I gasp. The comb must be enchanted, because it turns my hair instantly dry. The strands are smooth and tangle free. I laugh aloud. Magical combs like this would sell for a fortune among mortals. I finish my hair, then use the cosmetics, which glide on more smoothly than those I've tried in the past.

That done, I return to the bedroom and open the bureau, choosing some underthings. Like the dresses, they're all too large. I groan and put on some lacy drawers. As soon as I pull them up, they shrink to fit me. I gasp in delight and slip on a silky corset. Not only does it adjust to fit me perfectly, it also laces and ties itself. I giggle the whole time, then let out a luxurious sigh when I realize it's the only truly comfortable corset I've ever worn.

I have high hopes for the dress now. It doesn't disappoint, tailoring itself to my figure. I stand before the mirror and watch over my shoulder as the laces tighten and tie themselves. After donning a pair of shoes that mold themselves to my feet, I return to the mirror.

I look at myself, head to toe. I'm . . . I'm beautiful.

In the last two years, I've felt strong. Resilient. Intelligent. But I haven't felt beautiful.

I start crying. With a gasp, I try to stop. I worked too hard on this makeup for it to smudge. But it stays in place, because *of course it does*. The Fae seem to have figured out how to get past every annoyance we humans suffer through, even smudged makeup.

The clock on the bureau says it's only four o'clock. Two more hours until I have to face Tor and my fellow contestants. So I let myself have a good cry—I deserve it after what I've been through.

Then, trusting this Fae-made fabric not to wrinkle, I lie on the bed. Just for a moment, I think.

I promptly fall asleep.

And I dream. Of a stunning Fae male—royalty of some sort, I'd guess, based on the band of gold around his head. He's tall and broad shouldered, with smooth, pewter-colored skin. His eyes are bright blue, his hair black and wavy. Muscles ripple all over his beautiful form. Black-feathered wings, like those of a raven, spread behind him. He catches my eye and gives me a dazzling smile. "I'm so glad you're here," he says.

I wake, heart pounding. Am I . . . blushing? Over a dream? Oh, yes, I am.

I let out a low laugh. "Well, I guess I'm glad I'm here too."

I look at the clock. It's time to go downstairs to chat with my host . . . and scope out my competitors.

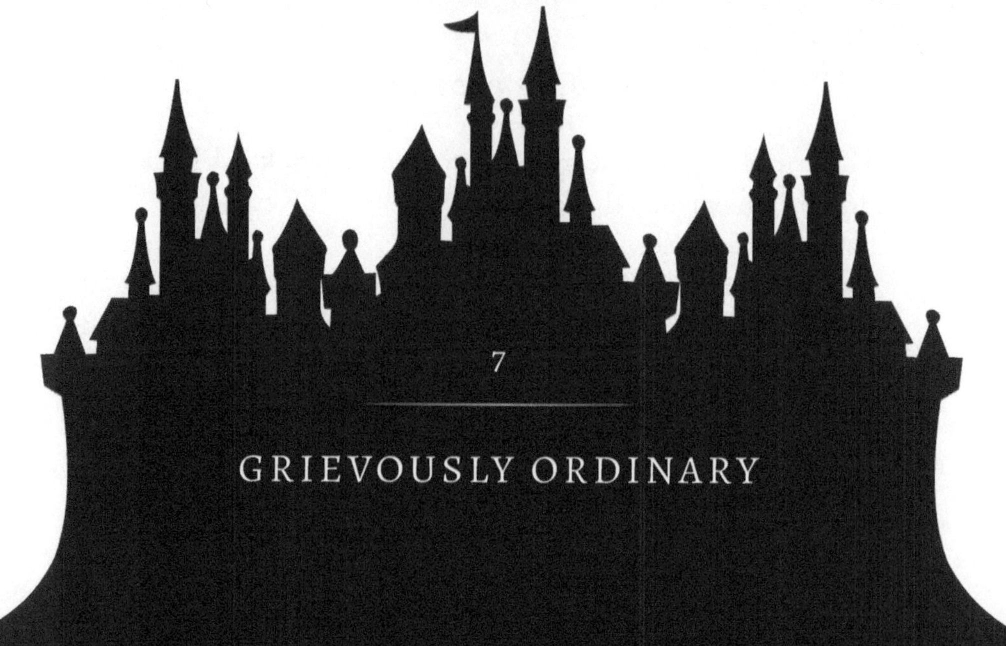

7

GRIEVOUSLY ORDINARY

I feel beautiful and—dare I say?—a little excited. I'm ready for this competition to begin.

The birds lead me down to the first floor, into a wing I didn't walk through earlier. We stop at an open door. The hallway is fairly dark, so I stand in the shadows and let my gaze wander over the room I'm about to enter.

The space is impeccably designed and decorated. It's a parlor with cozy seating areas scattered throughout. Four fireplaces blaze with orange flames. Lit candles glimmer in a large, golden chandelier. Intricate rugs lend warmth to the marble floors. Along the entire back wall is a glossy wooden bar, full of food trays, plates, drink bottles, and glasses.

I guess we'll have to help ourselves to drinks and appetizers. What an odd castle this is, full of every typical luxury but servants.

The room's stunning features are nothing compared to its occupants: four female faeries. A moment ago in my room, I felt pretty. In the presence of these four Fae, I'm reduced to *plain*. Grievously ordinary.

Each of them shines with unique, otherworldly beauty. There's the tall, fit female with short, black hair, reddish-brown skin, and eyes so green they light up the room. She's chatting with an equally athletic looking faerie whose taupe skin is offset by lavender hair. A pair of dragonfly wings catch my eye next. They're attached to a smiling female with luminous, deep-brown skin and purple hair that's so dark, it's almost black. Standing at the bar is a short, curvy faerie with intelligent purple eyes and silver skin. She has two small, white horns that are pierced in several places, with silver hoops and chains decorating them.

My turquoise dress and carefully applied cosmetics aren't going to cut it in this crowd, are they?

There's a little twitter at my ear, and one of the birds nudges me with its beak. The action makes me laugh, which knocks me out of my insecure stupor. No, I don't have beautifully tapered ears or exotically colored hair. What I do have is a *why*. I'm here to provide for my family. And I can't let these gorgeous faeries get in the way of that.

I walk in. Four sets of eyes turn toward me. Two of the faeries—the winged one and the one with decorated horns—smile.

The two fit faeries who were chatting with each other just stare at me. As I pass them on my way to the bar, I hear one of them murmur something about a "mortal contestant." The other says, "Well, I guess we know who's going home first." They both laugh.

I lift my chin and curse my fair skin, which I'm certain has turned red. At the bar, I choose a bottle of wine and pour myself a small glass, hoping it isn't any more intoxicating than the wine my family used to enjoy years ago, back when little luxuries were commonplace. I sip it and let it warm my insides as effectively as the females' harsh words warmed my skin.

The dragonfly-winged faerie with dark purple hair strides up to me. A big smile on her face, she murmurs, "I've known Margot and Ninette all my life. Don't let them bother you; their only goal in life is to be the worst bitches they can be."

I almost spit out my wine. "Noted," I say.

She winks, and it sends a glow of hope into my chest. Am I already making my first friend in this place?

She holds out a hand. "I'm Justyne."

I shake it, and of course her skin is fantastically soft. I have no idea how much Fae heritage I have, but couldn't it have come with silky skin at the very least? "I'm Aeryn."

"I take it you're mortal?"

"Mostly." I find myself smiling—her friendliness is rapidly slicing away at my intimidation.

Over the next couple of minutes, we watch the rest of the contestants arrive. They're all infuriatingly stunning. One of them walks right up to Justyne and me, her perfectly formed lips smiling. "Hi, Justyne." She turns to me. "I'm Rochelle." To my surprise, she holds out her arms. "I'm a hugger. Are you?"

It's such an ordinary, human-like thing to say, and I can't help but laugh. "Sure." I give her a quick embrace. Her skin is dark tan, with a luminous, pinkish-gold sheen. Long lashes draw attention to her deep-blue eyes. Her hair is her best feature—long, glossy spirals in a beautiful shade of violet-red.

She and Justyne tell me the names of all the other contestants. I'm too overwhelmed to remember any of them. Some of them look at me like I'm a rat invading their party, but Justyne keeps insisting the problem is theirs, not mine.

I'm on my second glass of wine when Tor's large frame fills the doorway. He steps in, and the room goes quiet.

He lifts his clawed hand, a smile overtaking his stark-white face. "Welcome. One of you is my future wife, and I'm pretty damn curious to figure out which one. So let's get this party started."

Melodic laughter fills the room. Several of the women step towards Tor. They're graceful—I don't think faeries know how to be anything *but* graceful—yet I see the fierce, competitive determination in their long strides and sharp gazes.

"I almost forgot," Tor says, holding up a hand. All the contestants halt. "I must insist on one ground rule for this competition. You may not use curse magic or otherwise harm your fellow contestants. Or me, of course. If anyone breaks this rule and you are affected, please report them. *Now* the party can begin."

A blue-skinned faerie, who's gorgeous despite her goat legs, reaches Tor first and leads him to a secluded seating area.

"No curse magic?" I say under my breath. "I won't have any trouble following that rule."

"Just how mortal are you?" Rochelle asks. "Do you have any magic at all?"

Her open, easy manner leads me to trust her. "I'm so mortal that I didn't know I had any Fae blood until today."

Her beautiful mouth drops open, and she shakes her head, making her violet-red curls tremble. But she's smiling when she says, "You're the first mortal I've ever met. I knew this competition would be fun, but I didn't know it would be this exciting!"

I laugh. "I can't see how meeting an ordinary human with no magic could be remotely thrilling."

"Well, when you're almost five hundred years old, you don't encounter new things very often."

I halt with my wine glass halfway to my mouth. "Five hundred?"

"Three years short of it. Figured it's about time I settle down." Her dark blue eyes dance with amusement. She scans the room and turns suddenly serious. "Watch Margot."

"Which one is that?"

"The one with the short, black hair."

Oh, right. One of the ones Justyne labeled a bitch. My eyes find her.

"See who she's staring at?" Rochelle asks.

I follow Margot's gaze to two faeries. One is Justyne. I hadn't even realized she'd left my side. She's laughing with a short, cute faerie with pale pink skin and white hair. Most of her hair is buzzed short, with botanical designs cut into it, but above each ear is a small section of long hair. She's twisted those locks around a pair of spiraled, golden horns.

"Desiree is the white-haired one," Rochelle says. "She's young, in her fifties, I think . . . and for some reason, Margot hates her. I think it's because Margot is practically elderly—she's a couple of hundred years older than me—and she's jealous of anyone who's smarter than her. Desiree is a genius. Reads more books in a week than I read all year."

I look back at Margot. Her eyes are still locked on Desiree.

"She's cursing her!" Rochelle hisses.

"How can you tell?"

"Margot lifts her pointer finger a little bit when she curses. It's her tell."

I'm about to ask what sort of curse she's placing, but I don't need to. The hair that Desiree has twisted around her horns is moving—tightening, by the looks of it. Desiree's white eyebrows pull together. She remains still, but pain is written all over her face. She whispers something to Justyne.

Then those two sections of long hair, which she must've spent years growing, tear away from her scalp.

I gasp and look back at Margot, who's now facing away from Desiree, a satisfied smirk on her lips.

There are tiny dots of blood on Desiree's head. Justyne's eyes have gone large, and Rochelle and I are still shamelessly gawking. No one else seems to have noticed them.

Justyne is urgently saying something to her friend, but Desiree shakes her head adamantly. More quiet words from Justyne. This time, Desiree nods. Justyne gently touches the two places where Desiree's hair was ripped out. The injured female's skin somehow sucks the blood back in, and it looks like nothing ever happened there. She pulls the hair off her horns and shoves it in a pocket of the green dress she's wearing. When Justyne points at Margot, Desiree shakes her head again.

"I don't think she's going to turn Margot in," I say.

"Probably not," Rochelle replies. "I don't know Desiree well, but she's always struck me as someone who stays pretty quiet. She wouldn't want to make a scene."

"But Margot will get away with it!"

"She's spent three-quarters of a millennium getting away with all sorts of things."

I look back at Margot, who's giggling with her lavender-haired friend. By the time I shift my attention back to Desiree and Justyne, they're sitting on a small sofa, chatting easily with each other. You'd never have known someone just pulled out entire chunks of Desiree's hair without even touching her.

How am I supposed to compete with females who can curse and heal and do who-knows-what else?

I don't have time to think much about that, because Rochelle is tugging at my arm, telling me she wants to introduce me to more of the contestants. We end up spending most of our time with a faerie named Harmonie. She's short, lithe, adorable, and far too sweet for this competition. Her skin is almost the same shade of turquoise as my dress. Her ancestors, she explains, were mermaids, so she has blue, fishlike scales on her shoulders, cheekbones, upper chest, and the tops of her hands. There are even small gills on her neck that allow her to breathe underwater for an hour or so.

As we chat, our eyes frequently find Tor. Margot whisks him away as soon as he finishes his tête-à-tête with the goat-legged faerie. I know I should get closer to him, find a way to get him alone . . . but this place and these people are all too overwhelming. I'm struggling to keep my focus on the competition and the male at the center of it.

At some point, I need a break. I set down my wine and slip into a hall-way, then go through a door that leads outside. A beautiful porch awaits me. I descend a few stairs into the grass, then find a tree to hide behind. In moments, I've connected with Jackie through my half of the mirror.

She quickly flies to the little shack I call home and holds the mirror up to the window. My throat clogs with tears—my family is eating a sumptuous dinner, with my father at the head of the table.

His leg is bandaged and splinted, and while his eyes look tired, he's laughing with my three siblings.

"Thank you, Jackie," I choke out.

"I've cast an enchantment that will provide them with food every day you are gone," she says. "I gave them each two new sets of clothes and a pair of shoes, as well."

"Wonderful. Can I see them again tomorrow?"

"I'm sorry, but you won't be able to reach me after tonight."

A jolt of panic goes through me. I'll be stuck here with no way to check on my family? "Why?"

"I have other things to accomplish."

Before I can ask more questions, her image in the mirror disappears. I'm now looking only at my own face.

Jackie is keeping up her end of the deal. I need to keep up mine. But how? The other competitors are beautiful and magical. They're all older than me—in some cases, older than I'll ever be. They have life experience on top of their other qualities.

What do I have? Using the faint light from a sconce on the porch, I examine myself in the mirror. Humans consider me pretty, but I'm nothing compared to the Fae. I purse my lips and tilt my head, seeking my most attractive angles. As if angles are the only thing separating me from the faeries around me.

"You're going to cut yourself on that broken mirror," a warm voice says.

I jolt, and sure enough, my hand slips. The edge of the mirror slices into my thumb. I drop the mirror back in my pocket, stick my bleeding thumb in my mouth, and turn to find Tor standing next to me.

"It seems I'll need to heal you every time we talk!" His back is to the light, and I can't see his facial expressions, but I can hear his smile. "May I?"

I remove my thumb from my mouth, and he touches it gently. The cut closes.

"Such handy tricks you Fae have," I say.

"You may learn to do magic one day."

"I'm guessing my Fae lineage was generations ago, based on how utterly human I feel."

"Magic can be awakened, even when there's not much of it."

That idea brings a smile to my face. I step toward him, not stopping until I'm so close, I can feel the warmth emanating from him. "I'm sorry I left the party."

"I'm not." When he brings a palm to my cheek, he doesn't even graze me with his claws. "It gave me an excuse to come look for you."

My breath hitches in my chest. With him in the shadows, I can't see his unsettling features. But I feel his soft hand, hear his rich voice, smell his compelling, spicy cologne.

And I like what my senses are telling me. Enough that I wonder if one day, I could get used to the sight of him.

"You intrigue me." His warm breath falls on my forehead—he certainly is tall, isn't he?

"The feeling is mutual," I whisper.

He lets out another of those lovely laughs. "Well, I'd say that's a good start, isn't it?"

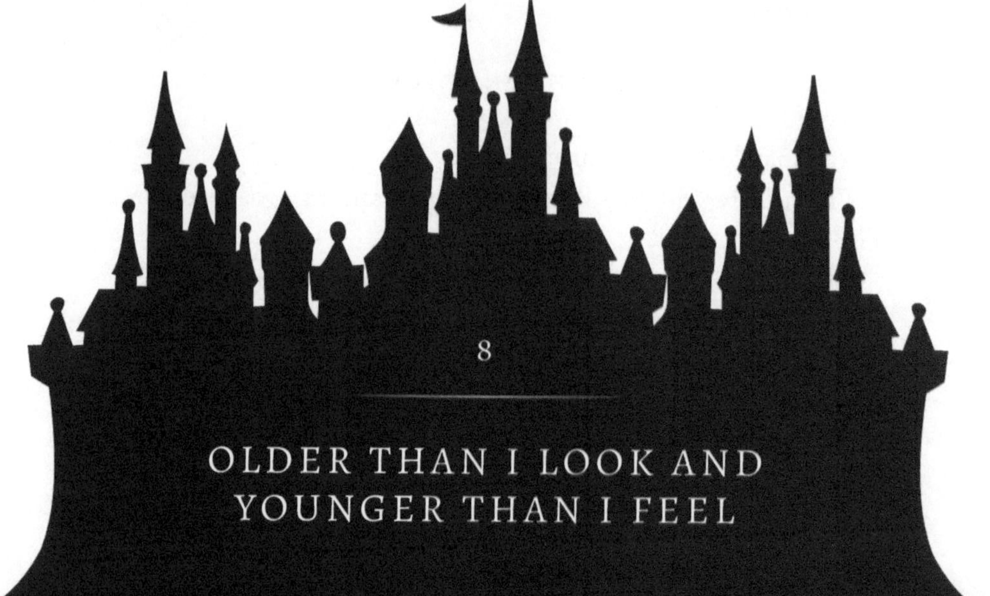

8

OLDER THAN I LOOK AND YOUNGER THAN I FEEL

Dinner is as delicious as I expected—soft bread dripping with butter, fork-tender meat, and the fluffiest strawberry cream pie I've ever tasted. I eat as much as I want, but I drink only water.

Despite the minimal alcohol in my system, my brain is filled with fog as thick as the barrier around this property. My senses are overwhelmed, and I fear I'll feel like this the whole time I'm here. How could I not, when I'm sitting with jaw-droppingly beautiful faeries; eating fragrant, flaky pastries; and listening to melodic voices as they chat with a literal beast? And then there's the magic. It fills this place —serving plates that refill at the touch of Tor's hand, spilled sauce that disappears without a trace, music filling the room with no discernable source.

I listen to as many dinner conversations as I can, determined to know a bit about each of my competitors. There's Sylvie, who was a dryad before converting into her current form. Her connection to the trees is evident in her long limbs, deep-green skin, and multi-toned brown eyes. Her perfectly-shaped head is totally bald, and it suits her; hair would distract from her unique beauty. The goat-legged, blue-skinned female who captured Tor's attention in the parlor is Felia. And Karine is the one with decorated horns and silver skin who smiled at me when I first arrived in the parlor tonight. As dinner winds down, I silently repeat the names of all nine contestants, committing them to memory.

At last, Tor stands. When a few of us start to push back our chairs, he holds up his large, clawed hands. "Please remain seated. Stay as long as you like. I must go—you've given me a lot to think about tonight."

Margot, the short-haired one who cursed Desiree, speaks up. "When will you start sending competitors home?" I have to give her credit—she's audacious.

Every faerie in the room goes silent until Tor gives Margot a sad little smile and says, "Tomorrow." As he leaves, I notice a couple of females tense up, like they're about to rise and follow. In the end, no one does. I suppose we'll all spend this competition trying to find the perfect balance in our pursuit of Tor. Not enough boldness, and he'll overlook us. Too much, and we'll be annoying. Tonight, I think we all sense our host needs time alone.

So do I. I say goodbye to Rochelle, who's sitting next to me, and Justyne, who's across from me. When I step into the hallway, I see numerous birds in all colors. Each contestant must have her own flying guides. The blue ones lead me back to the stairs. "I think I can find my way from here," I say. They fly off.

I stand still for a few seconds, considering my options. The comfortable bed in my room is calling to my tired body . . . but I suspect my mind is too busy to sleep. Instead of ascending the stairs, I follow the path I took earlier today, eventually exiting out the rear of the castle into the garden. I need to walk, and this is the most peaceful place I can think of.

The stars above are the same ones I've always looked at. There's no moon, so the garden should be quite dark. But gentle light brightens the pathways that wind through the plants and statues. I remember seeing the purple rose petals glow earlier, when I was following the path Jackie made for me. And now I realize that's not the only plant glowing—at least a third of the flowers here glimmer with magical light. I'm running my fingers along the soft, illuminated petals of a bright-blue iris when I hear Wyatt's voice.

"Originally, there was only one luminescent plant in this garden —a red daisy. I've spent years experimenting with cross-pollination to bring that trait to other flowers too."

I turn to find him dusting off the shoulder of a male statue. In the soft light of the flowers, Wyatt's blue skin is even more striking than it was in the daytime. "So you're the only servant at this castle," I say.

"I am."

"Why?"

"Yet another excellent question."

"One you can't answer?"

He nods.

"If you're the only servant," I say, "why choose the garden? Why not be a chef or a butler? Do you like plants that much?"

His smile turns mysterious. "I like *statues* that much."

I almost ask why, but I know he wouldn't be able to answer. I wander past several statues. Even in the faint light, I note how detailed they are—the strands of delicate hair on an arm. A tiny chip at the corner of a tooth. These statues are more than stone, I would swear to it.

I return to Wyatt, who's standing in the same place as before. His brows furrow as he gently rubs his fingers along the statue's hand. "There's a little weathering here," he says. "Tomorrow, when it's light, I'll repair it."

"Why?"

He meets my gaze. "I like to keep them in good condition. How was your night?"

I flinch at the quick change of subject. "Enlightening."

He chuckles. "I'm sure. Quite a group of females in there." He gazes at my face for a few seconds. "I see you used the strategic items Jacqueline provided."

"Jacqueline?"

"Pardon me—it seems you know her as Jackie. It caught me a bit off guard when you referred to her in that way earlier. She usually only gives her nickname to those of us who've known her a long time."

That tidbit sends warmth into my chest. "She's the one who left the cosmetics and clothes?"

"In a sense. She stood in this very garden and used her creation magic to enchant the castle in advance of the competition. The other contestants brought their own garments and such, but her spell allows the castle to . . . fill in the blanks, so to speak. You didn't bring luggage, so the castle created what you needed. Jackie's magic produced the birds who lead you around. Thankfully, she enchanted the kitchens as well. We're eating better than we have in years."

"I wish I could thank her. The food was delicious, and this dress is amazing." I gesture at the turquoise fabric that hugs my torso and glides over my hips.

It isn't until I direct his attention to the dress that he looks below my face, and even then, he doesn't let his gaze linger. When his eyes return to mine, there's appreciation in them. He nods a bit awkwardly. All he says is, "You chose well."

I sense that Wyatt wanted to look longer but was anxious to respect me. That he wanted to say more but held back—by choice this time. The interaction reminds me of how young men back home used to react to me, back when I had the money to keep up my appearance. Except those men weren't always so respectful.

Wyatt's brief moment of awkwardness makes me question my assumption that he's an old faerie who's worked in this garden for many decades or centuries. "How old are you?" I blurt.

His brows rise. When he opens his mouth, no words emerge. At last, he shrugs and releases a short laugh. "Older than I look," he says, "and younger than I feel."

"That could mean almost anything!" I protest. "All the faeries I met tonight looked about eighteen or twenty, whatever their true ages were. And I have no idea how old you feel, so that doesn't help me."

Wyatt grins. I bask in the brightness of his smile—until he speaks. "You should go, Aeryn."

"Oh, right." I look away. "I'm sorry I intruded."

"I don't mind you being here," he says quickly. "But you told me you want to stay here a while. You need to focus on the competition, and you need rest."

"I suppose you're right." I turn to go, but quickly pivot to face him again. "I was out of my depth in there, Wyatt." I'm not sure what it is about him that makes me trust him, but the words keep spilling out. "The other contestants are so exotic and beautiful. And they all know each other. I'm the new one, the plain one. Do you—is there anything you can tell me that will help me?"

He steps closer, and his bright smile turns gentle. "I already told you. Be yourself." His eyes wander over my features. "It's enough, I promise." His face goes somber. "I also—I should tell you . . ." He trails off.

Without thinking about what I'm doing, I bring my hand to his upper arm. The muscle there is firm under his simple, coarse shirt. He goes very still. Suddenly self-conscious, I pull my hand back to my side. "What do you want to tell me?"

"I'm"—his tongue comes out briefly to moisten his lips—"I'm trying to determine what I can say. Do you . . . are there mirrors in your quarters?"

"Of course. I used them when I got ready. There's a full-length one in the bedroom and a smaller one in the bathroom."

He smiles, but there's tension in his eyes. "You don't need mirrors. Your clothes will arrange themselves perfectly. Mirrors—they aren't really necessary, are they?"

"I do like using them when I'm applying cosmetics," I say with a little laugh.

"Oh, I—well, you could try it without," he says. "Couldn't you?"

There's so much he's not saying, but I see the warning in his gaze. "I've heard sometimes mirrors have magic," I say.

His eyes light up, seemingly in confirmation. "That's an interesting thing for you to have heard."

"If I'd brought a small mirror with me," I say slowly, "maybe I could use that instead of the ones in my room."

His expression sparks with curiosity, but all he says is, "I'm sure that would be sufficient for applying cosmetics."

"And I could turn the larger mirrors around."

His smile widens. "You could."

All at once, I remember Jackie told me not to use her mirror inside. "If the mirror I have happens to be of Fae origin," I say, "is it safe to use it in the castle?"

"In your room, it is," he says, "after you've taken care of the other mirrors."

"Thank you." I don't understand the advice he's giving me, but I sense it's important.

His warm gaze holds mine. "Good night, Aeryn the Mostly Mortal." He says it like it's a title.

"Good night, Wyatt Who Won't Admit His Age."

He laughs, and I feel his gaze on me as I walk back to the castle.

9

SMEARED LIPSTICK

The blue birds are in the corridor, perched on my door frame, when I return to my room. "I'm not sure if you can do this," I say, "but I'd love for you to wake me an hour before breakfast."

Their twittering responses tell me nothing.

In my room, magical lanterns provide plenty of light. "First things first," I say, walking across the space. The full-length mirror is on a heavy iron stand. I grunt and sweat as I turn it around. The mirror in the bathroom is lighter, and I quickly remove it from the wall, then prop it in a corner, facing away from me.

"Now if I can just figure out how to get this dress off," I say.

At once, the laces untie and loosen themselves. The rest of my clothing is just as accommodating. After putting on a nightgown and washing my face, I return to the bedroom.

"Lights, any chance you could turn off?" I ask. They comply. The slight glow of the garden reaches me through the window, making me smile as I crawl into bed.

The next morning, I'm woken by a lovely serenade from the birds outside my door. I take my time getting ready, silently thanking Jackie

58

as I use her broken mirror to apply cosmetics. I put on one of the simpler dresses provided for me. It's bright blue, with seams that situate themselves into all the right places. Fae dresses, I decide, are the most flattering garments I've ever worn.

The birds lead me down to the same dining room we used last night. Rochelle greets me, her lips curving into an enthusiastic smile. She's dressed in pink, which brings out the shimmer of rose gold on her tan skin. Her violet-red curls are piled atop her head, accenting her long neck and beautifully tapered ears. Two other faeries are at the table with her: Karine, who's wearing black jewelry on her white horns, and Sylvie, the green-skinned former dryad.

I sit and fill a plate with fruit, fluffy eggs, and toast. I've barely started eating when Tor comes in. He's wearing a burgundy suit, tailored to his huge form. His odd face, with those red eyes and a nose that's split in half, shocks me a little less than it did yesterday, and his smile is as warm as ever.

He chooses a chair two seats away from me, next to Rochelle. She asks him what fabric his suit is made of. He responds eagerly, and they get into a detailed discussion about his clothing preferences. Out of the corner of my eye, I see her running a hand along one of his broad shoulders.

He leans closer to her. "Would you care for a private tour of the castle?"

"I'd like nothing more," she breathes.

As they rush off, the castle's magic whisks away their plates.

"Three thousand years as a dryad," Sylvie says dryly, "and I'm expected to compliment a man's fabric choices to get his attention?"

My mouth drops open. "Three thousand years?"

Sylvie gives me a wry grin. "Good to know someone here thinks it's impressive. I've only been in this form for ninety-seven years, and I'm afraid I'm still terrible at flirting. I guess I'd better fix that if I want any 'private tours' with Tor."

We finish breakfast, and I wander through the castle corridors until I find an exit I haven't used before. A quick walk in the grass outside brings me to the porch I found last night. Margot, Ninette, and Felia are standing in a circle. I have no idea what they're up to, but I can't look away.

Goat-legged Felia has a look of intense concentration on her face. She's holding a stone cube, each edge about six inches long. Ninette, Margot's lavender-haired friend, is watching the cube, whispering something.

My eyes shift to Margot just in time to notice her lifting a finger. There's a sharp *pop*, and the square cube turns into a puff of black smoke. Felia and Ninette groan, while Margot laughs.

"What in the world?" I murmur.

"They're playing with their magic."

I turn to see who spoke. It's purple-haired Justyne. She's with her friend Desiree, the smart female with curled horns and pale, buzzed hair. Harmonie is accompanying them, the patches of blue scales on her skin shimmering in the sunlight.

"How does it work?" I ask Justyne.

"You mean magic?"

I nod.

"Let's sit." She leads us all to a table. When we're settled, she says, "There are four types of magic: curse, blessing, creation, and nature. Most faeries have some abilities in all four areas, but your first major spell determines your specialty."

I look back at Margot, Felia, and Ninette, who are paying us no mind. Felia is busy creating another stone cube. "I take it Margot specializes in curse magic?"

"She does." Desiree sends Margot a glare.

I almost ask why she didn't turn Margot in yesterday, but then Harmonie says, "Felia is trying out creation magic today. I think she wants to specialize in it, but she hasn't managed any major spells yet. She's only twenty-five, so her magic is still pretty weak."

"What about Ninette?" I ask.

"Blessing magic, believe it or not," Justyne says. "I think she was blessing the cube Felia made, trying to make it strong enough to withstand Margot's curse. Ninette is a little over a century old, which means Margot is way more powerful than either of them."

"She's over seven hundred, right?" I ask.

"She is indeed," Justyne replies.

I pull my attention back to the faeries at the table. "What do the three of you specialize in?"

"Blessing magic," Harmonie says with a sweet smile.

"Creation magic," Desiree says. She holds out her hand and whispers a word, and a tiny vase, holding an equally miniscule rose, appears.

"And nature magic for me," Justyne says. She waves a hand over the rose Desiree created and says, "Grow!" It grows so swiftly, the vase breaks into several clay pieces. "Sorry!" she says, but they're both laughing. Desiree waves her hand over the rose and the vase, and they disappear.

The other three faeries at the table chat about their magic—the first time they remember using it, their first major spells. They try to draw me into the conversation, but I stay mostly silent, because the only thing I want to say is something I refuse to speak aloud: *I don't belong here, and I never will.*

Eventually, the conversation shifts. We chat for about an hour, while the three faeries across the porch continue playing with their magic. Then, all at once, everyone goes quiet.

I look up and find Tor in the doorway leading to the castle. Rochelle is behind him.

"Come into the parlor," Tor says. "It's time for the first elimination."

Those of us on the porch follow Tor and Rochelle inside, then into the parlor. The other contestants are already waiting.

I look around, relieved to see a few females who appear as tense as I feel. Even those with confident stances can't quite hide their nerves. Curse-happy Margot is lightly tapping a foot. Justyne's dragonfly wings are fluttering just a smidge.

We arrange ourselves in a semicircle. Several feet away, Tor stands before us and spreads his burgundy-clad arms. "Thank you for meeting me here. We've come to the difficult part of the competition." Despite his words, he's the only one who looks truly at ease—his features are calm, his muscles loose. I suppose he hasn't had time to bond with whoever he's sending home. While he may shatter her dream, he'll have nine more chances to find his own happily ever after.

"I've enjoyed getting to know you all," he says, his gaze traveling through the room to briefly connect with each of us.

Rochelle holds his attention a second longer than anyone else, and I can't help but notice much of the lipstick she was wearing at breakfast is gone. Maybe her Fae-made cosmetics aren't as good as the ones in my room. Or . . . maybe she wants us all to know her lips have been busy? A picture flashes in my mind of her in a passionate embrace with the beast we're competing for. Along with it comes a flash of acidic jealousy. I draw in a deep breath and make a point to smile at her. I won't let this game turn me into someone consumed by bitter envy.

"Any of you," Tor says, "would make a wonderful wife. But in order to find the right person, I have to send people home as I discover they might not be the best fit for me. It's time to go from ten to nine." He takes a deep breath. "Rochelle."

Her mouth drops open, and though she's standing across the room, I swear I see a shimmer of tears in her eyes.

"Will you stay?" Tor asks, holding out his hands toward her.

A laugh, full of relief and a little giddiness, leaves her mouth. "Yes!" She approaches and gives him her hands. He kisses them both, then gestures for her to stand next to him.

"Ninette," Tor says, "will you stay?"

As Ninette strides to him, her athletic form full of confidence, I hold back a groan. This method of narrowing things down seems needlessly dramatic. What would it feel like to be one of the final two, standing there, wondering if you're the one about to be humiliated?

A couple of minutes later, I find out. Tor has called every name except mine and Harmonie's. Her turquoise skin is paler than before, and her blue scales seem to have faded a bit. Her lips are pressed together, fear evident in her expression. I wonder if I'm hiding my nerves any better than she is.

"Harmonie and Aeryn," Tor says, "I want you both to know how glad I am you came. Aeryn, as I've said before, you intrigue me. You're unique, not just because you appear mortal, but . . . there's something else about you."

I try to smile, but I recognize the truth behind his words: he can't explain what that *something else* is, because he hasn't had time to get to know me yet. Maybe I should've tried harder to get him alone. I vow to myself I'll do that . . . if I get the chance.

"Harmonie," Tor says, "I think everyone in this room would agree with me, you're the sweetest one here."

I nod. Harmonie doesn't display any of the guile faeries are known for. Last night and this morning, she had a smile for everyone, and even now, her trembling lips curve up. She's smiling at Tor as she awaits her fate. I can't manage to do the same.

Tor looks between us, pressing his lips together, seemingly deep in thought. Harmonie and I stand there quietly, awaiting his decision.

THERE'S A LIBRARY

"**A**eryn," Tor says, "will you stay?"

My breath exits my chest in a loud huff of relief. Margot and goat-legged Felia smirk. I approach Tor and let him kiss my shaking hands. Then I join the other females.

Tor walks off to the side with Harmonie to chat quietly with her. The one thing he said about her was that she was sweet, and I can't help but wonder if that's why she's going home. Tor is a physically powerful figure. And while I don't know his history, his bearing and voice are regal. Maybe he's looking for someone more assertive than Harmonie.

Can I ever be what he wants?

The question sends my heart beating even faster than it already was. Until now, I've tried to be myself, like Wyatt told me to do . . . and being myself almost got me sent home. I have no idea how to become the person Tor is looking for.

Overwhelming fear sweeps into me, nearly choking me. Fear that I'll try everything, and it won't be enough. That Tor will send me back to my poverty-stricken family, causing Jackie's promised provision to dry up. That I'll fail them, like I failed my mother. When she was sick, I tried everything. I traveled by foot to numerous other towns and villages. Talked to their midwives and doctors. Knitted hats and scarves to trade for herbs.

I tried so hard to save her that I wasn't even home when she took her last breath. I was in a town thirty miles away, begging someone to give me more medicine.

Harmonie exits, and the room goes quiet. Senseless panic sends tears into my eyes and tightness to my chest. I can't breathe deeply enough to calm myself.

"I'd like to spend the day with one of you," Tor says. "Margot, will you come with me?"

The meanest one—that's who he chose to spend an entire day with? She's what he wants?

I can't do this.

I have two choices: stay and burst into tears, or try to make it to my room before the weeping begins.

I spin on my heel and rush out of the parlor.

In my room, I have a long cry, then spend the day caught in a stranglehold of helpless anxiety, trying to come up with a strategy for staying in this competition. I'm too panicked to think clearly, though. I'm terrorized by images of Tor and the other faeries and my dying mother and my siblings and my father. Is Jackie keeping her promise of providing for my family?

Around mid-afternoon, I trudge down to the kitchen. I should be impressed by the food that appears on the countertop when I ask for it, but I'm already getting numb to the magic of this place. I take a full plate back to my room.

I eat and take a long bath that brings me no peace. When the sky outside my window goes dark, I spend a few minutes gazing into the garden, watching Wyatt repair a statue. Then I go to bed.

I dream that I'm in the corner of a large room, watching the same princely faerie as before. He stands before a mirror as he puts on a deep-blue dinner jacket. It's cut low in the back, as is his cream-colored shirt, to accommodate his raven-like wings. The suit beautifully sets off his pewter-colored skin, blue eyes, and black hair. He brushes a bit of lint off the front of the jacket, then spends a few minutes arranging his wavy hair before putting on the gold band that serves as his crown.

When he looks as perfect as any being could, he turns away from the mirror. His eyes meet mine, and his beautiful lips spread into a wide smile. "You wore the gown I had made for you."

I look down. My dress is the same beautiful cream color as his shirt. It's long and slinky and very flattering, if a little more daring than I would've chosen for myself. I look up to find the faerie standing before me, hands outstretched. I place my hands in his.

"All eyes will be on us when we enter," he says.

I'm about to ask where we're going when a knock wakes me from the lovely dream. It's not the tap I heard before, caused by bird beaks. This is the solid rap of knuckles on wood.

"May I have some light, please?" I ask. The room's lanterns flare to life, and I blink against the brightness. I don a soft robe that ties itself around my waist as I cross the room.

I open the door and pull in a little gasp. "Tor!"

His broad shoulders nearly fill the doorway, and the lantern light casts fascinating shadows on his features. "I'm sorry I woke you," he says as he enters.

"I . . . it's okay." I gesture to the chair before the desk. "Would you like to have a seat?" There's only one chair, so I sit on the edge of the bed.

Tor pulls the chair over to sit in front of me. "I know it's late, but I saw you rush out of the parlor this morning. I wanted to check on you."

I focus on his eyes. The red irises are strange, yes, but I'm getting used to them. And his gaze holds what appears to be concern. My mouth widens into a smile. "Thank you for checking on me. I'm doing better now." I almost tell him he woke me from a lovely dream, but then he might ask me what I dreamed about. I'd feel silly telling him about the faerie prince inhabiting my imagination.

"What was wrong?" he asks.

A short laugh leaves my mouth, but I quickly realize he's serious. "You . . . you almost sent me home."

He smiles, and I admire his full lips and straight teeth. Thank heaven he doesn't have sharp fangs to match his claws. "And me almost eliminating you from the competition was enough to upset you that much?" he asks.

"Yes, and you don't have to look so happy about it." As soon as the words come out, I bring my hand to my mouth. Am I determined to stay on the bottom of his list?

He releases a hearty laugh. "I'm not happy you were panicked. I'm happy you want to be here. I know I'm probably not what you pictured in a future husband." He's still smiling, but there's a hint of wobbly uncertainty in the curve of his lips.

I'm not sure how to respond. He's been nothing but kind to me, but our interactions have been so brief. I can't give him any grand assurances of my affection. So I settle on, "You've been a wonderful host, Tor. I want to know you better than I do. Of course I want to be here."

That seems to be enough, because he lifts a clawed hand and carefully cups my face. The soft pad of his thumb glides over my cheek. It's a sweet, light caress, and I lean into it.

"Good," he says, "because I want you here too."

I swallow hard, unable to reply. When I lived a life of privilege, I had a wealthy, handsome young suitor. I try not to think about him too much these days, because as soon as the money was gone, he was too. Now, when I see him in town, he doesn't sneer at me. It's worse— he looks through me. Like I don't exist.

Tor's red eyes fix on me with gentle affection. His words, simple as they are, fill a gap that's been in my heart these last two years.

I find myself wanting to feel his lips press against mine. Would this beastly faerie's kisses make me feel as good as his words? But then I picture him kissing away the lipstick on Rochelle. I imagine Margot's long arms caressing him as he nuzzles her neck.

I don't know what he's doing with these other women, but the possibilities cause me to hold back. It's enough to know he wants me here and to let him know I want to be here. I'm not ready for more than that.

The sweet moment passes, and he pulls his hand away from my face. I tilt my head to the side, seeking a topic to break the silence. "Have you always lived in this castle?"

He blinks and gives me a mysterious smile. "Interesting question."

"Not a hard one, I'd think," I say with a little grin.

"Until ten years ago, a prince lived here," he says. "Back then, this estate was in Faerie—a realm in what we Fae call 'the middle region of air.' It's under the same sky as Earth, but in a different, hidden reality. If you talk to the other females, I'm sure they'll share all the stories they've heard of how the royal castle came to be on Earth, in the possession of a beast."

I wait for him to go into more detail, but all he says is, "We both need sleep."

I remember the promise I made to myself earlier, that I'd actively seek more time with Tor. "Actually," I say, "I have questions about people like me—humans with Fae blood."

His hairless brow rises. "I don't know much about that. But there's a library here where you can find all the information you need." He stands and extends a hand. "Shall I take you there?"

11

A BORING PLACE FULL OF UGLY BOOKS

"You might have seen the main library with its high ceilings and large windows," Tor says as we walk down the stairs, our path lit by wall sconces that light themselves as we approach.

"Yes, I walked by it yesterday. It's beautiful."

"It is. And it's not where we're going."

I stop. He follows suit, and though he's on a stair below mine, he's still quite a bit taller than me. All at once, I'm very aware of how alone we are in this dark house. "Wh—where are you taking me?"

He laughs. "As I told you, Aeryn, we're going to one of the libraries. The one you saw yesterday is full of the books typical guests might enjoy, mostly novels and illustrated history books. I'm taking you to the library vault in the basement. It's where the less popular books and other records are stored. Genealogies, dry nonfiction, things like that. It's a boring place full of ugly books, but I think you'll find whatever information you're seeking."

Maybe the basement library isn't Tor's cup of tea, but his description makes my heart stutter in anticipation. Yes, I loved the faerie tales my father brought home to read to us, but when he asked what books he could purchase just for me, I requested what the faerie before me would classify as *dry nonfiction*. In my formative years, I spent blissful weeks digging into the history of the places my father's ships traveled—not the sanitized, glorified stories that ended up in school texts, but the real history, told in handwritten battlefield journals and other books that the eventual victors tried to burn. I even once spent an entire week comparing different versions of royal genealogies.

"I'm glad I got a nap," I say with a grin, "because I get the feeling I'm not going back to sleep tonight."

When we reach the first floor, Tor leads me through several hallways. At last, we approach an unmarked, plain wooden door. He pulls out a set of keys and unlocks it. Opening it, he says, "Lights." Bright, golden flames, contained in glass balls mounted to the wall, shed light on a downward staircase. "The flames in this basement are all protected by unbreakable glass," he says. "That way, they'll never start a fire. The books down here may not be popular, but they're more valuable than the ones upstairs."

We descend the stairs, then turn into a room that's far larger than I expected, about half the size of the ballroom I saw yesterday. It's full of bookcases made of reddish-brown wood with a lovely, swirly grain. The wood is the only beautiful thing in this room. Everything else is purely functional—smooth, black tiles on the floor, walls painted in white, and a plain, low ceiling. It may not be a fancy space, but the leather bindings give the room a warm, familiar scent that takes me right back home to the library where my father and I stored all our books.

Hanging above the shelves are black signs with white letters and numbers painted on them. More spherical lights are mounted on the ceiling and walls and on poles throughout the room. The last thing I notice is that each bookcase is covered in glass and protected with a lock.

"Will you be staying to open the bookcases for me?" I ask.

"I thought I'd loan you the key instead."

"This place is too boring for you to stick around?" I tease.

He laughs but doesn't deny it as he pulls a key off the ring and hands it to me. "This will open both the door and the bookcases, so you can come back whenever you'd like," he says. "I'd give you a tour, but I rarely venture down here, and I have no idea where to find scholarly books on humans with Fae blood. But over here"—he gestures to the right of the door—"is a cabinet that will help you find what you need."

I step to the cabinet. It's long, with dozens of small drawers. I pull one open and find it full of cards, each one representing a subject or book, along with codes that match up to the letters and numbers labeling the sections of the library. It's a brilliant organizational system, one I'd love to share with the keeper of our tiny library back home.

I'll spend plenty of time reviewing the cards in this cabinet, but first, I have to explore a bit. I walk to the nearest bookcase and use the key to unlock it. When I slide the glass door open, the smell of leather and old paper wafts out. I close my eyes and draw the scent deep into my lungs. A joyful smile parts my lips.

From several feet away, Tor says, "Maybe one day you'll react to me that way."

My eyes fly open, and I turn to him. "Only if you're lucky."

He smiles. "I'll leave you to your research. Be sure to lock the door when you're done—though I'm not too concerned about anyone else sneaking down here."

I laugh lightly. As he leaves, I wonder what he really thinks of my enthusiasm about this place. Based on the beautiful library upstairs, I'm guessing plenty of faeries love reading. But if the land of Faerie is anything like the mortal world, few people are passionate about true research. I doubt Tor is looking for a bookish bride.

That bothers me a bit, but not enough to squelch my enthusiasm for the massive number of tomes at my disposal in this beautiful place. Because it *is* beautiful, despite the plain walls and utter lack of romantic ladders leading to high shelves. There's a wealth of knowledge in this place, and knowledge has always made my heart soar even more than unique art or wonderful stories.

I return to the cabinet full of cards. I told Tor I wanted to know more about humans with Fae blood, and that's true. But my interest is more specific than that.

I want to know whether humans who are part Fae ever successfully integrate into Fae society . . . especially if they enter it through marriage. I came into this competition not seriously considering the possibility of winning it. But as I watched Harmonie leave and promised myself I'd try to spend more time with Tor, I began to realize something.

If I'm truly committed to this competition, I have to consider the possibility, however unlikely, that Tor will choose me as his bride. I'm not sure I could bring myself to say no after he'd sent home so many others—and knowing Margot, she'd probably get revenge if I tried such a thing. But what would it be like to marry an immortal male?

I spend at least half an hour at the cabinet, searching for books that might answer my questions. At last, I find a card for a book called *Partial Fae: A Study of Faeries With Mortal Ancestry*. I note its location, then venture deeper into the library, where I easily find the proper shelf.

The book doesn't have any of the information I'm looking for; it focuses solely on the varying physical characteristics of faeries who have human blood. But on the same shelf are other books that might be more likely to answer my questions. I flip through a few, then find one that's so old, I can't read the title stamped into the leather until I step closer to a nearby lantern. The book is called *Inter-Realm Mates*. Now that sounds interesting.

I carry the thin book to a small table that's lit by yet another lamp. After settling in the plain wooden chair, I open the ancient book carefully. The pages have uneven edges that appear to be crumbling with age. But when I turn them, I find they're far sturdier than they look. I suspect an enchantment is keeping this book from falling apart. What kind of faerie would be capable of such a spell? Maybe a blessing faerie. I like the idea of a faerie who uses magic to protect books.

I begin reading. The language in the book is archaic, but I'm skilled at reading such words and phrases, since my father sometimes bought books that were hundreds of years old.

It begins by explaining that many mortals with Fae spouses have some Fae blood themselves. I read eagerly as the text goes into detail about the life spans and magical skills of those who are part Fae. A mortal who is half-Fae can live a few hundred years. Those with less Fae blood enjoy shorter, though still extended, lives. Mortals who are one-sixteenth Fae generally live no longer than typical humans and have little or no magic. And most faeries who are one-sixteenth human enjoy the level of magic typical of full-blooded Fae, along with exceedingly long or even immortal life spans.

Based on my utter lack of magic and my mortal physical characteristics, I'd be surprised if I were more than one-sixteenth Fae. But would Jackie have been able to detect that tiny amount of Fae blood in me?

I return my attention to the text, which goes on to discuss marriages between Fae and mortals—those with or without Fae blood. As I read, my heart drops. By the time this book was written centuries ago, such marriages were strongly discouraged, as they tended to end poorly. The majority of Fae–mortal marriages resulted in divorce. Then there were the tragic cases of mortals committing suicide due to the heartbreak of feeling their own bodies age as their spouses stayed perpetually young. And several infamous, heartless faeries even killed their aging spouses.

My heart aches with the weight of this knowledge, but I can't stop reading. In the next section, the book assures me that a small minority of Fae–mortal marriages were so characterized by love that they continued until the mortal's natural death. I turn the page and encounter a detailed drawing of one such couple. A male with pointed ears, a square jaw, defined muscles, and unlined skin sits on the edge of a bed where a wrinkled, feeble human woman lies. He's feeding her soup as she looks up at him with sad eyes. The faerie has a tear running down his cheek.

The image goes blurry, and I push the book away before I mar its pages with my tears. The ending shown in this image is surely more tragic than divorce or early death. I imagine myself lying in that bed, watching the one I love grieve as I die. And what about the years leading up to such a moment? Would I turn scarlet with humiliation as my worn-out knees and hips began crackling with every step? At what age would I step out of a bathtub and feel the need to hide my wrinkled body from my ageless, virile husband?

My throat tightens, but I wipe at my wet cheeks and take a deep breath. I keep reading, grabbing another book when this one turns too discouraging.

The cases described in the other texts are all the same. There is no happy ending for mortals who marry immortals. There is only grief and despair.

If this were just a game, none of these possibilities would matter. But it's not. It's my life. And with that picture of the strong faerie and his decrepit wife branded in my mind, I can't keep pretending I want to win.

12

A SOFT HISS

I read all night. By morning, I have a plan. I return to my room with heavy steps just as the rising sun bathes my room in pink light. I dress for the day, then stand in the center of my room and rehearse what I'm going to say to Tor.

"You don't have any servants except the gardener. And while the castle's magic is impressive, the other females here would love to be waited upon. I have an offer for you. Keep me here for the rest of the competition, but not as a contestant. Instead, allow me to serve you and the others however you see fit. At the end, you can pay me a fair wage, and I'll return to my family."

It's the best solution I can think of. I assume my family will continue to be cared for as long as I'm here. And if Tor is willing to pay me for my service, I'll end this process in a better place than I started it . . . without being forced to pretend I want to marry a faerie.

I put on cosmetics and do my hair, keeping everything simple. My goal isn't to seduce. It's to build trust with Tor so he'll say yes to my plan. I walk toward the door, hoping to meet him at breakfast.

A soft hiss causes me to go still. Everything is silent. After several seconds, I convince myself I imagined the sound. I'm about to move again when a snake slithers out from behind a chair. I yelp and scamper backward. The snake coils itself right in front of the door, lifting its head and hissing again.

I draw in a deep breath. I've encountered plenty of snakes in the woods and even a couple inside our tiny house. I'm always startled when I see one, but snakes don't truly frighten me unless they're venomous. This one looks nothing like the dangerous species I'm familiar with.

She has brownish-bronze skin and intelligent green eyes. (I'm not sure why I think of her as a female, but I do.) Her pink, forked tongue, which keeps darting out of her mouth, is remarkably cute. I have a decent instinct for danger, developed during my foraging expeditions in the woods. And I don't believe this snake will hurt me.

I step toward her. She hisses louder, lunging.

I halt. Voice calm and even, I say, "I need to speak with the head of this house." I know she can't understand me, but I continue talking, hoping my tone of voice calms her. Most animals can sense danger. I want her to know I'm no threat.

She hisses again. Then she unwinds and slithers closer, stopping nearly at the edge of my long dress. Her head lifts higher than before. Her tiny eyes fix on my face, and once again, she hisses.

"Persistent little thing, aren't you?" I ask with a smile. "I wish you no harm. I like snakes. But the conversation I need to have with Tor is important."

Her head sways back and forth, like she's shaking it. Her next hiss is even louder. And maybe this crazy, magical place is making me go mad, but I have this odd sense she's trying to communicate with me. Trying to stop me from following through with my resolution to leave the competition.

But that can't be . . . can it?

"I'm sorry if you disagree with my choice," I say, keeping my voice as soothing as possible, "but believe me, if you'd read the books I found in that basement library, you'd see the wisdom of it. Now, pardon me, it's time for breakfast."

Having an instinct that she's not harmful is one thing. Acting on that instinct is another. My pulse accelerates as I turn to walk past the snake. She lets me pass, though she hisses until I leave the room.

I'm going to breakfast earlier than I did yesterday. Hopefully Tor will do the same, and I'll catch him alone.

The birds fly with me through the corridors, singing a sweet song the whole way. Though I don't need them to lead the way anymore, I enjoy their presence. According to Wyatt, Jackie used magic to create them. Does that make them more or less real than normal birds? They're certainly more intelligent, since they can follow the simple instructions I've given them.

The dining room has double doors that were open for our previous meals. This morning, they're closed. That probably means I'm the first one here. I wave at the birds and grasp one of the door handles. It swings open on smooth, silent hinges.

The room isn't empty.

Tor is sitting in the chair at the head of the table. Margot is on his lap, straddling him, her blue dress hitched up to her thighs. Her long, lean arms are draped around his neck, and she's kissing him. Passionately.

He doesn't seem to hear me, but one of Margot's green eyes opens and locks onto me. Her lips, still connected to his, curve up a bit, and she presses her body tighter against him. She continues to watch me with that cold eye as she pulls her mouth off Tor's and presents her neck for him to kiss. He responds enthusiastically, his wide mouth latching onto her skin like he's a sucker fish. She releases an overly dramatic moan.

I've been kissed like that, but I've never watched others do it. I can't help but wonder . . . did it look that disgusting when my old suitor used to hold me on his lap and kiss my neck? Heavens, I hope not. At least I can comfort myself in the knowledge that no one saw us. We had the respect to stay out of public areas. I suspect Margot hoped to be caught in the dining room.

As I exit, I hear the rip of fabric. Tor's gripping the back of

Margot's dress so tightly that one of his claws has caused a tear. I close the door, Margot's moans following me out.

My stomach is roiling, and I can't explain why. I came to this room to tell Tor I *don't* want him romantically. It shouldn't bother me if a fellow contestant is having a bit of fun with him. Even if she is the bitchiest one here.

Does he realize how horrible she is? Should I tell him?

I'm still considering that when Justyne rounds the corner. She smiles, and I hold a finger up to my lips as I hurry to meet her. Her long, dark-purple hair is coiled about her head in numerous thick braids. The look might be old fashioned on others, yet on her, it's somehow the most modern hairstyle I've seen since arriving here.

"What's going on?" she asks.

"Tor is in there."

"Good, we can all eat breakfast together."

"Margot is with him. The only thing they're eating is each other's faces." When Justyne snorts, I say, "Sorry, that was crass."

"A little crassness makes a person more interesting." She looks around the empty hallway. "Let's wait out here for a few minutes. I don't think I want to see what you just described."

"Trust me. You don't."

We stand quietly for the next several minutes, but Tor and Margot still don't emerge. My imagination is terrorizing me with all the thoughts of what they might be doing. At last, to distract myself, I step a little closer to Justyne and ask, "What can you tell me about the history of this place? How did Tor come to live here?"

Her eyes widen. "Oh, that's right, you've never lived in Faerie. You haven't heard all the rumors."

"Well, I did you a great service by preventing you from getting that picture"—I point at the dining room—"seared into your mind. Want to return the favor by telling me what you've heard?"

"Sure," she says. "I should warn you, it's nothing more than what you humans call a faerie tale. Nobody knows what really happened. But I'm happy to pass on some gossip."

A TALE OF TWO PRINCES

"This estate," Justyne begins, "used to sit at the center of a small, well-established kingdom in Faerie. I met the king and queen when I was a girl. They'd been on their thrones for hundreds of years by then. Several years after I met them, the queen gave birth to a boy named Fabien. Two years later, his brother, Luc, came along. Siblings born so close together are almost unheard of in Faerie, where we're not as skilled at procreation as mortals are."

I laugh softly. She grins and continues, "When the princes were young adults, the king and queen, who were both over a thousand years old, decided it was time to transition."

"Transition?" I ask.

"Yes—when elderly faeries get tired or bored after living such long lives, they move to what we call the spirit realm. If they stay in that realm for several years, their spirits leave their bodies. From then on, they live unencumbered by the limitations of their physical forms. They're just as alive, but it's a different type of life.

"Fabien, the eldest prince, became prince regent when his parents departed. He had all the authority of a king, and he should've officially been crowned once his parents transitioned to incorporeal forms—which I'm assuming they've done by now.

"But shortly after they left, this castle and estate disappeared from Faerie. One day, it was there, the next, a formless gap was in its place."

"How long ago was that?" I ask.

"About ten years. A rumor quickly spread that Fabien had died of a fever, and a Fae beast took over the estate and moved it to Earth. I didn't know whether to believe it until I arrived here for the contest. While I can't confirm what happened to Fabien, Tor's presence seems to support the story I've always heard."

"What happened to the other prince?" I ask.

"Nobody knows. Luc was notorious for being power hungry, and he always seemed angry that he wasn't first in line to inherit the throne. I met him once, when he was fifteen years old, and even then, I could see his drive to achieve. Some people think the beast drove him away, and now he's hiding somewhere to build up enough magical strength to take over this estate and move it back to Faerie. Others say he died along with his brother."

I nod slowly, then say, "This castle must've had a lot of servants. What happened to them?"

Justyne looks away, and her deep-brown skin turns a shade paler. A swallow ripples through her throat before she turns back to me. There's tension in the set of her mouth and shoulders, though she's clearly trying to hide it. "The servants disappeared from Faerie along with the castle. I expected to find them here, working for the beast. I couldn't believe the castle was practically empty when I arrived. I figured it out when I walked through—" She stops, blinking rapidly and pulling in a harsh breath.

"The garden?" I ask softly. "The statues?"

She nods and pushes her words through her tight throat. "I don't know how it happened. It would have to be a curse, and I don't think Tor could've done it. He's Fae, but he's young. He hasn't had much time to grow his magical abilities. In fact, I don't even know if he has as much magic as other faeries. I've never seen another beast like him, so . . ." She shrugs and trails off. "Anyway, someone turned all the servants to stone. Except the gardener."

"I wonder why Wyatt was spared."

"I don't know. But yesterday, I saw him repairing a crack in one of the statues. I'd like to think he's preserving them for when the curse is reversed. At least . . . I hope there's a way to reverse it." Her voice falters.

"You hope?" I ask gently.

She smiles, though it's a little wobbly. "Of course I do. Who wouldn't want to get all those people back to their loved ones?"

I sense there's more to it than that, but before I can say anything, the dining-room doors open. Justyne and I leap to our feet.

Tor comes into the corridor. "Ready for breakfast, ladies?"

"Actually," I say, "I'd like to speak to you. Alone."

"I can't let you do that," Tor says after I offer to become his servant.

My mouth drops open. We're standing on the same covered porch where I watched faeries practice magic yesterday. He's leaning back against a marble column while I stand before him.

"Why not?" I ask.

"Aeryn." He stands up straight and takes my hands in his. One of his claws barely scrapes the underside of my forearm, and it's a surprisingly nice sensation. Voice low, expression solemn, he says, "This house's magic provides all we need. It even cleans itself. I don't need a servant. *I need a wife.*" A smile mitigates the intensity of his words. "I mean . . . I *want* a wife. I'm here to find love."

"But if you fall in love with me, I'll be old while you're still young. That's what I learned in the books you let me look at. Please, Tor. Don't put either of us through that."

He shakes his head. "It'll be decades before you're old. Aeryn . . .

there's something special about you. If you end up being the one for me, I'll appreciate however many days we have together. Yes, I would eventually lose you, but wouldn't the joyful years be enough to make the grief worth it?"

For hours, one image has been stamped on my brain: that awful drawing of an elderly mortal woman and a young Fae male. Now, however, I allow myself to imagine what that couple's early years together might've been like. When they laughed together while taking walks and winked at each other over the dinner table and shared intimate moments at night.

If Tor and I came to an understanding, could we enjoy all the sweet moments and avoid the variety of terrible endings I read about? I take a deep breath and say firmly, "I will not allow myself to become a burden to someone who's still young when I'm old. Perhaps I could spend my youth with a faerie. But not my elderly years. I couldn't do that to you . . . to anyone who couldn't grow old with me."

A sweet warmth enters his odd red eyes. "I'm figuring out why I'm so drawn to you, Aeryn. It's your selflessness."

It would be humble to deny it, but I can't. I've given up so much to keep my family fed. It's what I love most about myself. I've searched the woods for food, even when it meant freezing in the winter or getting sunburns in the summer. I love that my hands have ached for weeks at a time from knitting hats and scarves.

But it's never enough. We suffer through too many hungry days. If I fall in love with Tor and he with me . . . surely he'll provide for my family for the decades he and I are together. I could finally care for them in the way I've wanted to.

Food for my family . . . along with true love? That would certainly be an acceptable conclusion to this unlikely adventure. The romance itself wouldn't end happily, but maybe the benefits would outweigh the eventual grief.

"Okay," I say. "I'll stay. If you'll let me. We'll take it day by day."

"That's all any of us can do." Tor releases my hands and pulls me into a tight, warm hug. Then he whispers, "I have to go. Karine is waiting at the door for me, and I told her I'd sit next to her at break-fast. I promise you this, Aeryn. At tomorrow morning's elimination, I won't send you home." He ends the embrace and gently holds my shoulders, his gaze finding mine. His whisper is even softer than before. "But every other female *wants* to be here. If you want to be safe at the next elimination . . . you need to show me you truly want to be here too."

What does he mean by that? A picture of Margot on his lap returns to my mind. Is that what he desires from me?

He's watching me expectantly. I'm overthinking this, and in this game, I can't afford such a luxury. All I need to do is convince him right now that I'm committed to him and to the competition. I'll figure out exactly what that means later.

"I hope I'll get more than a few minutes alone with you so I can prove how much I want to be here," I whisper with a smile I hope is both friendly and flirtatious.

He returns the smile. "Time alone? I can make that happen."

He kisses my cheek, then walks toward the door. Sure enough, Karine is there, her silver skin glowing, the chains on her small horns tinkling as she raises her chin to greet Tor with a smile.

I turn away. My appetite for breakfast is gone. I can't torture myself watching Tor flirt with a table full of females who are vying for his heart. I'll stand here instead, soaking up the sun . . . and antici-pating the time together Tor promised me. Hours alone with a Fae beast—I never knew such a prospect could excite me so much.

A soft hiss draws my attention. The snake I saw before is coiled around the porch rail next to me. "Well, hello," I say.

She peers at me through bright-green eyes. As before, I sense she's more intelligent than a snake should be. "Do you understand me?" I ask.

The movement of her head looks very much like a nod.

Perhaps I'm mad . . . but I honestly believe this snake witnessed and understood my conversation with Tor. I hold out my hand, and she rubs the underside of her head along it. Her skin is cool and soft. Soothing.

And I know she approves of my decision to stay in the competition.

14

THEY'RE JUST VIVID DREAMS

Just as Tor promised, he doesn't eliminate me the next day. Instead, he sends Sylvie home. The choice surprises no one. Three thousand years as a dryad gave Sylvie a no-nonsense attitude, and she couldn't throw herself into the flirtations required for this game. It's too bad; while she and I didn't get to know each other well, I sensed she was trustworthy. That's more than I can say of some of the other females here.

After the elimination, Tor speaks to the eight of us who are left. "I have an activity planned with one of you."

I fully expect him to say my name. Yesterday, he assured me we'd spend some time alone. His gaze meets mine, and I smile.

Then his attention shifts to the right. "Ninette, care to come with me?"

Ninette? The lavender-haired faerie is Margot's best friend here, and while she's not overtly cruel, she's certainly not kind. I force my mouth to retain its smile as Ninette and Tor walk away. Then I make my way to the main library, seeking distraction in the form of fiction.

As my eyes scan book titles, I can't focus. When Tor said he'd arrange for us to spend time together, did he mean it? Or is it a promise he's made to every other female here? The fact is, I don't know what he's telling them or what he's doing with them . . . except when I glimpse their interactions, like Margot's disgusting display with him in the dining room yesterday morning.

I'm spending all my time focused on one male, while he's happily juggling eight suitors. We're only six days into this competition, and it's already gotten old. He has more choices than he knows what to do with, and we're all expected to put our hearts on the line for him. The risk is entirely ours. It's the definition of *unfair*.

"He'll ask you to spend time with him soon, I'm sure of it," someone says.

I turn to find Rochelle standing behind me. "Apparently I wear my heart on my sleeve," I say with a rueful smile.

She grins. "I'm just good at reading people." She takes my hand and squeezes it. "Try not to think about it, Aeryn. It's all part of the game."

I want to protest that it's a whole lot easier for her to relax than it is for me. She's gorgeous, with her tall figure, tan skin that shimmers with rose gold highlights, and that stunning, violet-red hair. And I'm pretty sure she already kissed Tor, so she's created romantic memories with him. The kiss he gave me on my cheek yesterday was . . . brotherly.

But I don't say any of that, because she's right—this is a game. And maybe the rules are unfair, but I want to win. I can't do that if I show my weakness to the other contestants.

I paste on a smile. "I'll be fine. I thought I'd find a good book to read today, but I'm not familiar with Fae literature. Any suggestions?"

Her dark blue eyes sparkle. "Want to read to each other? I have a particular one in mind." When I agree, she finds the book and pulls it down. "Come on, let's grab that window seat over there before anyone else does."

We sit, and I quickly discover the reason she chose this book: it's hilariously awful. It's a romance novel written by a male who's clearly never spent time with a real female—his descriptions of her body, her reactions, and her desires are groan worthy. We spend most of the day laughing uproariously as we do dramatic readings from that book, then from another by the same author. It's the most fun I've had since I got here.

After dinner, I go to bed with another book, one that draws me in with its beautiful writing. I fall asleep early and immediately dream of the raven-winged prince.

He and I are wearing the same formalwear we had on in my last dream. We're sitting on a settee in some sort of little alcove. Curtains provide privacy. The prince's hands are cupping my face, and he's leaning in, eyes closed.

I think he's going to kiss me.

"Oh, my," I murmur, pulling away from him.

His eyes pop open.

"I barely know you," I say. "Maybe we should save the kissing for later."

His dark brows lift in surprise as he releases my face.

I can't help but laugh. "I'm guessing women don't refuse you very often."

He laughs too, and he doesn't deny it. "What would you like to know about me?"

I ask a question, and that's all it takes. He tells me all about his hobbies, his favorite foods, the fencing tournament he's training for . . .

He's still talking when I wake. I sit up in bed. My fingers come to my lips, and I laugh softly. I haven't been kissed in over two years; I should've taken the opportunity the fictional prince offered.

I review the conversation from my dream. I pull in a quick gasp as I realize something: the prince's voice was familiar to me. Perhaps it's my memory playing tricks on me, but I think . . . I think he sounded like Tor.

According to the clock, I only slept for a few minutes. But I can't stop thinking about the dream, so I rise and pace. I end up at the window, gazing into the garden. Wyatt is there, pruning one of the luminescent plants.

He must get lonely working out there by himself all the time. I put on a robe and my shoes, slip from the room, and hurry to the garden.

"Aeryn!" Wyatt glances at my clothing. "Did you have trouble sleeping?"

"Yes. Well, actually, I did sleep, but a dream woke me, and I'm wide awake now. I thought you might like some company."

"I'm finishing up for the night." He makes one more snip with his clippers and gestures to a nearby bench. "Care to sit?"

"Sure."

We both get settled, and he gives me that warm smile again. "Good dream or nightmare?"

"Good. I've been having such vivid dreams since I came. This is the third time I've dreamed of the same person."

"Well, that's intriguing. Who were you dreaming about?"

"No one I knew." I laugh a bit awkwardly, but as before, I find myself eager to open up to Wyatt. "I've been dreaming about a Fae prince, of all things."

Wyatt goes serious. "Really? What does he look like?"

"He has skin the color of pewter, black hair, and black-feathered wings."

"Handsome?"

"Very." A little laugh comes out of my mouth.

Wyatt nods, like he'd expected that answer. His gaze is intense. "These dreams, Aeryn . . . how do they compare to your normal dreams?"

"They're far more real than any dreams I've ever had." When he nods again, I say, "Is there something significant about that? You look so serious."

This time, he's the one who laughs. "I'm sorry, I'm just surprised. What you're describing . . . it's dream magic, Aeryn. It's a rare type of magic, and I've never heard of a faerie developing it before they reach their five hundredth birthday."

I blink. "That can't be it. I seem to have little Fae blood, and I'm certainly not old. They're just vivid dreams."

"I'd agree with you, except . . ." He shakes his head. "Suffice to say, I'm certain it's dream magic."

My gaze roves over his skin and eyes, which both look more gray than blue at night. I try to read something in his expression. "You can't tell me why, can you?"

"I'm sorry."

"Can you explain dream magic to me?"

"That, I can do. Magical dreams never show the whole truth, but they do *contain* truth. The people in them are real, though the locations and situations may not be."

"So the prince is real?"

That mysterious smile tugs at his lips again. "These dreams show you who a person really is, things they might hide in real life. Through dream magic, you can know their true character."

I nod, mulling over his words. What have I learned about this prince's character in my dreams? I'm not sure yet. I've seen him so little.

In the distance, I hear a dull *boom*. "What was that?"

Wyatt is sitting up straight, tension in his taut muscles. "Jackie told me—but I don't want to worry you—"

"About the people trying to breach the barrier?" I've hardly thought about that since arriving, but now, my heart is pounding. "That's what we heard, isn't it?"

"I suspect it was. Please don't worry. The barrier is magical; explosives won't affect it at all. But they must be getting desperate if that's what they're trying."

"What can we do to stop them?"

He looks to the side, and I know he's again searching for words he's allowed to say. When he turns back to me, his eyes pierce mine.

"Aeryn, continue to take this competition seriously. Listen to your dreams. Keep your heart open. Please."

I don't know how that will keep Fae soldiers from entering the estate, but I nod. "That's what I'm doing."

"Good." He lets out a little sigh. "I'm glad you're here."

"So am I." I can't pull my gaze from his. At last, I stand, and he follows suit. "I'm not sure what I'd do without your help, Wyatt."

"It's my pleasure." He offers me his right hand. When I take it, he lifts my hand, like he's going to kiss it. Then he suddenly lowers it and shakes it firmly. "Good night. I think I'll do a little more work after all."

He avoids my gaze as he releases my hand and walks away.

15

IT'S BEEN WAY TOO LONG SINCE I'VE BEEN KISSED

The next morning, all eight of us who are still in the competition enjoy a leisurely breakfast with Tor. I'm sitting next to him, determined to catch his attention. As soon as there's a lull in the conversation, I touch his arm and speak on the first topic that comes to mind. "I spent quite a lot of time in the beautiful library yesterday."

"The *beautiful* library?" he says, and we share a secretive smile. As far as I know, no one else here has been to the other library, the one he said was full of ugly books. "Did you enjoy it?"

"So much. It has more books than any other I've visited."

Tor's smile widens, and he tells me in enthusiastic detail how many books the library holds, how rare and valuable some of them are, and even the history of the well-known faerie who designed the space. I barely get a chance to speak, but I love witnessing his passion.

At last, he returns his attention to the rest of the contestants. "I'd like to spend the day in the kitchen with four of you, making dinner for tonight." He stands. "Ninette, Justyne, Rochelle, and Karine, will you come with me?"

Again, my heart drops. Does Tor even remember promising me we'd spend time together?

As they're leaving, he turns back to the four of us who are still at the table. "Tonight, after dinner, I'll spend time with just one of you." His eyes fix on me, and the smile he gives me fills me with warmth.

When he leaves and I return my attention to the others, Margot is glaring at me with those sharp green eyes. Her straight posture and short hair make her long neck appear positively regal, and despite the hatred currently suffusing her gaze, I can see how Tor might find her attractive.

She turns to Felia, who's on her right. "I overheard a conversation two days ago between Aeryn and Tor. She wanted to quit the competition and become a servant in this house."

Desiree, who's sitting next to me, straightens. The light above us glimmers off her golden, spiraled horns. Her wide eyes find mine, a question in them: *Is this true?* I probably shouldn't admit it, but I find myself nodding.

"I'd hate for Aeryn to be disappointed." Margot says. Then she picks up her plate, which is full of a stack of feather-light pancakes, smothered in syrup. She lifts it high and flips it over, letting the food fall to the white tablecloth. "Oops," she says. Then she slowly pours her glass of grape juice on the table too.

She turns to me. "Clean it up." Her hands are on the table, and one of her pointer fingers lifts.

My heart drops. That's what she does when she curses people. My legs move of their own accord, forcing me to stand. My hands are next, reaching for the sticky pancakes. I have no control over my actions as I pick up one of them and return it to her plate.

"Oh no, that won't do," Margot says.

Another twitch of her finger, and I bend at the waist so forcefully, my face slams into the table. I grunt as pain envelops my nose. Then my head lifts and repositions itself. My jaw opens and closes around a pancake. Tears roll from both my eyes as I carry the pancake with my teeth and drop it on the plate.

"Stop!" Desiree says.

"Shut up, Tor will hear you!" Margot snaps as I pick up another pancake with my teeth. Juice soaks into the bodice of my yellow dress every time she forces me against the table.

Desiree shouts this time: "*Stop!*"

All at once, I regain control over my body. I drop the pancake and turn to Desiree. "Thank you."

Her pale-pink skin is a few shades darker than usual. I remember it looking that way when Margot cursed her on our first night here. She touches my sore nose, healing it. Empathy and anger battle for prominence in her eyes.

Margot speaks in a low, chilling voice that pulls my attention back to her. "You will not speak of this to Tor." Her finger twitches, and I know that's her way of threatening me. Yes, there's a rule against curses. But what's the use of getting her kicked out of the competition if she kills or maims me as she leaves?

Out of the corner of my eye, I see a bit of movement. Thinking it's Tor, I turn. All I see is a mirror on the wall. No one is sitting over there. Yet . . . I saw something. Wyatt's warning about mirrors returns to me, and my throat goes tight as I wonder who might be watching us through the mirrors in this house. Who saw Margot's attack and my humiliation? Whose side are they on?

I flee, holding in tears until I reach my bedroom. As soon as the door closes, I start crying quietly.

I didn't even cry this much when I was a little girl. What is this competition doing to me?

A familiar hiss reaches my ears. I look down. When the brownish-bronze snake slithers toward me, I don't try to move away. She stops at my feet, and I don't know why, but I kneel and hold out my arm.

She slithers to me, spiraling her cool body onto my forearm. The action feels like a hug, and when she hisses, it reminds me of when my mother used to calm me with a gentle "Shh." I run my fingertips along the snake's smooth body, and my tears subside.

I'm still in this competition. And if I'm lucky enough to get time with Tor tonight, I won't let Margot or anyone else stop me from making the most of it.

When I arrive at dinner, Tor is already there, along with the four faeries who helped him prepare the food. He's wearing a royal-blue suit and a cream-colored shirt. The outfit isn't identical to the one the raven-haired prince in my dreams wears, but it's similar enough to catch my attention.

Tor's hairless head, red eyes, and split nose aren't what I'd consider handsome. But the strength in those broad shoulders, the way the fine fabric outlines his muscular arms . . . Just as I'm thinking, *Not every part of him is beastly,* I catch a brief glimpse of his hairless tail, flicking the air behind him. I flinch. I could probably get used to that rat-like feature, but it might take a while.

Before Tor sits, he picks up a glass of wine and makes a toast in honor of the eight of us who are left. Once again, I focus on that familiar-looking suit. Wyatt said the people in my dreams are real. What does that mean? Both the prince and Tor have the same regal confidence. They share the same voice, if I recall correctly. Could the prince in my dreams be Tor? It makes sense that my imagination would convert him into a more appealing form.

Dinner is pleasant enough, though the food isn't as consistently good as usual. At the end of the meal, Tor stands. "I'd like to have a drink with one of you in my quarters." His red eyes slowly travel over the four of us who didn't spend the day with him. Then his gaze settles on me. "Aeryn, will you do me the honor?"

A drink. In his quarters. Just him and me. *Hell, yes!* I shout in my head. But I manage a demure nod and say, "Of course."

He walks to my seat, pulls it out, and offers his arm. I take it. Rochelle, who's sitting on my left, winks.

Then we're in the hallway, and good heavens, the arm I'm holding is firm as stone under the smooth fabric of his suit. As we walk, I tell Tor the title of a book I spent the day reading. He commends my choice and shares stories he's heard about the author's eccentricities.

We're both laughing when we arrive at a broad, tall door decorated with golden leaves and flowers. Tor opens it and gestures for me to enter.

His sitting room is more luxurious than any room I've ever seen. Gilding is everywhere—on the furniture, the ceiling, and the frame of the massive mirror mounted on one wall. Even the floors boast wide, golden seams between the large sheets of marble. All the paintings on the walls feature the castle and grounds. In one corner is a tall, golden statue of a faerie female wearing only garlands of flowery vines. None of it is the style of décor I'd choose, but it's undeniably lovely.

Tor leads me to a crackling fire in a gilded fireplace, before which sit a small couch and three chairs. "Please, make yourself comfortable," he says.

I choose the couch, hoping he'll take the hint and join me. With a smile, he does.

There's a small table in front of us containing a crystal bottle with a stopper that looks like it's made of a single, large ruby. He pours red liquid into two gorgeous crystal glasses. They look like wine glasses, but smaller.

"Dessert wine," he says, handing me one, "made from the flameberry, which grows only in Faerie."

We clink our glasses together and drink. I can see where the berry got its name; the drink has a spicy bite to it that sets my mouth on fire. I love it.

Tor takes a few sips, then puts his glass down. I do the same. He turns to me and says in that rich, warm voice, "We're finally alone."

"This room is beautiful," I say.

"It's my sanctuary."

My brows rise at that. "Until the competition, you and Wyatt were the only two living here. I would think the entire castle was your sanctuary."

A low laugh. "That's true. But this is the place I feel most at home."

I don't know when I'll get more time with him, and I'm determined to make the most of what we have. I shift so that I'm facing him, and he does the same.

"You look lovely tonight," he breathes.

That brings a genuine smile to my lips. I expect him to touch me—we're sitting so close to each other—but he doesn't move. Maybe he wants me to take the initiative. Normally, I'd wait for him to at least draw closer to me, but this competition requires boldness . . . and the wine provides it to me.

I bring my right hand to his stark-white cheek, and when he leans into the touch, I get bolder, running my fingers along the folds of his pointed ear. He closes his eyes and lets out a pleased sigh.

"Were you lonely?" I whisper. My fingers move to his neck and trace little swirls on the smooth skin there. "Before we came?"

He opens his eyes and meets my gaze. "I was. Terribly."

"At least you weren't totally alone . . . but I suppose you don't have much in common with a wise old gardener."

A rumbly laugh emerges from his chest. "I've never thought of him as wise, and he's certainly not old. We're near the same age."

My hand stills on his neck. I try to remember why I assumed Wyatt was old when I met him. Was it just because he's a faerie, and so many of them have lived for hundreds of years or longer? Was it the wisdom I sensed in him?

Knowing now that he's younger, many of his actions take on a different meaning. The looks he's given me, the way he seemed to feel he needed to escape from our last conversation, the time he—

Tor interrupts my thoughts. "But you're right, I have little in common with Wyatt. We rarely talk."

I force my attention back to the faerie I'm sitting beside. My other hand rises to his neck, and I trace his skin along the edge of his collar.

He's not wearing a tie. On a whim, I grasp the first button of his soft shirt. "May I?" I whisper.

He nods. I release the first button, then the second. My fingers trace the smooth, firm, white skin I've exposed.

Until now, Tor's hands have been in his lap. In a flash, one moves to my back, pulling me to him. The other cradles the back of my head, tilting it up toward him, his claws tickling one of my ears.

His eyes drop to my mouth. Then they close, and his lips descend toward mine.

I almost push him away, like I did with the prince in my dream. It's only my tenth day here, and I've gotten very little time alone with Tor. I hardly know him.

But I don't want to refuse him. His warm laugh has seeped into me, and his arms are so strong, and, damn it, it's been way too long since I've been kissed.

So I close the gap between us and press my lips to his. Parts of Tor are beastly, but his lips are perfect—warm and soft and full. We kiss each other gently, sweetly. It's not enough. I press myself closer to him, opening my mouth and teasing his lips with my tongue. It takes a moment for him to react to that, but then he responds in kind, and we're both tasting each other, sharing heavy breaths and soft moans.

I'm enjoying myself, but my brain, as always, gets in the way. I know I didn't imagine his brief bout of hesitation when I tried to deepen the kiss. I'm more eager than he is, and my racing mind tells me that's a danger sign.

But my thoughts and fears have driven all my decisions for the last two years of my life, and I'm tired of it. If I want to win this prince's heart, I won't do it by overthinking things. He told me to prove that I wanted to be here. So I shove every doubt from my mind and push Tor back against the arm of the couch, kissing him with even more urgency, running my hands over his wide shoulders and thick arms.

He's responding with just as much passion now, and as his hand slides along my back, I feel a tug and hear a rip—he's caught the fabric with his claw. *Just as he did with Margot*, I think. In an effort to banish the memory, I speak his name against his lips.

He brings his mouth to my ear. "Is this what you thought I meant when I asked you to come have a drink?"

I laugh and capture his lips with mine again.

Minutes pass—how many, I don't know. Time isn't the same in the realm we've entered, a universe of insatiable lips and roaming hands, of quiet words and loud breaths. My mind wanders into more heated territory. I unbuttoned the top of his shirt; should I undo the rest? How would he respond if I asked him to tear open the laces of my dress with his claws?

I bet he'd keep me here longer if I did that. The thought rings through my mind, so loud that it's almost audible.

And that's when I pull my lips off his. Because I realize something. I don't want to give myself to Tor in that way. The deepest things I know about him are that he dislikes nonfiction books, and he likes gilded picture frames. Kissing him has been fun. But I won't bare my body and my soul for him, just for the sake of this game. I can't.

I sit up. Tor does the same. He's still breathing heavily as he picks up his wine and hands mine to me. "That was fun," he says.

I laugh. "It was." My mind is spinning, as usual, so I bring up a topic I suspect he'll be happy to talk about with little input from me. "Tell me more about the décor in here."

"Let's walk around, and I'll show it all to you."

Again, he offers me his well-formed arm. My pulse returns to its normal pace as we stroll through the sitting room and then his bedroom, stopping frequently for him to tell me about the artists who created everything—not just the paintings and statues, but the furniture too.

When I catch him yawning, I say, "We should both get some sleep."

He walks me all the way to my room. At the door, he takes my hands. "Thank you for the lovely night, Aeryn."

"I should be the one thanking you." I stand on my tiptoes, and when he leans his head down, I give him one more lovely kiss.

A door closes nearby. Someone was watching us, I know they were.

And maybe it makes me as bitchy as Margot, but my pulse races in delight. My time with Tor went well . . . and one of my competitors knows it. I'm finally in this game, really and truly.

"Good night, Tor," I say, before slipping into my room.

When I open the door, the snake is slithering away, and I wonder if she was watching us beneath the gap of the door. "You win," I tell her, kneeling and holding out a hand. "I'm glad he didn't let me be his servant."

She winds herself around my arm, and I stroke her smooth skin. "I still barely know him," I whisper, "but someone who kisses that well is worth sticking around for."

Her hiss sounds almost like a laugh.

16

FIND YOUR MAGIC

I'm still on a high from Tor's kisses when I get to breakfast the next morning. Justyne and Rochelle are already there, which further lifts my mood. Maybe Margot will sleep late, and my morning will be almost as enjoyable as my evening was.

I grab a buttery pastry and a big spoonful of berries. I bite into the pastry. Sweet filling, made of red fruit I've never tasted before, bursts into my mouth. I groan with delight.

"You look like you're enjoying that as much as you enjoyed kissing Tor last night." Rochelle smirks and flutters her lashes at me. When I blush, she gives me a wide smile. "I was about to leave my room to grab a snack, and I saw you. I thought you deserved to know."

I chew and swallow. This room is feeling very warm. "I'm sorry to subject you to that."

She grabs my hand and squeezes. "No apologies necessary. Good for you, Aeryn! You're in the game!" She leans in closer, grinning. "He's a good kisser, right?"

That's all the confirmation I need that Rochelle has kissed him too. I glance at Justyne. She's gone totally still, from her black braids that she's formed into a headdress, to her filmy wings. And in that moment, I'm certain of two things—she hasn't kissed Tor, and this conversation is making her feel like an outsider.

Maybe I'd relish that if she were someone else. But Justyne is my friend, and my heart aches for her. I give Rochelle a friendly smile and a wink. After all, she's just having a bit of fun. "I don't kiss and tell," I say. Then I return my attention to Justyne, determined to change the subject. "I was thinking about all the rumors we discussed the other day. About the history of the royal family who used to live here."

She perks up immediately. "I wish we could be sure what really happened."

"I don't," Rochelle says. "Fiction is always more interesting than the truth." She lifts her cup of coffee as if making a toast. We all clink our cups together.

"I was thinking about the mystery of Prince Luc," I say to both of them. "I came up with an explanation for what might've happened to him. It's probably ridiculous, but I've got way too much time to think up wild tales in this place!"

"I'm sure it's no more ridiculous than a beast taking over a dead prince's domain," Rochelle says.

"Exactly," Justyne says. "What's your theory?"

I set down my coffee and lower my voice. "What if Luc has somehow disguised himself . . . as a gardener?"

Rochelle's eyes widen, and she smiles with delight.

But Justyne shakes her head. "I visited the estate about twelve years ago. Wyatt was here then, looking just like he looks now. We chatted when I walked through the garden."

"Damn," I mutter. It would've been fun to solve a mystery—or at least to come up with a story believable enough to turn into a rumor.

At that moment, Margot walks in. I return my attention to my food, lamenting the end of my lovely morning.

Tor doesn't eat with us, but he enters the room after all the contestants have arrived. A small smile steals onto his lips when he sees me, but his expression quickly turns serious again. "In fifteen minutes," he says, "please come to the parlor. Two of you are going home today."

The room is mostly silent for the next quarter-hour. There are a few whispers as we walk to the parlor, and I get the sense no one feels confident today. The mood rubs off on me, and though Tor has given me every reason to think I'm staying, my heart is racing by the time the eight of us stand in front of him.

He's in a crisp, dark-red shirt and black slacks. The color combination against his white skin is somewhat macabre.

Today, he skips the introductory comments. "Aeryn," he says, "will you stay?"

I can't help the huge grin that takes over my face. I hadn't dared hope he'd call my name first.

He calls four more names, leaving three females with their fates undetermined—Margot, Karine, and Ninette.

First, he sends Karine home. The gold jewelry on her small horns glimmers as she leaves. I hate to see her go. She and I weren't close, but she seemed nice enough.

Ninette and Margot are both watching Tor, their eyes wide. One will go home, one will stay.

"Margot," Tor says, "will you stay?"

It wasn't the name I'd hoped to hear him say. But I'm still thrilled to see Ninette leave. The beautiful, lavender-haired faerie was Margot's best friend here, and I didn't remotely trust her.

I'm feeling fairly giddy when Tor comes back from telling Karine and Ninette goodbye. He clears his throat, and those of us who are left—Justyne, Rochelle, Felia, Margot, Desiree, and I—all go silent.

"Four are gone," Tor says. "One of the six of you will become my wife. From now on, this competition will include a series of challenges that will help me decide who to keep and who to send home. You'll be expected to use magic to win."

Every female in the room turns to look at me. I'm the one contestant who, as far as they know, has no magic. Even the magic I know about—my dreams—isn't likely to help much during these challenges.

My eyes lock onto Tor. When he meets my gaze, I hope he sees the betrayal there and the question that goes along with it:

Why would you do this to me?

After Tor's announcement, I spend the rest of the day with Justyne, Desiree, and Rochelle, who are practicing magic. I want to join in, so I make a fool of myself waving my hands around, breathing deeply, even lying on the grass, soaking up the sun. Nothing works. My new friends claim to feel mystical power around and within them all the time. I feel nothing.

When I go to bed, exhausted and frustrated, I have no trouble falling asleep. The beautiful Fae prince inhabits my dreams. We're still in our formalwear, but this time, we're standing on a balcony above a ballroom. On the dance floor below, dozens of faeries stand silently, gazes lifted to us. All their faces are blurry—the prince is still the focus of this dream.

His rich voice fills the room. "I'm pleased to introduce you to Aeryn."

The crowd applauds.

The prince takes my hand and lifts it, saying softly, "Give a little spin."

I spin once, showing off the slinky, cream-colored dress. The crowd cheers.

A wide, gorgeous smile takes over the prince's lips. "Music!" he commands.

A band plays, and he pulls me close, dancing with me on the wide balcony. My feet are light and graceful in this dream world, and I feel like I could dance forever.

The prince's mouth brushes my ear. "I knew they'd love the dress."

"It's beautiful," I say. "And it matches your shirt perfectly."

"By design." He spins me again, his admiring eyes fixed on my form. When he pulls me close and we continue our dance, he says, "If you marry me, Aeryn, do you know what that will mean?"

All I can think is that I could spend my life dancing like this, and I can't imagine anything more wonderful. "Tell me," I murmur.

"There have been no high-profile unions between Fae and mortals in generations. By marrying you, I would be bringing together two worlds. Two peoples. That would be my legacy. Isn't that marvelous?"

That's when I wake. I smile into the darkness as the prince's words anchor themselves in my mind. Again, I wonder if the male in my dreams is Tor, in a different form. I'd never thought of marriage with him from the perspective of bringing unity to humans and Fae. It's something none of the other contestants can offer.

But if I can't do magic, marriage with him will never be more than a dream.

My smile disappears, and it takes forever for me to get back to sleep.

The next day, we all spend time in various parts of the castle, Tor wandering between us. I hide out in the library vault, reading fascinating accounts of Fae history. Tor finds me after a couple of hours.

We sit in two chairs. Too frustrated for anything but bluntness, I blurt, "There's no way I can win magical challenges!"

"Are you sure?"

"I've been practicing with no luck."

"Some mortals who are part Fae have learned to use magic. I'm sure there are books here about it."

My voice rises in pitch. "Why is it so important to you?"

He leans forward and takes my hands. Again, his claws tickle the sensitive skin of my wrists. "I look forward to the day when this estate returns to Faerie. When that happens, I will be a king. My wife will need to lead as a proper queen. In Faerie, that includes magic."

My mind spins as I take in this information. Tor has never presented himself as a prince, yet he expects to become a king. Who is he really? I picture the gorgeous face of the prince from my dream. He looks nothing like Tor, but they remind me of one another.

Trying to shake off the confusing thoughts, I blurt, "This estate is returning to Faerie? I thought you wanted it to stay on Earth."

He shakes his head.

"I've never seen you use magic except when you healed me," I say. He flinches, as if the words hurt him, but I keep going. "Why would you expect your queen to be powerful when you don't seem to be?"

His hands tighten on mine. "Many things will change when I marry. Things will be as they're meant to be."

"What do you mean by that?"

All he says is, "Find your magic, Aeryn."

I expect him to steal a few kisses, but he just squeezes my hands again, then leaves.

I brush off the disappointment and set off in search of books. The information I need isn't hard to find.

It's also not encouraging.

Yes, some mortals with only a bit of Fae blood develop the ability to cast spells. But no one knows how to make it happen. The only advice I find boils down to *relax and stop worrying*.

I read all day. A couple of hours past sunset, my eyes are stinging from overuse. I put away the final book and trudge to the garden.

"Tor wants us to use magic in the competition," I say when I see Wyatt. "Any idea how I can develop mine?"

He looks up from the statue he's dusting. "The best thing you can do is relax." My glare must be toxic, because he holds both hands up defensively. "I'm sorry, Aeryn. If I had a better tip, I'd share it. I know of nothing you can do to force your magic to develop." He tilts his head and gives me a gentle smile. "Why don't you sit out here for a while? Enjoy the garden."

It feels unproductive, but I don't have any better ideas. I plop onto a bench. Wyatt sits next to me. We don't talk, but as the minutes pass, I feel my muscles loosening. I take note of the fragrances wafting from the flowers. My eyes wander over the luminescent species that light up the garden with their gentle, colorful glow, and a small smile steals over my lips.

After perhaps an hour, I stand. I didn't find magic. But I did find peace. "Thank you, Wyatt," I say.

"Sleep well, Aeryn."

I do—so well that I wake late. I must've slept through the birds' wake-up taps on my door. All the other contestants, along with our host, are in the dining room when I arrive.

As soon as I sit, Tor stands. "Our first challenge is today."

17

IT FEELS LIKE A WARNING

"You must each create a work of art that is also practical in some way," Tor tells us. "For materials, you may use anything you find in the house, though you may not enter any occupied living quarters. In judging, I'll give more credit if you use your magic to create or alter materials. However, you may not use the house's creative magic."

Damn it. The house has provided whatever we need since we arrived. If I can't take advantage of that, how will I find art supplies?

Tor continues, "You may work in pairs if you wish, though you must each create your own work of art, and you will be judged separately. Three winners will spend the entire day with me tomorrow."

I shift my gaze away from Tor, looking for someone to work with. Immediately, I realize I waited too long. Justyne and Desiree are nodding and smiling at one another; it's clear they are partners. That doesn't surprise me, since they often spend time together. I would've thought Rochelle might pair up with me . . . but Felia has grabbed her hand, and they're quietly agreeing to work together.

That leaves me. And Margot.

Our eyes meet. Then her cold, green gaze slides over to Tor. "I'll work alone."

Tor says, "You have until lunchtime to complete your project. The rule about not cursing or harming each other still stands."

"Tor!" Margot's voice is quiet, but I see the tension in her face. "Curse magic is my specialty."

"You have other magic too, even if it's weaker. You may use that." His gaze sweeps over all of us. "The challenge starts now. Bring your completed projects to the parlor when you're done."

I don't have time for breakfast. Along with the other females, I hurry out of the room. Running through the house, I frantically search for supplies, preferably yarn. I'm a fast knitter, and with the right supplies, I can have a hat made by dinner. It'll be both beautiful and practical.

But as I rush from one room and floor and wing to another, my breaths growing more urgent and panicked, I find no yarn. I do come across a well-lit painting studio that no one else seems to have found. Unfortunately, I'm terrible at painting. I keep searching the house, desperately grabbing items that catch my eye: a pretty gilded lampshade, a pillow made with fine damask fabric, a crystal wine glass.

I have no idea what I'm going to do with all this stuff.

I sit on a couch in a random room, cradling my items and catching my breath.

Margot runs in, panting as hard as I am. Her rust-colored skin is flushed a shade darker than usual. She scowls at me, then puts her hands on her hips. "We're both at a disadvantage. You have no magic at all, and I can't use my primary power. We have to work together. Maybe as partners, we can figure something out."

She's probably right. But . . . she's *Margot*.

She lets out a frustrated sigh, sweeping her toned arms to the side. "Aeryn, I'm not allowed to curse you. It's one thing to play a prank on you at breakfast. I wouldn't risk something as important as this challenge by breaking the rules. We've already wasted an hour. Come on. Let's work together."

I pause. Something touches my ankle, and I recognize the sensation of snake skin. She must've been waiting under the couch. I remain still as she wraps around my ankle, tighter than ever before.

It feels like a warning. But I'm sitting here holding a lamp shade, a pillow, and a glass. Clearly, I need help. I tuck my ankle under the couch and shake it gently. When the snake doesn't move, I shake her harder. She releases me and slides away, though I can somehow sense her continued disapproval.

"All right," I say to Margot. "Let's do it."

She sits. We're two partners, thrown together by necessity, who don't trust each other even a little bit. Neither of us seems to know what to say.

Hesitantly, I tell her I want to knit something. Her gaze is as distrustful as mine as she informs me she's skilled at painting. We glare at each other.

I break the silence. "I found a painting studio with plenty of supplies."

Her eyes widen briefly. She blurts, "I saw a knitted blanket in a sitting room. You could unravel it."

We nod, and in that moment, it feels like we're true allies. She leads me to the blanket. I grab it and take her to the painting studio. Wordlessly, we separate, our brief partnership having fulfilled its purpose.

In an unused study, I find several pencils I can use as knitting needles. I sharpen them with a knife that was sitting in a drawer.

Then I get to work unraveling the blanket and winding the yarn into a neat ball. The wool fiber is high quality, and it feels amazing on my fingers. It's a warm, soft connection to home. Soon, I'm knitting quickly, designing as I go, working intricate cables into the hat. I have no magic to bring to this project, but creativity is magical in its own way. I finish half an hour before dinnertime and bring the hat to the parlor.

Justyne and Desiree are already there. My heart drops when I see their proud smiles. Justyne is a nature faerie, and Desiree's specialty is creation magic. That's a lot of useful power between the two of them. I hold my hat behind my back, crumpling it.

They show me their projects. Justyne has created an herb garden that's enchanted to grow with or without sunlight. Interspersed with the herbs are miniature flowers. It's a work of practical art, fitting Tor's requirements perfectly. Desiree is holding a stone sculpture of an adorable baby faerie with wings. She tells me that when someone pours water in its cupped hands, the stone will purify it.

"Where's yours?" Justyne asks.

I try to smile as I hold it up.

They *ooh* and *aah*, claiming they've never seen a knitted item that was so beautifully designed and stitched. Their words give me a bit of hope.

Margot enters next. She shows off a water pitcher that she's painted with a gorgeous floral design. Though curse magic is her specialty, she successfully used blessing magic to enchant the pitcher to obey when she says, "Pour."

She asks to see my project, and I hold it up. Her eyes widen, and for a split second, I can see the true admiration there. Then her expression goes cold.

She lifts a finger.

The stitches in my hat turn sloppy and uneven. It unravels at the crown. The cable design now has innumerable errors in it.

The beautiful item that I spent hours crafting is ruined. My gaze finds Justyne and Desiree. They're chatting with each other, oblivious to what just happened.

"I thought you'd be able to do more with that yarn," Margot says, her voice sweet as syrup.

My face heats with an angry flush. "You cursed it!"

My exclamation brings Justyne and Desiree over. "Margot cursed it?" Justyne asks, ire blazing in her dark eyes.

"I most certainly did not," Margot says. "Aeryn has no artistic skill, and I refuse to take the blame for that."

"We saw the hat before you came in!" Justyne says.

"The light in here is terrible," Margot snaps. "You only think I cursed her because she's claiming it. If you try to accuse me of that on hearsay alone, Tor will never believe you."

Sweet, smart Desiree, who was a silent victim of Margot's curse magic on our first day here, walks right up to me. "I'll stand up for you."

"It won't work," I say. "We have no proof. You didn't even see it happen."

"But if I—"

Tor walks in. "Don't worry about it," I whisper to Desiree. At least there's no elimination attached to this challenge.

The other contestants arrive, and the judging goes quickly. Tor doesn't shame me for my awful hat. He just glances at it, then ignores it. Somehow, that feels worse than outright disapproval. He names Desiree, Margot, and Rochelle as the winners.

As we're leaving the room, I glare at the pitcher in Margot's hand. My chest goes suddenly hot, and I nearly gasp at the strange sensation.

The pitcher cracks loudly. Half of it falls to the floor and shatters.

We all halt. "Who cursed my pitcher?" Margot demands. She glares at the group, but she hardly spares a glance for me. Everyone knows I don't have magic.

No one replies.

At last, Tor says, "Your enchantment must've weakened it, Margot. I'm afraid I'll need to choose a different winner. Justyne, I hope you'll honor me by taking her place tomorrow."

It's all I can do not to grin. I'd never have cursed someone on purpose, not with the rules Tor has set up. But it seems my Fae magic has awakened.

And if it chose Margot as its target . . . well, I'm certainly not complaining.

DON'T TRUST THE GARDENER

The next day, Tor and the winners have a private breakfast together somewhere in the castle. I eat with Margot and Felia, then spend a lovely, quiet day exploring the castle. My favorite discovery is a tiny courtyard hosting an overgrown rose garden. It's stunning in its wildness.

The three of us join each other again for dinner. Afterward, I get a glass of wine and sit on the large porch I've visited before.

I've been relaxing there for an hour or so when Rochelle finds me. She sits in a chair next to me and tells me all about the day she had. It was full of delicious food and fun games, and Tor spent quite a bit of time alone with each of the three contestants. As I listen, I try to brush away the envy bubbling inside me.

"Oh, I forgot," Rochelle says, "before lunch, Tor brought us to the ballroom to teach us a dance. Felia was there, and she looked pretty angry when he kicked her out." She leans toward me and says in a low voice, "Working with her yesterday was awful. Every time she speaks, I get the feeling she's lying. I don't think she really cares for Tor. She may seem a little nicer than Margot, but she's covering up a lot of deviousness."

Just then, Margot and Felia step onto the porch, so Rochelle and I can't continue our conversation. Not long after that, I go inside, intent on getting some good sleep.

I'm finally getting a better feel of how the castle is laid out, so I send the birds away and take a circuitous route to my room. As I cross through a gallery full of gorgeous portraits, I see movement in the corner of my eye. I pivot to identify what caused it.

I'm facing an oval mirror with a frame that looks like it's made of twisted, dried vines. It doesn't match the opulence of the rest of the room. For a moment, I examine myself in the mirror. That must be what I saw—my own moving reflection.

Then, all at once, the face I'm looking at is no longer my own. It belongs to a stunning Fae female. She has high cheekbones, violet-blue eyes, and pointed ears emerging from long, curly black hair. The only creases in her flawless bronze skin come from the wide smile she's giving me. "Hello, Aeryn," she says in a melodic voice that's as beautiful as she is.

"Um . . . hello."

She laughs softly. "I'm sorry, it's terribly rude of me to call you by name when I haven't introduced myself. My name is Cerise. I'm a friend of Tor's. He and I often speak at this mirror. What a delight to meet the mortal woman he's told me so much about."

"He talks about me?"

"Of course. You fascinate him."

Wyatt's warning about mirrors blares in my mind. Has this female really heard about me from Tor, or has she been watching me from mirrors throughout this castle?

"You look a bit frightened." Kindness shines from Cerise's eyes. "I know this must be startling. But if you're willing to speak with me, I'd be honored to help you through the competition. Tor thinks you're special, and that means I do too."

I'm not sure what to say. Based on Wyatt's words, I'm hesitant to trust anyone who speaks to me through a mirror, with the exception of Jackie. Cerise exudes genuine kindness, and I want to believe her, but should I?

After several seconds staring at her, I say, "You're Tor's friend?"

Another lovely laugh. "Yes, and please be assured, I am nothing more than a friend. I care enough about him to want to ensure he chooses a wife he will be happy with. You may be that person. Will you let me assist you?"

I try to discern any deception in her features, but her expression is open and friendly. "I'm listening."

"You don't know how much I appreciate that. I'll give you two bits of advice, and if they're helpful, I hope you'll come back for more." When I nod, she says, "I know you don't have any magic."

That statement proves she's not omniscient. She doesn't know about my dreams or the inadvertent curse I placed on Margot's vase. "I'm certainly at a disadvantage," I say.

"You should join forces with one or two other contestants. I'm sure you know by now who is trustworthy. Agree to help one another stay in the competition. That will give each of you a higher likelihood of being the one Tor chooses."

It's sound advice, and I know who I'd want to partner with: Justyne and Rochelle. They've been there for me from the beginning; making our alliance official just makes sense. "What's your second piece of advice?" I ask.

Her smile disappears, replaced by a look that's somehow mournful. "Don't trust the gardener."

My eyes widen. "Wyatt?"

"I see your shock, and I understand it. He puts on a front of genuine kindness. But he will not lead you in the right direction, Aeryn. Be wary around him. Wyatt is not a true friend, as much as he seems to be one."

I try not to let my confusion show. "Thank you for the help."

"Thank you, dear Aeryn, for listening." One more smile, and she's gone.

And I have no idea what to believe anymore.

After a restless night, I leave my room half an hour earlier than usual the next morning. Quick steps bring me to the garden.

Wyatt is kneeling, buffing the nose on a statue of a child. He looks up as I approach, and the smile that spreads across his face is as kind as ever. Surely this gardener, who's welcomed me from the start and cares for the people trapped in these statues, couldn't be false, as Cerise claimed.

Or could he?

"It's an early morning for you," Wyatt says.

I stop a few steps away from him and blurt, "I met Cerise last night."

The hand holding the buffing cloth goes still. Wyatt stands slowly. The blue skin between his brows creases as he meets my gaze. He says nothing.

Questions flow from my lips, one after another. "I assume you know her? That she's the reason you told me to be wary of mirrors? Is she watching me through the other mirrors in the house? Is that the only one she can talk to me through?"

"Aeryn," he says softly.

I love hearing his voice speak my name. For a moment, it softens my heart, but my tension returns when he says nothing else. "Wyatt!" The frustration in the word is readily evident, though my voice is quiet. "Please tell me more! She's giving me advice, and some of it makes a whole lot of sense. I need to know if I should trust her!"

He rests his hands on my shoulders, his touch gentle and warm. "You don't need me to tell you more. You—*you*, Aeryn—have what it takes to navigate this." I pull away, and his eyes go wide. "I'm terribly sorry, I shouldn't have touched—I'm sorry."

I huff, briefly squeezing my eyes shut before meeting his gaze again. "I'm not angry that you touched me. I'm angry that you won't tell me more. You're hiding things from me, and *I don't know why*."

Up until now, I've assumed that magic prevented him from telling me pertinent details, but now I wonder if I was wrong about him this whole time. What if his reticence is part of some manipulative plot he committed to from the start? *Get the contestants to trust you,* I imagine him telling himself. *If you lie, you'll get caught, but if you simply refuse to say anything, they'll think you're helpless. They'll feel sorry for you.*

"Be yourself," Wyatt says. He looks at the castle, then gazes toward the tall, foggy barrier in the distance, where soldiers are supposedly trying to break through. "There's so much on the line."

Words like *be yourself* were encouraging to me when I first got here, but today, I need more than bland, feel-good advice. And it's just cruel to talk about a lot being on the line when he offers me so few details.

Embracing my anger, I turn to go. Then I halt, remembering the other thing I wanted to talk to him about. After accidentally cursing Margot, I thought Wyatt would be the one person I could confess to. Now I'm wary to do so . . . but I can't talk to anyone else either. I might get kicked out if I even hint to Tor that I sabotaged a fellow contestant. And while I trust Justyne and Rochelle, I don't want them to know I broke the rules.

I need answers. Maybe it won't hurt to ask Wyatt a general question. I face him again. He's standing still, hurt written all over his face.

I lift my chin, trying not to let his expression penetrate the walls I've built. "I've heard that when someone does their first major spell, that determines their magical specialty," I say. "What does *major spell* mean?"

He blinks at the sudden change in subject. "It's a powerful spell, one that causes a profound change. I know that's hard to measure, but when we perform our first major spell, we feel it. Something shifts in us. It feels different from all the smaller types of magic we've used before that."

"*Smaller types of magic,*" I repeat. "Are those minor spells ever unintentional?"

"Yes, especially at the start." A moment of silence passes as we stare at each other. "Did you use magic unintentionally?"

Hope has entered his eyes. How I wish I could believe it was real. But there's too much he won't tell me. I've lost the trust I'd placed in him.

"Goodbye, Wyatt," I say, and I don't look back as I walk out of the garden.

I'm sure of one thing: whatever Cerise's motivations, she's right about the wisdom of making an alliance. After breakfast, I invite Rochelle and Justyne to my room. We sit on my bed and agree to be true allies in this competition. We'll help one another during challenges, and if one of us gets information on a fellow contestant, we'll share it with each other. Maybe that'll result in all three of us staying here longer.

I can't trust Wyatt. I can't trust the faerie in the mirror.

But I know I can trust the two friends I made the first night I was here.

When they leave, the snake slithers out from under my bed. I kneel by her and hold out my hand. She wraps around my arm, giving me another of her comforting hugs. For now, that's enough confirmation that I'm headed in the right direction.

19

HERE'S TO BEING DIFFERENT

The next several days go by in an odd blur. I find myself thinking more about my father and siblings at home than what's happening in the castle.

Is Jackie still providing for my family? How is my father's health? Are my sisters making and selling knitted items, or is our brother's laziness rubbing off on them?

I have to believe the answer to the first question is *yes*. I can't entertain the idea that Jackie was lying about caring for my family. And winning is the best way to keep providing for them *after* the competition is over. I've got to focus on that.

But focus is hard to come by these days, when everything is so uncertain. I don't know if I should trust Wyatt or if Tor truly cares for me. I have no idea how to access whatever magic I have. I can't decide whether Cerise is an ally or an enemy. At least once a day, I visit the room where she talked to me. I don't see her in the mirror.

The only exciting thing that happens is that Tor gives us another challenge. It will test our creativity and grace, two qualities valued by the Fae. We must each move across the lawn in a unique way, preferably utilizing magic. We're competing individually, but this time, he doesn't give us any rules on how many people we can partner with as we prepare. Justyne, Rochelle, and I join together to brainstorm and help each other however we can.

When I was young, I took tumbling classes with other wealthy children. Hopefully I'm still capable of doing a nearly perfect cartwheel—or rather, many of them, enough to get me across the lawn. I go to my room and ask the magic of the house to provide me with some pants for this particular competition. In one of the wardrobes, I find a pair of flowy silk trousers, gathered at the ankles.

After dressing, I return outside, where all the competitors practice. I'm most impressed with Desiree and Rochelle.

Desiree uses creation magic to make a chariot. It has no wheels; instead, dozens of tiny propellers carry it through the air. She constructs it quickly, and I suspect she spent years working on the design before she came here.

Rochelle holds flowers in each hand, and her blessing magic causes colorful, vaporous ribbons to extend from the petals. When she does an intricate dance, the misty ribbons flow and twist. It's one of the most beautiful things I've ever seen.

After an hour or so, Tor calls us back together for our performances. Right before my turn, Rochelle enchants me using her blessing magic. The spell gives me a sense of near weightlessness, and my whole body goes slightly airborne each time I kick my legs up. Halfway across the lawn, however, the enchantment wears off, and I'm back to my hard-won, human skills. I finish my turn and smile, hoping it was enough.

I end up in fifth place. I'm content with that . . . because Margot is the one contestant who performs more poorly than I do. Her curse skills are useless in this task, and she spent so much time using her limited creation magic to make flowers for her hair and dress, she had little time to rehearse her dance across the lawn. Her stumbling steps aren't graceful enough to impress a human audience, much less a Fae one.

Desiree and Rochelle come in first and second place, as I

expected them to. As a reward, Tor spends the next morning with Desiree and the afternoon with Rochelle. I try all day to connect with my magic, but I'm still unsuccessful.

The day after that, Tor invites Justyne to come with him for a private picnic. As they leave, Rochelle and I whisper to each other, wondering why he chose her. I'm so tired of overanalyzing these things, yet I can't stop myself.

I spend hours alternating between both libraries, looking for books that will help me understand how Fae minds work. More often than not, the words seem to swirl around on the pages, their meanings lost to me.

On the morning of our twentieth day here—halfway through the forty-day competition—Tor informs us he'll be spending the morning with me and Felia. I try to smile brightly at the news, but inside, I'm just tired.

I get ready in my room. The magic of the house is becoming passé; I barely feel a thrill when my clothes adjust to fit me. As I'm finishing up my cosmetics, the snake slithers in, then coils herself at my feet, her head lifted expectantly. I pat a bit more powder on my nose, then put down Jackie's broken mirror and pick up the snake.

She immediately begins slithering up my arm, and I sense she's headed for some specific destination. I stay still, letting her move as she will. She anchors herself around my bicep, then slides her head across the skin of my upper chest, which is exposed by the square neck of my dress. At last, she stops, her head resting at the top of the furrow between my breasts. I laugh softly, wondering if she'll venture further, in search of a warm, cozy place to hide. But the snake stays right where she is.

Then warmth seeps into my skin. It immediately strikes me as odd. Snakes are cold blooded; I know that from a book on nature my father brought me years ago. In this cool room, she shouldn't have any heat to share with me.

Her warmth must be magical.

As the sensation grows stronger, I get an odd feeling that I've experienced it before. Recently.

All at once, it comes to me. This is how I felt right before I unintentionally used magic to break Margot's pitcher. The snake is directing me to the source of my power. Even now, I feel a hum within my chest, a vibrating awareness of magic that's waiting to be used.

I want to try to access it now. But as I consider how I might experiment with it, I hear the taps of bird beaks on my bedroom door, followed by loud twitters.

It's time to go meet Tor.

As I join Felia and Tor in the garden, I glimpse Wyatt dusting a statue. He quickly moves out of sight.

The three of us sit in metal chairs around a small stone table. There's tea and an impressive array of pastries waiting for us. "May I?" I ask, lifting the teapot.

"Please," Tor replies.

I pour for the three of us. Tor takes a sip, then says, "I'd like to know why both of you agreed to join this competition."

Felia's blue skin darkens to purple, the shade I normally only see on shadowed areas like the underside of her jaw and the hollows of her cheeks. There's an odd fire in her eyes. For a moment, I think she's angry, but then she grins and says, "Jacqueline described you to me, and I was intrigued. I hoped you'd be different from other faeries I've met." She raises her cup. "And I was right."

Tor's full lips curve in a smile. "Here's to being different."

I lift my cup, and we all drink. Tor seems satisfied with Felia's response, but I get the feeling she's lying. There's something false in her tone and even as she smiles, her shoulders remain tight. I remember what Rochelle said about her not being trustworthy.

"And you?" Tor asks me.

I'm tempted to lie, but I don't know if Jackie found a way to tell Tor what she knows about me. So I settle for a light version of the truth. "My family doesn't have much money, and Jackie said she'd provide for them while I'm in the competition. When I came, I discovered you were worth knowing, Tor. My motivation for being here expanded."

His wide eyes tell me he knew nothing of my agreement with Jackie. My heart thuds as I wait for his response. He sips his tea, takes a bite of a buttery pastry, chews, swallows, and finally speaks. "Your family is lucky to have you, Aeryn."

Oh, thank heaven. That could've gone very badly.

When we finish our tea, we wander the garden together. Felia is pleasant but seems oddly tense. She often makes Tor laugh, however, and his admiring gaze fixes on her when she begins dancing along the path, her goat feet moving in intricate steps.

Felia slows to walk with us again, and Tor asks me what my life was like back home. I hesitate for a moment, not wanting to share something so personal around a competitor. But I have to take advantage of every opportunity to connect with Tor, so I tell him about my family's history and our recent troubles. Both he and Felia seem sympathetic, although I'm certain her kindness is manufactured.

Felia then talks about her own childhood, growing up on her family's farm. Between the two of us, we have plenty of engaging stories to tell. Tor continues to ask us questions, but he skillfully sidesteps our inquiries about his own past. I still wonder if he's the prince in my dreams. Could he even be a beastly version of the supposedly dead Fabien? I tamp down my annoyance at his refusal to give me any hints. Is anyone at this castle, besides Rochelle and Justyne, willing to be themselves and open up?

We come to a bush covered in gorgeous orange roses. I bend down, intending to smell them, but stop when I see a wilting blossom hidden in the shadows.

I want to do something about it.

Touching my chest, I sense the simmering magic inside me. I bring my other hand to the flower and brush my fingers across the petals. I have no idea what I'm doing, but I draw in a deep breath and try to connect with whatever magical instincts I have.

Warmth enters my chest, then travels across to my shoulder and down my arm, all the way to my fingers. The blossom perks up. Its color brightens. Additional petals sprout, quickly growing to make the flower one of the largest on the bush.

"Aeryn." The word is a breath on my neck.

I spin around. Tor is right there, giving me a smile of wonder. I'd forgotten all about him and Felia for a moment, and now I realize he was watching it all. He saw me use magic.

"Come," he says, holding out a clawed hand.

I take it. As he leads me away, I glance at Felia. She's watching us, one brow raised.

He stops when statues hide us from Felia's sight. "Aeryn," he says again. He takes my face in his hands, keeping his claws away from my skin, though I feel a couple of them catch my hair. He brings his mouth to mine.

The kiss begins soft and sweet, but he quickly deepens it. There's a new intensity to his actions, far different from the first time we kissed. It sets my heart racing, and I press myself to him, my hands winding behind his neck. I devour him as surely as he's doing to me, and when we separate, I'm breathing hard.

He takes my hands and gives me a sly little smile. "You liked that?"

Keep going, I want to say, but I manage a bit of coyness instead. "As much as you seemed to like my magic."

"I did indeed. However . . . I've seen magic countless times. I certainly hope you haven't been kissed like that countless times."

I laugh. "I haven't."

He leads me back to Felia. She makes Tor smile more than ever the rest of the morning, and the competitiveness she exudes is nearly tangible. Tor's clear connection with her leaves a sour taste in my mouth. I have to keep reminding myself of the kiss we just shared. It was special . . . right?

When Tor leads us both back to our rooms, he drops me off first. I see the devious, hungry look in Felia's eyes as she tugs him down the hall. Tor seems a bit too enthusiastic to go with her.

I close my door, trying not to think about what their goodbye might look like.

2 0

FELIA IS A LIAR

ate the next morning, Tor knocks on all our doors and instructs us to come to the parlor for an elimination. No warning, just a summons. I skipped breakfast, so I'm still in my pajamas. I dress quickly, knowing I'll probably be the last to arrive.

I'm so damn sick of my heart beating this fast, I think as I traverse the castle's hallways on my way to the parlor. Tor's kiss yesterday burned through the ambivalence I'd begun feeling. Now, once again, I care deeply about staying here.

As my feet move along a path they've grown used to, I try to calm myself by analyzing my reactions. That kiss mattered to me. Why? I press my lips together, remembering what his mouth felt like. I try to remember what he said to me before and after the kiss, but I can't quite recollect it.

All I know is that he felt as warm as a blanket that's been hanging in front of a fire, and he was as strong as a well-trained knight. "It felt so good to be held by someone," I whisper to myself.

My brows draw together when I realize I said *someone,* not *him.* Would I have been just as captivated by any other pair of warm, strong arms? By the pressure of someone else's lips? I don't want to

125

believe I would, but the fact is, I know so little about Tor. I think I like him. I know I enjoy kissing him. But beyond that?

He's a mystery.

I want to mull over that fact for much longer, but I've reached the parlor, and I can't delay my entrance.

As I expected, the five Fae females are already there. Tor is at the door, beckoning me in, and his eyes go straight to my mouth. A small smile pulls at his lips. His reaction makes me nearly certain he'll keep me here, at least for now.

Still, I'm shocked when he opens his mouth and says, "Aeryn, will you stay?"

First to be called. Again. A thrill that I'll need to analyze later sets my whole body abuzz. "Of course." I approach him with my hands extended. He takes them and kisses my fingers softly.

Next, he calls Desiree, who holds her spiral-horned head high and doesn't even smirk at our mutual enemy, Margot. Desiree may be the most kindhearted of those of us who remain, and I'm glad she's still here.

When Tor says Felia's name, I groan internally. I recover quickly, however, when he calls Justyne . . . and my pulse quickens when I realize that Rochelle and Margot are the final two. My breathing turns shallow and quick as I wait. *Don't send my friend home. Don't keep my enemy here.*

"I've enjoyed getting to know you both," Tor says. "Rochelle, you are kind and lovely. Margot, your intelligence, coupled with your beauty, has always drawn me to you." His expression goes somber. "I recently heard some news, however, that disturbs me. One of you has broken the rules of this game, and I must send you home."

I'm lightheaded, but I can't seem to control my breathing. Margot deserves to be eliminated for cursing her fellow contestants, but until now, she's hidden her antagonism from Tor. Did someone talk to him about her? Or did she, in an effort to protect herself, blame Rochelle for the curses?

Tor's sad eyes find Rochelle, and my pounding heart tells me my fear is about to be realized. Margot backstabbed Rochelle. Anger sends hot blood into my cheeks. That conniving, heartless female. How dare she—

"Rochelle," Tor says, "will you stay?"

Her mouth drops open, as does mine. As Rochelle releases a peal of high, giddy laughter, my attention shifts to Margot. There's hatred in the curl of her lip, and I know she's dying to find out who tattled on her. Her glare slides from one competitor to the next, as if the sharpness in her eyes can cut the truth out of us.

She turns to face me, then strides toward me. I instinctively step back, expecting a curse. I know Justyne would want to defend me, but she's far less powerful than Margot. And Tor is too busy hugging a delirious Rochelle to pay attention to the female he just eliminated.

"I'm not going to hurt you," Margot murmurs.

I have no reason to believe that, but I must control my fear. It makes me look weak. I straighten my spine and watch Margot approach. She leans in, bringing her lips to my ear. No one else is close enough to hear what she says.

"Felia is a liar. I'd rather see anyone win but her—even you. If she consumes milk, she'll get sick. Use that information as you will."

She glides out of the room, leaving Tor to rush after her and say whatever goodbye he has planned. I watch them leave, not turning back to the others even when the door closes behind them.

I don't trust Margot. But there's one thing I'm sure of: she enjoys hurting others. I suspect she's telling the truth about Felia. She's doing her best to ensure that when she walks out of this place, she leaves chaos behind.

Now I just have to decide what to do with the information she gave me.

21

———

FEARLESS

*P*ale, golden-gray light streams through my window early the next morning. I groan and roll over, wishing I'd remembered to close the drapes last night. It's too early to get up.

Apparently my mind agrees, because moments later, I'm again dreaming I'm with the handsome, raven-winged prince. This time, I'm aware it's a dream. As always, it's more vibrant and realistic than my dreams used to be.

I'm watching the prince as he stands before a mirror, surrounded by three tailors who are pinning the seams of a burgundy dinner jacket to fit him. He gives them instructions—"Tighter here at the waist . . . No, no, I won't be able to move unless you let out the shoulders a bit."

After several minutes, his gaze finds mine. He gives me a sparkling smile. "I would never have signed up to be a prince if I'd known the tailoring sessions would be so involved."

I laugh. "It looks wonderful, just as it is."

"I'm not going for *wonderful*. I'm going for *perfect*." He winks and turns back to the tailors to give more instructions.

128

My smile fades. My dream body is famished, and I feel like I've been standing here, waiting, for hours.

Just as I'm about to go eat without the prince, he declares the jacket is, at last, "perfect." The tailors carefully remove it from him, and he replaces it with a yellow day jacket that's striking against his wings. "I'm starving," he says as he approaches me, holding out an arm.

I slip my hand into the crook of his elbow. The cloth-covered muscles under my fingers feel terribly familiar.

He leads me through nondescript hallways into a dining room. The walls are blurred, so I assume the details of the room aren't important to this dream. Several people are already at the long table, and as we enter, they stand. The prince sits at the end, the place of honor. He gestures to the chair on his left. A servant pulls it out. I sit, and the other guests follow suit.

Just as blurred as the walls are the faces and forms of the guests and servants. Even the food is indistinct and unidentifiable. I suspect my magic is creating the only real, important part (the prince), while my subconscious mind fills in the blanks with the setting and secondary characters.

I look down at my plate, thinking how much I'd love to eat the roast chicken, buttery potatoes, and creamed spinach our old chef used to make. My blurry plate fills with the exact things I was imagining. *There are some benefits to dreaming*, I think. I pick up my knife and fork and start eating.

The prince is telling everyone at the table about a new tapestry he's ordered for his bedroom when someone else walks in: a male faerie with a detailed, realistic face. No blurred features here. That must mean this person represents someone in the real world, if what Wyatt told me about dream magic is accurate.

The newcomer is handsome, though not breathtakingly so. He looks approachable. Friendly. Gray eyes sit beneath wavy, dark-brown hair that falls over his forehead. Unlike the prince, this faerie's muscles are average sized, and his shoulders aren't at risk of getting stuck in any doorways. His skin is bronze, with a hint of luminous shimmer. I'm convinced it's his nicest feature, until he smiles. That open, kind expression is really what sets him apart. It's impossible, of course, to discern his age.

The prince must realize the attention of his guests has shifted, because he stops talking mid-sentence. "Join us," he says to the other male.

I watch the bronze-skinned faerie closely. The prince didn't tell him where to sit, and I assume he could choose any open chair, including the one at the prince's right hand. Instead of sitting, however, he picks up a decanter of wine and refills a few empty goblets. That done, he sits between two guests, near the center of the table.

I turn to the prince, opening my mouth to ask who the newcomer is. Before I get the chance, I wake in my warm bed.

The sun is brighter now, and I sit up and stretch, intending to wake slowly while I ponder the dream. A couple of distinct, repetitive sounds make me freeze.

Squeak. Scrape. Squeak. Scrape.

My gaze drops to the floor. It's completely covered in uncountable gray rats, their feet scratching the floor, their noses upturned as they look at me, squeaks emerging from their mouths.

I hate rats.

I can deal with spiders. Snakes. Roaches. But ever since my family's very first morning in our awful shack, when I woke to a rat biting my ear, I've found them more frightening than wolves or wild boars.

I want to scream, but I'm breathing too fast to let out anything but a few small squeaks. That only panics me further, since—damn it—I sound like a rat. I huddle in the middle of my bed, panting and squeaking, watching in horror as one fat, intrepid rodent crawls atop on a mound of its friends, trying to climb up my bed frame.

Then, above the scratches and squeals, I hear a hiss.

Tingling relief washes over me. It's irrational, since one snake can't eat hundreds of rats. But at least I'm not alone.

My gaze sweeps the room until I see the snake sliding in under the bathroom door. The nearest rats try to skitter away, but the floor is too full for them to get far.

The snake pulls back her head, then strikes. Her sharp teeth close on . . . nothing.

I blink, my breaths slowing as my logical brain distracts me from my fear. How could the snake's strike have missed with that many rats around her? I haven't come up with any answers when she strikes again . . . and misses again. This time, I see her head go *through* the rodent she was targeting.

The truth hits me: the rats are fake. A horrifying, magical illusion. The product of curse magic, I suspect.

Magical warmth builds in my chest. I need to end this curse, and as much as I love to analyze things, I'm learning that when it comes to magic, I have to follow my instincts. I crawl across the bed. Grimacing, my heart pounding, I sit at the edge and reach my feet toward the floor. Based on what the snake just did, my mind knows these rats aren't real. But my gut, which cares little for logic, is anticipating the *squish* of warm rat bodies.

My feet go right through the rats and contact only the cool floor. Letting out a giddy laugh, I stand up straight. What I need is a blessing to counteract this curse.

I place both hands on my chest and feel the warm swell of magic there. I force myself to meet the beady eyes of the rats, even when a few of them appear to be attempting to climb my legs. A deep breath, and then I thrust my hands out towards the rats and speak one word. A blessing spell . . . or at least I hope it counts as one.

"Fearless."

The rats disappear.

For a moment, I'm elated. Then the intensity of it all drives me to my knees. I'm panting again. I have to sit and put my head between my knees so I don't pass out.

The snake slithers up to me and wraps herself around my ankle. Her touch calms me, and I sit up straight.

The only enemy I still have here is Felia. Supposedly she has very little power and has been trying to increase her creation magic. What if that's not true? What if she's really a curse faerie who's been hiding her true skills?

It's the only answer that makes sense.

I look at the clock. Breakfast won't start for another half hour. I dress quickly, pondering how I should respond to Felia's curse. I don't want to bring harm to anyone here . . . but I can't just ignore her hateful curse. While I'd never initiate an attack on someone, defending yourself is different . . . right?

My stomach is queasy, and my heart insists that what I'm considering goes against my personal moral code. But I'm here to care for my family, and maybe that'll require me stretching beyond the person I always was.

So I lift my chin and hurry to breakfast. I'm the first one there. The table is already full of food, including a particularly smooth porridge I've seen Felia eat several times. Remembering Margot's final words to me—and ignoring the throbbing of my conscience—I pick up a carafe of milk and pour some into the porridge. A quick stir mixes it in.

Right after I finish, Felia walks in. Barely looking at me, she sits, serves herself some porridge, and takes a few bites.

Then, groaning and holding her belly, she stands and staggers from the room.

22

I DIDN'T PLAN TO CLIMB
THROUGH YOUR WINDOW

My appetite is gone. I try to tell myself it's because seeing someone else who's sick makes me feel sick too.

It's not that, though. The ache in my belly is guilt, with a side of self-loathing. Putting milk in the porridge is what Margot would've done. As much as I try to convince myself that Felia deserved it, my conscience won't let me off the hook.

Rochelle walks in. One glance at me is all it takes for her to place a warm hand on my shoulder. "Are you all right? You look like you don't feel well."

I force a smile. "I'm fine, just not very hungry. I think I'll go back to my room."

In the corridor, I pass Tor. He gives me a big smile. Who knows, maybe he'd be proud of me. It's possible he'd appreciate a bride who knows when to break the rules, one who relishes revenge.

But I don't want to be that bride. I don't want to be that *woman*.

I wish I'd realized that before I poured the milk.

When I get to the corridor where all the contestants' rooms are, I walk right past my door. At Felia's room, I stop and knock.

There's no response. That makes me feel even sicker. I'm not sure what I was going to do if she let me in. Confess? Hold her hair while she vomited? All I know is, I wish I could do something.

In my own room, I flop on the bed. There's no snake to comfort me. No book to distract me. It's just me and my memories—of the rats and Felia's groans and Tor sending Margot home because of the stories he'd heard about her. Despite my thoughts when I passed him earlier, now all I can think is that he might eliminate me next if he finds out what I did. If he does, I deserve it.

Felia deserves it more. You have to be truly evil to curse someone with hundreds of rats. The thought doesn't settle my aching stomach.

I lie there for an hour or so before I can no longer stand the emotional torture I'm putting myself through. I've got to do something besides thinking about what a horrible human I am.

Human. That doesn't describe me anymore, does it? The magic I've been doing proves I'm more than human. How Fae am I?

That question drives me to the library vault. There, I find a book on humans who are part Fae. I sit and read the same page six times before giving up. It's impossible to lose myself in a book when I know Felia is suffering and it's my fault.

I leave the vault and roam through the castle, ending up at the small rose-garden courtyard I found a week ago. As I enter, the twittering of birds covers the sound of my steps. Rochelle is there, her back to me. I'm about to greet her when I realize what she's doing . . . and it freezes me in place.

Her hand is outstretched, fingers extending toward a bush full of yellow roses. As I watch, she whispers something, and an entire section wilts. Brown petals fall to the ground.

Without really thinking about what I'm doing, I quietly move behind a massive rose bush. When I stand just right, I can see Rochelle through gaps in the twisted branches. She continues using magic until the whole bush dries up and dies.

Not just any magic. Curse magic.

Why? Rochelle told me she's a blessing faerie, though not a strong one. Is she practicing a few darker skills in case she needs them?

She shifts a bit, enough for me to see one side of her lips. They're curled into a smirk. She's enjoying this destruction. And while I know it's just a plant, it still seems odd for her to get a thrill out of killing it.

Her gaze shifts to the ground. Outstretched fingers point downward, and again, she whispers. Several spiders, each as big as my hand, appear at her feet. Rochelle lifts a foot and stomps it on one of the eight-legged monstrosities. Her shoe goes right through the illusory spider. A delighted laugh bursts from her mouth as she continues to stomp.

It's just like the rats in my room. They seemed so real until the snake tried to touch them.

Rochelle stills. With a flick of her wrist, the spiders disappear. She lifts her gaze, and I freeze, heart pounding. She spins slowly, looking around. I struggle to control my breaths as she turns in my direction.

Her gaze meets mine. I stop breathing, waiting for her to raise that hand and curse me.

Her eyes sweep past my position. Cool relief washes over me. *It was the bush. She was looking at the bush, not me.*

Thank heaven. She can't know I'm here, because as much as I'd like to deny it, I'm sure of one thing: Felia didn't curse my room with rats.

Rochelle did.

I slip out of the courtyard as quietly as I can. Then I ascend several levels and run through unfamiliar hallways, no particular destination in mind. I end up in the portrait gallery. My legs and lungs are burning, so I come to a halt and bend over, hands on my thighs, gasping for breath.

"Aeryn," a smooth female voice says.

I stand and turn. Once again, Cerise's face is in the mirror. Her violet-blue eyes are wide and full of concern.

"Are you all right?" she asks.

I catch my breath. "Yes . . . No . . . I will be, I think."

"I know what happened."

The words send stiffness to my muscles. What exactly does she know? I try to sound casual when I reply, "You do?"

"It was a bold move, attacking another contestant."

My head drops. "It was wrong."

"No, dear." Her voice is so very kind. "In matters of the heart, you must act courageously. I'm proud of you. I wasn't sure you had it in you."

I meet her gaze again. It's as guileless as it was the first time I met her. All I see there is encouragement and wisdom. It confuses me more than ever.

"Thank you," I say.

I return to Felia's room and knock again.

"Who is it?"

"Aeryn. I wanted to check on you."

"Go away!" she shouts.

I go to my own room to tackle the only task I feel capable of right now: taking a nap.

I sleep through lunch and spend the afternoon in my room, trying to read. The words don't stick in my muddled mind.

A couple of hours later, it's dinnertime. I dress and walk slowly to the dining room. Everyone but Felia is there. Again, my stomach churns. I manage to eat, and I pray it stays down.

Justyne, Desiree, Rochelle, and Tor go to the porch after dinner. I know I should join them. Isolating myself at this point of the competition is just plain stupid. I can't bring myself to socialize, though. I'm too distracted by what I did to Felia and what I know about Rochelle. I return to my room and get ready for bed, but I'm too unsettled to do anything except pace.

Cerise is probably right. This competition requires boldness. Felia didn't deserve what I did, but maybe we all need to get a little brutal as we try to win Tor's heart.

The problem is, I don't think I'm strong enough for more brutality, even though four people at home would benefit greatly from my marriage to Tor. In caring for them these last couple of years, I've done a lot of things I never thought I'd do. I've hunted. Begged people to buy my knitting. Once, I took moldy bread from the trash bin behind a bakery so my family and I could eat the unspoiled parts.

Until today, however, I had never hurt someone else to help my father and siblings. I'm not sure it's a line I can cross again.

When I'm tired of pacing, I go to bed. Every time I close my eyes, however, I see Felia's miserable face as she ran from the dining room.

I crawl out of bed and open the window. There's a chilly breeze, and I gaze at the stars, welcoming the goosebumps that rise on my skin. The night sky holds no answers, but I keep staring. Perhaps if I stay there long enough, I'll figure out what to do next. Eventually, maybe I'll feel proud instead of guilty.

"Aeryn."

This time, it's a male voice. I look down. Wyatt is standing there, face upturned, eyes fixed on me.

I don't trust him. He's secretive, and Cerise told me to be wary of him. I left our last conversation hoping I'd never talk to him again.

So why does the sight of his face—that soft smile, that blue skin that looks silvery in the starlight—send a jolt of relief into me?

"You've been standing there a long time," he says.

I sigh. "It's been a hard day."

"You look like you could use a friend." He pauses, and his throat throbs with a swallow. Hesitation lends softness to his voice. "I could come up. If you'd like."

There is no situation in which it would be appropriate for me to invite the gardener to my room. Not when I'm striving to win the affections of the only other male at this castle.

"Come up?" I ask. "To the fourth floor? What if someone sees you?"

"I wouldn't come through the house. There's a tall ladder in the garden shed."

No one would have to see him. It would be safe.

And still highly inappropriate.

"Come on up," I hear myself say.

Starlight reflects off his smile. He rushes off and returns a few minutes later, carrying a ladder that's hinged in several places. After unfolding it, he leans it against the marble wall of the castle and begins to climb. At the top, he grasps the window frame and gracefully pulls himself in.

He's standing right in front of me, close enough that I can feel his breath. I can't bring myself to move.

His blue eyes search my face. "Are you all right, Aeryn?"

I feel my forehead crinkle as a lump lodges in my throat. I refuse to cry, though. Giving Felia milk was my choice, and I won't beg for pity. "I'm fine." The words come out a bit choked.

A gentle smile pulls at his lips. "You don't have to lie to the person who keeps telling you to be yourself."

That snaps me out of whatever spell was keeping me so near him. I pivot and stride to the chair. Sitting, I snap, "You shouldn't chide me for a white lie when you're the one who keeps hiding things. I don't even know why I let you come up here."

He looks at the window. "Do you want me to leave?"

"No." Again, my response escapes my mouth before I can think it through. "You can sit. If you'd like."

He looks around, but I have the only chair. So he takes the only other option: my bed. The sight of him sitting there sends an unexplainable flush to my skin. My heart racing, I demand, "Why are you here?"

He holds his hands wide as a huff exits his lips. For the first time since I met him, he looks exasperated. "I didn't plan to climb into your window tonight, Aeryn. I looked up, and you were standing there, and you looked . . . lost. I wanted to check on you. That's it."

His reply softens my heart. I rest my elbows on my knees and stare at the floor. Words tumble from my lips, a quick recounting of the curse I woke up to, the supposed revenge I got on Felia, and my realization about Rochelle.

"I messed up, Wyatt," I say. "My best friend in the house is really my enemy, and I hurt someone who may have never been an enemy at all. And I . . ." I hunch over even farther. "I'm so tired of trying to figure out all you faeries. I don't fit in with any of you, and I don't even know if I want to be here, and I kind of hate myself after what I did, and I . . ." I trail off, realizing there's nothing more to say. My gaze rises to meet Wyatt's. I can't read the emotions in his serious eyes, can't tell if he's disappointed or worried or something else.

"You made a big mistake," he says.

"I'm aware." There's venom in my voice. "That's why I said—"

"Please let me finish," he interrupts calmly. When my mouth closes, he says, "You made a mistake, but you know you did, and I certainly don't want to make you feel any worse than you already do."

Deflated, I nod. "I want to make it right, but if I tell her I did it, Tor might send me home. And my family needs me here."

"Felia is fine, Aeryn."

"What?"

"She came outside when she was sick. I saw her and healed her."

I stand and dash across the room, sitting next to him. "She's fine? Oh, thank heaven. I didn't even think about the possibility of someone healing her."

Smiling again, Wyatt takes my hands. "I'm glad you reacted that way."

I should pull away, but his skin is warm, his touch comforting. I tighten my grip. "Why?" I watch his blue thumb as it runs across the top of my pale hand. The sight of it entrances me.

I look up. His smile has turned a bit wistful. "I felt from the start that you were kind and good. Felia knew you were likely the one who put milk in the porridge. You were the only other one in the room, after all. When she told me that, I started questioning my judgment about you."

Just like I've been questioning his character. In this moment, however, I'm struggling to dredge up any distrust for him. "Why do you care whether I'm kind or not?" I ask softly.

"Tor needs a kind wife."

The words remind me why I'm here. I guess they have the same effect on him, because we both loosen our grips, then pull our hands apart.

I look at the sliver of bed between us. What the hell was I thinking? Inviting him up here, sitting on my bed with him, holding his hands . . . knowing tomorrow I'll be courting and maybe kissing the beast who rules over this castle. I stand and hurry back to the chair.

Wyatt sighs in what I can only assume is relief.

The sound sends a dart of pain into my chest. "You really want him to choose me, don't you?"

"You would be good for him. If he loves and marries someone who's good for him, that will be good for everyone."

I release a short groan. "You're being mysterious again. Can't you just speak clearly?"

A sigh makes his shoulders droop. "Aeryn, have you ever considered that I might feel as helpless as you do about all the things I can't tell you?"

Anger. Frustration. The negative emotions he's showing me tonight send an odd relief into my chest. I'm finally seeing the true Wyatt, even if he can't share everything with me. So I decide to open up further to the male who's sitting on the edge of my bed.

"I don't know what I'm doing here." My voice is quiet, but I know his Fae ears can easily hear the words. "I want to win Tor's affection, but I don't want to lose respect for myself in the process. I know you can't tell me everything, and that probably means I shouldn't trust you. But for some reason . . . I do. So, please. Tell me what to do."

He props his elbows on his knees, the same position I assumed earlier. His eyes meet mine, and all at once, it feels like he's right in front of me, instead of sitting halfway across the room. "You trust me?"

"I do."

"You don't know how much I appreciate that." His gaze drops a smidge, and I swear it settles on my lips. Then he sits up straight, crossing his arms and glancing to the side. He's all business when his eyes return to me. "Be yourself. It's what I've told you from the start. It's the best advice I have. Just be yourself."

He stands and rushes to the window, his only goodbye a quick wave. He's on the ladder before I can say a thing.

I watch him descend. It takes everything in me to stifle the urge to invite him to stay longer. "Thank you," I say as he stands on the lawn and folds the ladder.

He nods and walks away.

I return to my bed. I know my next step—I'm going to talk to Felia tomorrow. She may report me to Tor. I might get sent home. Those are terrible risks to take, but I can't avoid them. Because I can't stay here if it requires being someone I'm not.

I'll always find a way to care for my family. But I won't lose myself in the process.

23

WHEN FAERIES STARVE

The next morning, I knock on Felia's door, intending to confess to her before she goes to breakfast. If she's going to tell Tor, I want to get it over with and get back to my family. There's no answer, so I knock again.

Down the hall, Desiree's door opens, and she steps out. "Felia joined us last night on the patio. She mentioned she'd be going to breakfast early from now on."

Nausea stabs my stomach. Presumably, Felia went down early to guard her porridge. My prank scared her, and I couldn't regret it more.

Justyne exits her room and greets us. As the three of us walk to the dining room, Desiree and Justyne laugh together about something Tor said last night. I watch them closely, anxious for any signs that they've created an alliance. I've had no reason to doubt Justyne and her loyalty to me, but since finding out Rochelle cursed me, I'm hesitant to trust any of my fellow contestants.

When I enter the dining room, Felia's gaze finds mine. Her glare is so intense, I expect it to burn a hole through my head. Bubbling dread fills my gut, and once again, my appetite flees.

I sit next to Tor. He's in a cheerful mood, and the other contestants seem eager to talk and laugh. Between small bites of fruit, I try to join in, but I can't drum up any true enthusiasm for talking or eating. When Rochelle arrives, I avoid looking at her.

Halfway through the meal, when everyone else is in the middle of a heated debate over which type of cheese is the best, Tor turns to me and says quietly, "We missed you last night."

"*We?*" I challenge with a little smile. "You think the females I'm competing against were concerned about my absence?"

That low, rumbling laugh leaves his chest. "Well, I missed you." Not taking his red eyes off me, he reaches under the table and takes my hand.

The touch sends my heart racing. I slide my fingers between his, careful to avoid his claws. His thumb rubs the back of my hand.

The feeling brings me back to the night before, and I find myself imagining it's Wyatt's blue thumb gliding across my skin. When I realize the direction I've allowed my thoughts to go, it sends me into a brief panic. I pull my hand away. This is what comes of letting the gardener into my room.

Tor lifts his brows, then turns to the other contestants and joins in their conversation.

Damn it. That was a meaningful moment, and something in my brain insisted on messing it up.

Why would I think of Wyatt at a time like this? I'm here for Tor. I've kissed him and possibly even dreamed of him. Maybe it's the lure of the forbidden. Falling for the gardener would get me sent home. All I'm experiencing is a bit of juvenile rebellion, an irrational response to Wyatt's innocent visit. I won't allow myself to indulge in such thoughts.

Tor's attention is still on the others. I reach under the table and take his hand in mine. He laughs at something Rochelle said, then turns to give me a tiny smile and a wink.

His thumb continues its previous motion over my skin. I hang on to him tightly, enjoying the warmth of his touch. My mind goes to my family, and I send up a silent prayer that Felia won't tell Tor what I did. If she does, Tor will send me home. I need to stay. The longer I'm here, the longer my family will be cared for.

After breakfast, Felia declares she's going to practice on the harp in a nearby sitting room. A minute or so after she leaves, I casually leave the room, then rush to meet her. Felia is just settling herself before the instrument.

I stop just inside the doorway. "I'd like to talk to you."

Felia comes to her feet with her customary grace. But there's nothing gracious about the look she gives me as she strides toward me. Her blue skin has turned purplish, like it did in the garden that day. There's rage in her eyes, in her clenched fists, in her rapid steps. Her goat hooves click on the marble floor, and the sound sends trepidation into my heart.

She stops in front of me, grabs my chin hard, and pulls back her fist. Then it flies toward my face.

I should duck or sway or fight back. I've never been trained to do any of that, though. Panic takes over, and I freeze, eyes wide.

Her knuckles stop a fraction of an inch from my cheek. She stands there, perfectly still, eyes ablaze. My chest is heaving, but other than that, I don't move.

At last, she speaks. "It wouldn't be worth it to get sent home for hitting you. *You're* not worth it." She drops her fist to her side, pivots away from me, and stalks back toward the harp.

I reach behind me and close the door. "I'm sorry," I say firmly.

Not deigning to look at me, Felia sits at the harp and starts playing. The beautiful notes that come from the strings would take my breath away if our confrontation hadn't already done that.

I cross the room and stand next to the instrument. "I'm sorry, Felia. I thought you'd cursed me, and I wanted to pay you back. I know I was wrong." Her fingers pluck the strings with more force, and I raise my voice over the glorious music. "I'm ashamed of how I acted, and I won't do it again. Even if you had been the one to curse me, hurting you still would've been wrong."

Her fingers go still. When she looks up, I notice her skin has returned to its customary blue shade. Her brown eyes are unreadable, but the anger seems to have left them. "You mean that."

Though it's not a question, I nod.

"Then let's talk." She stands.

I glance around the room. There's a mirror over the fireplace. I won't risk being spied on. "How about my room?"

Her eyes narrow, but she nods her assent. We walk silently, and in my room, we sit on the bed.

"You thought I'd cursed you?" Felia says. "I'm not a curse faerie. I've always been better at creation and blessing spells."

I want to look away, but I force myself to hold her gaze. "I know. I convinced myself otherwise. I'm sorry."

"How did you know I can't tolerate milk?"

"Margot told me."

Felia nods, like she expected that. "I'm glad she's gone. She's far too talented with curses. I suspect a certain other contestant will eventually reach that level." Her gaze slices into me, challenging me to confess what I already know.

"Rochelle," I say, my shoulders drooping. After a few seconds of silence, I ask, "Are you the one who told Tor that Margot was using curse magic?"

"I am."

She answered that question readily enough, so I try another. "I heard Wyatt healed you. Why didn't you come to dinner last night?"

A smile overtakes her face, and it looks different from her other smiles. More genuine. "You've probably noticed how purple my skin looks when I'm angry, and last night . . . I was mad as hell, as you mortals might say. Couldn't have Tor seeing me in such a state."

I grin. "Tor has seen that shade on you before, and so have I. When we had tea in the garden—I think it was when he asked why you joined this competition."

She blinks, but her eyes stay closed just a smidge longer than usual. A fleeting vulnerability overtakes her features before she schools them into a passive mask. Her gaze finds mine again. "Every female came here for a reason. Maybe a couple of them were just hopeless romantics, but I suspect it goes deeper for most of us. I know it does for you, based on what you told Tor in the garden."

I sit quietly. I'm not even sure I want to know her reason. I've been so convinced I'm the one who deserves to win. I'm here for my family. What if her purpose is just as compelling?

Felia says, "When this estate was still in Faerie, Prince Fabien won a game of chance against my father."

"What did he win?"

"Most of my family's lands." She swallows hard. "He took them, then forgot about them. All we had left was a small lot containing our home and a tiny garden. Surrounding us were fields that used to be ours. The forest started taking them over. When Fabien died, we tried to farm the lands again, but other Fae have prevented us from it."

"Why?"

"There hasn't been a monarch over our kingdom since Fabien died. Everyone expects either Tor or someone else to eventually take over. When that happens, all those people keeping my parents from farming will come forward and brag about how they protected the royal lands."

It's all coming together in my mind. "But if you're married to Tor, and he claims the throne, you can return the land to your family."

She nods. Her gaze drifts across the room, and she says quietly, "There's been so much hunger in our little house. Do you know what happens when faeries starve?"

"No."

"They get thin and weak, but they don't die. Their memories falter, but they don't die. They sleep too little or too much, and they stumble around as if they're drunk. But they don't die."

My brows draw together. "That's horrifying. But it doesn't describe you."

Her eyes find mine again. "It describes my parents. They gave nearly all of our food to me. This is my chance to repay them for their sacrifices."

"Oh, Felia . . ."

She shakes her head hard. "Don't pity me, Aeryn. Work with me. Work with me, so one of us can win the prize and save her family. Work with me, so that whoever wins can protect the other."

Can I trust Felia?

I don't know. In fact, I can't guarantee anyone here is trustworthy, and that fact infuriates me.

Yet I know this: Felia just opened up to me in a way no one else has. I'm not saying she's guileless; I know she's not. I simply sense her guile isn't directed toward me.

So I choose honesty too. "I've already allied with Rochelle and Justyne. After what happened yesterday, I'll never trust Rochelle again. Justyne, though . . . I think she's still loyal to me, though I've been noticing she's also close to Desiree." All Felia does is nod and wait, so I continue, "I do want to ally with you. But we need to bring in Justyne too, and maybe Desiree. Together, we can try to get rid of Rochelle."

Felia crosses her legs and casually draws circles in the air with one of her hooves. "The more people we bring in, the more likely someone will betray us. Drop Justyne. She doesn't have to know you've ended the alliance."

"I won't turn against her unless she betrays me. Not when I gave her my word."

That genuine smile returns to Felia's lips. "Good."

"Was that a test?"

"You passed with perfect marks."

I nod. "Then let's expand this alliance."

Fifteen minutes later, I've fetched Justyne. Ten minutes after that, she's convinced us Desiree is trustworthy too. Soon, we're all sitting on my bed, staring at one another.

I take a deep breath and tell them about the rats in my room and Rochelle's curse magic in the courtyard garden.

Justyne shakes her head. "Rochelle is a curse faerie?"

"And you can use magic now?" Desiree asks.

My stomach twists. I've spent my life weighing facts, risks, and rewards so I can make the most logical decisions possible. Trusting people to this extent is frighteningly risky. But I don't see any other option. "Yes, Rochelle fooled us," I say. "And yes. I'm learning to harness my magic."

Felia lays out our plan: we'll all do what we can, within the bounds of Tor's rules, to get Rochelle sent home. When one of the four of us marries Tor, we'll care for the others' needs.

"If we're going to make such an agreement," I say, "we need to be open about our true reasons for joining this competition. I suppose I'll start."

When I finish my brief synopsis of my family's predicament and how marriage to Tor might help us survive, Felia tells us about Fabien taking her family's lands. The two of us then turn expectant gazes on Desiree and Justyne.

Desiree is sitting totally still, her golden, curved horns lending her a regal air. "You know there's a Fae invasion team outside the barrier," she says quietly. "My father is on it. I don't know who hired them—someone looking to take over these lands, I suspect. I believe he was tricked into joining. I'm afraid he'll get killed out there. He's a gentle faerie, and I can't imagine him threatening anyone, much less hurting them. I came here hoping I could somehow find him and bring him home. But I didn't even see him before Jacqueline brought me to the castle."

"I'm sorry," I say.

Before Desiree can respond, Justyne blurts, "My brother used to be on staff here. He's one of the garden statues now—I visit him every day. I don't know how to reverse the curse on him and the others, but I'm here to find a way." There are tears in her eyes, threatening to spill over.

The next thing I know, Felia is gathering us all into an awkward, wonderful hug. We let go, and each of us agrees to the alliance. We're a team. As long as one of us wins, we'll protect the others.

For the first time in days, I feel true hope.

The next morning, Tor announces another challenge. It will last four days. And it will put my new alliance to the test.

24

———

FIVE FAE REVELS

or stands in front of me and the other contestants, the tip of his tail peeking out from behind his back. "This challenge," he says, "will take four days."

Five mouths, including mine, drop open.

He continues, "I will assign each of you a room. You will transform it, and on the final evening, you will each host a revel." His eyes find mine. "Do you know what that is, Aeryn?"

I smile. "A Fae party. They're legendary in mortal lands."

He nods and laughs. "They can get wild, though with so few of us in this castle, ours will be tame compared to the stories you've heard. As a group, we will spend one hour at each revel, and at the end of the night, I will judge which is the best."

"What criteria will you use?" I ask.

Tor gives me an approving smile. "Excellent question. Your event must encompass all the qualities of the best Fae celebrations—creativity, entertainment, and magic. It should be a feast for all the senses. It must also reflect the best of who *you* are. After all, my bride and I will entertain many in this castle. I'd like a glimpse into my possible futures.

"Please use items from around the castle, supplementing with things created by the house's magic. Most importantly, bring your own magic to this project. As before, you may help one another if you wish.

"Your birds are in the corridor, waiting to take you to the rooms I've assigned to you. The revels begin at seven o'clock on the evening of the fourth day."

Tor's smile disappears, his expression turning grave. "Much is at stake in this particular challenge." He meets each of our gazes, then exits without explaining his final statement.

Felia, Justyne, Desiree, Rochelle, and I hurry into the corridor. Our birds bring us to the third floor, then to a hallway at the rear of the building. My blue birds halt above an open door, beyond which is a large, empty bedroom with a bathroom attached. The other contestants stop at neighboring rooms.

I enter. Double doors on the far wall lead to a balcony, and there's an inviting fireplace, bordered in marble, on the right side of the room. A large chandelier promises lovely nighttime lighting.

As I walk through the space, Justyne and Desiree join me, followed shortly by Felia. We agree to assist each other throughout the challenge. But I sense some tension in them all, and I feel the same. Based on Tor's last statement, we know this challenge is somehow important. Taking breaks to help each other might not be the most natural thing to do, but it's the best way to give ourselves an advantage over Rochelle. I'm still committed to this new alliance, and I sense they are too.

After they leave, Rochelle enters with a bright smile. "I'd be happy to lend you some magic if you need it."

I can't bring myself to stoop to her level of deceit. Instead, I meet her gaze. "I don't need the type of help you give."

Her eyes narrow. She stares at me for a few seconds, then spins around and heads for the door, muttering, "So much for loyalty."

Exactly.

Since this room is supposed to represent me, I decide to include décor, foods, music, and flowers that remind me of the parties my parents used to host. I bring in things I've seen in my wanderings around the castle: a small statue of two humans embracing, drapes that remind me of those my parents had, books that retell human myths. Using the magic of the house, I add stringed instruments, tables covered in luxurious linens, and more.

Wyatt helps me harvest flowers identical to those from the garden my mother once had. His friendliness and laughter cut the edge off my tension, and I find myself wishing I could skip the challenge and stay in the garden with him. But he hands me the large bag of cut flowers and urges me back inside, where I collect vases from around the house.

Every few hours, I check in with my friends. We gather items for each other and share ideas. By the time we've filled our rooms with décor, it's the end of the second day. Rochelle has kept her door closed most of the time, but Felia tells me she peeked in once when Rochelle was leaving. Apparently her room isn't nearly as beautiful or luxurious as the other four. Our plan is working.

On day three, I wake and eat a hearty breakfast with the others. We have two days left. It's time to add my magic to everything I've gathered. When I reach my assigned room, I close the door to help me focus. Movement in the corner draws my attention.

"Well, hello," I say to the snake. She's kept herself distant since the challenge started, but she must sense I need her strange brand of support. She slithers toward me over marble and rugs. I pick her up and drape her over my shoulders. Once again, she rests her head on my chest, where I always feel my magic. Her presence gives me confidence.

Delicious, potent warmth gathers in my chest. Making a point not to think too hard, I walk around the room and speak quiet words, adding magic wherever I go. Flowers burst into bigger blooms. Gorgeous illustrations show up in the margins of the books. Glittery stars dance over the drapes, and merry flames spring to life in the previously cold, dark fireplace.

They're all small spells, and when I try to do anything more major, like creating an entire statue, I fail. Still, I'm enjoying being able to do any magic at all.

I still don't know what my magical specialty is. Dream magic is the first power I displayed, but it isn't one of the four official categories of Fae magic. I can easily cast small nature, creation, and blessing spells, and I'd like to eventually identify with one of those types of magic. Based on how I damaged Margot's pitcher after our first challenge, I know I can use curse magic, the final type. But I'd rather use that skill as little as possible.

The snake is pointing her head into one corner, so I walk in that direction, stopping at the instruments. I'd hoped Felia might play each of them during the revel, as she told me she's skilled with all stringed instruments. But the snake's little nose continues to point insistently. An idea comes to my mind. This time, I don't speak. I simply hold my hands out and beckon my magic to do something I'm not even sure it's capable of.

All four instruments and their bows rise, as if musicians are holding them. They begin to play quietly, the hushed notes perfect and pure. I squeal in delight, then urge the magic to halt. I don't want Rochelle to hear and steal my idea.

For two days, I play with my magic, bringing my room to life. When I get tired from casting spells, which happens frequently, I improve the room in other ways.

My allies and I frequently visit each other's spaces, lending magic and suggestions to each other. Our collaboration brings greater depth to the beauty we've all created. As our deadline looms closer on the fourth day, I stand in the middle of my room, a silly, satisfied smile on my face. This place looks like me, but it also holds all the magic of a true Fae revel.

I fetch my friends. We've agreed to go to the kitchen together to request food and beverages, since it's where that particular magic works best. As we pass Rochelle's room, she's leaving. A quick peek into her space shows me tables piled with food. She's already visited the kitchen, so she must be going elsewhere to grab an item she forgot.

Rochelle catches my eye and gives me a little smile. It's just as friendly as a hundred other smiles she's given me. For some reason, this time, it sends a bit of dread into my heart.

I won't let her falsity disturb me. Along with the allies I've chosen, I hurry downstairs. In an hour, the revels will begin.

In the kitchen, Desiree whispers, "What if Rochelle curses our rooms?"

As Justyne shakes her head, the kitchen's lamplight glimmers on her long, deep-purple hair. "She's smarter than that. It would be too obvious she was the one who did it if hers is the only room left untouched."

I hope she's right, though I can't seem to shake the unsettled feeling I've had since seeing Rochelle's smile. Desiree's pale brows are drawn together, which tells me I'm not the only one unwilling to drop my guard.

Desiree uses her creation magic to make a smaller version of the flying chariot she used for a previous challenge, when we all had to move creatively across the lawn. We load up the chariot with food and beverages, then follow it upstairs. I let out a sigh of relief when I see that my room is untouched.

When we've unloaded and set up our food, we return downstairs for more. After adding it to our tables, we meet again in the hallway. "One more load should do it," Justyne proclaims.

The third time we get upstairs with food and drinks, we hear Rochelle singing a merry, wordless tune from behind her closed door.

Desiree frowns. "She seems quite cheerful for someone who's about to lose." A current of dread carries her words along.

My heart pounds as I open the door to my room. A single word escapes my lips: "Hell."

All the best parts of my décor are gone. The most beautiful flower arrangements, the loveliest paintings, the finest crystal. The corner that held self-playing instruments is starkly empty. My room looks plain.

I run into the corridor. Felia, Justyne, and Desiree are exiting their rooms. Their wide eyes confirm what I suspected: their hard work has come to naught, just like mine.

As one, we turn our attention to Rochelle's closed door. She must've heard Justyne saying we'd be bringing one more load. While we were gone, she raided our rooms with frightening efficiency . . . minutes before the starting time Tor gave us. Without a word, we step toward her door to confront her together.

"Almost time!" Tor calls from the stairs. "Are you ready?"

His voice makes us halt. It's too late to confront Rochelle, and we have no proof to bring to Tor. "Nearly ready!" I say to him, my smile full of false brightness.

I arrange the last of my food in the room. It's the only thing to do. The others follow my lead. Felia's skin has turned deep purple with anger.

I spend our final few minutes of preparation time numbly doing all I can to make my room look inviting. The snake emerges again, curling comfortingly around my arm and hissing in the direction of Rochelle's room. When I set her down, she slithers off into the shadows.

A distant clock strikes seven times. Tor calls us all into the hallway. I do my best to keep up my fake cheerfulness as he informs us we'll visit my revel first.

My allies gush over my room, but I can see Tor's disappointment as we try to celebrate in the quiet, under-decorated space. It's certainly not a feast for all the senses. At least the food is good, and we all do our best to enjoy it.

My allies' rooms mirror mine. Not spectacular, barely magical. Not cursed, merely unimpressive. Rochelle undermined us in a way that wouldn't arouse suspicion in Tor.

Felia can't hide her fury. Her smiles look like grimaces, and her voice goes shrill and loud when Rochelle spills wine on the single carpet left in the room. I notice Tor watching Felia, his lips turned down.

Rochelle's room is the last one we visit. It's nothing short of marvelous. Everywhere I look, there's beautiful artwork. The instruments she stole from me are playing, and I wonder if she somehow stole my enchantment too. Flowers fill the room with glorious scents and colors. My hands continually encounter luxurious textures.

Despite my anger, I get caught up in the perfection of it all. I find myself laughing at Tor's jokes, then humming along with the music. When Tor asks me to dance, I get lost in the wonderful sensation of his hands—one holding mine, the other warm on my waist.

Rochelle's revel lasts for hours and accomplishes everything a good party should. When it winds down and Tor declares her the winner, no one is surprised in the least. Felia, however, is purpler than ever, and anger lights up her eyes. She barely looks at Tor as she leaves, but his gaze is fixed on her.

Back in my room, I can't sleep. I'm too angry. When I finally calm down, my stomach growls loudly enough to startle me. It's been hours since I ate, and I built up an appetite dancing, not just with Tor, but with my friends too.

I'm craving the berry-filled hand pies I served at my revel. I return to that room and eat two in quick succession. As I depart, I hear the low rumble of Tor's voice. I tiptoe down the hallway, looking for him.

In the room where Justyne hosted her revel, I spot her and Tor. They don't notice me; they're too busy kissing. It's a sweet, passionate kiss, and I watch for several seconds before tearing my eyes away.

This feels like a betrayal, since I've been friends with Justyne since I first arrived. I know that thought is silly. I've kissed Tor too, and I don't think I'm betraying her. But I'm not built for this. I want love; I'm just sick of competing for it.

25

NOT GOING DOWN WITHOUT A FIGHT

Tension thickens the air at breakfast the next morning. Justyne and Desiree occasionally whisper to each other, but no one wants to talk much. Tor is next to Rochelle, and they're sharing frequent, syrupy-sweet smiles. Felia sits apart from all of us, her skin still flushed an angry purple. Perhaps it stayed that shade all night long.

"What are our plans for today?" I ask brightly, because I don't know what else to say.

The room goes silent, even the clink of silverware fading to nothing. Every eye is on Tor.

He clears his throat. "Well, I was going to announce our plans at the end of breakfast so everyone could enjoy themselves first."

I nearly burst out laughing, as this is not a room full of people *enjoying themselves*.

He continues, "After breakfast, there will be an elimination."

My breath catches. With twelve days left in the competition, I was hoping he'd wait a little longer before reducing our numbers again. I know he won't send Rochelle home this time. Not after she was the obvious challenge winner.

After breakfast, we gather in the parlor. I remember the first elimination, when there were ten contestants lined up in here. It feels almost empty with only five.

With no preamble, Tor says, "Rochelle, will you stay?"

Again, I flash back to that first elimination, when she was the first one called. She blinks away tears, just as she did then. This time, the sight makes me want to roll my eyes. I resist the urge.

"Of course I will," she gushes, before giving him a tight hug and a kiss that's far sweeter than I know her to be.

Damn, I hate watching him kiss other people. But I keep a slight smile on my face, unwilling to risk my own fate by showing him my disgust.

My whole body loosens with relief when Tor calls my name and asks me to stay.

Next, he calls Justyne. Her smile looks strained. After Tor kisses her hand, she joins me and Rochelle. But her focus is on Desiree, who's standing very still, awaiting her fate along with Felia.

"I told you much was at stake in yesterday's challenge." Tor's voice is low, his expression somber. "Winning was important—I now know Rochelle can host a revel fit for royalty." He gives her a brief smile before turning back to the two remaining contestants. "You may have noticed that, though I chose a winner, I did not rank the rest of you. I wanted to see how everyone except the winner dealt with losing an intense challenge."

The muscles in Desiree's shoulders and arms are tensed, but she doesn't allow emotion to cloud her placid expression. Her golden, spiraled horns are perfectly still. Felia, on the other hand, has widened her eyes, and she's avoiding Tor's gaze.

"Desiree," Tor says, "you handled the loss with equanimity, as did Justyne and Aeryn. That is the type of emotional control a leader requires. The type of emotional control a *queen* requires. Will you stay, Desiree?"

Felia squeezes her eyes shut and tightens her hands into fists as

Desiree whispers, "Yes." Tor kisses Desiree's hand and sends her to stand with the rest of us who are staying.

Then he turns to Felia. "I'm terribly sorry. I've enjoyed your time here. But I cannot have an angry wife."

She's dark purple now, like blackberry wine has stained her skin. Her only response is a nod. Tor walks to her and speaks in a whisper, then ushers her out of the room. She holds her head high the whole way, avoiding everyone's gazes.

Uncertainty bubbles in my gut. Is that what it takes to be an effective queen . . . an ability to hide negative emotions? None of us felt we should explain our anger to Tor last night, and based on how much he values our supposed serenity, I suspect we were right not to share.

But Felia . . . she was here to reclaim her family's lands so her parents will no longer starve. Every bit of her emotion yesterday and today was justified. Rochelle's thievery kept Felia from caring for her family. I redouble my commitment to winning this competition. Not just for my family, but for hers.

I'm still disquieted when Tor returns to us and says, "Relax today. You deserve it after all the work you did the last four days."

I drop onto a couch, hoping everyone will leave and give me a bit of time alone to think. Rochelle saunters out. Justyne and Desiree ask if I'd like to spend time with them, but I quietly decline. They exit the room.

I bury my face in my hands. I've always known the Fae were beautiful. Now I wonder if they value image over everything. *Stay pretty and calm, and if you have negative emotions, don't show them.* It's not quite what Tor said, but it's the impression I got. Maybe I'm simply unfamiliar with this aspect of Fae culture. Yes, I hid my anger, but it was briefly, for the sake of the competition. I would hate to wear that mask all the time.

I thought I wanted to be alone, but all at once, I have the urge to get someone's input on this situation. I stand and head for the garden.

When I arrive, however, Justyne and Desiree are already there, chatting with Wyatt. None of them turn my way.

I sigh. I'd love to chat with Wyatt alone, but I don't have the energy nor inclination to be with a group right now, even if it does include my allies. I return inside to wander the castle halls. At some point, the snake joins me. She slithers ahead of me, as if she's leading me somewhere.

Eventually, we end up in the vicinity of the portrait gallery. Should I go in? I don't trust Cerise, and I'll be careful about taking any advice she gives me. However, she seems to understand this competition. That gives her words a certain amount of value. The snake continues leading me in that direction, which surprises me. I'd expect more caution from her.

I walk up to the doorway. Just as I'm about to step in, I halt, drawing in a silent gasp. Someone is already in the gallery . . . standing before Cerise's mirror.

Rochelle. Her arms are crossed, her chin lifted, as she talks to Cerise through the mirror.

I quietly move out of the doorway and stand flush against the wall, breathing as silently as possible, listening for their words.

"You should have told me!" Rochelle's voice is barely above a whisper, but it's full of indignation.

Cerise's gentle tones glide straight to my ears. "Told you what, Rochelle?"

"That Aeryn and Justyne betrayed me. That they allied with Desiree and Felia! I was humiliated when I realized no one would work with me during that challenge."

There's laughter in Cerise's voice. "You certainly recovered well. I watched you through the mirrors as you rushed from room to room, absconding with their decorations. Brilliantly played; I was positively overcome with merriment. As I've told you, sometimes magic should be the last resort, not the first."

"Yes, but they almost caught me. I could've been sent home! I needed to know about their alliance; you could've told—"

Cerise interrupts her. "Stop acting like a petulant child. I would have told you, but I did not know until the challenge. I believe they solidified their alliance in a room I am unable to view. Even if they were elsewhere, I cannot constantly monitor everything that happens in this castle."

Rochelle sighs. "So you're still on my side?"

That sweetness enters Cerise's voice again. "Of course I am. I always have been." She sounds completely sincere . . . as sincere as when she first offered to "help" me. "Continue to give me information about the other contestants, and I will continue to assist you in this competition. We make an excellent team."

I want to vomit. Cerise is manipulating both me and Rochelle and has been for some time now. It hurts more than it should, as does the knowledge that Rochelle has been actively betraying me by talking about me to Cerise. She continues to prove she was never the person I thought her to be.

I close my eyes, breathing deeply and quietly, pondering what to do next. I was hoping to continue to benefit from Cerise's knowledge and her willingness to help me. That's no longer an option. I can't trust her for a second. I renew my commitment to being careful around all the castle's mirrors. Cerise is not only spying on us, she's passing along her observations to Rochelle. I'll have to meet with Justyne and Desiree in my room to share this information with them.

A split second after I realize the portrait gallery has gone quiet, a hand grips my arm tightly. My eyes snap open. Rochelle is standing there, her dark-blue eyes full of ire.

"What are you doing?" she hisses.

She yanks me through the door into the portrait gallery. Good heavens, she's strong. I'll have five bruises on that arm in the morning. She grabs my other arm just as hard and shakes me. "What are you doing?" This time, it's a shriek.

"Nothing," I blurt. "I was wandering through the halls—I just got here—"

Rochelle releases my right arm and shoves a fist into my gut. Pain screams through me, and I embrace myself with my free arm, doubling over. A deep groan leaves my throat.

She shoves me hard. I slam into a framed painting. Both it and I crash to the floor.

I look up. Through pain-glazed eyes, I see Rochelle looming over me. Righteous anger replaces my pain, sending bolts of energy through my whole body. Magic floods my chest with warmth.

She may be stronger than me . . . but I'm not going down without a fight.

My chest is bursting with magic. I refuse to curse Rochelle, but I can use magic in other ways to defend myself. My panicked eyes scan the room, alighting on a vase of roses on a marble pedestal.

I thrust a hand toward the flowers. "Grow!" I shout, ignoring the pain in my gut from Rochelle's punch.

The flowers obey both my spoken word and my unspoken desire, the thorny stems extending and shooting toward Rochelle's arms. All I need them to do is wrap around her and hold her tight so I can get out of here.

But my actions were far too obvious. Rochelle spins, holding out a hand.

The roses and stems immediately wither and fall to the floor, pulling the vase down too. It lands on the marble floor with a crash.

"Damn it," I say, just as Rochelle turns back to me. My mind scrambles for another way to use my magic to escape. I know she'll halt my efforts, though, like she just did with the flowers. I'm brand new at this, and Rochelle has had nearly five hundred years to build her skills.

In that moment, I realize how naïve I've been, allowing myself to feel confident with my new magic. Truth is, I don't even know what I'm capable of, much less how to accomplish it.

I come to my feet, grunting at the pain in my belly. Rochelle just watches me, which scares me more than if she'd tried to keep me down. Once I'm on my feet, I lift both my hands.

I'm not sure if I'm planning to push her or punch her or use my magic again. I don't get the chance to do any of those things. Her own hands snap up, and she grabs my wrists. Eyes locked on mine, she hisses one word: "Agony."

Pain enters every part of my body. Muscles, skin, bones, even my eyelids and toenails light up with unbelievable torment. Rochelle releases my wrists, and I slump to the marble floor. The pain is so debilitating, I can do nothing but curl into a ball, drooling on the floor, praying to die.

I have to combat her curse with a blessing. Just like I did when she put the illusory rats in my room. I can feel the magic in my chest, strong and warm and ready for me to call on it. But any movement of my hands is so painful to my muscles that darkness invades my vision. When I try to speak, all that emerges is a moan. I can't move my tongue or lips, can't speak a spell without passing out.

I cursed Margot's vase without speaking or moving my hands— but I don't know how I did it. I have no idea how to access my power.

My heart, thank heaven, is still beating. It's pounding, in fact, like it's begging to leave my chest. My lungs still work, though every quick, shallow breath feels like a stallion stomping on my chest.

Rochelle kneels and brings her head all the way down, placing her face a few inches from mine. Seeing her twisted, rage-filled features, I want desperately to scream, but I can't even manage that. She's going to torture me even more, I know it.

Help me, help me! The words remain in my head, far from my tongue. Magic continues to build in my chest.

Rochelle sits up, and all I can see is the blue fabric stretched over her knees. Her hands find my throat, grip it, and squeeze.

My lungs can no longer pull in any air.

I was wrong. She's not torturing me. She's killing me. She could probably do it with magic, but I feel her hatred in the intensity of her grip. This is personal.

I'm delirious with panic, but my cursed body remains stiff with pain, preventing me from fighting back. Black spots encroach on the edges of my vision. My lungs are burning; my eyes are bulging; my face feels like it'll explode.

And all I can do is lie there. Gazing at a spot of blue fabric that, every moment, gets blurrier and smaller as my consciousness fades.

I hear shouts, but it sounds like they're coming from miles away.

My vision goes dark.

My thoughts cease.

ALMOST IMMORTAL

The next thing I'm aware of is someone shaking me awake. My vision is blurry, but I can make out Justyne's glossy, dark-violet hair and, behind her back, her lovely dragonfly wings. My swollen throat makes it impossible to get enough air. Breathing feels like sucking mud through a tiny tube.

I'm aching all over, but I can move again. I have to heal myself. I bring my hands to my throat and release every bit of magic that's built up in my chest. It leaves me in a massive *whoosh* of power.

Nothing happens.

Justyne says, "We can't heal ourselves. I don't know anyone who can. Let me heal you, Aeryn." She pulls my hands off my throat. Then she's touching me with cool fingers, sending relief into me. The pain fades to nothing as I desperately suck in as much air as I can.

She helps me sit. My vision has cleared. I meet her gaze, finding tears in her eyes. She asks me, "Are you hurting anywhere else?"

"My stomach. She punched me. And I think my arms are bruised where she grabbed me."

Justyne's quick touches heal those areas too.

"How long was I unconscious?" I ask.

"Only seconds."

"Rochelle—" I gasp.

She points.

Desiree has Rochelle backed against the wall of the gallery. Desiree is short; her golden horns don't even come to the top of Rochelle's head. She's shaking her finger at my attacker. It would be a funny sight if I had any sense of humor right now.

"I was trying to help Aeryn," Rochelle says calmly. "I don't know who hurt her. Perhaps there was an intruder."

"That's a lie!" Studious Desiree has never sounded so angry.

Another voice—soft and soothing—fills the room. "Calm yourself, young faerie."

Justyne and Desiree flinch, looking for the source of the voice. Rochelle and I turn to face the mirror. With Justyne's help, I stand. Together, we cross to the mirror. Everyone else joins us.

I speak directly to Cerise. "I heard you and Rochelle. I know you're helping her in this competition."

"Rochelle?" she asks, like she doesn't even recognize the name.

Oh, so that's the game she's playing.

"Who are you?" Justyne demands.

"My name is Cerise. I live far away, but I find joy in coming to this mirror to meet with Tor and help him however I can."

"Did you see what happened in here?" Desiree asks.

Cerise's voice is as soothing and believable as ever. "I did not arrive until just before this lovely female with violet-red hair came to save the mortal." Her eyes find Rochelle's. "She owes her life to you."

"It's a lie." My voice is soft, but there's force behind it. "Rochelle and Cerise were talking. I was watching them. Rochelle saw me and attacked me, both magically and physically. I knocked down a painting when she pushed me against the wall." I turn and point.

The painting is back on the wall. My eyes widen. Perhaps this is part of the house's magic. It does clean up our messes, after all.

"You must be remembering incorrectly," Cerise says. "You don't appear to be hurt."

"I just healed her!" Justyne's voice is nearly a shout.

"I'm afraid you're mistaken. That's not what I observed." A note of warning enters Cerise's voice. "If I must, I will tell Tor what I saw. Who do you think he is likely to believe?"

The corner of Rochelle's lips lifts with the barest hint of a smirk.

My gaze drops to the marble floor. Hopelessness washes over me. I have magic, yes, but it's so weak. When I needed it most, it failed me. Rochelle tried to kill me, and she almost succeeded.

Because I'm mortal. Sure, I've got some sort of magical blood, but I'm drastically different from the other contestants. We're not even playing the same game. They have powerful resources, magic they've used for decades or centuries.

I'm just a little girl playing pretend.

I turn to Justyne and Desiree. "Thank you," I say softly. "I need some time alone."

Not waiting for a response, I stride out of the gallery. In the hallway, my steps grow brisker until I'm running. I don't stop until I'm in my room.

I grasp the key Tor loaned me, pressing it into my palm hard enough to leave an impression. Then I return to the palace corridors and rush to the library vault.

Inside, I take a moment to catch my breath. The scent of leather and old paper brings me a measure of calm. I've always used my mind, my wits, to survive. I have to get back to that strategy. Something in these books will help me.

And I'm not leaving until I find it.

I stop at the cabinet of cards, but before I can open any drawers, my ankle begins to itch. I reach down to scratch it and find the snake nudging me.

"Well, hello." I reach down to pick her up.

She darts away from my waiting hands.

I kneel and cross my arms, asking playfully, "Is that how this is going to be?"

She slithers a few inches, then peers back at me.

"You want me to follow?"

Another short slither. Another look at me with those intelligent green eyes.

Chuckling, I stand and follow her. She takes me to a bookcase near the back, one I haven't explored. I pull out my key and open the glass door protecting the books.

"Which one?" I ask.

She slithers along in front of the bookcase, and I take small steps after her. After a few seconds, she stops and nudges a book in the bottom row. I drop into a squat and pull out the book she's indicating, a blue volume that's about the size of my hand and no thicker than my thumb.

I lift the snake so her eyes are even with mine. "This one?"

She nods, which elicits a laugh from me.

"Well, let's go read."

Back in my room, I settle into bed, cushioning my back with pillows, and open the book. It's a journal, filled with handwritten words that are clearly ancient based on the vocabulary and penmanship style. I'm immediately captivated by the anonymous human woman's story.

The journal begins when she's sixteen years old, and she starts to feel like a stranger in her own skin. She talks to her mother about it, expecting to be brushed off. Instead, her mother tells her they're both part Fae.

The journal continues, telling of the woman's quest to strengthen her Fae qualities. She's brilliant and cunning and ends up tricking a Fae male into bringing her to Faerie, where she meets a part-Fae man who mentors her. Eventually, she learns to use her magic in powerful ways. She also notices her aging seems to have slowed.

There's one final entry squeezed into the margins of the last page. I squint to make out the words written by a trembling hand: "I have lived in Faerie for nearly four centuries. Now, my life draws to a close."

My jaw drops. The writer of this journal was only one-eighth

Fae. From what I've read before, I didn't think it was possible for someone with so little Fae heritage to develop that much magic, much less to live for so long. Four hundred years . . . In my mind, that's almost immortal.

I turn back to the pages where she explained what her mentor taught her. The method of connecting with her magic was simple. She spent nearly all her waking hours in isolation, both indoors and outside, meditating.

For years.

It's not the solution I wanted. But she says it didn't take long for her power to begin increasing. Maybe I'll never develop the type of magic she did. Maybe I'll never increase my life span to several times what a human's should be.

But if I spend time alone in this castle, meditating . . . perhaps I'll get enough power to defend myself if Rochelle tries to attack me again. Or at least enough to convince Tor I'd be a worthy wife.

The snake is coiled in my lap. I lay my hands on her, taking comfort in her presence, hoping she can remain with me in my isolation. The fact that she hasn't moved makes me think she approves.

I close my eyes and breathe.

It turns out meditation is hard to do.

I've always solved problems by using my mind—researching and strategizing and planning. Being rational. Thinking so hard that my head aches.

Sitting in bed, attempting to "release the myriad chattering thoughts filling my mind" (as the writer of the journal put it), I realize that, as hard as thinking can be, *not* thinking is much harder. Just when I seem to be getting it, urgent thoughts intrude:

Is Rochelle planning an attack on me right now?

How important is magic really to Tor?

Would I be better off spending time with my allies than trying to boost my magic?

Is my family okay?

I've been sitting there an hour or so when it finally comes together. I'm breathing deeply, and my mind is settled, and I'm thinking about nothing at all.

Luxuriating in the peace washing over me, I lie on my back. I'm still, so still. Even the snake, who remains on my lap, is at rest. When she eventually slithers off me, I barely notice.

At some point, I hear the tap of bird beaks on my door. It brings me back to awareness, and I sit up slowly. My stomach aches with hunger. It must be time for lunch.

A glance at the window, however, tells me it's neither lunchtime nor dinnertime. The sky is black. I've spent many hours meditating, lying there in a state of relaxation so deep, it was almost like sleep. The birds must think I'm starving.

I, on the other hand, am glad I missed both meals. Conversation would've pulled me out of this meditative state. Even as I stand, I feel pleasantly heavy, like my limbs are simply too relaxed to move quickly.

I slip into the hallway, and the birds lead me to the kitchen. The house provides all the food I ask for. When I'm done with my solitary dinner, I glide back to my room.

The door is open. Justyne and Desiree are both there. Justyne squeals when I enter, then pulls me into a tight hug. "We were so worried about you!"

"Where were you all day?" Desiree asks.

Their loud voices threaten to pull me out of the placid state I've been cultivating. I step away from Justyne's eager embrace. If I engage in conversation, I won't be able to recapture my calm. I settle for five simple, quiet words: "I need to be alone."

I see the hurt in Justyne's frown and in Desiree's furrowed brow. "Aeryn," Justyne says, "we're allies. Talk to us. If you're struggling with something, don't hide it."

I shake my head slowly, willing myself to let her words glide over me.

"You're not acting like yourself," Desiree says. "Are you all right?"

"Yes," I murmur.

"I don't believe you," Justyne says.

When I don't respond, they exchange a look, shake their heads, and leave.

I put on a soft nightgown and open the window, fixing my eyes on the moon. My breaths slow again, and I feel I'm at one with the soft breeze and shimmery moonlight.

"Aeryn," a voice calls from below.

It's Wyatt; I don't have to look down to know that. I can recognize his kind voice even when he's speaking one word only. I don't reply.

"Are you all right?" he calls.

Again, I ignore him.

"Should I come up?"

My heartbeat quickens in a distinctly non-meditative manner. Flashes of memory warm me: him sitting on my bed. His hands holding mine. Desire, as delicious as it is inappropriate, sparks in my chest.

2 7

I DON'T WANT TO DANCE
WITH TOR

*N*o, I tell myself. I can't let Wyatt come up to my room again. He's far too distracting. I keep my gaze stubbornly on the moon, though I no longer feel connected to its light.

"Are you all right, Aeryn?" he calls again.

I nod and wave him away, hoping the gestures tell him that yes, I'm fine, and no, I don't want company. That last part is a lie, of course. I would love for him to visit my room again.

But I must return to my calm state. I must do whatever I can to increase my magic. Then I can defend myself against Rochelle. Win Tor's admiration and his heart. Provide for my family.

I return to my bed and try to get back to the calm place in my mind where I spent most of the day, but even when the snake curls up next to me, my thoughts race until I somehow fall asleep.

The next morning, I wake and begin meditating again. Like yesterday, I'm able to achieve incredible relaxation, though it takes longer than I'd like. I barely even notice the periodic knocks on my door, and when Justyne pokes her head in and tries to talk to me, I easily ignore her.

Mid-afternoon, I make my way to the kitchen alone and collect

172

enough food for two days. By now, it's been over twenty-four hours since I began meditating. The author of the journal said she felt an increase in her magic after just a day. I return to my room and try a bit of creation magic. All I want to make is a single flower.

I attempt it until my head aches. It doesn't work.

For a few hours, I try other magic. I'm about as successful as I've been in the past—I can cast small spells only.

And that frustrates me so much, I've lost my ability to meditate.

I go to bed early, then toss and turn much of the night. The next day is very similar, right down to my failure to do anything magically impressive. At least I do manage to meditate through the evening this time.

By the time darkness falls, I'm more bored than I've ever been. I'm not sure I can stand being still and silent for one more day. I'm craving conversation or a good book or *something* to make my mind feel alive again. How in the world did the woman who wrote that journal spend years thinking of nothing?

I refuse to give up on my new strategy this early, but at least I can follow more of the advice I read in the journal. I can go outside to spend time in nature.

Breathing deeply, I slowly make my way through the castle's marble hallways. There are many ways to leave this beautiful building. I find myself drawn to the exit that leads to the garden. It's a dangerous place to go; Wyatt may want to engage me in conversation. I'll have to avoid him. I'm convinced the flowers will bring quiet back to my mind.

I see no one in the garden, so I walk along the paths, letting the blooms, some of them luminescent, fill me with peace. My fingertips glide along soft petals, and I breathe deeply of their fragrance. Eventually, I sit on a bench near the edge of the garden. Beside me are beautiful flowers; above me, twinkling stars; before me, the dark grounds of this estate. I bask in the beauty, then close my eyes and let the breeze wash over my skin.

All is silent . . . until it's not. Female laughter finds my ears, and while I should ignore it, my eyes pop open, and my head swivels toward the sound.

In the distance, someone has set a few lanterns on the lawn. The light illuminates Justyne and Tor, dancing. My heart drops.

"Hi, Aeryn," Desiree says as she sits next to me.

I didn't even hear her approach. "Hello."

"Oh, you're talking again?" As she turns to face me, light from the magical blooms around us shimmers off her golden horns.

I sigh and meet her gaze. I'm far too distracted now to get back into a meditative frame of mind, anyway. "I'm sorry. I know I've been distant."

She laughs softly. "That's one way to put it." Her gaze finds Tor and Justyne. "He was going to spend the evening with you, you know."

My eyes widen. "He was?"

"He knocked on your door. You didn't respond."

My shoulders slump. Three days of meditation, and not only have my magical skills refused to blossom, I also missed out on time alone with Tor.

"What's going on?" Desiree asks.

I let it all out. My sense of helplessness when I couldn't defend myself against Rochelle. The book I found. My three days of boring, useless meditation. The only thing I don't mention is the snake. By now, I suspect everyone would think me insane if I told them an animal is guiding me.

"And now," I say, "I've not only failed to keep Tor close, I've pushed you and Justyne away too."

Her slim arm slides around my waist, and she leans her head against my shoulder. I drape my arm over her shoulders and rest my head on hers. This is the most purely comforting touch I've gotten since I arrived here.

Desiree's voice is soft when she asks, "Are you jealous that he's dancing with her?"

The question snaps my newfound serenity into sharp pieces that dig into my chest and gut. I don't like seeing Tor dance with someone else, but I'm not sure what I'm feeling is jealousy. It feels more like . . . the ache of failure.

I can't bring myself to say that aloud, so I ask, "Are you?"

I've never sensed that Desiree had a deep connection with Tor, so it surprises me when her voice sounds choked, like she's holding back tears. "I . . ." she begins. I feel her shoulders shudder under my arm. "I . . ."

I pull back so I can look into her eyes. They're swimming in pained tears. "What is it, Desiree?"

She pulls in a long breath and holds it while she wipes the tears from her eyes. She exhales slowly, then swallows. At last, she speaks.

"Yes. I'm jealous."

I nod. "It's understandable. We're all fighting for the heart of the same person. I've been jealous of most of the other contestants at one time or another."

Her gaze, locked on mine, is bold. Yet her words are soft. "I'm not jealous of Justyne. I don't want to dance with Tor."

My head tilts to one side, and I know she can read the questions in my eyes.

Desiree lets out a short little breath, like she can't believe she has to spell it out for me. She looks away and lifts one of her hands to her buzzed white hair. Her finger traces the swirly design that's shaved into it.

I watch her, mulling over what she said. She's jealous, but she doesn't want to take Justyne's place. What else would she be jealous of, unless . . .

I think of all the times I've seen Desiree and Justyne together, whispering or laughing. Eyes wide, I take her free hand. "Are you in love with her?"

Her forehead wrinkles, and she presses her lips together. I expect her to cry, but she avoids it as she nods her head slowly.

"Oh," I breathe. "Does she feel the same?"

She bites her bottom lip and nods again.

"But . . . but you're both here to win the right to marry Tor." I'm stating the obvious, but I can't seem to find anything else to say.

Desiree yanks her hand away. "Don't judge us! You know why we're really here. I was hoping to get my father away from whoever manipulated him to join the soldiers out there"—she points into the darkness, toward the distant, foggy barrier—"and I'm still hoping to find a way to do that. Justyne wants to somehow free her brother from being a statue. And it's not like you're here for Tor; you told us you just want food and other provisions for your family!"

Finally, I get a chance to speak. "I'm not judging you, Desiree. If anything, I'm jealous that you've found love here. It's certainly more than I've accomplished! But I'm concerned about your heart—Justyne's too. Could either of you be happy marrying a male?"

She wrings her hands. "I've only ever been attracted to females. I'd be miserable with Tor. Justyne has fallen for all sorts of people, so she came here hoping she might learn to love him. But the longer she's here, the more she realizes he doesn't suit her."

"And you do," I say softly.

She sighs. "We've known each other for years, and there's always been a spark between us. It wasn't until we got here that we finally admitted it to each other." Her whole body seems to deflate as she hunches over, propping her elbows on her knees. "Honestly, Aeryn, I want to leave with Justyne and trust that you'll win this competition and save my father and her brother. But what if . . ." She trails off.

"What if Rochelle wins?"

"Yes." She looks up, and tears slip from both her eyes.

"I'd like to assure you that won't happen, but based on my utter failure to improve my magical skills, not to mention the fact that I don't know if Tor really cares for me beyond enjoying a few kisses here and there . . . I'm not confident in where I stand." I gently wipe the tears off her cheeks. "I don't have any advice for you, Desiree. But I can make two promises: I'm still trying to win. And your secret is safe with me."

"I know," she says. "I trust you."

I trust her too, more than ever. She gave me information I could use to hurt her chances of winning. That's a gift, one I won't forget.

I smile in a way I hope is encouraging. "You make a beautiful couple, you know."

She returns the smile, though hers looks a bit pained. "We do, don't we?"

We give each other a tight hug, and she looks over at Justyne and Tor one more time before groaning and excusing herself to go to bed.

As soon as she's gone, Wyatt approaches and stops at a statue next to me. By the light of the moon and the luminescent flowers, he begins to carefully clean the statue's eyes. I think he's going to ignore me entirely when at last, he sighs and looks my way.

"Aeryn," he murmurs, somehow imbuing those two syllables with both sadness and yearning. He shakes his head and turns back to the statue.

I'm brought back to last night, when he asked to come to my room and I brushed him off. It was the right thing to do, I suppose. But it doesn't seem like it benefited me. My hours of meditation didn't give me any magical powers. And while staying away from Wyatt helps me focus on Tor, right now, that doesn't seem to matter. Not when Tor is across the lawn, dancing and laughing with another female.

All at once, I want the friendship Wyatt has offered me, crave it more than I've ever craved anything from the beast I came here for.

"Wyatt," I say, "will you sit with me?"

He turns his head to look at me. One of his black brows arches, and there's something about the movement that sends a thrill through me.

"Are you certain you want company tonight?" he asks dryly.

My mouth drops open, and I can't seem to reply.

He shakes his head and lets out a short sigh. "Forgive me, Aeryn. That was petty of me. I was . . . flummoxed by your response last night."

I get the feeling by *flummoxed*, he means *hurt*. That knowledge squeezes my heart.

Wyatt tucks his dust cloth in his pocket. "Of course I'll sit with you."

He lowers himself to the space recently occupied by Desiree, though his presence makes my heart pound in a way hers didn't. He's not quite seated when I blurt out, "I was meditating, Wyatt. That's why you couldn't come up. I was meditating, very poorly, not realizing it was a waste of time."

A smile tugs at his lips. "Why were you meditating?"

The truth tumbles out—not just about the journal I read, but about how useless my days of quiet were and how they did more harm than good, causing me to turn away my allies, Tor, and Wyatt himself.

When I finish, Wyatt says, "Meditation is a wonderful practice for calming the mind if you feel anxious. It can also be an effective way for some faeries—and part-Fae, I presume—to increase their magic. Not everyone experiences such magical effects, however."

"They don't?"

"Magic is very personal. Did you feel like yourself as you meditated?"

"Not really. It felt unnatural. It was a lot more difficult than I expected."

"You should feel *most* like yourself when you're connecting with your magic. If you want to better use your magic and catch Tor's heart, all you must do is be yourself."

I throw my hands up. "You keep telling me that. It's not working."

"There were ten of you here. Now, you're one of the final four. Plus, you do have magic; you've used it repeatedly. How is being yourself not working?"

I could tell him all about my fight with Rochelle and how out of place I feel in this castle. I could tell him all I want is an easy way to win this competition so I can care for my family. And I could tell him that while I have some magic, it's not impressive enough to make me truly stand out to Tor.

I don't, though. He'd just keep coming back to his advice to *be yourself*, and I need something more practical than that. More concrete.

I know he means the best, so I smile and briefly squeeze his hand, trying to ignore how his skin's warmth seems to travel straight to my heart. "Thank you, Wyatt."

Then I walk briskly into the castle, back to the one person who seems to be powerful enough to actually assist me.

2 8

THE DEAL IS SET

"Cerise?" I call as I stand in front of the mirror in the portrait gallery. The only face in the glass is my own. "Are you there?"

I have to call a few more times before she appears. She's wearing a loose, silver nightgown. Her skin is free of cosmetics, but she looks as perfectly beautiful as ever.

"Aeryn, I did not expect to see you again."

"You lied to me. Told me you'd help me when you were really working with Rochelle."

Her gentle laugh rings through the room, causing me to glance around to ensure the noise hasn't attracted anyone else. I confirm we're alone.

She says, "You weren't interested in my help. You rarely visit me. Rochelle comes daily."

I swallow and lick my dry lips as I ponder the devious faerie in front of me. I can't trust her, but I sense her great power. If I can get her to use that power to benefit me, I can win this competition and provide for my family. Then I'll never have to speak to her again.

I don't know what she'll ask in return, but I promise myself I won't do anything immoral. I won't betray those I care about. I'll be myself, just as Wyatt keeps telling me to do.

"I'm here now," I say. "And I need your assistance."

Cerise's violet-blue eyes narrow. "You expect me to help you? Why would I trust you when you've avoided me for so long?"

My snort is undignified, but it's the only appropriate response. "Why would *I* trust *you* when you've lied to me? I'm not proposing we trust each other. I'm proposing we make a deal. Isn't that something faeries like to do?"

A sly smile lifts the corners of her lips. "I'm listening."

"I'm at a disadvantage compared to the other contestants. I'm the only mortal, and I don't have much magic. I need information that will help me win Tor's heart."

"You're demanding something from me and offering nothing in return. I'm not sure how things work in mortal lands, but in Faerie, that's not considered a deal." Condescension drips from every one of Cerise's words.

I don't let her tone offend me. "I told you what I need. I'm waiting for you to do the same."

She gives me an approving nod. "Very well. I propose an even trade. I will answer your question. You will answer one of mine. We will both be honest, of course."

The deal sounds remarkably fair, and for some reason, that scares me. "What's your question for me?" I ask.

She smiles again. "I don't know yet. You'll find out when I ask it."

"How do I know the information you'll give me will truly be worthwhile?"

She somehow looks beautiful even as she's releasing a long-suffering sigh. "I'm not trying to trick you, Aeryn. However, I understand your hesitation. I'll add this caveat: if you choose not to act on my information, you owe me nothing. Alternatively, the moment you do act on it, the deal is set."

I look away for a moment, my eyes sweeping over the gallery's portraits. I need time to consider this.

There are plenty of things I'd prefer not to disclose to Cerise, but if she asks something I'm hesitant to tell her, I can answer honestly without giving her the full truth. I got plenty of practice doing that when I was growing up, every time my parents tried to be more involved with my life than I wanted them to be.

If the information Cerise shares with me is useless, I'll ignore it. I won't be any worse off than before I walked in here tonight.

At last, I turn back to her. "It's a deal. Or it will be, if I use the tip you give me."

Delight fills her eyes. "Wonderful! I will fulfill my end now." Her voice lowers. "Tor did not always have those claws. In the past, he loved cooking. He spent hours upon hours in the kitchen, creating new dishes. It's hard for him to do that now, but if you cook with him, just the two of you, with your hands and his creativity . . . it may be the most meaningful time he's spent with anyone here."

I remember early in the competition, when he cooked with four of the other contestants. Two of them are still here: Justyne and Rochelle. If that time was special to him, how much more would he value time with just one woman, doing what he loves?

"Thank you," I say, then turn away.

"Wait," Cerise says.

I look over my shoulder at her.

"Return every night. I'll ask my question when I'm ready."

I nod and leave.

I can hardly sleep, but I'm still full of energy when I go to breakfast early the next morning. Tor is the next to arrive, and I smile at my luck.

I turn to him. "Would you like to cook dinner with me tonight?"

Pure joy fills his red eyes, and the smile he gives me is radiant. Behind his chair, his tail swishes through the air with a flourish. He doesn't have to say a word for me to realize Cerise's information was accurate. I've found Tor's passion.

He carefully takes my hand. One of his claws glides along my wrist, sending a delightful shiver through my body. "I would love that," he reassures me in that warm, rumbling voice.

Cerise's words from last night echo in my head: *The deal is set.*

I shiver again.

29

JUST A DREAM

After breakfast, I crawl into bed, wanting to ensure I'm rested before my scheduled time with Tor in the kitchen. Unlike last night, I immediately fall asleep.

Hours later, I wake, a dream fresh in my mind. My most recent dreams about the prince have all been short and not very memorable, but this one was as detailed and real as the ones I had my first couple of weeks here. I sit up in bed, silently remembering what my sleeping self just experienced.

The raven-winged prince has brought me to a lush garden. We are to be married in two weeks, and today, he wants the royal florist, who's accompanying us, to practice making the bouquet. The florist is nothing but a blurry, person-shaped figure, with no discernible features.

I gaze at the myriad of vibrant, healthy blooms in the garden. "They're all gorgeous!"

The prince brings a hand to my cheek and cups it gently. His thumb sweeps across my skin. "I can't even look at the flowers. You're the most beautiful aspect of this garden."

I feel my face grow warm. When I reach up and caress his wavy,

184

black hair, he kisses me. It's both sweet and fervent, and I find myself wishing the florist wasn't standing nearby. I'd love some privacy with my prince.

Stepping back, he gestures at the riotous colors around us. "Choose what you like. The florist will cut them for you."

I step up to a rose bush covered in pink blooms. They're small, but something about them makes me smile. "Let's start with these."

As the florist is cutting them, my eye is drawn to some delicate, bell-shaped blue flowers on a vine that's crawling up the legs of a nearby bench. "Oh, those are perfect!"

I continue through the garden, pointing out several more flowers. None of them are the most traditionally beautiful. The blooms are all small but unique, pairing well with the original pink roses.

After pointing out some miniature purple daisies, I finally look at the prince, expecting to see him delighting in my joy.

He's glowering at the florist, his bright blue eyes cold, the hint of a flush on his pewter-colored skin.

I go still. "What is it?"

He turns to me, his expression instantly shifting into a warm smile. "My darling, you've seen yourself in the mirror, have you not?"

"I—of course I have."

"Well, then, you know about the hint of red in your golden hair and the creaminess of your luminous skin. You're stunning. In fact, I need not wear even a bloom in my lapel on our wedding day, because you are my flower. You must carry a bouquet that enhances your beauty! Every one of the plants you've chosen is one I plan to soon remove from the garden. They're plain, my dear. And you . . ." Desire fills his blue eyes. He licks his lips. "You are not plain."

He offers me his muscled arm. I take it, though less eagerly than usual. He leads me to a rose bush covered in massive orange flowers. "These will look incredible with your hair and skin. And those—and those." He points out flowers of red and yellow, so large, they're ostentatious. "You'll carry a bouquet of flame-colored blooms, as bright and beautiful as you are."

As the florist rushes to cut the large flowers, the prince leans down and whispers in my ear, "When I walk into our wedding with you on my arm and that bouquet in your hand, every jaw in the room will drop."

My stomach has turned sour by the time I finish recalling the dream. How dare he tell me I could choose whatever I wanted, then try to flatter me into agreeing to his choices instead? And that final comment, when the prince mused about how I'd look on his arm— clearly he considered me beautiful, but he appreciated my beauty not for its own sake, but for how it would make him look.

I shake my head. *Stop being silly, Aeryn. It was just a dream.*

Yet I know that's not true. Wyatt told me the people in my dreams are real, even if they're unrecognizable. I've always thought the prince might represent Tor.

I must have been wrong. The beast who brought me here, the one who healed my wounds upon my arrival and has kissed me with such passion, the one who gave me access to his library, would never display such arrogant vanity.

Would he?

The tapping of bird beaks on wood echoes through the room. I curse under my breath as I leap out of bed. Calling, "A moment, please," I rush to the bathroom to freshen up.

It's time to meet with Tor. I don't have time to change my clothes, but I can't imagine meeting him in a slightly sweaty dress.

He can wait, I decide.

Approaching one of my wardrobes, I say, "I need something prac-tical enough to cook in and pretty enough to distract Tor if my cooking is awful." When I open the door, I see a new purple dress. The neckline is square with a little notch cut in the middle. I put it on and find that cunningly shaped darts in the bodice highlight my curves. It's soft and a bit stretchy, and I can move in it well. The fabric drapes smoothly over my hips.

I hurry downstairs and am a bit out of breath when I reach the kitchen. I can feel the flush in my cheeks, which is fortunate, since I'm wearing little makeup.

Tor is leaning against a countertop, his thick arms crossed. His gaze travels over my form, and his well-formed lips curve into a smile. "Worth waiting for."

I made a deal with a faerie to get this time with Tor. I'd better make the most of it. So I walk up, slide my arms around his neck, and say, "Kiss me?"

He complies eagerly, bringing his hands to my waist and his mouth to mine. His lips part almost immediately—he's hungry for more than food tonight. I respond in kind, deepening the kiss, thinking of nothing beyond the taste of his mouth and the softness of his lips.

His breathing is as heavy as mine when he breaks the kiss. "Is that what you were looking for?" he asks in that rumbly voice I've liked since the day I arrived.

"I hadn't planned it, but then I saw you standing there, and . . ." I shrug. "I couldn't help myself."

Tor's satisfied smile tells me it was the right thing to say.

He walks to a countertop that's full of ingredients. "We'll be making fish. I know a delicious way to prepare it." He must see something in my expression, because he says, "You do like fish, right?"

"It's . . . not my favorite. I could introduce you to a chicken dish I grew up with. It has a delicious sauce—"

Suddenly, he's in front of me, gripping my shoulders. "Trust me on this. It will taste like no fish you've ever had. I made it dozens of times before—well, *before*." With one clawed hand, he gestures, like he's referring to a story that's not worth telling. "I'll need your help because of these damn claws, but I can give you instructions every step of the way."

I guess it's settled, then. "What can I do?"

We quickly get into a routine. He tells me what to do, and when I don't get it quite right, he corrects me gently, always with a smile. I chop vegetables, sear fish, and stir sauce.

A few times, I make suggestions. "What if we added a bit of carrot? Shall I put in another pinch of salt?" He brushes off every idea, assuring me his method will have the best results. He's kind about it, but I soon learn to stop offering my opinions. Tor is certain the recipe is perfect as is.

A little too certain, I can't help but think. But I brush the thought away. Cooking is his hobby, not mine. He just wants to be sure the meal turns out the way it should.

When we're done, I plate the fish and side dishes according to his specifications. We sit at a small table right there in the kitchen, and Tor takes a bite. His red eyes roll blissfully. "It's *perfect,*" he says after swallowing. "Try it."

I do. And while it's seasoned well, I've had better fish. Considering my ambivalence towards seafood, I know I'll have a hard time eating my whole serving. I can't bring myself to lie outright, so I give him a bright smile and say, "It's a good recipe." And it is, if you like fish.

He grins and gives me a quick kiss. "I told you it would be the best you've ever tried." Then he returns his attention to his plate.

Thankfully, he's so wrapped up in enjoying his meal, he doesn't seem to notice I'm mostly eating the vegetables, not the main dish. I'm also watching him. And thinking.

Earlier this evening, I told myself the prince in my dreams, who insisted I carry a bouquet of his choice, was nothing like Tor. But now I think of the confidence they both have. Confidence that their way is the best way, that if I just follow their advice, I'll be happy. Maybe *confidence* isn't the right word—though when my mind replaces it with *arrogance,* I squirm at the thought.

To get such pointless musings out of my mind, I ask Tor what other dishes he once enjoyed cooking.

For the next hour, he regales me with tales of gourmet dishes he's made and the enthusiastic reactions from other faeries who tasted his offerings. It's the clearest glimpse I've gotten into the life he used to live, before he was isolated in this castle. He doesn't tell me any details about who he was then, but it's clear he enjoyed lavish entertaining. I enjoy the stories, and he clearly loves having someone to listen to him.

When our conversation lags, Tor stands, and I join him. He pulls me into his arms. I lean against his broad, hard chest, enjoying the closeness.

"Thank you, Aeryn," he says into my hair. "Cooking with you . . . this was the most special night I've had since this competition began."

I accept his kiss, then find myself returning it passionately, getting lost in the firmness of his lips on mine and the gentleness of his hands sliding over my back and hips. This is what I've always wanted, a partner who desires me. My body responds quickly, yearning for more from him.

Tor brings his mouth to my ear and starts whispering about how beautiful I look tonight.

His words break the spell I allowed to come over me. Yes, he's saying all the right things, but all I can hear is his voice from earlier, when he brushed aside my ideas.

His mouth returns to mine. Again, I kiss him back, but this time, I can't seem to drum up the passion I felt moments before. I enjoy the sensation of his lips, his tongue, his hands, but my body isn't begging to go further now. And the longer he holds me, the more my mind fixes on how he responded to me as we cooked together. My eagerness wanes, the movements of my lips and hands turning rote.

Before he can pick up on my mood change, I break the kiss and give him a smile. "I enjoyed cooking with you," I say, and it's true. At some level.

Those red eyes are full of warmth and desire. His hand comes up to my cheek, and when a claw glides over my ear, I can't help but shiver.

"Aeryn." His tone, both growly and breathy, tells me he wants to return to what we were doing just now.

An instinct deep inside me screams what I know to be true: if I kiss him again, he'll ask for more. Maybe even invite me to return to his room with him. I should want that. If I'm considering marrying this male, the thought of losing myself in him should be delightful.

Yet at this moment, it's not.

"Good night, Tor," I say. Then I turn and walk away, hoping he didn't see the truth in my eyes.

I begin climbing the stairs to my room, but at the first landing, I stop abruptly and descend again. I need to ponder what just happened, but I don't want to stare at the walls in my room for the rest of the night.

Instead, I exit the castle and wander the grounds aimlessly. Clouds cover the stars, so I walk slowly, lest I trip or run into something. My skirts swish on the grass, and I draw deep breaths of the brisk air, hoping it'll bring clarity to my mind.

Who is Tor? I ask myself.

I don't mean, *Where did he come from?* or, *Is he the prince in my dreams?* No, all that feels secondary now. I want to know who he really is, deep inside. What's his true personality? More importantly, what is his character?

I review my significant interactions with him. There are far fewer than I'd like, considering I've been here thirty-three days. I suppose that's the hazard of competing with other people for a potential mate. I focus on the limited time we've shared, trying to draw conclusions about who he is.

When I came, he welcomed me with true kindness. He healed me—the only time I've seen him use magic, other than the magic of the house. He was gentle and warm.

Perhaps our most meaningful time together was on my second day here, when Tor brought me to the library vault. I felt *seen* by him that night and acknowledged for who I am.

I walk even slower as I relive the kisses we've shared. That one night in his quarters. In the garden after I used magic. In the kitchen tonight. Our kisses have been pleasant, even passionate. Tor has never pressured me for more than I wanted to offer.

He's proven he desires me. So why am I now, with one week left in this competition, struggling to see him as a future spouse? Why am I questioning whether I'd be happy with him?

I shake my head and walk faster, despite the darkness. Maybe I'm just scared. This marriage would be good for me and my family. Perhaps all I need is to keep focusing on Tor's positives. I try to relax my mouth into a small smile as I shift my focus from kissing to conversations. What have Tor and I talked about during my time here?

All at once, the truth strikes me so soundly, I stop in my tracks.

Nearly every conversation I've had with Tor has been focused on him, not me.

Yes, he asked Felia and me why we were in the competition. But looking back at it now, I doubt he was truly interested in us. He simply wanted to discern how committed we'd be to him if he chose one of us.

We've discussed lighter topics too. The artwork in his room and the fish recipe. But has he ever shown true interest in *me*? Even when he brought me to the library vault, he didn't stay. I want to believe he took joy in showing me a place he knew I'd love, but now I wonder if he was just trying to appease me, to ensure I stayed content in the competition.

I need to talk to someone who truly knows him.

At that thought, my feet shift direction, leading me toward a glow in the distance: the garden with its luminescent plants.

As I walk, my mind spins. My breaths come too quickly. My heart pounds.

This competition was a mistake.

I'm fighting for the love of someone I'd never choose on my own, if it weren't for my family's needs.

I don't think he's a villain, but neither is he a hero. That might be okay if he loved me . . . but I don't think he does.

He's arrogant, and if I try to tell him that, he'll just send me home.

What am I doing? What am I doing? What am I doing?

I'm out of breath, my whole body warm despite the breeze, when I arrive in the garden. Someone is whistling a mournful tune. I follow the sound. In the glow of a bush of small red roses, I find Wyatt, carefully cleaning the hands of a female statue.

He stops whistling as I approach. He turns, and when he sees me, he smiles softly. "Aeryn."

"I don't think I want to marry Tor," I tell him between my quick breaths. "And I need you to convince me otherwise."

30

OH HEAVENS, HE CAN KISS

Wyatt's eyes go wide. There's an odd panic in them, and when he responds, his voice is trembling. "Why—why wouldn't you want to marry him? What's going on?"

I cover my face with my hands and attempt to control my breaths. "Can we sit?"

"Of course."

We settle on a nearby bench. My breathing slows a bit. "He's arrogant, Wyatt. At least that's what I see in him. But you know him better. Please tell me I'm seeing this wrong."

He swallows hard. "Why do you think he's arrogant?"

I take a deep breath. "I've been walking the grounds, reviewing every meaningful interaction I've had with Tor. I'll tell you all of it, good and bad and in between. Then you can honestly tell me what you think. Is that all right?"

Wyatt nods.

I talk for a very long time. He doesn't interrupt, but he responds silently, smiling when I tell him of the library vault and grimacing when I talk about Tor's focus on himself in conversations. I don't want to admit I've kissed Tor, but I force the words out, knowing how

193

important those moments were. At those points of my retelling, Wyatt's face goes oddly blank.

Finally, I recall how Tor insisted I do things his way as we cooked tonight. Wyatt's shoulders droop, and I wonder why he looks so disappointed.

At last, I go quiet. All I can hear is crickets for a minute or two before he shakes his head. "I don't know what to say."

"All I'm asking for is honesty. Please. You've known him longer than I have."

"I'm so . . . so confused, Aeryn. This vanity you're describing, it does sound like the person Tor used to be. But I thought he'd grown past all that. I thought he'd improved himself. I'm encouraged by some of what you've told me—that gentleness you describe wasn't always there. So he's . . . he's headed in the right direction, I think."

"Are you trying to convince me or yourself?"

A short, humorless chuckle leaves his mouth. "I'm not sure." His warm hands find mine, and an odd intensity enters his gaze. "He needs to find someone who will love him, Aeryn. That goal, it's not only important to him, it's vital for others too—" He cuts off abruptly. "I can't say more."

I'm trying desperately to ignore the warmth swirling low in my belly from the touch of his hands on mine. I should pull away, but I don't. Maybe if I keep talking, my body's irrational reactions will fade. "He isn't just in this competition for his own benefit," I say.

It's not a question, but Wyatt nods.

"I'm here for others too," I say. "Marrying Tor may be the only way I can ensure my family is provided for."

He nods again, somehow imbuing the simple motion with deep care and understanding.

"I know there's good in him." I unconsciously squeeze Wyatt's hands. "There really is. He's treated me with gentleness. And if you're telling me he's a better male than he used to be—"

"He is," Wyatt interrupts, his voice fervent. "I know he is."

"Maybe I can still give him a chance. For the sake of all the people counting on me and on him."

Wyatt smiles, but I swear there's a bit of sadness behind it. He pulls his hands away, and all at once, I'm aware of the chilly breeze again. Voice casual, he says, "Inviting him to cook with you was a great idea. That was always one of his favorite things to do."

I look down, then blurt out, "Cerise told me that about him."

When I raise my eyes back to Wyatt's, his expression is somber. "Did Cerise require anything in exchange for her assistance?"

I sigh. "Of course she did. At some point, I'll have to answer one question of hers honestly. I thought through it before agreeing to it, and I think it'll be fine. If she asks me something I don't want to share, I'll just be careful how much I tell her. I'll tell the truth without telling the whole truth."

He watches me for several seconds, his blue eyes liquid in the light of nearby flowers. At last, he says quietly, "That's not how Fae bargains work."

"What do you mean?" I ask as a bit of dread settles in my heart.

Wyatt sighs. "I tend to forget you haven't had much experience with Fae ways. When Cerise asks you her question, you'll be compelled to tell her the full, absolute truth. Fae bargains are powerful, imbued with very old magic. You can't trick your way out of this."

His tone is kind, and there's no judgment in it. Yet his words slice into me like swords. Here I am, trying to do what's right for my family. Maybe even what's right for me. And now I find out I've made an error, possibly a big one, simply because I didn't know how faerie bargains work.

For the hundredth time since my arrival, awareness slams into me of just how inadequate I am. The one mortal in this competition, with enough Fae blood to do a bit of magic but not enough power or experience to make success likely. Once again, I cover my face with my hands. My body is heavy with hopelessness.

"Aeryn," Wyatt's voice is as gentle as ever. I hear him scoot closer on the bench. Heat emanates from him as he settles right next to me. "What is it?"

I pull my hands from my face and cross my arms tightly against the chill. "I'd leave if it weren't for my family. I don't have what it takes to be here, wooing a Fae beast and competing against gorgeous females with amazing magic. I certainly don't have what it takes to negotiate with a faerie in a mirror. I don't belong here. I don't want to be here!"

His eyes are locked on mine, and I see indecision in his pursed lips and furrowed brow. He opens his mouth as if to speak, then closes it.

Then he pulls in a short breath and lifts his chin, sudden certainty taking over his expression. He's made whatever decision he was struggling with.

He opens his arms wide.

I fall into them, wrapping my arms around his waist.

His warmth covers me like a blanket. One of his hands cradles the back of my head and the other rubs my back, and I have never felt so safe. I press my ear to his chest, smiling when I hear the rapid beating of his heart.

He murmurs in my ear, wonderful words about how I'm enough just as I am, how my differences are what make me special, how I don't need to be anyone but myself. I soak it all up, silently begging him not to stop. Then he says, "You do belong here, Aeryn. You do."

I pull back just far enough to look up into his eyes. One of my hands rises to his face, and my fingers trace some of the faint spots there—the areas that, in the sunlight, look slightly darker blue than the rest of his skin. Out here, near a patch of luminescent pink flowers, he appears a bit purple. I like it.

"I belong here?" I whisper.

"You do."

"Where is *here*? On this estate? Or in your arms?"

He doesn't answer. His hand, which had been rubbing my back, goes still. His throat bobs with a swallow.

I should let it go. Instead, I hear myself ask, "Which one, Wyatt?"

He licks his lips, drawing my eyes down to his mouth. Once my gaze is fixed on it, I can't look away. His lips are perfectly formed, with a lovely little indentation in the center of the bottom one. I want to touch it, but I don't.

Finally, he speaks, his voice quiet and rough. "You shouldn't belong in my arms."

"I know." My hand finds the back of his neck, and my fingers gently stroke it, eliciting a shiver. I meet his gaze again. "But I do, don't I?"

His nearly imperceptible nod gives me just enough confidence to lift my chin and bring my face closer to his.

It's an invitation. For several seconds, I suspect he'll decline it. He's so very still.

Then his eyes drop to my lips.

"Please." I don't mean to say it. It just slips out, hovering in the chilly air between us.

I feel his warm exhale on my mouth, followed a moment later by his lips, pressing to mine.

And oh heavens, he can kiss. There's confidence in the way his lips move over mine—he's clearly in the lead. But when I open my mouth, he hands the reins to me. I feel him smile beneath my lips as I taste him, exploring his perfect mouth. Then he's in charge again, pressing me against the back of the bench, his tongue as eager as mine.

It's not a battle for control—no, it's give and take, gentle pulls and teasing pushes, a perfect dance of equals.

His kiss is remarkably revealing. This Wyatt, the one who's adoring me with his mouth—he is my home and my adventure. He's comfort and excitement. Questions and answers. Hunger and sustenance. He's the thrill of fulfilled desires and the ache of those still unmet.

And I'm in big trouble, because there is no part of me, body or mind, that wants to stop kissing him. I lie back on the seat of the bench, and Wyatt follows me down, pressing his body to mine, moving his lips to my neck, my ears, my eyelids, before bringing them back to my mouth.

I never would've guessed this gentle gardener had so much passion in him. When we're both out of breath, our kissing turns languid—deep kisses that taste like rich dessert. I feel more than hear a growly moan that rumbles in his chest, and I breathe my own happy sighs into his mouth.

We're wrapped up in each other like that for hours, our kisses only broken by occasional soft, affectionate words. I've never kissed someone for so long before, yet it's not enough time. I think we'd continue until dawn if we could. But all at once, my body stiffens, and some force pulls my head up, knocking my face against Wyatt's.

He's blinking, eyes wide, as he quickly stands. "I am—I am so sorry. I knew I shouldn't kiss you, but I thought I would do it just once, and that one turned into—"

I'm standing by that time, the same force from before having pulled me to my feet. I want to reply to him, to tell him there's no need for apology, but my feet are acting on their own, striding briskly away.

As my head clears, I realize why I'm being tugged away from Wyatt. Still walking, I shout over my shoulder, "I told Cerise I'd go to the mirror every night!"

I hear his footsteps running behind me. He catches up and slows his strides to match mine. "It must be close to midnight. It's the magic of the bargain, pulling you back."

"I know. But, Wyatt, there's so much I want to say—"

Then I'm inside, and there's a closed door between us. I let out a furious grunt as my feet carry me to the portrait gallery.

31

TELL ME NOW

The magic pulling me to the portrait gallery is so strong, I can't help but run. Several times, I nearly trip over my own feet. When I arrive in front of the mirror, I'm winded.

Cerise is waiting, black brows raised over her violet-blue eyes. "Were you even planning to come if I hadn't compelled you?"

"Yes, I just lost track of time—"

She interrupts me. "I was happy to see you using the advice I gave you. Where did you go after your dinner with Tor?"

I wonder if she watched us make and eat dinner. If she spied us kissing each other. Is there a mirror in the kitchen? My journey here flushed my cheeks, and now, heat creeps up my neck too.

"I went to the garden," I say. Thank heaven Cerise can't observe me when I'm outside, far from mirrors. My kisses with Tor might amuse her, but I suspect she wouldn't react the same way to the passion Wyatt and I shared.

She purses her lips. Her incisive eyes bore into me as if she suspects something. I stand straighter and remain quiet.

"I'm ready to ask my question," she says at last.

My heart beats in a rapid canter. After Wyatt's warning, I'm terrified to fulfill my end of the bargain.

"What one fact do you most want to hide from me?" she asks.

My throat goes tight. I don't want Cerise to know why I'm in this competition; something tells me she'll use that information to harm those I love the most.

Then I realize that wasn't her whole question—she was simply taking a long breath. Toying with me. Her gentle voice completes her inquiry: ". . . regarding one or more of your competitors who is still in this contest?"

No. No, no, no, no, no. I repeat the word silently, frantically trying to drown out the secret that threatens to overtake my mind: the liaison between my two friends.

I won't tell her. I won't. I'll find something else to share.

"Tell me!" Cerise shouts, and I could swear there's magic in her powerful voice. "Tell me now!"

I draw in deep breaths as I try to remember if Rochelle told me anything worthwhile before she found out I no longer trust her. I wouldn't mind harming her chances of staying here. It doesn't take long for me to realize, however, that she never shared many personal facts with me. Her friendship was always an illusion.

I scramble to think of something relatively harmless I know about Justyne or Desiree, something significant enough to satisfy Cerise. I recall Justyne telling me the true nature of the statues in the garden. Anyone could've guessed they were more than stone, especially those who'd visited this place when it was still located in Faerie. Surely it wouldn't hurt Justyne if the faerie in the mirror knew she'd figured out the truth.

"*Now!*" Cerise's voice booms through the room, so loud I wonder if the whole castle heard it.

I cannot wait any longer. The power of our bargain, and of this beautiful faerie's voice, compels me to speak. I open my mouth to tell her what Justyne figured out about the statues.

"Justyne and Desiree are in love," I hear myself say.

I snap my mouth closed so fast that I bite my tongue. The taste of copper invades my mouth. I swallow down the blood, wishing I could swallow my words too. Shame weighs down my shoulders and fills up my throat. I drop my gaze to the marble floor. A tear slides down my left cheek, cooling the flushed skin along its route.

I promised not to tell Desiree's secret. Desiree, who's here to save her father, a peaceful male who is even now outside the foggy barrier, risking his life to steal this land for someone else. Desiree, my friend.

I promised.

But what strength does a mortal promise have compared to a faerie bargain? None, apparently. None at all.

And now I've betrayed not only Desiree, who shared the information with me, but Justyne, too. My most faithful friend in this place. My stomach twists, and I fear I'm going to be ill.

A chuckle sounds from the mirror. I raise my eyes, fixing them on Cerise's delighted countenance. "No wonder they both covered the mirrors in their rooms," she says, before giving in to her laughter, letting peals of it fill the air around me.

All I can do is swallow my blood-tinged saliva and try not to sob.

When her amusement at last dies down, Cerise gives me the gentle, kind smile she's sported since our first meeting. It's only now that I discern a cunning glint in her eyes.

"Tor will be here soon," she says. "I assured him I would have compelling information for him, and you did not disappoint. Would you like to stay for our conversation?"

I stare at Cerise's smiling face. "No," I choke out. "I do not want to stay for your conversation with Tor."

I rush out of the room, but as soon as I enter the hallway, I hear footsteps on the nearby stairs. Wanting to avoid a confrontation with Tor, I slip inside a small sitting room. I try to control my breathing as I listen through the cracked-open door.

The footsteps get louder. Then they stop, and I hear Tor's deep voice.

"You said you'd have information for me?"

"I'm so glad you came," Cerise purrs. "When I see you, it's always the highlight of my day. Or my night."

"Get on with it, Cerise," Tor snaps. His tone makes me smile. I may be struggling to trust him these days, but I'm relieved that he doesn't seem to like the faerie in the mirror any more than I do.

"Oh, my sweet beast." She's crooning now, and sharp nausea floods my gut. "I've been helping you through this whole competition, and you can't spare me a smile? Your mouth is the only beautiful part of you; you really should use it for good."

"You know why I won't *spare you a smile*," Tor says. "And since you're clearly toying with me, I'm going to bed."

"Wait!" Cerise's command rings through the hallway, resounding in my ears. "You'll want to hear this."

"Then tell me!"

His voice is loud, the pitch higher than usual. He's not someone who's used to bowing to the whims of others. I desperately wish he'd get angry enough to give up, that he'd refuse to hear the secret Cerise is taunting him with.

Of course, I'm not that lucky.

"Two of your contestants are in love," Cerise says.

"They are?" All trace of annoyance has left Tor's voice. He sounds excited. Desperate. "Oh, thank the gods; I couldn't tell if any of them loved me yet. Which two? Tell me! I'll narrow it down to them, and then I'll make my choice."

Cerise's laughter is rich and musical. "I didn't mean they're in love with *you*, my sweet beast."

Silence follows her words. At last, she breaks it. "Beautiful Justyne and bookish Desiree—they're the two who are in love. With each other."

"*What?*" The word is almost a roar. "They're—they're playing with my heart? Do they have any idea what's at stake?"

None of us know what's at stake, I think, tuning out Cerise's laughter and words. *Not for Tor, anyway. We don't know why he's so desperate to find a wife. One who loves him, apparently.*

I'm well aware of the stakes for Justyne, Desiree, and myself, however. We all have good reason to be here, fighting for Tor, and I can't let my friends suffer from my mistake. I have to talk to them.

I'll confess everything. If they know Tor is going to confront them, he won't catch them off guard. Surely it won't be too hard for them to convince Tor that Cerise's words are lies. That they truly want him.

I pull the door open and scamper through the corridor as silently as I can. The voices of the faerie in the mirror and the male she calls *my sweet beast* get quieter as I climb the stairs.

I make it to the hallway where all the contestant rooms are. First I knock on Justyne's door. There's no response, so I try Desiree's.

She opens the door and squints at me. "Aeryn—what is it?"

"Is Justyne here?"

She nods slowly.

"Good. I need to talk to both of you."

Desiree opens the door wider. As I enter, she turns on the light. Justyne is sitting up in bed, blinking her dark, bleary eyes. Her dragonfly wings are folded neatly at her back, and her deep-purple hair looks tangled.

My expression must show my distress, because Justyne asks in a voice that's far gentler than I deserve, "Aeryn, what's wrong?"

It's strange how little time it takes for me to ruin two people's dreams. In just minutes, I tell Desiree and Justyne about everything. The deal with Cerise, my date with Tor, my betrayal of their secret, Tor's conversation before the mirror.

I don't skimp on the details of Tor's selfish behavior in the kitchen. My friends deserve to know that. I do skip over my kisses with Wyatt. Not because I don't trust the two faeries sitting on the bed with me, but because I want to keep those perfect moments close to my heart for now.

"I wanted you to know immediately," I conclude, trying to keep my voice level despite my grief and shame, "so you can be prepared to deny it when Tor confronts you. And I"—damn it, I can't stop my throat from tightening with emotion—"I can't express to you how sorry I am. I know my words will never make it right, but, I—I'm so, so sorry."

Their hands are clasped, fingers intertwined. Both of them stared at me, wide eyed, during my whole recitation. Now, they look at each other, communicating without words.

When Justyne's gaze finds me again, she says, "You think we should deny it?"

"Of course. Assuming you still want to be in this competition."

Another wordless conversation between the two of them. Then Desiree turns to me. Her skin is naturally pink, but emotion has further rouged her cheeks. "There are two problems with that. First of all, it sounds like Tor needs someone to actually love him."

I nod slowly. "Based on his response to Cerise, I think that's true. This is about love, not just marriage."

"I can't speak for Justyne," Desiree says, "but loving Tor is out of the question for me."

"Me too," Justyne quickly agrees. "I realized that on my first night here."

"Before you fell in love with Desiree?" I ask.

She lets out a wry laugh. "Absolutely. Tor can be kind and gentle when he wants to be, but underneath it all, he's a bit of a cad."

Desiree is nodding emphatically. "You saw that tonight, Aeryn."

"I wish I'd noticed it earlier."

After a brief pause, Desiree says, "There's one more problem with denying our relationship. If Tor looked in my eyes and asked if I loved Justyne, I couldn't say no. I couldn't betray her like that."

"But you were considering marrying him," I say slowly. "That's . . . not a betrayal?"

Desiree shrugs. "I planned to tell him eventually, after the wedding. It's common in Fae marriages for one or both parties to have other relationships."

"I planned the same if he chose me," Justyne says. "We just didn't want him to know yet, because why would he choose one of us, when he has contestants here who are unattached?"

Unattached. After my time in the garden with Wyatt, that doesn't describe me anymore, does it? I feel my cheeks go warm and hope they don't notice.

"Of course," Justyne continues, "based on what he said to Cerise, I doubt he'd have ever accepted such a thing. That shouldn't surprise me. He doesn't seem like the type who wants to share."

I roll my eyes. "Right. He expected all of us to share him, but he'd never do the same."

We all laugh, but then Justyne's expression turns serious. "This is it for us. Tor will kick us out, or we'll leave before he can."

"I'd rather the second option," Desiree says.

"Me too." Justyne's eyes burn into me. "That leaves you, Aeryn. We certainly can't depend on Rochelle to find a way to free my brother, or protect Desiree's father, or provide sustenance for your family, or give Felia's family's land back to them. There were four of us working together, and you're about to be the only one left. Are you up for this?"

"You . . ." I swallow. "You're asking me if I can fall in love with someone we all agreed is a cad."

Justyne leans toward me. There's passion in her eyes, and I know she's thinking of her brother, stuck in stone. "Plenty of people fall in love with cads. You've connected with the good parts of him—he healed you when you got here. He shared one of his passions with you, cooking. You've admitted you enjoy kissing him. Sometimes he can be self-centered, yes. He's used to getting his own way. Maybe you can love him despite that?"

"If you can't," Desiree interjects, "tell us now. We'll understand. But we'll have to find another way to meet our families' needs. So be honest with us, Aeryn. Is there any chance you could truly love Tor?"

I look between them. There's so much hope in their eyes. Hope . . . and kindness. They're not angry at me. I don't deserve their continued trust, but they're offering it anyway. I want to be worthy of it.

This was never about Tor for any of us. It was always about our families, about caring for all of them by ensuring one of us marries a wealthy beast.

Is that still a possibility?

Wyatt's face fills my mind. My body goes warm remembering his kisses. What do I feel for him? It can't be love; I haven't known him long enough. We're bound together by desire and sweet friendship. Can I let go of my attraction to him and return my focus to Tor? Not for myself, but for my family. And for Felia, Justyne, Desiree, and the people they love.

Justyne is right. Imperfect people (cads, even) fall in love and get married all the time. I certainly have my own foibles. Wyatt must too; I just don't know him well enough to see them yet. I don't think all of Tor's kind acts have been fake. Can I focus on the gentleness and passion I've seen in him, instead of his less-than-desirable qualities? That's what I'd want my own partner to do for me.

My mother used to say, "Love grows over time." Maybe my love for Tor will sprout and grow over the final six days of this competition. Surely it will, if I want it badly enough.

But can I stop wanting Wyatt?

I push that question away as I turn to Justyne and Desiree. "I think—well, I hope—I can learn to love Tor. I'm definitely going to try."

32

WE CAN'T TOUCH

My sleep is fitful. When I do manage to drift off, I don't have any magical dreams about a faerie prince.

Instead, I dream of my mother.

More specifically, of the days when she was ill and I traveled from village to village, looking for help. I begged doctors and midwives for herbs and tonics and *knowledge.* Anything that would save her from her mysterious illness.

She died at home . . . . while I was away, frantically failing at helping her.

When I wake in the morning, my head aches, and there are tears on my cheeks. I wipe them off and think of Justyne and Desiree. I'm just as helpless to save them as I was with my mother. And it's my fault that my friends are in trouble. My whole body feels heavy as I put on clothes and makeup and trudge to the dining room.

Justyne and Desiree are both waiting there. Tor and Rochelle haven't shown up yet. It's just me and the two females I betrayed.

I sit and force myself to meet their gazes. Based on their blood-shot eyes, I doubt either of them got any sleep after I left. "I can't tell you two how sorry I am," I say. "I never would've made the bargain if I'd realized—"

"We know it was a mistake," Justyne interrupts. "We've forgiven you. But . . ." She exchanges a glance with Desiree, and I can tell they've talked about this already.

Desiree says, "But sometimes mistakes have big consequences. It hurts, Aeryn."

I don't know how to reply. They don't seem to be angry. Instead, they both look truly sad, and I think that might be worse. I did this to them, and I can't make it right.

Actually, I can. Hope swells in my heart for the first time since I woke. I can fix everything by falling in love with Tor, then marrying him and using my influence to help my friends. I'm more determined than ever to make that happen. I couldn't save my mom's life. But maybe I can save Justyne's brother and Desiree's father.

Just as I'm about to assure them I'm fighting for them, I hear Tor and Rochelle in the corridor, laughing. Justyne and Desiree stand, clasp hands, and turn to face the doorway. Their gazes have gone hard. Determined.

They aren't hiding anymore.

Tor and Rochelle enter. He stops in front of Justyne and Desiree and folds his arms.

"What's going on?" Rochelle asks as she pulls out a chair. She sits and begins filling her plate.

"Tor," Justyne says, "Desiree and I are leaving the competition to pursue our relationship with each other."

He shakes his head, and his wide shoulders droop. Is that genuine hurt I see in his eyes? "I learned the truth about the two of you last night," he says quietly. "I was planning to confront you today, but I wasn't looking forward to it."

Neither of them respond.

"I've been doing all I can to get to know every female here," Tor says. "To determine who I want to spend my life with. Can you imagine how disappointing it was—how humiliating—to find out two of you were lying to me?"

I analyze his expression and stance, trying to see a hint of the anger he showed last night. It's not there. Did he sleep it off? Or is he hiding it? I don't know, but the vulnerability in his voice makes my heart reach for him.

"I wish you'd told me earlier," he says.

Again, Justyne and Desiree remain silent.

"I'll walk you out," he murmurs.

That's when the stoic expressions on both my friends' faces falter a bit. They're hurting, and so is Tor, and it's all my fault.

As soon as they're gone, I stand to leave. None of the food looks appetizing.

Rochelle's voice stops me. "Did you know about them?"

I ignore her and head for my room.

I don't venture out until lunchtime. As we eat sandwiches, Tor is all smiles. He tells Rochelle and me he's looking forward to spending as much time with us as we can.

She and I stay with him all afternoon, playing board games and taking walks through the grounds. Despite the guilt eating away at my insides, I enjoy Tor's company. It helps that I'm consciously looking for his good qualities, and he has plenty of them. He's strong, intelligent, and at times quite witty. Yes, he tends to take charge of every situation he's in and to assume Rochelle and I will agree with his decisions, but when he speaks to us, it's with kind words.

I could learn to love him. Perhaps.

After dinner, he says he's tired and wants to go to bed early. I let out a sigh of relief. It's been a long day.

I take a leisurely bath and get ready for bed. When I pass by the window, I stop and peer into the garden. Wyatt is sitting on a bench next to a bush of glowing blue flowers.

He looks up. Even from this distance, I can tell his eyes are fixed on me. He points at himself, then at my window.

And, because I'm weak, I nod. *Yes, Wyatt. You can come up.*

He climbs through my window and stands right next to it, keeping plenty of distance between us. When I offer him a seat on the bed, he politely declines. Instead, he leans his back against the wall and crosses his arms.

They're slender arms, but they're strong from all his outdoor work. My eyes wander to the wiry muscles below his rolled-up sleeves. I force my gaze to meet his. There's a message in his neutral expression and crossed arms: *We can't touch one another.* As much as I know he's right, as much as my head agrees, my heart aches.

I'm here for Tor, I remind myself. *Only Tor.*

So why did I let Wyatt come up? And why did he offer?

"I know about Justyne and Desiree," he says. "The three of you were close. How are you doing?"

Ah, that's why he's here. To check on me. The knowledge that he's offering friendship both relieves and disappoints me. Friendship is good. But the kisses we shared were exceptional.

I force the thought out of my head and sit on the edge of my bed with a sigh. "You know why they left?"

"I know they approached Tor to admit they've fallen in love."

I bite my lip. Wyatt doesn't seem to know I'm the one who first revealed that secret. Something inside me urges me to confess. But would he look at me differently afterwards?

I can't bring myself to put the truth into words.

"I'm glad they found each other," I say. "I miss them, but I'll be okay."

He tilts his head in concern. "And your conversation with Cerise? How did that go?"

Oh, hell. Now I've trapped myself. If I tell him the truth, he'll wonder why I didn't volunteer the information as soon as he mentioned my friends. I don't want to lie, but . . . well, Wyatt's good opinion has become precious to me. I can't lose it.

"She asked me," I say, "to share my worst memory with her. I was compelled to tell her about the day I found out my mother had died."

"Oh, Aeryn. That was cruel of her. I'm sorry."

I close my eyes briefly, because I can't bring myself to look into Wyatt's soft eyes. I'm afraid his gaze will prompt me to do something stupid, like tell the truth. Or run up to him, smash my body against his, and kiss him.

Time to steer this conversation in a safe, practical direction.

"There's less than a week left in this competition, and I could use your advice," I say. When he nods, I give him a little smile. "Have a seat, please. You're making me nervous standing there."

He shakes his head. "Sitting next to you on that bed is a very bad idea if all we plan to do is *talk*."

Warmth floods my cheeks and neck. "I meant you could take the chair."

"Oh. Okay, then." He moves to the chair and sits, folding his hands tightly, like he wants to convince them not to reach for me. His blue skin has taken on a violet tinge, his version of a blush.

"Do you know why Justyne and Desiree joined this competition?" I ask.

"No."

I tell him about Desiree's father and Justyne's brother. "If I marry Tor, will I be able to help them both?"

"Regarding Desiree's father . . ." He sighs. "There's a lot I can't say. I'm trying to find the words that will break through the—" He halts and groans. "The words I can say." A long pause, and then: "I think we can safely talk about Fae battle strategy. I can't imagine any soldiers would attempt to take over Fae lands unless the ownership of those lands was in question."

I nod slowly. "No one knows where Tor came from. It makes sense others might try to claim ownership of this estate. Am I on the right track?"

His smile tells me I am. He says, "I think Desiree will be relieved if you win this competition." Again, I know there's more he wants to say, but he can't.

I take some time to think through his words. Then I mentally review all I know about Tor and all I've wondered about him.

Whether he's the prince in my dreams. Whether he's Fabien, the prince who used to live here.

A possibility enters my mind for the first time, and I blurt it out. "If Tor is Fabien, and somehow our marriage turns him back into his true form, the ownership of the estate would no longer be in question."

Wyatt goes very still. His wide eyes are fixed on mine. His mouth remains closed. His silence is more encouraging than all of the vague answers he's ever given me. Why would he be silent unless I'm close to the truth, and he's prevented from confirming it?

Tor is Fabien. This estate is rightfully his, and once the Fae world knows that, the soldiers will go home. Oh heavens, I hope I'm right.

Smiling widely, I say as casually as I can, "You said Desiree would be happy if I won. Do you think Justyne would be too?" He hears the unspoken question: *Can I break her brother out of the stone?*

His gaze leaves mine and travels to the window, where the statues of former staff reside. "People are generally happy when their friend encounters good fortune. And Justyne is a true friend."

Relief loosens my muscles. I lie back on the bed, reveling in everything Wyatt is not saying. I'd be willing to bet that if I win this competition, I'll be able to solve Justyne's and Desiree's problems. And mine too, of course.

I picture the prince from my dreams. If Fabien looks anything like him, and if Tor is really Fabien, our marriage will be a whole lot more pleasant than I've been anticipating. I've gotten used to Tor's red eyes, hairless head, and rat-like tail, but when he's in that form, he doesn't make me want to swoon like the dream prince does.

A sliver of caution slips into my heart: *That dream prince doesn't always treat you in a way that makes you want to swoon.* With effort, I shove the thought away and focus instead on wavy black hair and raven wings. On soft touches and words. I'd rather associate both Tor and the prince with their best attributes, not their worst.

I sit up. Wyatt is watching me, and I can't read the expression on his face. "You're a good woman—kind and strong," he says. "This estate needs someone like you."

I know the words come from his heart. But pain fills his eyes as he speaks them. He cares for me, I know he does. Yet pursuing me would be selfish, and that's one characteristic that doesn't apply to Wyatt.

More than anything, I want to comfort him. I stand and cross quickly to him, arms outstretched, reaching for his hands.

With Fae speed and grace, he stands and puts his hands behind his back. His lovely blue eyes lock on mine. "We can't" is all he says.

The words feel like a dagger to my stomach. But I know he's right. *No touching.* I step back, dropping my hands.

Without another word, he crosses to the window and descends his ladder to the ground.

33

THERE ARE NO SMALL LIES

*E*arly the next morning, I dream of the prince. We're at a ball, and he dances with me all night, taking particular pleasure in spinning me away from the faceless faeries who want to cut in. That stubbornness makes me a bit uncomfortable, but I relax in his arms, reminding myself how lovely it is that someone so handsome sees me as his. He's proud of me.

When we tire of dancing, we slip into a curtained-off alcove. He kisses me and touches me in ways that make me blush when I wake and remember them. Breathing heavily, I sit up in bed, remembering the feel of the prince's lips and hands. The way his soft hair glided over my skin as he did things to me no one else has done.

Pure *want* heats my skin and creates a delightful stirring in my belly. When Wyatt's blue skin and soft smile enter my mind, I purposefully replace those images with ones from the prince in my dream. Allowing the memories from my dream to stoke the heat simmering in me, I quickly get ready for the day, choosing a dress with a low, scooped neck.

Then I walk through the palace toward Tor's quarters. He should still be there; the sun just rose, and it's not time for breakfast yet.

I'm not quite sure what I'll do when I get to his room. All I know is, I have to take advantage of this moment, when I want desperately to be kissed and touched. Desire can turn into love, right? I'm certain it will if I create a moment that neither Tor nor I will forget.

I turn a corner and spy the golden leaves and flowers covering his door. My feet nearly trip over themselves in their eagerness to reach him.

When I'm almost there, the door opens. I halt, prepared to greet Tor.

It's Rochelle who walks out of the room.

Her long, violet-red hair is tangled. She's wearing a nightgown and robe, both made of luxurious silk. Her feet are bare. When she first sees me, she flinches. But she recovers quickly, closing the door behind her.

Eyes sparkling, she says, "I had a wonderful night."

Then she lifts one eyebrow and glides away.

The gut-wrenching disappointment that floods through me proves one thing: my desire for Tor was real. It's gone now, though, replaced with wicked jealousy. I don't want to feel hopeless, but—*a wonderful night?* Was she really there all night? Did they plan it—is that why Tor said he wanted to go to bed early?

A muffled screech sounds in my ears, and I spin to see Rochelle standing several yards away, hands on her mouth, eyes wide with terror.

The copper-colored snake is coiled in front of her, head raised as if she's getting ready to strike.

Rochelle backs away, ever so slowly, then turns and runs.

Stifling a smile, I walk to the snake and pick her up. She coils around my arm, and while the touch doesn't dissolve my anxiety and humiliation, it does bring me a certain measure of comfort. "I didn't know you'd followed me here," I whisper. "It seems Rochelle isn't fond of reptiles."

She opens her mouth, and her forked tongue darts out. It almost looks like she's smiling.

I return to my room, where I change into a dress with a high neckline, covering up the skin I'd previously exposed. After what I just witnessed at Tor's bedroom door, the thought of seducing him holds little appeal. As I dress, the snake slithers away.

It's still not time for breakfast, so I sit at the desk and try to read. It's a useless endeavor. My eyes fix themselves on the page, but all my mind can focus on is Rochelle's smug expression.

With a sigh, I set the book down and stride out the door. A few minutes later, I'm in the garden. Dark clouds loom above me, but the hidden sun provides me with grayish light.

I expected to be alone at this hour. Before long, however, I encounter Wyatt. He's kneeling, pruning a rosebush. As soon as he sees my face, he puts down his shears and stands. His gaze is full of concern. "You're upset." Not a question, a statement.

Good heavens, how can he read my expression so easily? I thought I was hiding my emotions.

"I saw Rochelle leaving Tor's room this morning," I say.

Bless the man, he doesn't even ask why I was at Tor's door before breakfast. His brows arch, and he asks, "This morning? Did she say why she was there?"

"No, but she . . . she was wearing a nightgown, and she told me she'd had a wonderful night. It wasn't too difficult to draw conclusions from that." Warmth floods my cheeks, and I'm not sure if it's from embarrassment or anger.

Wyatt releases a sigh and gestures to a bench. "Shall we?"

As we both sit, I blurt, "How am I supposed to fight for his heart if he's sleeping with my competitor?"

Wyatt shakes his head. "It would surprise me if that was truly what happened."

"Would it, Wyatt?" My voice is sharp, and I hope he realizes my anger isn't directed toward him. "I've never gotten the feeling Tor was the type who would say no if I offered myself to him."

Wyatt swallows. A purplish flush has darkened the blue skin of his face. "I . . . I know him," he says softly. "I know what he's been through. I don't think he would play with your heart or Rochelle's."

I peer at the gentle, kind gardener, trying to figure him out. He's always seemed to view Tor as someone who's noble and kind. And while I see hints of those characteristics in my beastly host, I've seen other qualities too. Ones that are far less complimentary.

One of us is viewing Tor from a cloudy lens. Is it Wyatt or me?

Wyatt's voice breaks through my reverie. "I've hardly spoken to Rochelle. Is she someone who would purposely deceive you?"

Hearty laughter exits my chest. "Absolutely."

"Then perhaps she was in Tor's chambers for some innocuous purpose, and she gave you the impression it was more. She may have wanted to elicit jealousy."

I shrug. "I wouldn't put it past her."

"When Tor started this competition, I knew it would bring out the worst in some people. Deceit was bound to be part of it, and it's unfortunate that Rochelle has embraced such tactics." Wyatt leans closer to me, the warmth in his blue eyes capturing all my attention. "I'm glad you haven't."

My lie from last night thrusts daggers of pure shame into my chest. This, I sense, is an important moment. Not for the competition, but for my own heart. My sense of who I am as a person.

Will I tell Wyatt what really happened with Justyne and Desiree, possibly losing his trust in the process?

Or should I keep my mouth shut and protect the one true friendship I have in this place?

"Aeryn?" Wyatt says softly. "What are you thinking about?"

In a flash of insight, I realize deceiving him won't protect our friendship. It'll dismantle it. How can I build trust with someone if falsehood is at the foundation of our relationship?

"I need to tell you something." Tears sting my eyes, but I don't surrender to them. My voice remains steady. "I lied to you."

Wyatt is still sitting next to me on the garden bench, but he crosses his arms, and suddenly it seems like he's miles away. "About what?" he asks quietly.

"Cerise didn't ask me for information on my family. She asked me to tell her a secret about one of the other contestants—the one secret I'd be most anxious to keep hidden. I told her about Justyne and Desiree. I tried not to, but the bargain pulled the truth out of me. After that, she told Tor. I warned Justyne and Desiree. They did choose to leave—but only because they preferred to leave on their own terms instead of waiting for Tor to dismiss them."

Wyatt's black brows draw closer together, creating small, vertical creases between them. His lips are taut and pressed tightly together, and his throat throbs with a swallow.

I can't bear the pain in his gaze, so I look down at my hands. "You're disappointed in me," I murmur. "I don't blame you." When he doesn't reply, more words rush from my mouth. "I hate that I ruined this for them. I'll never forgive myself. I betrayed their trust, and I—"

"Aeryn." His voice is soft, but it brings my rambling to an end. "Cerise manipulated you. You didn't willingly betray your friends."

My head lifts, and I meet his gaze again. "I never should've bargained with someone like her."

"Of course not. But you didn't know that. Now you do. You'll do better next time."

I tilt my head, studying his face. The sorrow I saw in it after my confession hasn't disappeared. And something in me knows the truth: Wyatt isn't disappointed in me for making an ignorant mistake. He's hurt that I lied to him. Unlike my confession to Cerise, lying was my choice.

My mother used to say, "There are no small lies, Aeryn." I don't think I ever understood that statement until today. My deception felt small, but it created a rift between me and a faerie who'd given me the gift of his trust.

I force myself to keep my gaze on Wyatt, as much as I want to escape his pained expression. "Lying to you was stupid. You deserve better." I can't come up with anything more eloquent than that.

He nods, but his tense form tells me things are still all wrong between us. "I appreciate that," he says. He's the one to finally break eye contact as he sweeps his gaze over the garden. "I have a lot to do today." His gaze returns to me. "Was there anything else?"

I want to beg his forgiveness. Beg him to still be my friend. But shame creates a knot in my throat, and the words don't come. I shake my head.

"Okay." Wyatt stands, pulling his polishing cloth from his pocket, and walks away.

I remain seated until his path takes him out of my sight. A breeze blows through the garden, and as I stand, I shiver. Hugging myself, I begin walking.

A raindrop plops on my right cheek. Another hits my nose. Then it's like a cloud exploded as sheets of cold water fall on me. I run through the garden, but my dress is soaked through by the time I reach the door into the castle.

I hurry to my room, where I pull off my wet clothes. If only I could strip off my guilt and shame as easily. If only the rain could wash away the wall between me and Wyatt.

I may have just lost my only friend in this terrible castle. And it's my fault.

It's time for breakfast, and at this point in the competition, I can't afford to avoid the male whose heart I'm fighting for. Despite my distraction, I dress in dry clothes and make my way to the dining room.

As the three of us eat, Tor invites Rochelle to spend the day with him. I should be disappointed, but I can't drum up any emotion but relief. I don't think I could pretend to be happy all day after everything that already happened this morning. Maybe Tor and Rochelle will spend the day in his quarters picking up where they left off . . . whatever that means. I don't have enough energy to be jealous.

I visit the main library and return to my room, where I lose myself in a novel. The rain continues, and it's still gently falling when I go to bed.

I dream of the Fae prince. He's hosting a dinner party. He tries to converse with me, but I spend the whole time looking for the brown-haired, bronze-skinned Fae male who visited one of my previous dreams. He's not there, and I can barely keep from weeping, though I'm not sure why.

I wake to find the snake curled up on my chest. Once again, she's warmer than an ordinary snake would be. I let her comforting body heat seep into me, but she can't take away my sorrow as I think of Wyatt, wondering if he has a dry place to stay when it's raining. Wondering if he regrets all the time we've spent together.

Wondering if he'll forgive me.

34

YOU HAVE NO IDEA

For two days, I spend as much time with Tor as I can. Rochelle does the same, and with Tor there as a buffer between us, she's surprisingly tolerable.

Tor's tendency to make plans without asking for input is working well for me now. Wyatt's hurting eyes fill my mind day and night, and I can't focus enough to make any decisions. So when Tor says we're going to walk the grounds, listen to magical instruments making music, or play a game, I smile and go along with it, hoping each new activity will distract me from Wyatt. It works. Occasionally. For short periods of time.

The second night, Tor spends time alone with me. We cook again —not fish this time, thank heaven. Determined to make the most of the night, I laugh with Tor and kiss him and even lick chocolate off his lips. It all delights him, and his gazes and touches stir my desires. All evening, I refuse every thought of Wyatt that tries to enter my mind. Instead, I keep my focus locked on the smiling beast sharing the kitchen with me.

I'm not quite in love, but perhaps I'm getting closer.

As Tor and I talk over a dessert of strawberries and cream, I

221

almost ask why Rochelle was in his room that one morning. I've seen the looks they've shared since then, and deep down, I suspect her visit to him was exactly what it looked like.

But I hold my tongue. Jealousy might push Tor away, and that's a risk I can't afford.

The next morning, as I'm getting dressed, I realize with a start that it's day thirty-eight.

Of a forty-day competition.

I've been so focused on staying busy with Tor over the last couple of days that I lost track of how close we are to the end of this thing. My emotions better catch up with my mind soon. I need to fall in love with Tor.

But I don't know if I can when I'm so distracted by what happened with Wyatt. I hurt him, and I've never been someone who could walk away without making amends. If I'm going to focus completely on Tor, I need to set things right with my friend, the gardener.

After breakfast, I go outside. Wyatt is once again polishing a statue, and a lump enters my throat when I see there's a missing button on the stone servant's cuff. Justyne once described her brother's statue to me, and I know this is it.

Wyatt turns. "Hello, Aeryn," he says, before returning to his job.

I position myself in his line of sight, though he makes a point to shift his eyes away from me. I speak anyway. "I've been thinking a lot over the past three days. And it strikes me, I admitted how stupid it was for me to lie to you. But I never told you I was sorry."

His hand stills, then falls to his side. His gaze finds mine, and he stands still. Waiting.

"I was ashamed of what I did to Justyne and Desiree," I say, "so I lied about it. It was wrong, and I'm sorry. I don't know if I'll ever see you again after this competition, but if I do, I can tell you this: I'll never lie to you again. You've been a true friend to me, and I wish I'd been one to you too."

He shoves his polishing cloth in his pocket and steps toward me.

"Thank you." A slow sigh leaves his chest. "It hurt, Aeryn. I won't claim it didn't. Not just that you lied, but that you left without even apologizing."

I scoff, and the sound clearly surprises him as much as it does me. "You made it clear you didn't want to hear anything else from me!"

His eyes widen. "I specifically remember asking if there was anything else you wanted to talk about."

"Yes, you did. Right after you told me how busy you were."

A sheepish smile steals over his mouth. "I did, didn't I? I'm sorry too, Aeryn. I was hurting, but I shouldn't have shut you out."

I blink. I haven't known many human men who will readily apologize. I don't know what's typical for Fae males . . . but of the two on this estate, I suspect Wyatt is the only one who would do so.

"I forgive you, by the way," Wyatt says.

"Thank you." My words are barely a whisper. "And I forgive you." I turn to a flower bush and brush my fingers against its bright-green leaves. "I've messed up a lot. First with Justyne and Desiree's secret, then with you. Actually, if we go back further, there was that prank I played on Felia . . ." My sigh is almost a groan. My eyes lift, meeting Wyatt's again. "I'm having a hard time living with myself, to be honest."

To my surprise, another soft smile creases the blue skin of his cheeks. "Aeryn." His tone is warm and full of acceptance. "We all make bad decisions. Big ones, sometimes. Life-altering ones. All we can do is learn from them. Forgive ourselves and try to do better the next time."

I roll my eyes. "I somehow doubt you've made any of those huge mistakes you're speaking of."

His smile falters. "You have no idea," he whispers.

I wait for him to explain, but he doesn't seem inclined to. Maybe it's one of the many things he can't tell me.

Wyatt holds out his arms, and I know I shouldn't, but I step into his embrace. It's warm and comforting and perfect. "I'm glad you came to talk to me," he says.

"Me too," I murmur into his shirt. Then I pull in a deep breath of his scent. It's both fresh and earthy, just like this garden, and it affects me in ways I didn't expect, awakening yearnings I've been trying to tamp down. I let go of him and step back.

"Two more days, huh?" Wyatt's casual tone sounds forced.

"Yep."

"Do you—" He clears his throat. Clasps his hands behind his back. "Do you love him?"

My shoulders lift in a little shrug. "I'm trying to."

I don't miss the tightness that enters his forehead and lips and shoulders. He nods and says in a low voice, "Good."

"I'll see you later, Wyatt."

I rush toward the castle to prevent myself from asking him to hold me again.

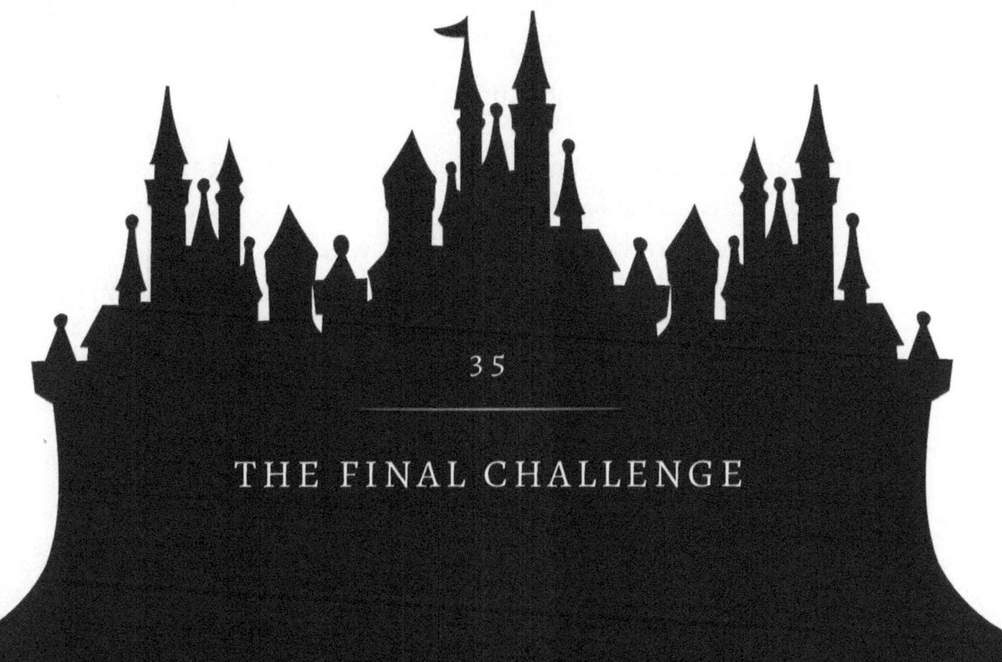

35

———

THE FINAL CHALLENGE

When I go to the dining room for breakfast, Tor is already there. He greets me with a smile, which I readily return.

"Last night was lovely," I say.

He takes my hand and presses a warm kiss to my knuckles. I shiver—not from his lips, but from the gentle scrape of his claws on the sensitive underside of my wrist. "And you are lovely," he says.

"Can we spend more time together today?"

"Actually, you'll be busy preparing. I spent time last night and this morning planning the final challenge of this competition."

It feels like the birds that led me here are in my belly, flying in circles. In two days, I will either commit to marrying Tor, or I'll go back to my family. My gaze sweeps over the bounteous food laid out before me, and it reminds me of our nearly empty table back home.

I need to win. I need to win. I need to win.

Rochelle interrupts my internal chant, sweeping in and sitting on the other side of Tor. She's wearing the tightest dress I've ever seen. The bodice is cut scandalously low, and there are cutouts on the sides at her waist and thighs. Her tan skin, with its rose-gold highlights, shimmers under the lights, and her violet-red hair sets off the purple fabric of her dress perfectly.

She's gorgeous. And she clearly wants to win.

I try to ignore the frank lust in Tor's eyes as he gazes at her. Why didn't I wear something more daring today?

Tor pushes his chair back and walks to the opposite side of the table, his hairless tail swishing on the ground behind him. His red eyes fix on Rochelle, then on me. He's smiling at both of us. "As much as I love sitting next to you, I want to be able to see you both as I tell you what I have planned."

I lean forward, waiting.

"The previous challenges have helped me evaluate the magical abilities and creativity of the females fighting for my heart," Tor says. "The two of you have risen to the top. Tonight, you'll compete head-to-head.

"After dinner, you'll go to your rooms. You may not leave until the birds tap at your door when full darkness falls. At that point, the challenge will begin. You must go to the lawn outside. From there, your goal is simple: climb to the pinnacle of the northwest tower. Whoever succeeds first will spend the entire day with me tomorrow. If you lose, you'll have to hope you've made enough of an impression on me to win the entire competition, because in two days, I'll make my decision. Aeryn, Rochelle"—he pauses for what feels like forever —"I'm giving particular weight to this challenge. It's a test of your ingenuity, strength, and persistence. All qualities my wife must have."

Rochelle looks at me. The gleam in her eye and wickedness of her smile tell me she'll do all she can to beat me tonight. Her gaze returns to Tor, and she slowly crosses her legs, the shimmery skin under the cutouts shifting in an entrancing way.

Tor watches her, his gaze so heated, I wonder it doesn't incinerate her dress. He clears his throat and continues, "Now for the rules. While you may use tools to help you get to the top of the tower, you must depend on your own strength as well. No flying machines or other tricks—this is a *climb*, not merely an ascent. As long as you stay within those guidelines, you may use any means at your disposal to win."

"Including magic?" Rochelle asks.

"Especially magic. As you know, I'm looking for a powerful wife. In fact, during the challenge, curses will be allowed. However, you may not kill the other contestant, and any injuries must be healable.

"The climb will be difficult. At any time, you may call my name, and I will ensure that you are returned safely to the ground. However, in doing so, you will forfeit this challenge and be eliminated from the entire competition. Do you have any questions?"

My mind is racing, not with questions, but with strategies.

When neither Rochelle nor I speak, Tor smiles at us and says, "Spend your day preparing. I will see you both tonight." He strides from the room.

I stack plenty of rolls, meat, cheese, and fruit on a napkin. As Tor said, I'll need to prepare all day for the challenge, and I'm certainly not going to waste time sitting in the dining room with Rochelle.

Twisting the ends of the cloth to close my makeshift pouch of food, I head for the garden. My magic is limited, and I don't have the physical strength of a faerie. In other words, I'm in desperate need of some wisdom.

I know who to count on for that.

"I need advice."

That's my greeting to Wyatt, who's pruning a bush that's practically exploding with roses in every shade of the rainbow.

He turns and smiles. "Hello to you too."

I laugh. "I'm short on time, sorry. Tor just told us about our final challenge."

I give him the rundown of the tower-climbing competition. By the time I finish, I'm standing right in front of him, our eyes locked together. I'm not sure how we ended up this close, but I don't move.

"You seem excited," he says.

"You know, I am. It's strange. Should I be scared?"

"Never." There's a bit of sadness in his smile. "It's good to see your confidence, Aeryn."

"Confidence is great, but I honestly have no idea how to get to the top of that tower. Can you help me? Give me some Wyatt wisdom?"

That makes him laugh. "I've pulled the wool over your eyes if you think I'm a good source of wisdom."

"Or maybe"—I suddenly realize I've taken his hand—"I see you better than you see yourself."

He rubs his thumb over the top of my hand. "Fight to win, Aeryn."

"How? I'll need to use magic, and I'm still not very good at it. I have the rest of today to prepare. What should I do to get ready?"

"You don't need to ask me that." He presses my palm against the center of my chest, over my heart.

Most of his hand is on top of mine, but the tips of his fingers are touching my dress, creating small, enticing points of warmth on the skin underneath. I shiver.

That brings a smile, one I'd almost call mischievous, to his mouth. The words he speaks are low and soft. "You know what my advice is."

My eyes rove over his blue skin. In the sunlight, I can clearly see the slightly darker, irregular spots all over it—on his face and neck, and on the *V* of skin exposed by his open shirt collar. I want to trace every little splotch with my fingers. Or my tongue.

Focus, Aeryn. My eyes return to his, and in their blue depths, I read the words he isn't saying. "You're telling me to be myself."

He nods.

"Why does it always come back to that?"

"Because you're so good at it." There's a new huskiness to his voice, and when I see his throat throb with a swallow, I want very, very badly to kiss him.

But that's not why I came to the garden today. I came for advice—advice it turns out I didn't really need. It was in my heart already.

In fact, maybe I'm here for a different reason entirely. Maybe I walked to this garden because I needed this moment—Wyatt's warm hand covering mine, his clear eyes telling me he believes in me, his presence reminding me I'm not alone. Every time we're together, he shares his strength with me.

No, that's not quite it. What is it, then? What keeps bringing me back here?

"You help me connect with my own strength," I whisper.

The smile that takes over his face is full of sweetness and desire and sadness.

"Okay," I say. "I'll spend today being myself. And tonight . . . tonight, I'll play to win."

"It's all you can do." Wyatt releases my hand and brings both hands to my cheeks. "It'll be enough."

He lowers his face, and for a split second, I get my hopes up, until I realize the angle is all wrong—his mouth isn't headed for mine. He presses soft lips to my forehead instead.

Maybe playing to win is indeed enough. Being myself? I'm starting to believe that's enough too.

But that kiss . . . on my forehead.

It wasn't nearly enough.

AT LEAST TEN POCKETS

I give Wyatt a smile that I hope is cheerful (but suspect is merely wistful). His hands drop to his side, leaving my cheeks colder than they were before he touched me.

I return to the castle. I'm going to spend the day by myself, connecting to the person I am. The person I've become through wealth and poverty, through joy and grief, through being a daughter and a sister and even a contestant in a strange competition.

Part of me screams that it's ridiculous to spend the day "just being myself" when I have a massively important challenge coming up tonight. I should be strategizing and preparing. But the voice in my heart is louder than the shrill antagonist in my head. My heart says I can only win if I'm fully *me*, and I won't get there by anxiously problem solving for hours on end.

Back in my room, I stand before one of the wardrobes and say, "Today, I'm doing what I want to do, and that starts with wearing what I want to wear. I'm tired of dresses. And of corsets—even the comfortable ones you've provided for me, which I'll readily admit are far better than anything mortals make."

I don't know how the house's magic works, but I know it's

listening to me. I continue, "I want to wear pants today. And I want a long-sleeved top. Something simple. Everything should be soft, warm, stretchy, and comfortable."

I didn't start this spontaneous design session thinking about the climb, but it occurs to me that what I'm describing will work well for that too. So I add, "I'd like for all of it to be snug, but not so tight that I feel constricted. Oh, and—pockets! Can there be pockets, please? Different sizes of pockets in the pants and the shirt, plenty of them. And I think—I think green fabric would be nice. A bright green that will bring out the hint of red in my hair."

I pull open the wardrobe.

Only two pieces are hanging there, and they're exactly what I asked for. I can't pull off my dress and corset fast enough. The grass-green top and pants fit perfectly. They're soft and snug on my curves, and between the two pieces, there are at least ten pockets. I pull out my little half-mirror, the one Jackie gave me. Expecting to find that I look silly, I hold it out, examining as much of my outfit as I can. The pockets—some closed with buttons, some open—are placed in such a way that they look artistic and flattering, not ridiculous.

I feel amazingly good in these clothes.

In the bottom of the wardrobe, I find green socks and a pair of black boots made of soft, supple leather. The soles are very thin, with a nubby texture made from some substance I can't identify. They'll be perfect for climbing. The creative magic of this house is caring for me well, meeting needs I didn't even anticipate.

"Thank you!" I say as I pull on the socks and shoes.

Next, I spend a full hour applying cosmetics and arranging my hair into coiled braids. I've always liked doing my hair and makeup, but it's been years since I spent so long on it. Reconnecting with this ritual, taking time to enhance my own beauty, feels *right*. I'm not doing it for Tor. Nor for Wyatt.

I'm doing it for me.

When I'm done, I grab the key to the library vault and put it in a delightfully tiny pocket on my shirt that seems made for it. I don't see

Tor or Rochelle as I stroll to my haven full of books, and I like it that way. When I enter the vault, I realize the snake is slithering in alongside me. I smile at her, and she curls up by the door, head lifted, watching me.

I don't go to the card cabinet. Instead, I explore the shelves aimlessly, pulling out books that interest me. I read bits and pieces of books about weather, baking, Fae anatomy, and sea monsters.

When I come across a book about snakes, I eagerly slide it from the shelf. It's ancient, and some pages feel thicker than others. As I examine it more closely, I conclude that some of them are stuck together. I don't dare try to pull them apart; it feels like the whole book might disintegrate if I did. The book starts with a section on non-venomous snakes. Each page contains the name of a snake, along with a hand-painted illustration. I lose myself in the gorgeous pictures that have retained their vibrance through the ages.

At some point, I decide I've had enough of snakes. "Except you," I assure my friend at the door. I have a sudden desire to read a book on climbing. I want to be ready for tonight—and that desire isn't born of anxiety or fear of losing, for I'm perfectly serene in this quiet room full of books. No, I want to read and know and prepare, because in this moment, it'll make me happy. Practical research is part of who I am.

The card cabinet leads me to an excellent illustrated guide to climbing. I sit in a chair, the snake on my lap, as I read. My stomach growls, but I ignore it. I'm entranced by the science and sport of climbing. Why didn't I ever try to ascend any of the small cliffs near my home? It's clear this sport will suit me well, the way it requires such focus and attention to detail.

Finally, my stomach's grumbling becomes too hard to ignore. I allow the snake to coil around one arm while I tuck the book under the other. Then I leave the vault, a smile on my face, and stroll back through the marble hallways of the castle.

I don't think I've ever spent so many consecutive hours simply being myself. When we had money, my days were consumed by my parents' expectations—to socialize, entertain, and learn mind-numbing skills like needlepoint. Then we lost our money, and I became consumed with ensuring my family survived.

This has been an exceptionally good day.

In my room, I eat. Afterward, I lie on the bed, arms and legs stretched out wide, grinning at how free I am to assume whatever position feels most comfortable. No constricting corsets, no cumbersome skirts. I close my eyes and release a long sigh.

And as I lie there . . . something builds in me. Something foreign yet familiar. Something powerful.

It's warm and peaceful, thrilling and entrancing.

I'm pretty sure it's magic.

I sit on the edge of my bed and put my feet on the floor. Looking down, I see the snake coiled nearby. Like she was waiting for me. A laugh, full of pure joy, bubbles from my chest.

"My reptilian ally," I say, wishing I knew her name, "It's time to play with magic. Will you stay here and help me?"

She glides over to me and climbs up my leg, coiling around my calf.

"I'll take that as a yes. And will you come with me when it's time for the competition? Will you try to help me?"

This time, her response is to crawl into a large, open pocket on my outer thigh. She's peeking out, her intelligent green eyes watching me closely. I slide my fingertip over the smooth, coppery scales on the top of her head.

I rest my hand on that now-lumpy pocket and close my eyes, drawing in a deep breath. My chest is warm, like it's been at other times I've connected to my magic. But this feels much stronger than anything else I've experienced. I'm connected to a deep sense of *potential* . . . like my whole body is a vessel, full of concentrated magic that's just waiting to be drawn upon.

I recall the four categories of faeries: blessing, curse, nature, and creation. If I were fully Fae, I'd specialize in one of those types of magic the first time I cast a major spell. Hopefully that's how it works for someone who's part-Fae too.

But it has to be a major spell. My previous magic has all been minor. Unimpressive. Am I capable of casting a spell that would be considered major?

There's only one way to find out.

Creation magic excites me the most. I think of the flying chariots Desiree makes. Such a feat would surely qualify as a major spell. But I'm not interested in a flying chariot. What should I create instead?

My face lights up with a grin as a design forms in my mind. I stand facing one corner of the room, and then I . . . well, I do magic. Moving my hands in ways that feel right, I murmur simple words, feeling the power within them: "Seat." "Carvings." "Tray." More specific words and phrases follow: "Cushioned." "Blue." "Smooth." The words flow from my mouth with little thought.

The whole thing takes perhaps five minutes—a big, complicated spell that comes from my heart and mind and is powered by that deep well of magic inside me. I don't know where my sudden knowledge and capabilities came from. All I know is, my magic works. When I'm done with my spell, I'm facing a chair I created.

It's not just any chair. It's wide enough to curl up in and has deliciously squishy cushions covered in soft, blue fabric. There's a tray attached to one armrest, and I even created a cup of hot tea to go on it. Two shelves for books are built into the opposite side of the chair, below the other armrest.

It's a reading chair, and it's so perfect that I cover my mouth to muffle a squeal of delight. I should go to the vault, grab a stack of books, and come back here to read all day and night, drinking tea and—

The squirming snake in my pocket brings my mind back to the present. As lovely as hours and hours of reading would be, that'll have to wait. I have a challenge coming up, a challenge that will give me more opportunities to use my new magic.

"Am I a creation faerie now?" I ask aloud.

I'm not sure how I'm supposed to answer that question. Wyatt said I'd feel different when I completed my first major spell, but I feel the same as I did before I made the chair.

Maybe another, stronger type of magic is waiting to be released in me. What could it be—blessing, nature, or curse magic?

There's only one way to find out. I need to cast more spells.

I'll try blessing magic next. There are no people nearby for me to bless, but I owe so much to this house that has provided for me for the last several weeks. *If I were a house, what blessing would I seek?*

I stroll around the room. This castle is lovely and in overall excellent shape, but my close perusal reveals a bit of wear and tear. I notice a small crack in a wall, near the ceiling. One of the wardrobes has a squeaky hinge. In the bathroom, the pipes attached to the tub are discolored.

So I walk—well, more like dance—around the space, letting my hands, voice, and instincts cast the spell. In minutes, my quarters aren't just repaired. They're remodeled, with strong plaster added to the walls, gorgeous new curtains, gleaming pipes, whisper-quiet hinges on the wardrobes, even a colorful rug that I somehow know this creative house will love.

Blessing magic feels a lot like creation magic, with an added element of selflessness. It's gratifying and beautiful, and it comes as easily to me as creation magic did.

Yet I still feel no different. I don't think I'm a blessing faerie.

I spend the next quarter-hour casting major spells in the final two categories, nature magic and curse magic. After gazing out the window at the garden, I use nature magic to recreate a colorful portion of it inside my room. Then I curse the plants, turning them all to ash. With a prolonged gust of wind (more nature magic), I send the ashes out my window and direct them to a neglected corner of the estate.

It's all easy—joyfully, astonishingly easy. But I don't feel like a nature faerie or curse faerie.

I pull the snake from my pocket. "Do I need to figure out what type of faerie I am?"

She shakes her head, and she looks so much like a person in that moment that a delighted laugh leaves my mouth.

Apparently there are bigger things to worry about than what category I fit into. I glance at the clock, trying not to stress over the time I wasted doing all those spells. "It'll be dark in about an hour. I suppose I should prepare."

The snake nods.

Mentally, I review the rules Tor set. I must use my own strength to climb to the top of the tower. I can't fly—which is unfortunate, as I'd love to see if my magic was up to the task of modifying my own body with wings.

I consider using nature magic to grow vines to climb on. Then I remember watching Rochelle in that little courtyard garden, using her curse magic to kill a rose bush. I'm not going to place my life in the hands of plants she could easily destroy.

So I open the book on climbing, my eyes eagerly examining diagrams of gear and descriptions of techniques. If I could magically create what may be the best reading chair in the world, I can certainly make ropes, rings, and a harness.

I speak the words that come to mind, drawing from the fantastically strong magic inside me. There's a lot of trial and error involved as I make ropes that are lightweight yet strong and create rings with no seams or weak points. The harness, too, is more complex than I expected. I wish I had a real one to look at instead of just diagrams. I groan at all my mistakes, but I also feel *alive* as I embrace the challenge of getting it just right.

As I finish creating my gear, a troubling realization strikes me: I'm no longer overflowing with magical potential. I suppose I'd hoped my new magical well was bottomless.

It's clearly not.

Instead of casting spells in all four magical areas, I should've saved my strength for preparing for and completing the challenge. I haven't depleted my magic entirely; I still feel stronger than I ever did prior to today. But I suspect I've used at least half of it, and I don't know how long the rest will last.

I hope my magic is enough. I hope *I'm* enough.

I put on my new harness and attach ropes to it, carefully following knot-tying instructions in the book. Then I have a conversation with the snake—me talking, her nodding her head. I'm going to need her help during the challenge, and she seems more than willing.

I look out the window. Dusk is already darkening into night. The time for preparation is drawing to a close.

I check all the connections between harness, ropes, and rings. After several deep breaths to calm my sudden nerves, I check it all again.

The last bit of gray in the sky turns to black. I rest my hand on the pocket the snake is in and murmur, "I wonder when—"

Tap tap tap tap tap. My room fills with the sound of bird beaks on wood.

It's time.

STRONG ENOUGH TO BREAK A CURSE

Gathering heavy loops of rope from the floor, I sense the magic inside the gear I created. I'm also suddenly aware of the trickle of power leaving my body. A horrifying knowledge fills me: my magic is maintaining my creation spell. If I use up all the magic within me, the gear will disappear.

Guess I'd better climb fast.

As I hurry to the door, I hear running footsteps in the hallway. The rhythmic pounding stops near my room. My door shudders, and the footsteps resume.

Dread sends a tingling numbness throughout my body. What did Rochelle do?

I turn the doorknob and pull. The door doesn't open. Rochelle did something to jam it shut.

With a furious shout, I slam my shoulder into the door. Bad idea. I shake out my aching arm.

Then I remember a few very important facts: *I can do magic. The door is made of wood. Wood is flammable.* I've never tried to make fire, but surely my nature magic is capable of such a feat.

Let's find out.

I wave my hands before the door, my fingers dancing as if they're flames. "Fire," I murmur. When the wood ignites, I let out a small chuckle. "Hotter," I command, my hands continuing their spell-casting movements.

No one taught me what gestures to use or which words to say. I don't understand this new magic, yet it seems to understand me.

The flames follow my continued commands, growing so hot that pieces of charred wood drop to the marble floor. When the fire threatens to burn the door frame, I shout, "No further!" It obeys.

Soon, I can see the hallway through great, gaping holes in the door. "Stop," I say. The flames cease. "Cold. Wet." Steam hisses from the burnt, broken wood. Then all is still.

Ignoring my continued magical depletion, I push through the blackened, damp wood, easily creating a hole big enough to step through. As I stand up straight, I spy a wickedly thick metal spike inserted into the door at an angle, pinning it to the frame.

I should run outside to begin my climb, but my feet are frozen in place. Rochelle is already proving she'll use any tools at her disposal to stop me. Am I really about to trust my life to the ropes I'm holding, knowing my enemy will try to break them? Tor said we can't kill one another, but I wouldn't put it past her to ensure I fall to my death. She could always claim it was an accident.

"Hell," I murmur. Then, "Damn." I throw in a few more curse words, but they do nothing to relieve my fear.

What if . . . ? An idea fills my imagination and stretches my lips into a smile. I lower my gaze to the snake, who's still peeking from my pocket. "Can I use magic to shield myself?

She shakes her head back and forth. Then she nods. Another shake, another nod.

"I'm interpreting that as *I have no idea*," I say with a sigh. I guess it's up to me to figure this out.

Rochelle is a curse faerie, so that's the magic she's most likely to use when trying to stop me. I counteracted her awful rat curse with a blessing. Maybe I can use blessing magic to prevent all her curses from reaching me.

I close my eyes, remembering the minutes I spent redecorating my room. The magic I used came with a particular feeling, a sense of fullness and rightness that warmed and invigorated me. Holding that sensation in my memory, I extend my arms and say, "Blessings. All over me, extending to the space around me. Repelling curses. Turning them to dust."

My entire body tingles with magic, from the crown of my head to the soles of my feet. I sense it extending from me, pressing into the surrounding air and even the floor.

"Wow," I breathe.

I hope this is a magical shield. Whatever it is, I can tell it's further draining my power. I doubt my magic is strong enough to maintain my magically created gear and hold up a constant shield, all while climbing to the top of a tower.

Eyes still closed, I speak from my heart. "Blessing magic, I'm grateful for you. I'm asking you to shield me, but only when necessary. Can you do that?"

There's no audible answer, but the tingling, reaching magic drops away. All I can do is hope it returns when I need it.

Hand on my lumpy snake pocket, I run through the hallway and down the stairs. It's time to conquer the tower—and hopefully Tor's heart.

I'm out of breath when I reach the northwest side of the castle. Tor is standing in the lawn, holding a torch with a bright, white flame.

"Welcome, Aeryn," he says. "Rochelle has already begun."

I press my lips together to prevent them from expelling a petty, whiny complaint about Rochelle trying to trap me in my room. The best way for me to move forward is to use my magic more creatively than she uses hers.

"You look beautiful," Tor says.

Warmth enters my cheeks, and for some reason, I wish he couldn't see my curves in these snug clothes. I shake off that thought and murmur, "Thanks."

I stand right next to the wall of the castle and look up. From bottom to top, the building is lit by occasional torches. Between the rounded pools of light are large areas of darkness. My pulse accelerates as I realize just how tall the tower is. The castle itself has five levels, and the tower appears to extend at least two additional stories into the sky.

Climbing this is just a task, I tell myself. *Like knitting a hat or hunting for food. It's one more way to take care of my family. That's all.*

Breathing as normally as I can, I pull the snake out of my pocket. Back in my room, I told her what her role would be in this challenge, and she seemed to be up for it. "Ready?" I whisper.

She nods.

My long rope is already attached to my harness. I offer the snake the other end of the rope. She opens her mouth shockingly wide, then bites it.

"Thank you," I say before placing her on the castle wall. Despite the marble's slickness, she slithers up at an impressive speed, still holding the end of the rope. What would I do without her?

My limbs tingle with the desire to climb, but I must wait. The snake needs to carry the rope to the tip of the tower, which I desperately hope is as narrow and steep as it's always appeared to be. If it is, she'll loop the rope tightly around it a few times. She'll then bring me her end of the rope, which I'll tie to a ring on my harness so I can start climbing.

While I wait, I peek around the corner of the castle. Immediately, I spot Rochelle. She's climbed all the way to the third floor using a tall ladder. It appears to be the same one I've seen Wyatt use. Clever of her to find it.

She's now standing on a windowsill. I can't make out her expression, but I discern fear in her stiff movements. She's reached the top of the ladder, and she's pulling the whole thing up so she can use it to climb the rest of the building. I'm not sure how she's planning to stabilize it once she gets it in place.

She'll be in even bigger trouble for the final portion of her climb. The tower is smooth and tapered, with no convenient features like windows or ledges to lean the ladder against or attach it to. Rochelle has loops of rope attached to her belt. She must be hoping to tie the ladder to the tower. The plan is questionable at best, and she'll need magic to make up for its deficiencies. Of course, my whole plan is based on using rope I created from nothing, not to mention the assistance I'm getting from a mysterious snake. I can't judge Rochelle for leaning on her magic.

She grunts as she pulls the ladder a little higher. Then she looks down, and her gaze finds mine. Somehow, she frees one hand and thrusts it toward me.

My newly formed shield, made of pure blessing magic, flares around me—*literally* flares, emitting a pale, purple light I couldn't see in the well-lit hallway earlier. A sense of well-being fills me as Rochelle's curse bounces right off.

I step back around the corner of the castle, out of her sight. I'm not anxious to test my shield more than I need to. Before long, the snake slithers back down the marble wall, still carrying the end of the rope.

"Did it work?" I ask.

She nods.

As soon as I can reach the snake, I pull her off the wall and return her to my pocket. Murmuring words of gratitude, along with effusive compliments for her excellent climbing skills, I tie the end of the rope to a ring on my harness.

A few adjustments, and I'm ready. I have a short rope attached to myself and to the long rope, to use as a brake. As I climb, I follow the climbing book's advice, continually adjusting the ropes. They help support my weight and allow me to control my ascent.

"Clever, Aeryn," Tor says.

"Thanks." I grit the word out, most of my attention reserved for the climb.

As I pull myself to the halfway point of the castle's first story, I let out a pained groan. I'm barely into this challenge, and I've already reached an undeniable conclusion: the book on climbing that I read prepared me in all ways but one.

It never mentioned just how hard this would be. My arms and legs are already protesting, and I haven't even reached the second story of the castle. There's no way I'll make it to the top of the tower.

38

DON'T LOOK DOWN

I can't see much in the dark. The images in my mind, however—instructions and diagrams from the book on climbing—are sharp and clear. I'm following them as well as I can, but this is all so new. My muscles are far too tense. I seem to be working against the ropes, instead of surrendering to their strength, letting them assist me.

Did I really think climbing would be fun? Now I just want to get to the top and be done with it. My trembling arms and legs taunt me every moment, insisting that finishing is impossible.

Breathing hard, I stop for a rest. Maybe I can strengthen my body with magic. It's the only reasonable option I can think of, and I both love it and hate it. Love it, because it may save my life and my position in this competition. Hate it, because I don't know if I have any magic to spare.

"I can't risk it," I murmur.

The snake slithers inside my pocket. Does she agree or disagree with my assessment? I shake off that question and continue climbing.

I don't even make it to the top of the second story before I have to

244

stop and rest again. I can't see Rochelle from here. Don't know if I have a chance of beating her.

She's heartless. If she wins, she won't use her power as Tor's wife for good. My family and Felia's parents will be destitute. Justyne's brother will remain a statue. There will be no one to advocate for Desiree's father. Those possibilities, growing more likely by the minute, set my heart to galloping in my chest. My lungs tighten. I can't get enough breath. This is no time to panic, but that's exactly what I'm doing.

Don't look down, I tell myself.

I can't help it. I look down.

Bad idea, Aeryn. The ground is much farther away than I expected. My eyes are drawn to a sharp rock that could easily crack my head open if I fall. Then I see Tor looking up at me. Over the weeks, I've learned to look past his beastly qualities. But in the torchlight, his bald head, red eyes, and clawed hands send irrational terror into my gut.

I'm at a Fae castle, trying to climb a tower, hoping to win the heart of a beastly prince who may or may not even care about me. *How did I get here?*

I'm breathing too fast. Too shallow. My heart is doing its best to break through my ribs.

I have to use magic to strengthen my body. Nature magic—maybe that'll do it. Grasping for the sensations I felt when I grew a garden in my room, I say, "Strength. Athleticism. Air. Endurance." I can't bring myself to let go of the ropes, even with one hand, but I move my fingers as well as I can, casting the spell through motions and words.

All at once, my body feels lighter, stronger, more agile. Air fills my lungs. I have so much energy, enough to climb ten towers. I resume my climb. It's blessedly, marvelously easy.

Dread tempers my relief, because my body is now using magic faster than ever. *Please let it be enough!*

I make it to the top of the fifth floor in what feels like no time at all. Grinning broadly, I pull myself onto the roof and run to the base of the round tower. I adjust my ropes and have barely started ascending when my shield flares purple again.

Rochelle.

In my focused state, I forgot about her. Forgot that making it to the top doesn't count unless I get there first. Looking to my right, I spot that damn ladder of hers, tied to the tower in several places along its height. I have no idea how she managed that, but she did. My gaze locks on the silhouette of her climbing form. She's halfway up the tower and ascending it quickly.

It's too dark to make out her face, but I hear her laughter. She should ignore me and keep climbing—she's so close. Yet she can't seem to stop herself from halting to curse me. My shield flares purple. Once, twice, three times.

With every curse repelled, I feel my magic lessen. After her fourth curse, the extra strength that got me this far sputters out. Once again, my body is weak, tired, and sore.

I still sense power draining out of me, keeping my gear-creation spell active. It's just a trickle of magic, but I can tell it'll dry up soon. Do I have enough time to make it to the top? I can't tell.

And Rochelle is climbing again.

There's one more thing I can try. Unfortunately, it'll require magic. But I'm hoping it'll so unsettle Rochelle, she'll have to stop climbing. The idea came to me when I read that book on snakes earlier today. As I looked at the gorgeous illustrations, I thought of Rochelle's terror when she saw the snake outside Tor's room that one morning.

I remove one hand from the rope and wave it like a slithering snake. Calling on my creation magic, I whisper, "Red diamondnose. Mottled constrictor. Blue-striped slider." Three non-venomous snakes whose illustrations I admired.

They appear on the tower, created from magic alone. Two of them start to slide down, and I realize they must not be climbing snakes. "Climb," I gasp, and I guess that's a good enough spell, because they begin slithering up the sharply sloped surface.

"To her," I say. They all glide across the smooth marble toward Rochelle.

I lose sight of them in the dark, but I know when they're within her sight, because her scream slices through the cool night air.

I don't take the time to gloat. Instead, I climb with all my human strength, determined to overcome my lack of experience through pure grit. My gear remains solid. The magic I'm expending is now maintaining two creation spells: one on my gear, the second on the snakes. Hopefully Rochelle is too scared to keep cursing me; I doubt I could put up a shield at this point.

She's still screaming, and sobs accompany the sound. Guilt swirls in my gut. If a snake bites her, though, it won't hurt her. My goal is to scare her, not kill her.

Not looking at her, I call, "Rochelle! Ask Tor to rescue you. I'll remove the snakes if you do." *And you'll be out of the competition,* I add silently.

"Never!" Her voice is shrill and breathless from her continued crying.

Fine, then. A quick glance tells me she's frozen in place. I just have to get to the top before she overcomes her fear. An additional burst of strength—born of desperation, not magic—fills me.

"It's venomous!" Rochelle screeches. Pure panic has replaced her sobs. "The striped one, we have those at home! It'll paralyze me! I'll fall! Oh gods . . . oh gods!"

No. It can't be true. I didn't even read the venomous section of the book. "You're lying," I manage to growl as I pull myself a bit higher.

"It's true! Please! Aeryn, please!"

Then I remember the pages that were stuck together. *Oh, no.* Could I have been reading the venomous section without realizing it?

"Snake," I say softly to the one in my pocket, "if blue-striped sliders are venomous, please wiggle."

Her body vibrates intensely against my thigh.

My heart clenches. If Rochelle falls, she'll die. I'm not a

murderer. I have to let go of part of my magic, the part keeping that blue snake alive.

The problem is, I've never done that before. I don't know how to cancel a creation spell. "Blue-striped slider," I say, "stop. Cease . . . cease being."

"Please!" Rochelle wails. Her voice drops to a hoarse whisper. "It's—oh gods, it's looking at me. It's going to strike. Please . . ."

My attempted spell didn't work. I don't know if it's because I said the wrong words . . . or if I'm simply too weak to cast any new spells. My instincts tell me I could let go of all of my magic, all at once. I'm holding onto it right now; all I'd have to do is release it. I know it would work, know it with the intuition that has guided me all day.

But if I do that, my gear will be gone.

The tower is made of marble. In its surface are golden veins that mar its smoothness, but none of them are deep enough to hold onto. I have no handholds. No footholds. My boots' soles have been gripping the marble just enough to help me climb, but it's the ropes that are holding me up. Once they're gone, I'll fall. All the way to the ground.

All the way to my death.

I can save Rochelle. But not myself.

It's funny how time slows during a crisis.

I first experienced such a phenomenon when my father gathered us all in his study two years ago. He was shaking so hard, I thought he had a fever. In a broken voice, he told us he'd lost everything, and we'd be living in poverty. I remember the stillness in the room after his revelation. My three siblings, my mother, and I inhaled in unison, and I grew immediately lightheaded, as if we'd sucked all the air from the room. After that dramatic breath, my mother spoke, asking practical questions in a strained voice. The pause between his words and hers had lasted only a moment, but it felt like an hour.

Months later, I had a similar experience. I stood outside our little shack, with empty hands and holes in my shoes, and opened the front door. I'd been traveling, seeking medicine for my mother. My brother looked up from his position by our small fireplace and informed me she'd died the night before. The distance from our front door to the bed where my mother's body lay was no more than fifteen feet, but it took an eternity to traverse it.

Now, as I cling to magical ropes holding me to a tower, time slows again.

Rochelle whispers, "Aeryn, please save me!"

How long does it take for her to speak those four frightened words? Maybe two seconds. Yet during that time, my mind is alight with images and sounds. Memories and imagination.

Sitting at the table with my family, splitting one dinner roll between us.

Justyne's brother, frozen in stone.

Desiree's father and other soldiers shouting outside the foggy barrier.

Felia's emaciated parents, stumbling around their home, giving their limited food to their daughter.

There are so many things I want to make right for my family and my new friends. Marrying Tor is the only way I know to accomplish it all.

"Please." The word escapes Rochelle's mouth as a sob.

At the same time, one more memory pierces my mind: *Cerise's peals of laughter when I betrayed my friends to her.*

When I'm in trouble, I analyze and strategize. I don't know any other way to deal with difficult situations. Analysis, however, takes time, and that's a luxury I don't currently have. I can't strategize. I must choose, and I must act.

The memory of Cerise's laughter carries with it a new, indisputable truth: allowing Rochelle to be bit by the snake, to succumb to paralysis and fall to her death, will change me. I don't know when or why Cerise became so manipulative and heartless, but I know that by ignoring Rochelle's plea, I will set myself on that same path.

Several seconds have passed since Rochelle said the snake was about to strike. Every additional moment makes her demise more likely. I'm the only one who can prevent it—if I'm willing to let go of all my magic. To fall instead of her.

I make my choice.

"Release," I say. There's no hand gesture associated with the spell, but I feel it working before my tongue forms the S. My spells are broken. I have no shield. The snakes are gone.

So is my gear.

That strange, slowed-down sense of time, that crisis-born clarity, hasn't yet left me. As gravity pulls me away from the tower's marble surface, I remember Tor said he'd save us if we called his name. I suspect there's nothing he can do to keep me from breaking apart on the ground, but the desire to live is more powerful than my cynicism.

"Tor!" I scream as I fall.

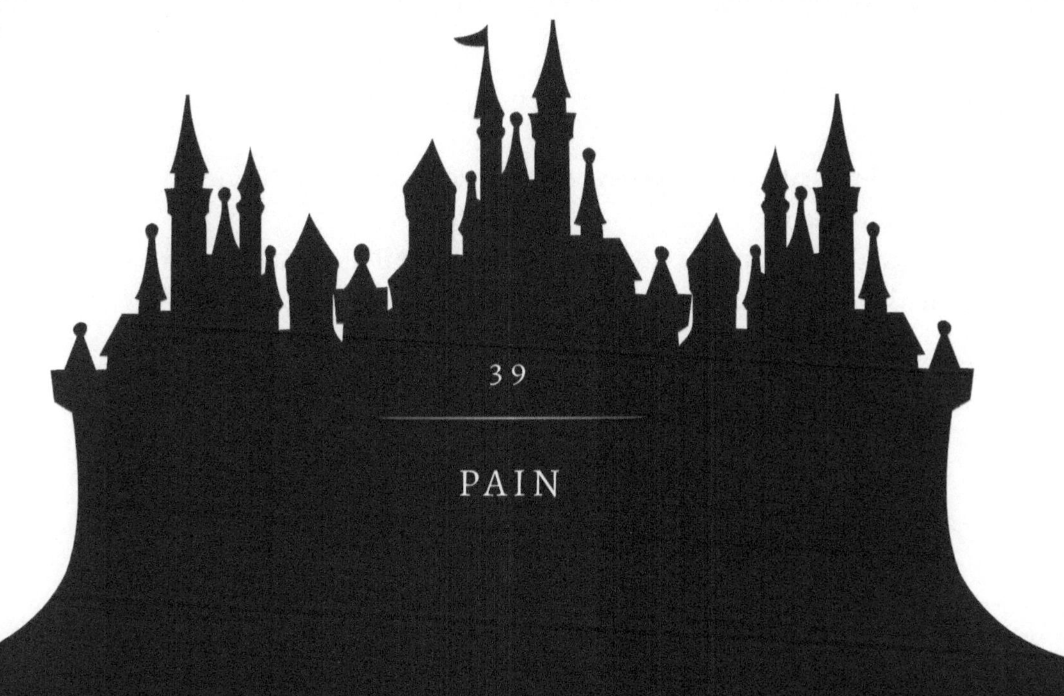

Tor's name barely leaves my lips before I slam into the roof below the tower. I hit it close to the edge, and I'm going far too fast to control myself. My body violently rolls, then tumbles over the last row of shingles.

I'm surrounded by nothing but cool, black air. My brief landing on the roof knocked all the breath out of me, so I can't even scream as I fall past windows and balconies, down, down, down—

I slam into . . . something. My whole body should break apart.

Instead, I bounce twice—once violently, once gently.

My body settles on a flexible, soft surface.

Pain hits me all at once—in my right hip, legs, ribs, and wrist, and, oh dear God, my head. All parts of me that hit the roof. I squeeze my eyes shut, as if that'll take the feelings away. A moan pushes itself from my lungs.

The agony is too intense for me to think clearly, but I'm half-aware of being laid on the grass. Of the brush of sharp claws and warm fingers against my skin. Of voices—Tor's and Wyatt's, both alternating between sharp and concerned.

Relief fills me as healing magic takes care of my injuries. Then I drift to sleep.

At some point, I return to awareness and open my eyes. It's still dark. I'm still on the grass.

Tor is kneeling over me. Light from a nearby torch reflects off his smile. "You're awake."

I'm terribly weak, so all I manage to say is, "How?"

"How did I save you?" he clarifies.

"Uh huh."

"Creation magic. I made a stretchy blanket of sorts and caught you in it. Then I healed you."

"You did magic," I mumble.

"You knew I could do magic. I healed you when you first arrived."

"But . . . since then . . ." Even those three words require so much effort, and I hope he knows what I'm saying: I haven't seen him do any magic since that day, until now.

"I have very little power, but if I let it build up for weeks, I can use it. Thirty-eight days was plenty of time."

It's not lost on me that both times he's used magic since my arrival, it's been to help me. This beast keeps surprising me. I still don't know quite what to think of him, and I'm too drowsy to ponder it.

"I thought I'd die," I say softly. Suddenly, I remember what I was doing when I fell. "Rochelle?" I ask, trying to sit up and finding I'm not quite strong enough.

He helps me sit. "She reached the top of the tower shortly after your fall."

"She won," I say.

A thoughtful look fills his eyes. "She did."

Not just the challenge, I think. In calling out to Tor, I eliminated myself from the entire competition. Rochelle will marry him.

The heaviness of failure saps what little strength I have. I lie on my back again. My family, what will come of them? What about Justyne's brother? Desiree's father? Felia's parents?

And what about . . . ? "The snake!"

"Yes, I saw the snakes you created. Rochelle told me one of them was highly venomous. They all disappeared when you fell."

I don't tell him I was thinking of a different reptile. Maybe he didn't see her when I sent her up the tower with my rope, or maybe he thought I made her with magic, like I did the others. All I do is pat the pocket where my snake was coiled.

It's empty.

Please tell me she got out. Somehow saved herself.

The sudden burst of anxiety has sharpened my thoughts, and I remember something else—the sound of Wyatt's voice after I fell. I look around, but he's not there. I don't dare ask Tor. I'm afraid he'd sense my feelings for Wyatt, and even though I'm now out of the competition, I fear his reaction.

"Let's get you to your room," Tor says.

He lifts me in strong arms, and I doze as he carries me inside, climbs the stairs, and lays me on my bed. I feel his lips, cool and soft, on my forehead. I hear his departing footsteps and the click of the door closing.

I should sleep. But my strength and alertness are returning, and along with them, despair takes hold.

I've been here for over five weeks. Thirty-eight days of loneliness, frustration, challenges I wasn't equipped for, and confusion. Of dreams and kisses and magic and feelings I can't hope to sort out.

And for what purpose? I hope Jackie kept her word and ensured my family was cared for this whole time. But I could've done that myself, like I've done for years. I came here to ensure they'd be secure for a very long time, not just a few weeks. When I return home, we'll be no better off than when I followed a path of purple rose petals to this faerie castle.

Then there are the others I wanted to help. Tears press at my eyes as I remember Desiree and Justyne and Felia. The secrets we shared and the promises I made to do everything I could for them and their families.

I failed everyone I care about.

What really makes my gut twist with anguish, however, is that I didn't just fail. I also betrayed Justyne and Desiree when I shared their secret. I nearly killed Rochelle up on that tower. And I suspect I may have broken Wyatt's heart. Not to mention my own.

Who am I? What has this place turned me into?

My tears finally fall, but they're gentle. Quiet. No sobs accompany them. I don't even have the energy for a proper cry.

At some point, I become aware of the sweat stains on my clothes. I take a quick bath and ask the house to give me another outfit as comfortable as this one, though I specify I don't need pockets, as I'll just be sleeping in it. I find a soft, stretchy blue shirt and leggings waiting in one of the wardrobes.

Once I'm dressed, I sit in bed and hug my knees to my chest, staring out the window and whispering wishes to the bright, familiar stars. "I wish I could relive the last thirty-eight days. Do one or ten or a hundred things differently." It's the first time I've wished on the stars since I was a little girl. I'm a woman now, and I know such wishes don't come true.

When I hear a hiss, I sit up abruptly. My gaze finds the snake coiled on the floor. "Oh, thank heaven," I breathe. She must've escaped my pocket as I fell.

I pick her up and lie down again, letting her curl up on my chest. But tonight, her magical warmth isn't comforting at all.

THAT'S THE YOU I'VE FALLEN FOR

I wake to the sound of something small striking the window.

The snake is gone. I don't know how long I've been asleep. It's still dark outside, though the room is lit by magical lamps I didn't bother to shut off.

In a flash, I remember the evening's events, and a despairing sense of failure returns, weighing me down.

Again, I hear the clink of an object hitting glass. I drag myself out of bed and trudge to the window. Opening it, I see someone standing on the ground below. It's too dark to tell who it is, though my heart beats in anticipation and hope.

"Aeryn!" Wyatt says.

The sound of his voice isn't enough to banish my disappointment in myself and this competition, but it takes the edge off. "Were you throwing rocks at my window?"

"Only small ones." I can hear his smile.

"Where's your ladder?" I ask.

"Tied to the tower."

"Still? Maybe I can make you one." I call on my creation magic, but nothing happens. "I guess my power hasn't replenished."

"It's all right. I just needed to check on you. I was afraid you wouldn't wake up." Emotion turns his voice rough.

The sound grabs my heart. "Stay there."

Not waiting for his reply, I leave the room and hurry down the corridor. I don't know where Tor and Rochelle are, but if they catch me, what will they do? They can't kick me out of a competition I already forfeited.

At that thought, a sense of freedom rushes through me. Immediately, I stifle it. I've failed my family and friends. I don't deserve to feel relieved.

My quick, quiet steps bring me down to the first floor, then outside.

Wyatt runs up to me, and we both skid to a stop. He takes my hands. "Should you be running? Are you sure you're all right? I had to wait to check on you until I was fairly certain Tor was asleep—I saw you fall, and I helped him heal you, but then he told me he didn't need any more of my assistance, and—"

He's never seemed this anxious before. I lay a hand on his cheek and interrupt his rambling. "I'm fine. Much better now than when Tor carried me to my room."

"Are you . . ." His throat throbs with a hard swallow. "Are you still in the competition?"

"No. I suppose I should be grateful he's giving me time to recover before sending me away." We're both silent for several seconds before I blurt, "Come to my room."

He pauses. I wish I could see his expression, but it's too dark. "Tor doesn't want me in the castle during the competition," he says at last.

A slight smile pulls at my lips. "That hasn't stopped you before. Is climbing the stairs so much worse than climbing a ladder?"

That elicits a quiet chuckle. "I suppose not."

He's still holding one of my hands, so I tighten my grip and tug him to the door. We make it to my room without incident. Once the door is shut, we stand there, staring at one another.

I'm not sure what he sees in my expression, but it's enough to prod him to ask, "What's wrong, Aeryn?"

The anguish I was wrestling with earlier tumbles from my mouth in a geyser of self-loathing. I tell him every single way I've failed, every single *person* I've failed, finishing with, "Then there's you. I kissed you when I was supposed to be fighting for Tor's heart, and I'm afraid I hurt you, and . . . I messed up everything, Wyatt. Everything."

His gaze drops to my mouth, and I don't know if he wants to kiss me again or if he's just remembering the night we both gave into that temptation. I hold my breath, waiting.

Wyatt doesn't move closer. Instead, he gives me a soft smile and says, "Let's sit."

I plop onto the bed, pull my legs up, and fold them in front of me. When Wyatt climbs up and takes the same position in front of me, knees almost touching mine, I allow myself to bask in a moment of joy. His closeness is a gift.

He takes my hands. "Why do you feel the need to fix everyone's problems?"

I swallow. Then, keeping my emotions as steady as I can, I tell him the full story of my family. How my father lost his money and my mother died. How the responsibility to care for my siblings and father came down to me.

"So," he says, "you spent years of your life planning the best ways to keep your family alive, then executing those plans."

I nod.

"And when you came here, you tried to do the same—taking care of others? Planning and executing?"

"Yes. And it didn't work." I swallow, determined not to cry. "Instead, I turned into someone I hardly know. Someone who's willing to betray my friends and who considered letting my chief competitor die so I could win."

"Aeryn." His volume is barely above a whisper, and the warmth of his tone is like a blanket wrapping around me. "I watched the challenge from the ground. It looked to me like you released your magic so Rochelle would live. Is that what I saw?"

I blink. "You must have very keen eyesight."

"All Fae do. When you let go of your magic, did you think you'd fall to your death?"

I manage a small nod.

Wyatt's smile is small but genuinely beautiful. "You didn't *turn into* anyone you should be ashamed of. At home, you risked everything for your family. Here, you risked everything for an enemy. If anything, you turned into someone who's even better than the person who arrived here—a person who was already very good."

I'm so tempted to believe his sweet words. Instead, I shake my head hard, pulling my hands from his and folding my arms. "My plans didn't work, Wyatt!" A stubborn tear works its way out of my right eye and slides down my cheek. "None of them worked! My family will still live on the edge of starvation. I didn't help Justyne or Desiree or Felia. I failed everyone, even you—I don't know why it was so important to you that I win this competition, but it clearly was. And once again, I failed."

"Yes," he says. "You failed to become Tor's bride."

My mouth drops open. This is not the type of encouragement I expected from him.

"But," he continues, "we all fail sometimes. Plans are tricky things—they're based on so many factors, many of which we can't control. All we can control is ourselves. Our hearts and morals and character. And, Aeryn . . ." His hands come to my upper arms, rubbing them soothingly. "You've succeeded there. Where it matters. Your heart—it's good." He must see that I'm about to protest, because he grins and adds, "I know you're not perfect. You've made mistakes, just like we all have. But underneath it all, you're kind and generous."

His words insist on worming their way into my despairing soul, bringing light and hope to my most fearful places. I exhale a slow breath, unfolding my arms. When I hold out my hands, Wyatt takes them. "Thank you," I whisper.

"It's just the truth. And one more thing." His thumbs slide along the tops of my hands as he speaks. "It was never your job to meet every one of your family's needs. It was never your job to meet every need that Felia or Desiree or Justyne had. It's wonderful to help the people you love. But no one can solve every problem they become aware of. I'm sorry you thought you had to."

"What about you?" I ask. "I know you'll say it was never my responsibility to win this thing, but I also know you wanted me to. Please be as honest and open as you can. How will my loss affect you?"

He bites his bottom lip and looks to the side, like he's trying to figure out what he can say. Eventually, his gaze returns to me. "If Rochelle marries Tor out of love," he says, "many things will change for the better. For me and others."

I nod slowly, though inside, I'm frustrated that once again, he's unable to give me details. "You've said it would help Tor to marry someone good. Rochelle, well . . ." A small laugh escapes my lips. "I don't think she qualifies."

He laughs but quickly turns sober again. "I'm concerned about how Rochelle will affect him." He squeezes my hands. "But I suppose that's not my responsibility, is it?"

"Or mine," I hear myself say, and the relief carried by those words is palpable.

Wyatt lifts my hands to his mouth. He kisses the tips of my fingers, one at a time. His lips on my skin light a flame in me, and for the first time since calling Tor's name, I allow myself to really consider how losing this competition might benefit me.

I'm no longer vying for Tor's affections.

No one is stopping me from following my own heart.

And there's only one faerie I truly want.

I crawl into Wyatt's lap, relishing the way his brows raise and his breathing quickens. I bring my lips to his ear and whisper, "Please stay. Stay with me until I have to leave."

His arms come around my waist, tightening, pressing me against him. "Aeryn," he says before laying feathery kisses along my jawline. His lips find mine for a brief, tantalizing second before he loosens his hold on me and meets my gaze. "I've wanted you since I first saw you in the garden."

The words stir hot desire in me. I approach for a kiss, but Wyatt smiles sadly and places a finger on my lips.

"However," he continues, "there is much I can't tell you about myself, about my past. If you give me all of you, you deserve all of me. I can't offer you that right now."

My body is screaming for him in a way it never did for boys back home. But somewhere deep in my soul, his words register as wise and true. He's considering my heart right now, rather than indulging his own desires. It makes me want him more, but it also gives me strength to hold back, just as he's doing.

I nod slowly. "Very well. But I'd like to make one request. If you need to say no, I'll respect that."

"I'm listening."

"I'm afraid I've fallen for you—the *you* that can't tell me everything. The incomplete *you*." I laugh softly. "The faerie that's looking at me like he can see everything written on my heart? That's the *you* I've fallen for."

His breaths are quick and shallow, and I see the tension in his body. He's holding himself back, and it's beautiful and selfless and so very *frustrating*. His voice turns low and rough. "You said you had a question for me?"

Reluctantly, I crawl off his lap, because as wonderful as it feels to sit there, it does nothing for my critical thinking skills. Or his, I'd wager. Sitting in front of him, I take his hands again. "I don't need all of you. Is there any part of you that you can share with me tonight?"

He cradles my face in his palms and lets his beautiful blue eyes roam over me before capturing my gaze. "I've kissed you before. I'd like to do it again. And then I'd like to hold you close until someone kicks me out of here. Is that all right?"

I respond by leaning in and pressing my lips to his. It starts gentle, but soon, our soft sighs and moans are filling each other's mouths. He guides me to lie down next to him, and we continue kissing until I have to bite my lip to keep from begging for more. Breathing hard, we gaze at each other wordlessly. It's like standing outside a bakery window, smelling the pastries. Delightful in its own right, but not at all satisfying.

When the heat between us has settled to a simmer, Wyatt asks, "May I hold you now?"

I flip so that my back is to him. His body curls around mine, and his breath warms my neck.

"I feel safer with you than I've ever felt with anyone," I murmur.

"It's the same for me," he says. "Thank you."

After some time, his breathing turns slow and even. Assuming he's sleeping, I whisper, "Wyatt, I didn't want to stop. Will there be a day when you can tell me all your secrets? A day when we don't have to stop?"

When he speaks my name, I jolt.

He chuckles. "I think you could pull me out of the deepest sleep just by saying my name." He presses a kiss to my neck. "I didn't want to stop either. And I hope the answer to your questions is not only *yes*, but *soon*."

The words are sweet, yet I hear his uncertainty. I release a long sigh and let his presence soothe me to sleep.

41

SOON

When I wake, mid-morning light is flooding the room. Wyatt is sitting in bed, propped up on pillows, reading the climbing book I borrowed from the library vault. He doesn't seem to realize I'm awake.

I slept next to Wyatt, I muse. *I woke next to him.* My heart stutters with the thrill of it.

My gaze slides over him, settling for blissful moments on various details. His white button-up shirt, wrinkled from sleep. The wiry muscles in his arms, visible beneath his rolled-up cuffs. His beautifully tapered ears. The subtle changes in the hue of his skin, from the lighter base color to the darker blue blotches.

The book in his hands is possibly the most attractive part of an overall splendid image.

"Planning on climbing the tower?" I ask. "It's a highly overrated activity."

He laughs and puts the book on the table by the bed. "No tower climbing for me." After pressing a gentle kiss to my lips, he gestures around the room. "I like what you've done to the place."

I look around my redecorated room. "I was practicing my blessing magic. Didn't you notice last night?"

His smile turns into a smirk. "I was a little distracted."

My fingers come up to my lips as I allow myself to relive the "distracting" activities we participated in last night. Yearning rises in me, a deep need to share more of myself with him. How much longer will we have together?

My gaze finds the door. "I'm surprised Tor hasn't arrived to announce his engagement to Rochelle and send me home."

Wyatt's brow furrows. "As am I. It's day thirty-nine. Maybe he's waiting until tomorrow to announce his engagement. But . . ."

I pick up where his words dropped off. "But why hasn't he sent me away?"

Wyatt nods. "Not that I'm complaining." He smiles again, but I see the strain in it.

My gut tightens. This sweet tension between Wyatt and me, this desire that woke me through the night, beckoning me to press myself closer to his warm body, is so fragile. Tor reigns over this estate, and he can separate me from the gardener in my bed any time he chooses.

Unwilling to dwell on that, I stretch, then get out of bed and walk to the bathroom. When I turn to close the door behind me, I see that Wyatt's attention is fixed on me. Naked desire fills his gaze until he realizes I'm watching him. He coughs and picks up the book again.

I push the door shut and lean against it, ultra aware of the tightness of my clothes and my lack of a corset. Maybe I should wear something more respectable today, but I can't bring myself to do such a thing. Not when these clothes are so soft, so free of constraint.

Not when Wyatt looks at me the way he just did.

I return to the room a few minutes later. "I'd like to get some food, but I don't know if Tor will see me."

"He already knows you're here," Wyatt replies. "If you're hungry, please don't starve yourself."

"And you? Are you hungry?" Heat enters his gaze again, and a flush fills my cheeks. "For food?" I clarify with a laugh.

He gives me a wry smile. "I am."

I don't really want Tor looking at me the way Wyatt just did, so I grab a robe. As I slip it on, Wyatt murmurs, "I like your outfit, Aeryn."

I grin at him. "I know."

In the kitchen, I gather bread, hard cheese, olives, smoked sausages, apples, and wine—enough for two people for a few days, though I know I'm fooling myself. Wyatt and I won't be able to hide away for that long. But I don't see Tor or Rochelle, so I suppose Wyatt and I can live in our fantasy world a little longer.

I carry everything to my room atop a wooden cutting board. When I arrive, I lay the cutting board on the bed. I shrug my robe off, and Wyatt and I settle in for a leisurely picnic.

"You said you decorated this room with blessing magic," he says. "And I know you used creation magic on the tower. It seems your powers developed overnight."

I tell him about the day I spent simply being myself and how my magic underwent a profound, powerful shift. Admiration fills his eyes, and I lock away an image of his expression in my mind, knowing I'll always treasure it.

"Has your magic replenished?" Wyatt asks.

I create a single rose and hand it to him. "I feel as strong as I did before the challenge."

"Are you still having dreams?"

All at once, lush, romantic images fill my mind. My fingers go loose, dropping the piece of bread I was about to bite into. "I . . . I just remembered." I can't meet his gaze. "I had several last night, but I didn't recall them until you asked."

He swallows a bite of cheese, and I can hear his smile when he says, "You're even more beautiful when you blush. Care to tell me about these dreams?"

I silently curse my pale skin and its habit of broadcasting any discomfort I'm feeling. I could tell Wyatt that the prince was absent from my dreams last night and that instead, the kind, bronze-skinned faerie filled my mind. But if I reveal that, he might want to know precisely what I dreamed about.

I can't share those details. Because the mysterious male consumed my nighttime imaginings with kisses and caresses that were full of exquisite gentleness and heart-stopping passion. Unlike Wyatt and me last night, the dream faerie and I felt no need to stop ourselves. We surrendered fully to one another, and even now, flashes of those beautiful moments fill my body with desire so exquisitely strong, it's almost painful.

I don't think Wyatt would be jealous of a character in my dreams, but I still can't bring myself to share. "Dreams are private things," I say.

His warm hand finds my warmer cheek, and I force myself to meet his gaze. "You're always free to keep them private, but please know you have nothing to be ashamed of." I nod, and he adds in a casual tone, "And remember, dreams represent reality. The characters in your dreams represent real people."

"Well," I mumble, "let's hope . . ." In my mind, I finish the thought: *Let's hope you were the one who showed up in my head last night.* I can't believe I almost said it aloud.

His eyes burn into mine. Somehow, I know he's trying to imagine what I saw in those dreams . . . and I doubt he's far off the mark. He moves the cutting board to the edge of the bed, leaving nothing between us but our warm breaths and a rumpled sheet. Never once does his gaze leave me.

He kisses me, and while it's as beautiful as it was last night, it's even more frustrating, because I desperately want to bring my dreams to life, and he's not ready for that. "Soon," he keeps saying.

We spend the day in bed, kissing and talking. The hours pass far too quickly. I need more of him. More of his lips. More of his words. More of his *everything*.

Between two breath-stealing kissing sessions, I tell him more about my life before the competition. Later, I share details about my experiences in the castle.

Wyatt is a wonderful listener. It turns out he's also quite the storyteller. He's still unable to give me meaningful details about his past and his family. But he shares what he can—adventurous anecdotes from childhood, books that made him see the world differently, and more.

The tales introduce me to him in a deeper way than any of our previous interactions. Wyatt is witty. Smart. He has a drive for adventure, something I've never had the opportunity to witness in him. He was quite mischievous when he was a child, and I suspect that part of him still exists, waiting for someone to draw it out.

Nighttime falls again. When we're too tired to talk, we simply hold each other. Wyatt lies on his back, and I curl up next to him on my side, my head resting on his chest, our legs entwined.

Though neither of us mentions it, I know we're both aware that tomorrow is day forty, the final day of the competition. What does that mean for us? We hold each other tightly all night, and I don't sleep much or have any dreams. Mostly, I lie there with my hand over his heart, relishing the feel of his heartbeat and the rise and fall of his chest.

The next morning, Wyatt rises first. He's in the bathroom when someone knocks on my door.

I pull on my robe. Then, heart pounding, I walk to the door, turn the knob, and pull it open.

Tor is standing there. His eyes hold an intensity I haven't seen in him before. My mind spins, trying to interpret the look.

"Aeryn," he says, "I've spent the last day and a half thinking." He swallows, then gives me a smile that's full of genuine sweetness. "Can we talk?"

I barely keep myself from turning to look toward the bathroom where Wyatt is waiting, silent and out of sight. The air in the room seems to have thinned. I pull in a sharp, deep breath and blurt, "What about Rochelle?"

Tor's gaze captures mine. "I sent her home."

42

————

I LOVE YOU

I stare at Tor, swallowing to bring moisture to my dry mouth.

"I sent Rochelle home," he repeats, as if I didn't hear him the first time.

"Why?" I whisper.

"I . . . may I come in?"

He takes a step toward me, but I put my hand up, halting him. I can't let him in here, not with Wyatt in the bathroom. "Can we, um . . . can we go to your sitting room?" I ask.

"Of course." He offers me his arm, and I slip my fingers in the crook of his elbow.

As we walk, he asks how I'm feeling, and I assure him I'm fine. Then I'm lost in my thoughts, and he doesn't make another attempt at conversation.

We arrive in his sitting room. I settle myself in a chair while Tor sits on the couch. The room's extravagant, gilded décor is overwhelming, further muddling my anxious thoughts. I stare at my hands instead of my surroundings, trying to come up with something to say.

Tor saves me the trouble by speaking. "I couldn't marry her, Aeryn."

I bring my gaze to his face. "Why not? She won the challenge. I forfeited. She proved herself. I didn't."

"No, you're the one who proved yourself." He sighs, his broad shoulders drooping. "I spent the last day and a half right here, in my quarters, remembering every day of this contest. Thinking about all the ways you and Rochelle acted, all the things you each said to me and to your fellow contestants. I recalled the gossip I've heard too." My brows rise, and he chuckles. "Plenty of tidbits were whispered in my ears by the females here, and I learned even more when I heard quiet conversations you had with each other. Then there were your actions on the tower. I considered those too." His thoughtful gaze settles somewhere beyond my left shoulder.

"And?" I prompt.

Those red eyes meet mine again. "And I realized Rochelle is intelligent and beautiful and driven. But she's also conniving and, far too often, cruel to those around her. Whereas you . . ." He leans forward, a small smile on his perfect lips. "Aeryn, you're *kind*. You have many other excellent virtues as well, but it's your kindness, your selflessness, that's important to me."

I study him, remembering the qualities he told us he was looking for in a wife. Things like magical power, perseverance, and the ability to entertain guests. "Why kindness?"

"Because it's never been a quality I had enough of in my own heart. And I want more of it."

That may be the most honest, vulnerable thing he's ever said to me. I can't seem to come up with a response.

"When this estate returns to its proper place in Faerie," Tor says, "my wife and I will reign over many people. Deep down, I've always known leaders should be kind and selfless. I need a bride who will pull me in that direction."

Hearing those words, my heart softens unexpectedly. Since

arriving at this castle, I've felt many things towards the beast who rules it. Gratitude. Annoyance. Passion. Confusion.

What I'm experiencing right now? It's true respect.

Tor must see it in my eyes, because his lips curve into a sudden, beautiful smile. He stands, and I move to do the same. "No," he says, "please stay where you are." He steps up to my chair, then drops to his knees and holds his hands out, palms up.

I place my hands in his. A few of his long, red claws make their way inside the wide sleeves of my robe, tickling my wrists. A surprisingly strong surge of desire sparks in me.

As I debate whether to welcome the sensation or tamp it down, Wyatt's face fills my mind. My stomach clenches with confusion and guilt.

"I know this is unexpected," Tor says, again reading the emotions on my face, though not quite so accurately this time. "I wish we had more time to build things between us. But there is much that is out of my control. And so there is a question I must ask you now." His grip tightens on my hands. "Faeries often marry out of obligation or for purely practical reasons."

"Mortals do that too," I say.

"I know, and that is why I must make myself clear. I'm not looking for that type of marriage." His expression softens with a hopeful smile. "I love you, Aeryn. So it's time for me to ask—will you agree to marry me? Out of love?"

I pull in an unsteady breath. "I . . . I need to think."

Disappointment flickers in his eyes for just a moment before he gives me an understanding nod. "Of course you do. I can leave and come back—"

"No!" I nearly shout the word.

His eyes widen. "I thought you might want privacy."

I'm certain of one thing: if I have too much privacy, my mind will fix on the blue-skinned faerie I left in my quarters. But it's not Wyatt who just proposed to me. It's Tor. He's the one I must focus on right now.

"Stay," I say. "I just need a few minutes to think."

The crease between his eyes betrays his uncertainty. He doesn't argue or pry, however. He merely stands and walks to the window, giving me the privacy afforded by his turned back.

My eyes scan the room, fixing on random details. Scrollwork carved into moulding along the ceiling. A gilded foot on a wardrobe. A pointed ear on a marble bust of a faerie.

With a frustrated sigh, I close my eyes. I have a decision to make, and I don't need distractions.

Marrying Tor would give me access to money with which I could provide for my family. That's why I came to this castle. I can't let a few kisses with an inconveniently kind, attractive male change that.

Warm, scaled skin glides across my bare foot, and I open my eyes and smile. I don't know why, but I want the snake to remain my secret, so I glance at Tor. When I confirm he's still turned away, I pick up the snake, hold her to my chest, and again shut my eyes to the world.

The sensation of the warm snake pressed against me reminds me of my magic. *I have magic now—I could use that to provide for my family.* I don't know why that thought didn't occur to me earlier, but now that it has, my heart speeds up. With magic, I could create food for my siblings and father. I could even travel to villages and make money performing spectacular magical feats.

I don't need Tor to care for my family. I can do it myself.

And maybe, just maybe, in between visits to mortal lands, I could come back to this estate and visit a certain gardener. Maybe there's a future for us.

The snake nudges my chin firmly. I open my eyes. She uses her face to point at the window. My brow furrows, and I stare at her, trying to discern what she's telling me. She only points more adamantly.

My heart drops. I gently place the snake on the floor, and when she's slithered out of sight under the bed, I say, "Tor?"

He turns. "Yes?"

"Are you looking at the statues?"

He cocks his head but doesn't reply.

"If they could listen," I say softly, "they'd care about my answer to your proposal, wouldn't they?"

His silence is response enough.

I may be able to care for my family with my magic, but I have no idea how to turn stone back into living flesh. Considering the bits and pieces of information I've picked up since arriving, I suspect someone must marry Tor for love if the curse on those servants is to be broken.

I would even be willing to bet that Wyatt would choose the servants' lives over a relationship with me. He loves them. I see it in the way he cares for their stone forms. Breaking the curse is the greatest gift I can give him.

Wyatt isn't the only one who wants to save those servants. Justyne's brother is out there. She was a true friend to me, and I promised her I'd do whatever I could to free her brother.

Then there's Felia's family. Without a kind wife by his side to temper his powerful will, would Tor return their land to them?

I need to consider Desiree's father too. Someone manipulated him into joining the fighting force that's trying to break through the foggy barrier. Desiree came here with the goal of bringing him home. Based on my earlier conversation with Wyatt, I have reason to believe that if I marry Tor, he'll return to his princely form, proving he's the rightful ruler of this estate. The soldiers will leave.

Yes, I can use magic to care for my family. But I can do so much more if I marry Tor.

No, marrying him isn't enough, I remind myself. *I must marry him out of love.*

I stand and cross the room, joining Tor at the window. Once again, he gives me that hopeful smile. I take his hand, sliding my fingers between his.

Marriage to him is the only answer. And if love is required, I will love him. It's what I must do. In fact, if the thundering of my heart is any indication, I'm already in love with him.

I tell myself that, shouting it silently, over and over. *I love Tor! I love him! I do!*

Before I can convince myself it's not true, I turn to him, pulling my hand from his. Both my palms find his cheeks, and our gazes lock together.

"I love you," I say. "And I would be honored to marry you."

43

IT'S THE LAST DAY

Tor's face breaks into a huge smile.

It doesn't last, though. Almost immediately, he pulls back, and my hands fall away from his cheeks. He lifts his clawed hands and stares at them. Shaking his head, he says, "I thought . . . I expected . . ."

"What is it?" I ask.

"Nothing, I—I thought when you agreed to marry me, it would . . ." He shakes his head. "But it didn't. Maybe it won't happen until we're married. But that means . . ." His eyes go wide.

Just finish a sentence! I want to cry. With forced patience, I ask, "It means what?"

He drops his hands, fixing his gaze on me. "We must marry today. It's the last day. My last chance." His breathing has gone shallow, and there's a strangely vulnerable look in his eyes. "Will you? I'm sure this urgency isn't what you dreamed of for your wedding."

A laugh bursts from my chest. "Tor, I'm standing in a Fae castle. I fell from a tower a couple of days ago, and in doing so, I lost a compe-tition—or maybe won it? I'm still not sure about that. And I've agreed to wed a faerie I met just weeks ago. None of this is the way I expected my life to go."

"What are you saying?" he asks slowly.

He's the one who's confused now. It's about damn time. Grinning, I say, "I agreed to marry you. I don't care when it happens. Today is fine."

In fact, I'd like to do it today, while the decision is fresh and firm in my mind. I'm not sure what will happen if I give myself the chance to ponder it too much.

I don't, however, tell him that.

Pure joy softens the strange lines of Tor's beastly face. A moment later, I'm in his arms, and his lips are on mine.

I give in to the kiss immediately. More accurately, I throw myself into it, desperate to feel connected to this male I've agreed to marry, this faerie I've proclaimed that I love. His lips are warm and pliant. When my tongue begs entrance, he opens eagerly, and I press my whole body against his as I taste him.

One of his claws tears through the fabric of my robe and the shirt beneath, then lightly scratches my waist, making me yelp. He murmurs an apology against my mouth. We both laugh, then go back to kissing.

It feels great, surrendering to his soft lips and hard muscles, letting myself enjoy the pure physicality of a good kiss. It gives me hope that maybe this relationship will be a happy one. He's not perfect, but heaven knows I'm not either. If we can connect like this, perhaps we can build something that will stand the test of time.

He's the one who pulls away. His chest is heaving as his gaze finds mine. "I've never planned a wedding before. I don't know where to begin."

I step out of his arms. "Perhaps I could return to my room to put some real clothes on?"

He laughs. "Will you meet me for breakfast after that?"

"Of course."

"Half an hour?"

I nod and turn to go.

"Oh, Aeryn—I almost forgot."

When I face him again, he's dropping to one knee. He pulls a ring out of his pocket and holds it out. "Shall we make this official?"

My heart pounds as I step to Tor and extend my left hand. He slips the ring on my fourth finger. It's a perfect fit. In a house full of magic, I suppose that shouldn't surprise me.

"It's beautiful," I say.

And it is, though it's not a style I would've chosen. The band is thick, shiny gold. Set atop it is a round ruby as wide as my fingernail. Small diamonds surround the red stone. It's flashy and luxurious, and it could buy enough food to feed my family for a year.

"I'd better get dressed," I say.

Tor nods. "I'll see you in half an hour."

As I rush through the castle corridors, my senses are more alive than ever. I'm aware of every patter of my bare feet on the marble floors. My eyes scan over the artwork on the walls and ceilings. My lips burn from the kisses I shared with Tor, and the ring makes my whole hand heavy.

Every one of those observations sets me on edge, though I can't pinpoint why. By the time I enter my room, my whole body is buzzing with anxiety. I can't seem to control my breathing as I slam the door behind me and run to the closed bathroom door.

"Wyatt?" I say in an urgent, hushed voice.

There's no answer.

I open the door. The bathroom is empty.

I should let this go. Wyatt is the last person I should be talking to when I just agreed to marry someone else. But my heart is shouting at me, and it's far louder than my reason. *I need to tell him! I need to explain!*

I find myself at my window, though I don't remember walking to it. My eyes scan the grounds below.

Wyatt is walking slowly along a garden path, hands in his pockets. My breathing slows as I watch him stroll to a bench and sit.

He looks up. His eyes widen as they meet mine.

I slip on a pair of shoes and yank off my robe. Then I open the window, point downward, and say, "Ladder." A long ladder forms, propping itself against the marble beneath my window and extending all the way to the ground.

A warning rings through my head: *Talking with Wyatt is a very bad idea, Aeryn.* I ignore it.

Exiting my window backwards is scarier than I thought it would be. I wish I had my harness, but it would take too long to make another one and buckle myself into it. I push past my fear, holding the windowsill, then the ladder, with tight fingers.

As I descend, I hear running footsteps behind me. It has to be Wyatt. I shouldn't smile. I shouldn't be doing this at all. But it's easy to disregard logic when I know how close he is.

I descend even faster, and when I reach the bottom, Wyatt is waiting, holding the ladder steady and extending his free hand to help me down.

Grasping his hand tightly, I hop over the final rung and land on the grass. I look up, expecting to meet his gaze.

He's not looking in my eyes. Instead, he's staring at the hand he's holding. My left hand. His thumb rubs across the large ruby for a moment before he releases his grip and brings his gaze up to my face. Resigned sorrow fills his blue eyes.

"Wyatt," I whisper.

He smiles, and it makes him look even sadder. "I knew you'd win him over."

I clasp my hands in front of me, tangling my fingers, suddenly unsure what to do with myself in front of the male who was lying in bed with me an hour ago.

My tongue darts out to moisten my lips before I speak. "I had to say yes. Not just for my family, but for Justyne and Desiree and Felia and . . ." With my chin, I gesture toward the garden. "And all of them."

Even to my own ears, my explanation sounds unsatisfying. I'm telling Wyatt the reasons I *needed* to accept the proposal. Tor, however, expects me to love him, not just need him. So I swallow down my uncertainty and allow my mouth to relax into a smile. "He was so kind when he asked, Wyatt. He appreciates me for who I am—he said I'm selfless. I can love someone like that. I do love him. I do."

Wyatt moves a hand as if to cup my cheek. I lean toward his palm, but he pulls back before making contact. He clasps his hands behind him, and I wonder if he's twisting his fingers together as tightly as I am.

"That's wonderful, Aeryn." The roughness of his voice belies his words. "Really wonderful. You love him."

My brisk nod brings my attention to my tight throat. "I do." I sound a bit hoarse. My vision goes blurry, and blinking doesn't improve it. "I don't know why I'm crying."

"People often cry from joy." It's a statement, but there's a question in Wyatt's expression.

I almost assure him that, yes, these are tears of joy. I can't, though. I won't lie to him. Not again. I shake my head just a little, and the hope that enters Wyatt's eyes cuts my heart in two.

"This is all . . . you and I . . . it's impossible," I say. "I'm marrying Tor—today."

Wyatt flinches, like my words are daggers. I hate hurting him. If only I could take it all back. I can't, though. Nothing has changed. Tor needs someone to love him and marry him, and I've chosen to be that person.

Why does that choice feel like a lead weight, threatening to yank my heart out of my chest?

Over the last two days, as I talked and laughed with Wyatt, as he held me and kissed me and we slept in each other's arms, my heart reached for him in a way it's never reached for anyone. I wasn't ready to give my feelings a name, but they were profound and beautiful.

And they haven't gone away, despite my commitment to Tor. I want Wyatt to know that. Whether or not he should.

I open my mouth, letting the words come as they will. "I'm

marrying him because I care about you, Wyatt. I see you with those statues. I know how important they are to you. I'm doing what's best for them and, by extension, for you." After swallowing hard, I repeat, "I care about you."

He steps so close, I can feel the warmth of his breath. "I . . . care . . . about you too, Aeryn."

I'm not certain of many things in this world. Yet I know, beyond any doubt, Wyatt didn't want to say *care*. We're both using that word as a substitute for another term. A dangerous term.

"Wyatt," I whisper. His name lingers between us, an apology and a request.

He pulls me to him tightly, his hands gripping the back of my shirt. His breaths have turned short and shallow. The brisk beat of his heart sends vibrations through my chest.

I dare to meet his gaze, and yet again, I'm certain. About two things this time.

He wants me to kiss him.

And I'm going to do it.

As I lean in, the desire in his eyes fades, replaced by caution. I halt. I should take the opportunity to flee, to climb the ladder and return to my room, but I . . . can't.

I run a finger across his lips and utter one word: "Please?"

Wyatt squeezes his eyes shut briefly, then meets my gaze again. His tiny nod is all the permission I need. Desperately, I kiss him, joining my lips so tightly to his, I can almost convince myself I'll never have to let go. I open my mouth, and he groans into it. I respond with a sigh that begs for more.

Wyatt's fingers dig into my hair, gently tilting my head so he can deepen the kiss further.

One of my hands finds his neck. The other travels down his back. I slip it under his jacket, then tug at his shirt, pulling it free from his pants. My hand slides under the hem. I glide my palm along his warm back, reveling in the smoothness of his skin. He shudders, and I laugh quietly against his lips.

Many women would feel guilty for kissing one person right after agreeing to wed another. Others would laugh at the audacity required to kiss two males in the space of half an hour. Maybe they'd compare the two experiences.

My mind, however, has no capacity for guilt or comparison. I'm too thoroughly wrapped up in this perfect moment. My ears are closed to the sounds of the outdoors; all I hear are Wyatt's gentle groans and the short gasps coming from both our lungs. I keep my eyes tightly shut—who needs sight at a time like this? As for my sense of touch, perhaps there's a breeze, but my skin is aware of nothing but Wyatt's lips and hands. I smell and taste only him.

Wyatt. In this perfect moment, he's my entire world. My very existence.

He pulls back, panting. "We shouldn't, Aeryn."

I open my eyes, blinking against the bright sun and shaking my head helplessly. "I know."

Then we're kissing again, and I have no idea which of us initiated it. It's different this time. His words—*we shouldn't*—have dug their claws into my mind.

So many people need me. To help any of them, I must return to Tor.

A gentle wistfulness fills my kisses. I sense the same shift in Wyatt. Tears slide between our cheeks, and I'm not sure whose eyes are the source. Maybe both of ours.

My senses reluctantly awaken to details other than the male I'm with. I hear birds. I feel the warm sun. When my eyes open, the statues in the garden nearby draw my attention.

Guilt fills me, a pressure so intense that it seems to burst from my chest, pushing me back. I let go of Wyatt and stumble, only saved from falling by his hand on my elbow. "This was a terrible mistake," I whisper.

"I know. Oh gods, Aeryn, I know." He releases me and steps back.

We both go silent for what feels like several minutes but might be only seconds. At last, Wyatt's mouth curves into an exquisitely sad smile. "I'm glad I had the chance to know you."

My throat tightens. "You're saying goodbye."

"I can't stay. What we just did—it was wrong. We certainly cannot act in such a way after you've wed. As soon as I have the freedom to go elsewhere, I will. But I'll leave my best wishes with you —truly. I want you to be happy."

I squeeze my eyes shut, pondering whether happiness is possible. *Of course it is,* I assure myself. *Despite my desire for Wyatt, I love Tor.*

And that will be my focus from here on out. My commitment to the faerie whose ring I wear. But first, I need Wyatt to know something.

I open my eyes. "You've made my life brighter." My hands find his. "No one will ever take that away from me."

Once more, I bring my lips to his. This is our true farewell. We linger longer than we should, but the kiss is gentle and chaste. This time, it doesn't feel like I'm betraying my fiancé. This is a kiss between two friends who want to remember what was—and honor what cannot be.

A roar, intense enough to shake the marble castle, fills the air.

Wyatt and I both gasp, breaking apart. We lift our faces, shielding our eyes from the sun.

Tor is standing at an open window, looking down on us.

He roars again.

44

PURE, WHITE-HOT FURY

The sound emanating from Tor's mouth is no louder than the roar of beasts I've encountered in the forest, but it's markedly different. His agonized noise could only come from a person with a soul that's capable of being ripped apart.

And I'm the one who did this to him.

I could find Tor and tell him the kiss he witnessed was a goodbye kiss. I could assure him it wasn't sensual in nature. It's the truth.

Only, he might ask if I've ever kissed Wyatt before. That final kiss was innocent, but the ones before it weren't. If Tor had come to the window a couple of minutes earlier, he would've seen two people utterly lost in one another.

I pull in a deep, shuddering breath and meet Wyatt's gaze. "How do I fix this?"

He shakes his head. "I don't know."

Above us, Tor bellows, "How dare you?" I have no idea if he's speaking to Wyatt or me. His next words make it clear. "You are mine! *How—dare—you?*"

There's more than pain in his voice. There's pure, white-hot fury.

Terror twists my gut. I hug myself tightly and bring my wide eyes to Wyatt. "Will he hurt me?"

He shakes his head hard for a moment, but then he stops, blinking rapidly. "I want to believe he wouldn't," he whispers.

"But . . . ?" I prompt.

"Oh, Aeryn." He turns and stares toward his garden. His mouth barely moves as he speaks softly. "All this time, I've cared for the garden. For the statues. I've tried so hard to be better than I once was. To turn myself into the male I truly want to be. Every day, I assumed he was inside that castle, doing the same. But now . . . I wonder if I've been blind."

There's an entire, secret history behind his words, but I know better than to ask for clarification he can't give.

I look up at the window. Tor fixes me with a fiery glare, then releases one more harsh, wordless cry before leaving the window.

It takes effort to push words through my tight throat. "I have to talk to him." I reach out for Wyatt's arm, then think better of it, dropping my hand. "There are too many people counting on me. I'm still determined to love him, Wyatt. If he'll let me. I have to try to make things right."

He turns back to me, his eyes full of so many emotions, I couldn't untangle them if I had an eternity to attempt it. His throat throbs with a swallow. "I'll come with you."

I step toward the ladder I made, then stop and shake my head. I'm trembling slightly and don't trust myself to climb anything more challenging than stairs. With a thought, I release the magic holding the ladder in place. It disappears.

I rush toward the nearest castle entrance, Wyatt close behind me. My palm tingles with the desire to take his hand, but I refuse the instinct. I'll let Wyatt act as my protector if he so desires, but he cannot be anything more.

I reach for the doorknob but stop when Wyatt says, "Wait."

"What is it?"

"We don't know where he is."

"Maybe his room?"

"Perhaps." He presses his lips together, looking off to the side before catching my gaze again. "I'm recalling conversations you and I had in the past. About mirrors."

My eyes widen. "You think he's talking to Cerise?"

He doesn't reply—can't reply, I suspect. That's enough to confirm it for me. "The portrait gallery."

"Let's go."

Together, we run through the palace, our steps echoing off the marble floors and art-filled walls.

We hear Tor before we see him. He's yelling—or ranting is more like it. "She said she loved me! She said it, I know you heard it too!" His voice lowers a bit, and I can't understand anything else he says until he cries, "Why didn't it work?"

Wyatt and I slow our steps, approaching the doorway as quietly as we can.

"If you'll stop ranting," Cerise's gentle voice says, "I'll tell you why."

Wyatt and I stand against the wall just outside the portrait gallery, eyes wide as we listen. The room has gone silent.

After several seconds, Tor snaps, "I'm waiting, Cerise!"

"So impatient." Her voice is as sweet as ever. "Do you remember why I turned you into a beast?"

My eyes widen. It doesn't surprise me that Cerise would do such a thing, but it's shocking to hear it revealed in such a casual way. My gaze finds Wyatt. He merely nods.

One less secret between us. Let's hope she'll keep talking.

"Did you hear my question?" Cerise asks.

"I heard but didn't deem it necessary to answer." Tor's voice is tight with restrained anger. "How could I forget? You cursed me because I wouldn't sleep with you."

I'm so riveted to the truths these two are sharing that I can barely breathe.

Cerise's musical laughter fills the air, turning my stomach. "Oh, my dear Prince Fabien," she says, and I stifle a gasp as she confirms my suspicions about his identity. "It's true your refusal was the catalyst. I wonder, however, whether you've ascertained why I chose this particular consequence. No? Very well, I see I've overestimated your self-awareness. I turned you into this because you were vain. What better punishment for a vain faerie than to be forced to live as a red-eyed, rat-tailed beast? It was so delightfully . . . poetic."

Tor—I can't think of him as Fabien—says nothing. I search Wyatt's face, as if I'll find more answers there. His brows are drawn, and he looks truly grieved.

Cerise says, "After I cursed you, however, I feared I'd done you a favor. Let's be honest—you're rather disgusting in this form. I feared you'd look at your new body and lose your vanity, thus turning yourself into someone more, well . . . likeable. Someone who, despite his obvious deficiencies, might attract a spouse. But I can see my fears were unfounded. The way you're making demands of me— you're as vain and entitled as ever. No wonder you had ten females here and couldn't get even one of them to fall in love with you." She *tsks*.

"What is your point?" Tor hisses.

"I'm simply giving you the opportunity for a bit of self-reflection. For the record, I owe you no explanations. But it grieves me to see your pathetic confusion, so shall we revisit your original question?"

"We shall." The words are a low rumble.

"Let us recall the instructions I gave you ten years ago on how to break the curse," Cerise says in a condescending voice. "I remember the exact words: *By the last second before midnight ten years from today, someone must agree to marry you for love. The curse will be broken when they verbally proclaim their true love.*"

" 'Verbally proclaim!' " Tor shouts. "Aeryn did that; she said she loves me! I'm sure you were watching through the damn mirrors; you heard it too!"

"Oh, Fabien." Sweet syrup infuses Cerise's words. "I said 'true love.' She was clearly lying."

My hand comes up to my mouth, and my gaze finds Wyatt. Hope and grief war in his eyes.

"Do you have any reason to suspect she doesn't love you?" Cerise asks.

"No!" Tor's response is too quick, too defensive. "No reason at all!"

Heat fills my face as I remember the kisses Wyatt and I shared outside. The passionate ones Tor didn't see and the sweet one he did. Apparently he doesn't want Cerise to know what he witnessed. I'm grateful for that.

"Magic knows the truth, my love," the honey-tongued faerie says. "It always knows the truth."

But I do love him! I do! my mind insists, even as my heart reaches for the male beside me. I press my hand tighter to my mouth, squeezing hard, determined not to release the sobs building in my chest.

"Wait!" Tor's voice is full of sudden hope. "You didn't say she had to love me romantically. It may be too soon for that, but I'm certain she loves me as a friend!"

Cerise laughs, and there's a bit of deviousness in it now. "If only you knew how often I've regretted not making that distinction when I cursed you. Yet it didn't matter in the end, did it? Here we are, on the final day of the decade I allotted you, and the woman you chose does not love you. Not as a lover, not as a friend. The curse would have broken if she did."

I squeeze my eyes shut and swallow hard, pulling in deep breaths through my nose, trying to steady the emotions rising in me.

She's right.

I tried so hard to love him. How can I, though? I barely know him. I care about him as a person, but would I sacrifice myself for him in the way I would for my family? For my true friends?

For Wyatt?

I wouldn't. Tor is not precious to me. Perhaps he could've been in time, but we don't have time.

The truth settles inside me, along with a heavy, resigned calm. I uncover my mouth and lift my chin to look at Wyatt.

It's all right, he mouths.

The words make me feel the tiniest bit better, though I know they're not true.

"So!" Cerise is suddenly cheerful. "Here we are, Prince Fabien. You have until the end of the day to find someone who loves you and will agree to marry you. Otherwise, you'll be stuck in that form for the rest of your life, and all the other elements of the curse will remain in place as well."

Wyatt's eyes flood with tears. I know he's thinking of the statues, and I have to look away, lest I lose my tenuous control over my own emotions.

"Smugness does not become you, Cerise," Tor mutters.

"It's not smugness," she chirps. "I'm joyful, my love, because I have wonderful news to share."

His silence is louder than her words.

"I have a gift to offer you," Cerise says. "Another way to break the curse."

"And what will you ask in return?" Tor asks.

"Oh, my dear prince, you know me well. Well enough, certainly, to know what I want. What I've always wanted."

"Me," he says.

That elicits hearty laughter from Cerise, peals of mirth that go on and on until my head is ringing. Wyatt's face takes on a look of comic agony that nearly makes me break into laughter of my own.

Stop! I mouth at him.

He responds with a sheepish smile.

At last, Cerise calms down and speaks again. "There's that vanity again, Fabien. It's time for you to hear the truth.

"It wasn't your heart I coveted ten years ago, it was your power—I wanted to be your queen, ruling your land with you. I assumed your bed was the fastest path to your heart and the throne. When you refused me, I was forced to consider alternate strategies. According to Fae law, I couldn't simply take your land and crown. So I cursed you and sent your estate to Earth, knowing you'd never find someone to love you this far from Faerie, especially surrounded by the foggy barrier. I assumed that after ten years living in that horrendous body, you'd be ready to make a deal."

"You didn't count on a friend of mine finding a way through the barrier and bringing me potential brides, did you?" Tor asks.

"Of course I didn't. But I adjusted, as I always do. I befriended the candidates I wanted you to consider—Rochelle, because she'll do anything to benefit herself. Aeryn, because as a mortal, she is weak. I knew whichever of them you chose, I could control her. I helped them find ways to become close to you. Had you married one of them, I would've taken her place eventually."

I roll my eyes. Cerise's view of *befriending* is far different from mine, and I'd like to think I learned my lesson about letting her control me.

"You would have killed my bride to take her crown," Tor states.

"Only as a last resort, my dear. You should know by now I prefer more subtle forms of persuasion." Cerise laughs lightly, then continues, "So, here we are. My desires haven't changed. I want to be your queen."

"Last I heard, I'm the prince regent, not the king," Tor says. "Are you telling me my parents have transitioned?"

My brows rise as I remember the conversation Justyne and I had weeks ago. She told me that the king and queen of this castle had moved to the spirit realm, where elderly Fae live their eternal lives. Once they transition to incorporeal form, the prince will become king.

Cerise sighs. "I expected your parents to transition years ago, but word from the spirit realm is that they've held out, believing you're still alive out there somewhere. Once I return you to your true form, I'm certain they'll move along and let you have the crown."

"Am I to understand," Tor says slowly, "you'll break the curse if I marry you?"

"Essentially," Cerise says, and I hear the satisfaction in her voice. "There are, of course, a few more terms for us to discuss. First, you will reach through this mirror and bring me into your home.

"Next, you will marry me immediately, here in this room. As part of our private ceremony, you will swear, using an unbreakable Fae oath, to be loyal and true to me in word and deed for the rest of our lives. You will also swear that, as prince and princess, then as king and queen, we will be equal in power.

"In return, I will restore your true form and all your magical power. I will also transport this estate to its rightful place in Faerie, where we will rule our kingdom together. And I'll remove that dreadfully foggy barrier and send my soldiers home."

"The soldiers trying to break into my estate are yours?" Tor growls.

"Of course they are, you silly male." She pauses, and I can easily imagine the condescending tilt of her head as she gazes through the mirror at Tor.

"I don't think you quite understand your situation," Cerise continues. "I *will* gain power over your estate and your people in Faerie. If you don't give it willingly, my soldiers will break through the barrier—I hear they're very close to doing so. I will enter, kill the terrible beast who stole this land, and return the estate to its rightful location, where I will rule it. I'd rather rule as your queen, for your people will follow me more readily with you next to me. But if I must seize power, I will."

Tor draws a long, shuddering breath as he considers her proposition. At last, he says, "Is that all?"

"Not quite. We must cover two other minor details."

"Details?" I hear the dread in his voice, and it fills my chest with the same.

"First," Cerise says, "there's a particular stipulation I wish I'd included with the original curse, and I'm happy to rectify it in this renegotiation. I'm sure it will come as no surprise that I cannot revert your stone servants to their fleshly forms. They would never forgive me for cursing them. I'd have to constantly watch my back for a maid with a fireplace poker or a cook with a knife, seeking to assassinate me."

My face crumples, along with Wyatt's. I take his hand and squeeze it tightly as we both shake our heads in despair.

"You're cruel," Tor says quietly. The bit of pushback gives me hope.

"I never claimed to be otherwise," Cerise replies.

Tor clears his throat, and somehow I know what that sound means. He won't fight her on this. Those statues are just servants—why would he risk his own freedom for them? Wyatt squeezes my hand harder, and I shake my head, hoping he sees my sorrow.

"Your final stipulation?" Tor asks.

"I'm surprised you haven't guessed it. Surely you haven't forgotten your brother."

I blink. *Luc.* The one who disappeared on the day of the curse.

Tor sighs. "I didn't forget."

"I've had ten years to ponder his character and his fate," Cerise says. "I've always thought his temperament was more malleable than yours. I knew you wouldn't lose your vanity in the span of a mere decade. Your brother, on the other hand? Yes, he was selfish. Power hungry. A real ass, if we're being honest. But I suspect he's made true changes in the last ten years. I cursed him in the way I did because I wanted to humiliate him . . . yet my instincts tell me he found humility rather than humiliation."

"Maybe he did," Tor growls. "Why would you care?"

"Because he never liked or trusted me. He won't support me as your queen, and he'll turn people against me." She sighs. "The bottom line is, if Luc has developed a heart and a sense of morality, he'll do whatever he deems necessary to protect the subjects of this kingdom. And that won't bode well for me."

"You're refusing to return him to his natural form and remove the limits on his magic?" Tor asks.

"Oh, my love, if only such limitations were enough," Cerise says. "I'm afraid Luc isn't trustworthy in any form, with any amount of magic. Therefore, once I've restored your power, you and I will walk out to that damn garden your brother has spent ten years caring for . . . and together, we will kill him."

45

REACHING THROUGH THE GLASS

I can't get enough air into my lungs.

Wyatt is Luc. And Cerise wants to kill him.

I turn to him and point down the hall. "Go!" The word is a harsh whisper. "Hide!"

"I won't leave you," he whispers back.

I clench my teeth, holding back a scream. Then my logical mind, the weapon that's gotten me through innumerable crises with my family, takes over.

Tor may refuse Cerise. But I wouldn't be willing to bet on it. If he agrees to her plan, she'll soon be standing in that room next to him. I can't let that happen.

I steady my breaths and stand still. As I wait for Tor's response, I summon my creation magic. A few flutters of my fingers, a couple of words spoken on a quiet breath, and the simple spell is complete. I'm prepared.

Inside the portrait gallery, Tor's voice rumbles, "I'll do it."

I spin into the open doorway, drawing back my right arm. In my hand is the iron ball I just created with magic. It's small and—I hope —heavy enough to break magical glass.

I take a moment to aim . . . and I gasp at what I see. Tor is already extending his hands toward the mirror. Cerise is reaching through the glass, the smooth, bronze skin of her hands and forearms visible.

I curse and let the iron ball fly just as Tor grasps Cerise's hands and pulls.

The ball hits the glass above Cerise's head, shattering the mirror. The beautiful faerie screams. Her arms and head are out. I hold my breath, waiting to see if I've prevented her from coming through.

Grunting, Tor tugs harder. Glass crumbles and falls to the marble floor. Cerise swears as glass shards slice her through the fabric of her dress. But she's still coming, pulled by Tor.

The glass broke. The magic didn't.

"Get me out of here!" Cerise shrieks. "I'll kill her!"

A warm hand grasps mine. I turn to find Wyatt tugging me. The panic in his eyes snaps me out of my frozen state. Hands clasped tightly together, we run down the corridor.

Cerise's voice follows us down the hallway. "We have to get them!" Her customary soothing tones are gone, replaced by a screech.

If we're still running down this long hallway when she leaves that room, she'll attack us magically. I'm certain of it. I twist a doorknob and pull Wyatt into a dark sitting room, slamming the door behind us.

"Open the window," I hiss.

"We're too high to jump!"

"Trust me."

We dash across the room, lean over the window seat, and pull the window open. In the hallway, Cerise shouts, and doors slam.

I climb onto the window seat. Wyatt, bless him, follows me. He has no reason to have this much faith in me, but I appreciate it . . . and I'm about to ask for even more of his trust.

"Hold me tight." I jump on him, straddling his waist. His eyes go wide, but he catches me and clutches me close. "Jump," I say.

I'm prepared for his questions, ready to explain in as few words as possible why we're jumping. I don't have to, though. Wyatt clambers onto the windowsill, not an easy proposition with me wrapped around his torso. He's entrusting his life to me, to a wild plan I haven't even shared with him.

I love him, damn it. I do.

Crushing me to him, Wyatt jumps. At the same time, I extend my arms wide and shout, "Cloth!"

I picture something I once saw in a book—a large piece of fabric, used to slow a fall. Before the spell fully leaves my mouth, my magic recreates the cloth above us, wrapping its ends tightly around my outstretched hands.

We decelerate—but not enough. The ground is approaching far too quickly.

"Wind!" I shout. A forceful burst of air presses upward into the large cloth, further slowing our descent.

We're drifting lazily towards the ground when, from the window above, Cerise bellows something unintelligible. The entire cloth bursts into a cloud of ashes.

I scream as I crash to the ground, along with the faerie holding me.

Cerise's laughter rings through the air as Wyatt and I groan in unison. We're lying on the ground, legs tangled together. My left wrist is on fire. I clutch it to my chest.

A bolt of lightning hits the ground inches from my head, searing a black furrow through the green grass.

Wyatt curses as he stands and pulls me to my feet. A fireball slashes through the air next to his head, scorching his hair.

"Run!" he shouts.

I don't have to be told twice. We both sprint to the garden. It's the only place nearby with plenty of barriers to hide behind. Wyatt is taller than me and could probably run faster, but he stays right at my side. Another bolt of lightning barely misses us.

We crouch behind a thick hedge, and Cerise's attack stops.

Wyatt pokes his head above the greenery. "She left the window. I'd wager we have a couple of minutes before they both get here. Where are you hurt the worst?"

I hold out my left hand and gag when I see the unnatural angle at which it's hanging. My wrist is broken.

Wyatt grasps it, whispering, "I'm sorry."

His firm grip draws a loud, animalistic groan from my throat. Blackness invades the edges of my vision. Then, all at once, sweet warmth replaces much of the agonizing heat in my wrist. There's a painful, yet satisfying *pop* as the bones click into their rightful places. I sense their broken edges joining back together. Wyatt releases me.

"Thank you," I whisper, rotating my hand. I'm only slightly sore. "Where can I heal you?"

"My ribs." He places his hand on his side, wincing at his own touch.

I slide my hand up his shirt. There's a slight bump in his skin where a rib is broken. Running must've been torturous.

"Heal," I breathe, hoping desperately it works. Warmth flows through my hand, and I feel his rib mend, just as my wrist did.

Wyatt's lips twitch in a small smile, almost a smirk. "Ever done that before?"

I shrug. "First time for everything."

His blue eyes burn into mine, and he shakes his head, giving me a smile full of tender admiration.

The moment passes all too quickly. "They'll be here soon," Wyatt says. "I don't have much power these days, but Cerise left me with a bit of nature magic to use in the garden. I'll do whatever I can to protect you."

Protect *me*. At this moment, he's weaker than I am and should be concerned with his own safety. I'd really like to slap him. Or kiss him.

I bring my focus back to our current situation. *Beast. Manipulative faerie. Coming this way.* "I'm going to shield us from her curses," I whisper.

His black brows rise, but again, he doesn't ask questions.

I speak words similar to the ones I used when summoning my first shield. "Blessings over Wyatt and me. Repelling curses. Turning them to dust." Magic tingles over my skin. "Do you feel it?" I ask.

Wyatt shakes his head.

I take his hand. "Now?"

"Yes!" His voice is full of wonder.

I squeeze his fingers tighter. "Don't let go."

We stand just as Cerise and Tor burst through the castle door. He's still a beast. She promised to break that part of the curse when he marries her, but I suppose I delayed their nuptial plans (and turned myself into a target) when I broke the mirror.

Tor's relative lack of magic in his current form will help us, but physically, he's stronger than Wyatt or me. Plus, I'd wager that Cerise's magic is more powerful than mine. She certainly has more experience. If I had to choose two opponents, it wouldn't be them.

"Well, this'll be fun," I murmur. Wyatt barks a short laugh.

Cerise runs toward us, hand extended, saying words I can't hear from this distance. The shield around Wyatt and me flares purple, protecting us.

"We need to evade her," I say as I pull him behind a taller hedge. "This shield depletes my magic quickly."

A second later, a fireball hits the hedge with a sizzle and a puff of smoke. Wyatt leads me through the winding garden paths, moving constantly.

"We have to get close to her, undetected," I whisper between quick breaths.

Wyatt nods.

Flashes of lightning and bright fireballs soar through the air randomly, telling me Cerise has no idea where we are. We must stop her quickly, before her curses strike any statues. Wyatt has spent ten years protecting those servants. I refuse to give up on saving them.

We halt, crouching behind a waist-high bush. Through the foliage, Cerise is visible, perhaps twenty feet away. She's wearing an emerald-green gown. It would be a beautiful dress, were it not for the bloody streaks across it that mark where the mirror cut her. She's looking around frantically, searching for us.

And she's alone.

"Where's Tor?" I whisper.

"I'm guessing he ran away."

I can't help but roll my eyes. *Of course he did.* "One less problem to solve," I mutter.

A whispered word, and I've created another iron ball like the one I used to break the mirror. It's not the most impressive spell, but I know it works, and it doesn't use much of my magic.

I meet Wyatt's gaze. He nods. We stand as I lift the iron ball, ready to attack Cerise.

46

THE FIGHT IS ON

I throw the iron ball. Just as it leaves my hand, I mutter two words: "White hot."

I'm not even sure which magic I'm using—nature? curse?—but the spell works, and the ball flares with intense, bright heat as it continues on its path towards Cerise's chest.

I'm certain it's going to hit her until, with typical Fae grace and precision, she spins around. She must've heard me. As if she's performing a dance she's done a hundred times, she leans back. The iron missile flies past her and lands in a bush, creating a charred, smoking depression in the leaves. Furious heat fills her eyes.

The fight is on.

"Whirlwind!" she screams. A funnel of dirt, grass, and small rocks forms in an instant. It heads straight toward Wyatt and me—a spinning, screaming monster made of air and debris. It's too large and fast to avoid.

As soon as it touches us, magic flares bright purple around us. The whirlwind stops spinning. Rocks and dirt fall to the ground.

"How?" Cerise bellows.

I don't have time to revel in the victory. I lost a lot of magic in that single flare of my shield. We have to get out of sight before Cerise depletes my power completely. I do the only thing my frantic mind can think of: copy my enemy.

"Whirlwind!" I scream, thrusting out a hand.

My twister isn't as big as Cerise's, but it does the job, stirring up enough dirt and greenery to block us from her sight. Wyatt and I duck and run, hand in hand, through the garden paths.

We're both panting when we stop and crouch behind a hedge. Again, we're close to Cerise, but she can't see us. The whirlwind I created is gone; I didn't have the focus to keep it going as we ran. Cerise is rubbing her eyes hard, so I know it found her before it disappeared.

Cerise is in the middle of an open circle of grass. I look around and recognize where we are—the center of the garden. The servants-turned-statues are scattered throughout the garden, but they all have one thing in common: they're facing the area where Cerise is now standing.

I turn to Wyatt, cup my hand around his ear, and whisper, "Is this where she was when she placed the curse?"

He nods, his expression somber.

"Did she turn the original gardener into a statue?" I ask.

He lets out a whisper-soft sigh. "She killed him in order to replace him with me."

Fury heats me from the inside out. "We need a plan to bring her down."

Wyatt pauses, then breathes, "I can use nature magic to create a vine with thorns that will put her to sleep if they prick her skin. Can you make it travel to her and attack her?"

Possibilities run through my mind, and one is particularly devious and delightful. Drawing on my nature magic, I'll strengthen the vine and send it tunneling through the ground until it reaches Cerise. Then I'll make it burst through the surface and twist around her ankle, piercing her skin.

I nod at Wyatt. He must see the fierce thrill in my gaze, because he smiles broadly, then grabs a branch of the hedge we're hiding behind.

Long seconds pass. Cerise is no longer rubbing her eyes. She's looking around for us.

A vine, covered in inch-long thorns, bursts from the branch in Wyatt's hand. Liquid oozes from the tips of the thorns, making me shudder.

I grab the tip of the vine, where there aren't any thorns, and thrust it against the ground. "Tunnel," I murmur, moving my fingers to direct the spell. "Grow." I picture the wicked vine breaking through the ground and wrapping around Cerise's leg, hoping my imagination is clear enough to make it happen.

The vine begins its trip through the earth.

All goes well until it's a few feet from Cerise . . . and the ground splits above the moving vine. I stifle a gasp and whisper, "Deeper!"

It's too late. Cerise saw the small crack form. With a screech, she charges towards it . . . then keeps going in the direction the vine clearly came from.

In seconds, she's reached our hiding spot.

Wyatt and I leap to our feet, vine forgotten. Cerise lifts her hands. With a word, she sends another bolt of lightning toward us.

Our shield flares bright purple.

I touch the hedge, shouting, "Fire!"

A small area of greenery explodes in flames, but they're less intense than I expected. My magic is running low. Cerise skirts around the fire until we're in full view. Her hands come up again, and she opens her mouth for yet another curse. I don't know if my shield can handle it.

"STOP!"

Hearing the familiar voice, Cerise, Wyatt, and I all turn. Tor is barreling through the garden toward us. Running close behind him are Justyne, Desiree, Felia, and Harmonie—all former contestants, all trustworthy.

I gape at Tor. I've witnessed his selfishness and pride many times.

Less than an hour ago, he pulled an evil faerie through a mirror, getting us into this mess. I don't trust him and probably never will.

But for some reason, when he could've fought his brother or fled from Cerise, he switched sides to defend Wyatt and me. This time, he did the right thing. Gratitude surges in my chest.

"There are more of us than you!" Tor shouts at Cerise. "Surrender, and we won't hurt you!"

Cerise lets out a short, bone-chilling laugh before gesturing violently toward the entire group and screeching, "Freeze!"

Tor and every female behind him stop moving, frozen in place by her curse.

With a roar, I lift my free hand, prepared to send heat to the group, hoping it will counteract her curse. In doing so, I make a grave error.

I take my eyes from Cerise.

She doesn't curse me this time. Perhaps she's guessed my shield's limitation: it can protect me from curses but not physical attacks. Cerise grabs my arm, yanking me away from Wyatt with such force, I scream in pain. Then she pulls me to her chest and covers my mouth with her hand, her grip unbreakable.

I can't speak. And while I did once accidentally cast a silent spell, I've never done it on purpose.

A word from Cerise generates a puff of air so strong, it knocks Wyatt to the dirt path. "Don't move unless you want to watch Aeryn die," she hisses. She kneels beside him, forcing me to do the same. With a knee, she pins his chest to the ground. She presses down hard, and pain fills his eyes. He doesn't fight back.

Freeze, I think, eager to place the same curse on Cerise that she used on my friends. But I'm tired and unfocused, and the silent spell does nothing.

"I knew you'd choose the do-gooder route," Cerise tells Wyatt. "Goodbye, young prince." She lifts her hand and pulls in a breath. She's going to kill him with the best weapon she has: her curse magic.

With every bit of strength I can dig up, I throw my head backwards. It slams into Cerise's nose with a violent crunch.

She screams in pain and falls backwards. Her grip on me is tighter than ever . . . but Wyatt is free.

"Run!" I shout.

He does. I wish he'd hide in a safe spot Cerise doesn't know about, but he won't. I know him well enough to be certain he's looking for the perfect moment to attack Cerise and free me.

He doesn't have much time, though. Cerise is on my back now, holding me down, and she's moved her hand to cover both my mouth and my nose.

I can't breathe. I can't do spells. With Cerise atop me, I can barely move.

She breathes a couple of words so softly, I can't understand them. But I see the result: a ring of fire surrounds us, keeping Wyatt away.

Blackness creeps into the edges of my vision. I hear shouts, like war cries. *A hallucination,* I tell myself.

"Oh, how lovely." Cerise is speaking into my ear, but her voice sounds muffled. Distant. "My soldiers must've finally broken through the barrier."

I try to breathe, try to sob, try to scream.

Cerise just tightens her grip and laughs.

COMING BACK TO BITE HER

My mind scrambles for purchase, attempting to hold on to its last shard of consciousness. But my efforts are useless. The blackness entering my vision wins.

I hear an odd sizzling sound just as I'm about to lose my grip on the last bit of my awareness.

Suddenly, the weight on my back is gone. And the hand that was smothering me—it's gone too.

I pull in a deep, desperate gasp, then another and another. My thoughts are still blurred as I push myself to my feet.

Cerise is on the ground, looking dazed. Her nose is swollen and crooked—it's clear I broke it. The fabric on her left shoulder is charred and smoking. The ring of fire around us is gone, and the ground is wet. Someone doused the flames, then somehow burned Cerise and forced her off me. I'm pretty sure Wyatt's magic couldn't do any of that.

I stumble away from Cerise. Who just saved my life? Why?

My mind clears further as I look around, and I gasp when I see several dozen Fae charging toward us. All at once, I remember the triumphant words Cerise spoke before my awareness slipped away. These must be her soldiers . . . but if so, who attacked her?

At the front of the group is a large Fae male with long, bright green hair. Hand extended, he sends a ball of fire toward Cerise. He must be the one who knocked her off me. She avoids the new missile with a scream.

They're on our side. Hope swells in me.

A hand grabs my arm. I pull away, panicked, until I hear a male voice say, "Come on. Get out of the line of fire."

"Wyatt!" I breathe.

His blue eyes are wide as he pulls me away from Cerise.

We don't go far before stopping to watch the approaching soldiers. "They're fighting against her!" I say.

At that moment, a female archer with buzzed blonde hair lets an arrow fly. It strikes the back of the male who attacked Cerise with fire. He falls to the ground with a grunt.

"Some of them are still on her side," Wyatt replies.

In moments, the soldiers are in an all-out battle with each other. Some of them protect Cerise. Others attempt to attack her.

A male with sharp, curved horns gores a fellow soldier in the chest. Another faerie creates a sinkhole that swallows a green-skinned male. Two flying faeries engage in a fierce, mid-air wrestling match.

Wyatt and I curse in unison, then turn to each other, looking for answers in each other's eyes.

Wyatt says, "If we can unfreeze the contestants and Tor—"

I interrupt him. "We'd just be putting them in danger. Why are the soldiers fighting each other?"

Cerise's voice brings our conversation to a halt. "Stop this!" Her bellow is barely audible over the sounds of battle. "You're my soldiers!"

"You tricked us to get us to come out here!" a female faerie returns. "We've been starving outside that barrier! No more!"

I almost laugh. Cerise's manipulation and cruelty are coming back to bite her.

A bolt of lightning strikes right next to her. She ducks behind two of the males protecting her, shouting, "Kill all the traitors!"

I can't let this go on. Can't watch faeries injuring and killing each other pointlessly.

"Stop!" I cry.

No one hears me. "Aeryn, what are you doing?" Wyatt asks urgently.

I don't answer. Instead, I run my fingers over my throat, muttering, "Louder." When I speak again, magic raises my voice above even the cries of the injured. "Stop!"

Many of the combatants look my way. Some of them even halt their attacks on one another.

Still using magic to amplify my voice, I say, "Let's negotiate. This bloodshed is unnecessary."

"Yes, I'm ready to negotiate." It's Wyatt, who's now standing next to me. He's not as loud as I am, but the fighting has calmed enough for everyone to hear him. There's a regal intensity to his voice I've never heard before.

"Negotiate? This land doesn't belong to either of you!" one of Cerise's loyal soldiers replies before throwing a punch into the gut of a male in front of her.

Cerise lifts a calming hand and speaks in that gentle, well-modulated tone that makes my stomach turn. "I'd like to know what this male has to say. Shall we temporarily halt our hostilities?"

It takes a couple of minutes, but the soldiers eventually stop fighting. They've gathered into two groups, about thirty with Cerise and twenty opposing her. I wonder if Desiree's father is in that second group. I'm relieved to see that on both sides, faeries are kneeling by the injured, tending to their wounds. Someone quickly heals the burn on Cerise's shoulder, her broken nose, and the gashes she got when she came through the mirror. Another faerie digs up the male sucked up by the sinkhole.

Glowing with confident strength, Cerise strides forward, eyes locked on Wyatt. He and I step closer until only a few yards separate us from her.

She's the first to speak. "Like you, I have no desire to see continued bloodshed on this land. I'll gladly allow all my soldiers to return safely to their families, even the mutinous ones. I'll return this estate to Faerie, where it belongs. All I require is that the two of you leave the kingdom and agree not to interfere as I assume leadership over its people in Faerie. I never desired such violence; I only wanted to help a kingdom that has been without monarchial leadership for a decade."

Wyatt says, "You know as well as I do that the firstborn prince is the rightful leader of this kingdom. If he cannot perform his duties, his brother will take his place."

"Perhaps you haven't heard the bad news." Cerise gives him a sweet smile and speaks loud enough for everyone to hear. "Fabien died ten years ago, and Luc disappeared."

Wyatt says nothing, though I sense his tension as he stands ramrod straight next to me. He confirmed his identity to me earlier today, after I overheard Cerise and Tor speaking of it. Yet it's clear the curse won't allow him to speak the truth to those who don't know it yet. Cerise is staring at him in true delight, reveling in his powerlessness.

It's time for someone to wipe that smile off her face.

Maintaining my voice-amplification spell, I say, "Cerise, you know very well that the male beside me is Luc, the second-born prince. The frozen beast over there is Fabien, the crown prince. You cursed them both ten years ago, forcing them to take on new forms."

Cerise's cheeks turn dark with anger. I know she'd like to strike me down right here, but such an action would only confirm the truth of my words.

She spins to face her soldiers. "Lies! All lies, conceived by weak people who are hungry for power. The royal family abandoned their kingdom ten years ago. All I desire is peace. I know you're all ready to go home. All I've ever wanted to do is return this estate to Faerie so I may provide the just, strong leadership they desperately need."

Every falsehood that leaves her lips stirs up my anger. But that's not the only thing I sense happening inside me. My magic, which was so depleted by my use of a shield, is regenerating. It's building in me, stronger than ever, and it's begging to be used.

That gives me an idea. One Wyatt won't like.

"Cerise," I say.

She turns to face me, arching an inquisitive brow.

I take Wyatt's hand. I have no right to negotiate for his land . . . yet, due to the curse, he's limited in what he can say or do. *Let me do this for you,* I beg silently.

I tell Cerise, "You brought these soldiers here, expecting them to fight for you. Yet this dispute has nothing to do with them. With Fabien incapacitated, this fight should be between you and Luc. Would you agree to a one-on-one battle for the estate and the kingdom?"

"The one you claim is Luc is merely a blue-skinned gardener pretending to be a prince. A faerie with little magic who's unwilling to even speak for himself." Her laughter peals through the air. "It would be a short fight."

"He may choose a champion to fight for him, according to Fae tradition." I remember reading about such a practice in a book my father brought me years ago. I hope it was accurate. "You're welcome to do the same."

Wyatt's grip on my hand turns fierce. I know his mind is whirring, considering the plan I'm putting forth and what it means.

"Clearly I don't need a champion," Cerise says. "But Wyatt would be welcome to ask any of my soldiers to fight for him. Not that it will matter. I'm not in the habit of hiring people more powerful than I."

I turn to the male next to me. "Will you agree to this, Luc?" It's the first time I've called him by his true name. As my eyes search his, I attempt to send magic from my hand into his. I'm not sure it worked until his eyes widen with wonder. Power is fairly bursting from me, and he feels it. He knows I'm as ready as I could ever be. He also knows what I'm offering—to be his champion.

Emotions flick across his face. Fear. Uncertainty. Gratitude.

And, finally, trust.

Wyatt cares for me far more deeply than he's been able to say. I know that to be true. Because of that, he despises the thought of watching me fight a powerful curse faerie. But he cares about the other people in this garden too. He'll risk his own heartbreak—and let me risk my life—because it's the only way to protect the innocents around us.

I really need to find a time to tell him how much I love him.

Wyatt turns to Cerise. "I'm open to a one-on-one battle. Let's talk terms."

48

WEAK

"**I**'m not giving you the servants!" Cerise screams.

Wyatt has been negotiating with her for at least a quarter-hour. Despite the grumbling of the hungry soldiers and Cerise's progressively worsening attitude, he remains calm. "Very well," he says, looking past Cerise. "Is everyone ready to fight?"

"Wait!" Cerise says. I'm sure her hesitation has nothing to do with concern over the soldiers. She's scared she'll get killed if there's an all-out melee. She gives Wyatt a sweet-as-sugar smile. "I'm open to returning the servants to their natural forms if you win. But if any of them try to get revenge on me—if they lay one finger on me—I will turn them back to stone."

"Only those who attack you?" Wyatt asks.

She releases a small huff, and I realize she left that part purposely vague. "Yes, of course."

Wyatt smiles, though his blue eyes are full of steel. "The terms, then: Regardless of who wins, you'll return this estate to Faerie." They'd agreed on that point pretty easily. Whoever ends up living on this estate, it doesn't belong on Earth. Mortals may discover it and learn too much about the Fae.

308

When Cerise nods, Wyatt says, "If you prevail, you'll become queen of the kingdom this estate has historically ruled over. You'll remove the freezing curse on Fabien and the four contestants and swear, with an unbreakable oath, not to lay a hand on him, me, Aeryn, or any of the other contestants for the rest of our lives. Fabien, Aeryn, and I will leave your kingdom, and neither we nor our descendants will ever be allowed to return."

Cerise's smile turns triumphant, like she's already won.

"If I win," Wyatt continues, "you will leave this kingdom, and neither you nor your descendants will ever return. You will never interfere in Aeryn's life or in the lives of anyone she cares about. And you will fully break the curse you placed ten years ago."

"Fully break?" Cerise's eyes go wide, as if in surprise. "Oh, my dear boy, I said I was *open* to returning the servants to their bodies, but we didn't agree on those terms. Your brother could have broken the entire curse, but he failed. I won't reward him for that. If you somehow win this challenge—a highly unlikely prospect—I will break the curse on the servants *or* on you and Fabien. Not both."

I suck in a short, shocked breath as I turn to Wyatt. Breaking the curse on the two princes was one of the first things he and Cerise settled on. If he wins, she can't expect him to live in a different form, with greatly reduced magic, for the rest of his long life—and to require his brother to do the same. In his beast form, Tor might not be able to convince his people he's their rightful ruler.

"That wouldn't even qualify as winning!" I blurt.

Cerise simply smiles. Shaking my head, I look at Wyatt, expecting him to refuse her terms.

His gaze is sweeping over the circle of statues around us.

Wyatt has spent ten years keeping them in perfect condition so the servants will be healthy when they resume their fleshly forms. According to Cerise, Wyatt—or, rather, Luc—was terribly selfish when she cursed him. Caring for these servants-turned-statues transformed him into the male he is today. Loving. Kind. Sacrificial.

I'm not remotely surprised when he says, "If I win, you will break the curse on the statues. We have an agreement."

I squeeze my eyes shut briefly, indulging in a moment of grief. Wyatt deserves the chance to live as the faerie he was born to be, full of the magical power that was his birthright. And Tor? Well, I'm not sure he's *good*, but he did the right thing when he brought the contestants back to attack Cerise. He deserves the chance to become the best male he can be, free from the beastly body he's inhabiting.

But Cerise's cackling assures me that the deal is now official.

"As we agreed upon," Wyatt says firmly, "the one-on-one fight will continue until one party surrenders or loses consciousness. Neither combatant may kill nor permanently injure the other. Breaking that rule will result in a death sentence for the guilty party."

Cerise nods, then looks Wyatt up and down, her lip curling in a sneer. "I assume you'll choose a champion?"

Wyatt squeezes his lips together. His throat bobs with a swallow.

He wants to fight for himself. I see it in his eyes. But he knows his limitations. I take his hand in mine and give it a squeeze. He turns to me, a mournful question in his gaze.

I nod.

Wyatt turns back to Cerise. "Aeryn will be my champion."

The beautiful faerie's laughter once again peals through the garden. "A mortal," she says. "It'll be a boring fight, but I'll enjoy it while it lasts."

Her words are bold, but she's tapping her thumb and finger together. There's a certain tension in her shoulders. Despite her arrogance, she's a little nervous.

I hope she has reason to be.

Wyatt clears his throat. "The soldiers and I will swear unbreakable oaths not to interfere in the battle."

Cerise agrees. When all the oaths are sworn, Wyatt walks up to me and leans in to whisper in my ear.

I expect him to thank me for fighting for him. To tell me how strong I am. To assure me I can win.

Instead, he breathes, "I love you."

He runs to join the soldiers before I can respond.

My mouth widens into a broad smile. Confident joy sends energy through my body. Wyatt loves me. And I'm going to fight with everything in me to win this challenge for him.

He and the soldiers stand in a wide circle around Cerise and me.

"Let the fight begin," Cerise says.

I push my hands forward, shouting, "Steam!" Great billows of steam form instantly, rushing toward my opponent.

"Reflect!" she cries, her own hands raised.

Her curse turns my spell back on me. Because I formed the steam with nature magic, not curse magic, my blessing shield doesn't protect me from it. The front end of the cloud blasts my hands with heat before I shout, "Fog!"

Cold mist and hot vapor sizzle as they meet, neutralizing each other.

Cerise throws a thunderbolt at me. That seems to be one of her favorite curses. My shield flares bright purple, depleting my magic noticeably.

With a quick spell, I cause the ground to tremble under Cerise's feet.

She falls, but it doesn't distract her from throwing another bolt of lightning. My shield flares again.

Cerise leaps to her feet, opening her mouth to curse me again. I allow my shield to defend me from yet another bolt of lightning, but I'm determined it'll be the last time. While she was down, I picked up a handful of soil. Now, I throw it, speaking a one-word spell: "Gag!"

The air obeys, launching the soil across the space separating me from Cerise and depositing it in her mouth.

It's hard to curse if you can't speak.

She begins digging out the densely packed soil with her fingers. I won't give her the chance to finish. I need to conserve my magic, so it's time to bring some pure physicality into this fight. I sprint toward Cerise. She reaches out to defend herself, but at the last second, I duck low. I slam into her pelvis and thighs, tackling her to the ground.

Cerise attempts to push me off, but I have strength born of righteous anger. I straddle her, pinning her arms to the ground with my knees.

I grab her face in my hands, and as soon as our skin connects, I feel more magic building inside me. My magical intuition shares a new truth with me: I can cast spells directly on her body when I'm touching it.

I grip her tighter and say the first thing that comes to mind: "Boils."

It's a curse, and a nasty one. Speaking it makes me feel sick. But the servants are depending on me for their lives, even if they don't know it. Wyatt and Tor are counting on me to defend their right to live in their family home.

Angry, seeping boils pop up all over Cerise's skin. Her eyes go wide, and she wriggles beneath me, trying to escape.

"Surrender, and I'll heal you," I say.

She finally yanks one arm free and drags her nails across my face, digging deep gouges into my skin.

I grunt as fiery pain flares on my cheek. Desperately, I try to pin her arm down again, but she's thrashing too violently beneath me.

I hear her spitting. When my eyes return to her face, it's too late. She's managed to spit out most of the soil-gag.

Her free hand forms a fist. She punches me hard in the jaw, causing me to scream in pain. Then she clamps her hand over my mouth, so I can't speak any spells. A curse leaves her lips: "Weak."

My shield flares. Anger turns her eyes bright as she repeats herself: "Weak!"

Another flare.

"Weak! Weak! Weak!"

My shield fails.

"Weak!" Cerise says one more time.

I slump atop her, barely able to move. My strength is gone. Years ago, I made a small doll out of yarn for a child who lived down the street. Cerise's spell makes me feel like that doll. Helpless, floppy, feeble.

"Poor Aeryn," Cerise croons. "A faerie would've known not to let someone with curse magic touch them. Curses are even stronger when skin meets skin."

She pushes me off her. A soft grunt leaves my mouth as I land on my back. Breathing requires every bit of the strength she left me with.

Cerise stands over me, watching me thoughtfully. "Clearly I'm going to win this battle, but I'm trying to decide the best way to finish it off. The rules say I can't kill you or permanently injure you. However . . ." A slow smile spreads across her mouth, causing a boil on her cheek to crack and leak fluid. I look away, gagging, but return my attention to her when she says, "I have a much better idea. You're going to hate it."

Despite my physical weakness, I sense that I still have a bit of magic left. Not enough to regenerate my shield, but enough to do . . . something.

"I'm going to curse you," Cerise says, "just like I did to Fabien and Luc."

She begins droning on about how much she loves curses. I'm not listening, though. I'm strategizing.

All at once, I remember the thorns Wyatt created. If one of them pierces Cerise's skin, she'll fall asleep. Wyatt will win. I just have to get the vine to her before she curses me.

One of my hands is lying in the grass. I somehow find the strength to send a tendril of magic through the ground and immediately sense the vine Wyatt made. It's only a couple of feet from Cerise, just underneath the surface of the ground. With great effort, I open my mouth and whisper one word: "Go." Along with the spell, I include my intention for the vine to emerge from the earth, wrap around Cerise's ankle, and prick her skin.

I sense the vine obeying me, traveling through the soil. It's slow, though. So very slow. My weakened magic can't manage anything more. Every time I allow myself a shallow breath, the vine briefly halts. But it always starts moving again.

I return my attention to Cerise.

"I performed almost no spells for decades," she says, "in order to build up enough power for my curse on this estate and its people." She kneels over me, smiling casually as if we're friends chatting about the weather. "Fellow faeries thought I had almost no power. They didn't know I was merely saving it up. In the last decade, I've conserved my magic. Not as completely as I used to, but enough to build up a fair amount of strength. Certainly enough to perform one impressive curse on one silly mortal. How would you like to spend the rest of your pitifully short life as a wild boar, Aeryn?"

Dread fills my weak body. Cerise doesn't just want to win. She wants to punish me—for daring to resist her manipulation. For allying myself with Wyatt. For being a mortal with magic.

I beg the vine to move faster. Thank heaven, it obeys.

"You'll be a lovely pig," Cerise says.

My magical senses make me aware of the instant the tip of the vine bursts through the ground, right next to Cerise's ankle. With her kneeling, it'll be so easy for the vine to wrap over her skin. *Please, please, please,* I beg.

She reaches out and takes my wrist. "It's time," she says.

The vine curls up over her ankle. The first thorn is about to emerge from the ground.

Feeling the vine with my magic isn't enough. I need to see it. Need to confirm it's doing as I've asked. My eyes shift away from Cerise.

It's the worst mistake I've ever made. Cerise must've noticed my gaze moving, must've looked to see what had grabbed my attention, because she scrambles to her feet and steps away from the vine, just as a thorn pushes through the ground. "Burn!" she screams, pointing down.

A stream of fire leaves her finger and incinerates the vine.

She turns back to me, looming over my weakened body. "It's time to end this," she hisses.

49

A WOMAN WITH A STRONG MIND

Cerise is bending down to curse me when a voice stops her.

"No! Please!"

It's Wyatt. His exclamation causes Cerise to straighten and look his way, but she doesn't forget me. She presses a foot, shod in a green leather shoe with a slender narrow heel, onto my chest. It feels like if I breathe too deeply or she shifts her stance, the heel will penetrate straight into my heart.

I'm too weak to breathe deeply. Or to push her damn foot off of me.

"I wondered when you'd speak up," Cerise calls to Wyatt.

"Take me." His voice is loud, rough, desperate. "Curse me however you'd like. Just let Aeryn go."

Cerise laughs, rupturing yet another boil on her cheek. "Don't be silly, Luc. I'm having far too much fun to change things now."

He continues to argue with her, but I stop listening. He's stalling, giving me the chance to find a way to win this battle. This extra time is a gift, and I must make the most of it.

The problem is, I used all my magic. I can't even sense the magical vine under the ground. I'm physically weak. Magically destitute. Breathing and speaking require all my strength. How am I supposed to stop a powerful faerie?

Cerise's long, loud laugh pulls my attention back to her.

"Isn't this pitiful?" she asks Wyatt. "All this weak human had to do was fall in love with your brother, and she couldn't even manage that. If she'd truly agreed to marry Fabien for love, all your problems would've been solved."

Something moves on my hand. I shift my gaze and see the copper-colored snake nudging me with her head. As soon as I see her, she stops and fixes her green gaze on me.

Pay attention, she seems to be saying.

To what? I mouth.

With her head, she gestures to Cerise. Then she slithers away.

"But somehow," Cerise is saying, "Aeryn fell for the gardener instead. The younger brother with less power, less personality, less *everything*." She shrugs. "There's no accounting for taste."

Wyatt again offers himself in my stead. As he and Cerise argue back and forth, I hear nothing that will give me the power to change my fate. I don't know what the snake wanted me to hear.

A question pops into my head: *What was Cerise saying when the snake got my attention?*

My body is weak, but my mind is still sharp. I fix my eyes on Cerise, begging my memory to return to the moment I felt that movement on my hand.

The curse. She was talking about the curse. About how if I'd married Tor for love, everything would've been fine.

That memory brings me back to another one—Cerise speaking to Tor through the mirror, repeating her original terms for breaking the curse. I need to remember exactly what she said, but can I? It takes a strong mind to remember specific words that were only spoken once.

A strong mind.

Who am I, if not a woman with a strong mind?

Wyatt told me over and over to be myself. So it's time to depend on that glorious mind of mine, the one honed sharp by reading countless books and by strategizing to keep my family alive. If I'm going to defeat Cerise, it will not be with my body or my magic.

It will be with my mind.

I close my eyes and ask myself a question: *What were the terms for breaking the curse?*

The words come to me—stored somewhere in my head, like a card in that delightful cabinet in the library vault, just waiting to be retrieved.

By the last second before midnight ten years from today, someone must agree to marry you for love. The curse will be broken when they verbally proclaim their true love.

Despite my weakness, my jaw falls open.

. . . agree to marry you for love . . .

. . . verbally proclaim . . .

. . . true love.

I know what to do.

Somehow, I find the strength to speak several words. "I agreed to marry Tor—Fabien—for love."

My voice is stronger than I thought I was capable of. It brings Cerise and Wyatt's argument to an abrupt halt.

Cerise glares down at me. She grinds her shoe even harder into my chest, and damn, it *hurts*. I clench my teeth, trying to hide my pain, but the pressure of her foot forces a breathy grunt from my lungs.

"That's a lie," she says. "Nice try."

Her foot makes it even more difficult to pull air into my lungs, but I manage it. My words are soft and strained. "You didn't say it had to be out of love *for him*. I agreed to marry him because I love my family. And Wyatt—Luc. And my friends. I'm willing to marry Fabien. And it's for love."

I've verbally proclaimed my true love, the reason I agreed to marry Tor. It should be enough to break the curse. And it certainly does *something*—the ground beneath my prone body begins trembling.

I don't have time to consider what that means, because Cerise throws herself to her knees next to me. She's bellowing wordlessly, her face twisted into a grotesque, oozing, angry scowl. She grabs my head in both hands, squeezing so tightly, it feels like she'll smash my skull.

"I curse you," she shrieks in a voice that's harsh and full of power, "to live for the remainder of your pitiful lifespan as—"

For a split second, I glimpse something large and black above me, moving in my peripheral vision. I see a flash of glossy, black wings. Whatever the creature is, it slams into Cerise, forcing her off me and pushing her so hard, she skids along the grass, carried by the momentum of the flying being.

Wyatt's voice reaches my ears. "You must render her unconscious!"

"Any reason you didn't already do that?" the black-winged creature replies in an annoyed voice. I can't see his face from my position, but he sounds human—or, rather, Fae, considering the wings.

"It was a challenge," Wyatt replies, "and I swore not to interfere! You swore no such thing! I'm naming you as my new champion. You can't kill Cerise—she must surrender or be unconscious to lose the challenge."

"Something tells me she won't surrender," the male mutters.

Both Wyatt and he go quiet, and I become aware of what else is happening in this garden. The ground is still trembling, though more gently than before. There are cracking sounds in the distance, loud and sharp. I have no idea what's causing any of it, and I can't move to get a good look.

A moment later, the male says, "It's done. She's unconscious. Your challenge is over."

As he's speaking, the ground at last settles. A certain measure of strength returns to my body. The weakness curse is broken, but I'm still exhausted from all the magic I used.

I hear multiple footsteps coming my way. The first person I see is Justyne, and I've never been so overjoyed by the sight of her deep-purple hair and dragonfly wings. She throws herself to her knees beside me.

"You're okay," I murmur.

She grins. "I'm not sure what that faerie did to us, but we're free now."

I shift my gaze past her and realize four others are kneeling around me: Desiree, Felia, Harmonie, and . . . someone else. A male faerie.

One I know from my dreams.

He has luminous bronze skin, dark brown hair that falls in waves over his forehead, and gray eyes. Heat floods my neck and cheeks when I remember the intimate moments I shared with him in one of my dreams.

"I have nature magic," he says. "I can use it to increase your body's strength."

I stare at him. He's speaking in Wyatt's voice, but I realize now it's a bit deeper than before.

"Do you know who I am?" he asks.

"Wyatt?" I whisper. "Luc?"

"Yes. May I touch you to give you strength?"

"Please. Touch me."

His smile is deeply familiar, and not just due to my dream memories. Wyatt's spirit, his goodness, lurks in that beautiful smile. He takes my hand in both of his.

Strength rushes into me, so strong and fast that I gasp. Good heavens, he's powerful. And this is the magic he was willing to forsake in exchange for the servants' lives.

I love him more than ever.

He gently heals my cheek, where Cerise scratched it. I open my mouth to tell him my heart is his.

Before I can speak, someone behind him asks, "What's going on?"

Luc turns. Behind him stands a tall, broad male with curly blue hair poking out of the bottom of a chef's hat. A huge grin takes over Luc's face. "Jules!"

At the same time, Justyne leaps to her feet, squealing, "Leo!"

I push myself to a seated position as Justyne runs to a male with bright red wings. She launches herself at him, in the process nearly knocking over Luc and Jules, who are also embracing.

The rest of the freed servants stand behind them, watching the reunions. I confirm they're all alive and whole. One of the small children who was trapped in stone along with his mother begins singing, seemingly unaware of how close he came to eternal imprisonment in this garden. I swallow a lump of emotion as his little voice soars, lisping and off key.

Luc releases Jules and brushes gray powder off the male's shoulders. "You broke out of the stone," he says in a voice thick with emotion.

So that's what the cracking noises were.

"I have a lot of questions," the chef says. "We all do."

"Well, there was a curse . . ." Luc begins. He leads the servants several steps away, speaking animatedly.

I turn to tell Desiree that the soldiers, including her father, made it through the barrier. I quickly realize she's already found him. They're sitting on a bench, holding each other's hands and chatting. The other soldiers are standing around peacefully, no longer at odds with each other now that Cerise is out of commission.

Felia and Harmonie begin asking me questions—"How do you feel?" "What happened here?"—but I don't respond. My attention has shifted several feet away, to where Cerise is lying.

The raven-winged Fae male is tying her wrists together using rope he must have created magically. His back is to me, and I can't see much other than his wings and his outstretched hands, but . . . I know those wings. I've seen them over and over in my dreams.

"He's Fabien, isn't he?" I ask no one in particular.

Felia confirms it, then launches into more questions.

I barely hear her. A fact I'd rather not dwell on has overtaken my mind: I committed to marrying Fabien. My promise to him was a crucial part of breaking the curse.

Fabien finishes tying the knot, then turns to face me. He looks just as he did in my dreams. Smooth, pewter-colored skin. Wavy black hair. Broad shoulders and muscles. He gives me a slow smile.

How would I describe him? *Devastatingly handsome* is too mild of a term. His Fae beauty and strength are glorious. He'll make a truly impressive king and husband.

At that thought, my chest tightens. . . because I don't want to be his wife when I deeply love someone else.

But Fabien is a crown prince. Marriage to him is still the best way to provide for my family and to ensure that Felia's parents get their land back. It may also be the only way to be certain the curse stays broken—that Luc and the servants he's spent years caring for remain in their true forms.

I committed to marrying Fabien, the raven-winged faerie who was once a beast. And I'll do it—for the people I love.

AN UNBREAKABLE OATH

Fabien stands and walks to me, his hands extended.

"Aeryn," he says, helping me up.

I can't think of anything to say.

He smiles and squeezes my hands. "You knew me as Tor, but I'm really Fa—"

"I know," I interrupt.

Silence stretches for far too long as his eyes search my face.

"Nice wings," I say at last.

"It's, ah . . . it's good to have them back."

I'm not sure why this feels so awkward. It gets worse with every second that passes.

He opens his mouth to speak again, but a female servant runs up to us. She has tight green curls, yellow eyes that sparkle like topaz, and rosy lips curved into a joyful smile. "We're back in Faerie!" she says. "Come, look!"

I drop Fabien's hands, and we follow the servant to a nearby spot where we can see past the garden shrubs all the way to the border of the estate.

The foggy barrier is gone. Beyond the estate's smooth lawn is a forest that looks nothing like the one I came through on the way here. The trees are brighter green. They're taller and wider, too. Older. I sense the magic in their stately forms.

Felia, who's standing behind me, says, "I suppose that's why the ground was trembling. The entire estate transported itself back home."

"The curse is broken. All of it." Rich satisfaction resonates in Fabien's words.

His mention of the curse reminds me that Cerise is lying on the ground nearby. I turn and confirm she's still unconscious. Fear sends my heart into a gallop. I clutch Fabien's forearm and meet his gaze. "Cerise told me she's conserved much of her magic for the last ten years. When she wakes, what's to stop her from placing another curse?"

"The rope binding her wrists is unbreakable," he says. "It will be difficult for her to move her hands enough to complete any powerful curses. But I'll gag her too, just in case."

We both kneel next to Cerise. Fabien waves his hands and whispers, creating a long, narrow black cloth. He places it in her mouth and ties it behind her head, murmuring spells under his breath the whole time.

As he works, my eyes roam across her oozing boils. *I did that to her.* Fierce, vengeful satisfaction fills my chest.

Another thought occurs to me. *Cerise would be just as pleased with my injuries if our roles were reversed.*

The smugness in my chest disappears, replaced with tight regret.

When Fabien finishes gagging Cerise, I place my hands gently on her cheeks. Oozing boils are less disgusting than blood, but only slightly. I swallow my gorge and whisper, "Heal," hoping my magic has recovered enough to complete this spell. "Everywhere."

When I sense warm power flowing through my palms, I breathe a sigh of relief. Cerise's skin returns to its former state of perfection.

"Aeryn," Fabien says, "she didn't deserve your healing touch."

I look up to find bright blue eyes that have turned hard and cold. I can't condemn him for his vindictiveness. Just moments ago, I felt the same way. All I say is, "I want to be as different from her as I can possibly be."

His brows knit together, but he doesn't reply. I can't tell if he approves or finds me naïve.

A sharp inhale draws our attention back to Cerise. Her eyes are open. She grunts and wiggles, trying to loosen her bonds. When she's unsuccessful, she lifts a foot to kick Fabien.

He grabs her foot before she can injure him. "None of that, or I'll tie your ankles too."

She stills, though the fury in her eyes tells me she hasn't surrendered.

"Before you go," Fabien says, "you must swear with an unbreakable oath never to return to my kingdom and never to curse or otherwise harm any member of my family or our descendants."

"Or anyone else associated with Fabien or his kingdom," I add, thinking of the servants and my fellow contestants. "And you must make an oath to free your soldiers from their commitments to you, without any repercussion."

"Yes," Fabien agrees. "All of that."

Cerise shakes her head violently.

"Or . . ." Fabien's voice shifts, a satisfied grin breaking over his face. "If you refuse to make these oaths, I'll send you away, but my loyal guards will follow you closely. The moment you make any effort to harm me or any member of my kingdom, my guards will bring you to me, and I will punish you in the manner I deem appropriate." He leans in closer. "Did you consider what would happen when you stifled my magic for ten years? It grew in strength—every single day. You don't want to see what I can do to you now, Cerise."

When her expression doesn't soften, he sighs and turns to me. "Scoot back, just a bit."

I move away. He does as well. Then he sweeps his hands over her and mutters a quiet spell.

A metal grid appears around Cerise. It's a cage, but like none I've ever seen. It's anchored in the ground, and it's shaped like her, molded around her prone form, nearly touching her. The metal glows a deep red color.

I hear gasps from the servants and soldiers. They've been fairly quiet, but they're clearly watching.

Cerise turns her head to glare at Fabien. There's a sizzle and a terrible smell of something burning. She gasps and goes still. After a moment, I find the cause of the sound and odor. A bit of her hair is smoking where it's now in contact with the cage.

It's a terrible, effective invention, and Fabien made it out of nothing. "You're a creation faerie, aren't you?" I ask.

He meets my gaze and nods with a little smirk.

A moment later, the cage disappears. Fabien leans in close to Cerise. "Are you ready to swear those oaths?"

She glares at him for a long moment. Her entire face softens with resignation, and she nods.

All my breath leaves my chest in a loud, satisfying sigh of relief. This all began ten years ago with a curse, and it's ending with a simple nod.

Fabien removes Cerise's gag long enough for her to make the oaths we've required. I ask why he doesn't force her to swear to never curse anyone again, and he explains that cursing is part of life in Faerie—but so are negotiations. This type of agreement is acceptable according to Fae law and custom.

"Your gag and bonds will disappear the moment you step foot out of my kingdom," Fabien says. "It's time for you to leave, along with your soldiers."

He gathers the soldiers and requires each of them to swear to never again work for Cerise or attempt to infiltrate his kingdom. I can tell he's pleasantly surprised to see how many of them aren't just willing, but relieved to make such a commitment.

Desiree pulls me aside and tells me she's leaving with her father. We embrace, and she returns to him. He puts an arm around her shoulders and squeezes.

All at once, I miss my father fiercely.

The soldiers leave peacefully, along with Cerise. Despite her gag and bound hands, she holds her head high. The garden remains quiet until the departing group is out of sight, swallowed by the bright green trees of the Fae forest.

I survey those of us who are left: contestants and freed servants, along with Fabien, Luc, and me.

Movement in the grass at my feet catches my attention. I smile as I realize it's the snake, lifting her head above her shiny coils.

Felia yelps and skitters away on her goat hooves. Several of the servants gasp and back away too.

"She's friendly," I assure them. "She helped me throughout the competition. I don't think anyone else saw her except Rochelle . . ."

I trail off as the snake's bronze body begins to change.

Gradually, she transforms into a different being. Her body shortens dramatically, then swells and morphs, changing color and form. The process is unnatural and somewhat grotesque, yet I can't take my eyes off her.

Four pale-orange nubs pop out of her sides, and her body lightens to the same color. At the same time, two purple bumps form on her back. They stretch out quickly, becoming long and thin. "Wings," I whisper. The pale-orange bumps lengthen into arms and legs.

Before long, a short faerie, no taller than the middle of my thigh, stands before me. Her flame-colored hair and purple wings glimmer in the sunlight. She flashes me a wide, familiar grin. It's Jackie, the pixie who brought me into this competition. She's as beautiful and friendly as ever.

She's also naked.

No one around me seems to care about her state of undress. Faeries aren't a modest bunch. As Fabien and Luc exclaim over Jackie's sudden appearance, I use magic to create a small, white dress featuring a cutout in back for her wings.

"It's great to see you," I say, kneeling, "but, well, in case you'd like us to see *less* of you . . ." I hand her the dress.

Jackie grins and pulls it on. Then she literally flies into my arms. "You did so well, Aeryn!" she trills. "You broke the spell. I knew you could!"

I barely get the chance to return her embrace before she releases me and says, "Stand up, silly mortal. I can come up to your level. Wings, remember?"

I stand, giving her a rueful smile. Wings fluttering, she rises along with me.

Fabien's arms are crossed, and he's glowering at Jackie, a fearsome expression that does nothing to reduce his handsomeness. "Why did you become a serpent?" he demands.

She flits over to him, propping her hands on her narrow hips. "Because I needed to stop Cerise."

"The risks, Jackie! You could've died—forever!"

"I know, but I passed the test."

I spread my arms wide. "Can someone please explain to me what's happening?"

Luc crosses to me. He stops a couple of feet away, and I barely keep myself from reaching out and pulling him closer.

"A strong curse can't usually be broken unless the terms are met," he says. "There are probably no faeries alive who could have broken Cerise's curse with magic alone."

"*Usually?*" I repeat. "*Probably?* Are you saying there are exceptions?"

He nods. "Some ancient faeries were strong enough to break or weaken other faeries' curses, but nearly all Fae transition into spirit form before they develop such a skill. I've never met a faerie with such an ability."

"What does this have to do with Jackie turning herself into a snake?" I ask.

"An ancient Fae law says even a young faerie may gain great power against curses by becoming a serpent and giving significant help to someone in need. If they succeed, they may return to their previous form."

"After that, they're able to break curses?"

"Break or weaken, depending on the strength of the one who placed the curse."

"Then why doesn't every faerie become a serpent, help someone out, and enjoy their new power?"

Luc's eyes turn very serious. "When someone undergoes the transformation, they lose nearly all their magic. The form they take also limits their physical capabilities, which makes it difficult to help others. Plus, they're vulnerable—faeries often aren't any fonder of snakes than humans are, and many will chop off a serpent's head without thought. If a faerie dies in their snake form, they cannot transition to a spirit form. They forsake their immortality."

My mouth drops open. Jackie risked her immortal soul in an effort to save Fabien. I turn slowly to her. "Why did you do it?"

She swipes a tear off her cheek. "I cared for Fabien throughout his childhood. I love him. For nearly ten years, I sought a way to free him from this curse. At last, I found the estate, discovered a weakness in the barrier, and started the competition. I couldn't, however, leave it all to chance. I decided to become a serpent and help the worthiest contestant."

Her mouth widens into a grin, though her eyes are still shining with tears. "I saw your dedication to your father, Aeryn. I knew Fabien needed a selfless partner like you. But my goal wasn't just to help you win Fabien's heart—it was also to ensure that you, a mortal, stayed alive in a competition I suspected might become dangerous."

When she takes a breath, I interject, "And you hoped that, even if I lost the competition, you would qualify to become a curse breaker?"

"Precisely," she says. "Cerise's curse, however, was strong. I'm terribly glad you broke it. I might have only been able to weaken it."

I give her another tight hug. "Not only did you keep me alive, but think of the power you have now! Next time Cerise attacks someone like she did ten years ago—"

"I'll do everything I can to nullify the effects of her curse, and I'll enjoy doing it," Jackie says firmly.

Fabien's voice interrupts our conversation. "You know, I've had a rough day. I'd like a hug from my governess."

Jackie laughs, flies to him, and flings her arms around his neck.

My gaze sweeps over the garden. Various servants are looking longingly toward the borders of the estate. They must be anxious to see their families. Then there are my fellow contestants. Justyne is happily talking to her brother, but I hear Harmonie and Felia whispering about going home. That makes me wonder about the five contestants still unaccounted for. As much as I dislike some of them, they deserve to return home too.

I approach Harmonie and Felia. "Where did you stay after you were eliminated?"

Harmonie smiles, the mermaid scales on her cheekbones catching the light. "In a house hidden by magic, tucked into a corner of the estate. We had everything we needed there. Tor couldn't let us go home while the soldiers were outside the barrier, lest they hurt us."

"Are the other contestants still there?" I ask.

"Yes." Felia arches a bronze-colored eyebrow. "Even Margot and Rochelle. But I think Fabien can safely release them. Losing took the fight out of them. Now, they just want to return home."

I nod and turn to suggest that Fabien allow everyone to leave. Someone else speaks before I can.

"Brother," Luc says, "I'm sure the servants and contestants would like to return to their families."

I smile at Luc and give him a nod of gratitude.

Fabien's wide-eyed expression makes it clear he'd forgotten all about the servants and contestants. "Of course—of course!" he says. "They're all welcome to go whenever they'd like. But there's a certain event some of them may wish to remain here for."

He crosses to stand before me, a hesitant smile on his lips. When he speaks, his voice is low and warm. "Aeryn, I didn't see you break the curse," he says. "But I know you did it, and I know that means you confessed your true love for me." He cups my cheek in his warm hand. "Will you still marry me? Today?"

DAMN IT, LUC

I knew this moment was coming.

Part of me hoped Fabien would decide I'm not worth marrying. He did, after all, witness me kissing his brother. Deep down, however, I knew it wouldn't matter. He's a prince. His parents raised him to claim his rights to get what he wants, to mold his world to meet his needs. For ten years, he couldn't do that. Why wouldn't he eagerly reclaim such privileges, now that he has the chance?

"Will you?" Fabien repeats.

"I must marry you." The words sound hoarse after passing through my dry throat. "It's part of breaking the curse."

Fabien's lips part, and he blinks several times. "The curse is broken, Aeryn. That won't change—not if we refuse to marry or even if one of us dies. You committed to marrying me for love. Your promise and your love broke the curse."

"Oh," I whisper. Emotions slam through my heart with such violence, I fear I'll fall over. *Relief. Confusion. Obligation. Guilt. Uncertainty.*

"Aeryn," Fabien says softly, "do you *want* to marry me?"

As I consider how to answer that question, Wyatt's words return to my mind: *Be yourself.* How can I follow that advice right now?

Well, I've learned a few things about myself, in my years caring for my loved ones and my weeks on this estate.

I'm a woman who keeps her commitments. I'm a woman who loves her family. I'm a woman who loves her friends.

I meet Fabien's gaze. "My family has suffered for years. They often don't have enough food to eat. Our house is in disrepair. If I marry you, will—"

"I'll ensure they're cared for," he interrupts. "Always. They won't just have what they need; they'll live in true comfort."

I nod, and a small weight drops away from my heart. *So why does it still feel so heavy?*

"Also," I continue, "years ago, you won a piece of land in a game of chance. It belonged to Felia's family." Seeing the surprise in his wide eyes, I continue, "I'm sure you didn't make the connection when Felia was part of the competition. You may also not realize that her parents are starving, since they cannot farm the land that was once theirs. If I marry you, will you return their land to them?"

As I was speaking, one of Fabien's large hands came to his mouth. "Oh, gods," he says, the words little more than a grunt. There's true remorse in his shining eyes. He turns to Felia. "I—of course I'll return their land," he tells her.

Her own hands rise to her mouth, stifling a sob.

Fabien faces me again and swallows, waiting for me to say more.

I am a woman who keeps her commitments, I think. I square my shoulders and say, "I committed to marrying you. I still intend to."

The next moment, his arms are around me, holding me close to his muscular chest. I place my own arms around his waist, leaning into him. He's going to be my husband. He's going to take care of my family. *I could do far worse than this imperfect faerie,* I tell myself.

Fabien rubs a hand along my back. A bit of serenity washes over my chaotic thoughts. In that moment, I remember something else that's true about me.

I am an honest woman.

I don't have to think about what I'm going to do next. It's the only thing I *can* do, at least if I want to be able to live with myself in the coming days and years.

I pull away from Fabien. He lets me go, but his questioning gaze holds me captive. I take both his hands and force the necessary words from my mouth.

"I will marry you, Fabien. But I must tell you the truth. I don't love you."

"Aeryn . . ." A short chuckle exits his mouth. "Of course you do. You couldn't have broken the curse unless—"

I place a hand gently over his lips, quieting him. "I did agree to marry you for love, but the love I felt was for others in my life." I don't go into detail. He already knows about my family and Felia's, and I don't want to hurt him by confessing the love I also hold for his brother.

Fabien's eyes close briefly before he looks at me again and clears his throat. "Could you learn to love me?"

I swallow hard. "I hope so. I'll certainly try."

"I'm glad to hear that," he says with a strained smile.

Then, it's as if he turns into a different person. As his back straightens and his gaze hardens, he drops the cloak of a gentle lover and replaces it with the mantle of an authoritative prince. He drops my hands and begins issuing orders.

First, he instructs a trusted servant to release the remaining contestants from the house where they've been staying. "Please escort them out of my kingdom so they may return to their families," Fabien says. "Keep an extra-close eye on the ones named Rochelle and Margot."

I try not to smile at that.

Next, he proclaims that anyone who wishes may return to their families. About two-thirds of the staff leave, along with Harmonie, who gives me a quick hug goodbye.

Fabien then instructs his steward to draft a document returning

Felia's parents' land to them. He tells Felia she can deliver it herself. The steward leads her to the castle.

With bright, intelligent eyes, Fabien surveys the servants who remain. "I'll need someone to travel back to the mortal realm right away to bring food and money to Aeryn's family."

Jackie flies up to him. "Before the competition began, I delivered food to them, along with funds to purchase enough provisions for several months."

This time, I give in to the grin pulling at my mouth. Jackie came through for me with more generosity than I'd dared hope for.

Fabien says, "I'm sure there's a story behind that, Jackie. You'll have to share it with me when we have more time. I'll send someone to visit Aeryn's family tomorrow. Today, we'll all be busy preparing for this evening's wedding."

This evening's wedding. Fabien continues giving commands to his servants, but those three words are all I hear. Yes, he asked me to marry him today. Yes, I agreed. I'd held out hope, however, that there would be a delay. If only I could have more time to adjust to the idea.

I look around the garden, like I'll find salvation in a hedge or flowering shrub if I search hard enough. My gaze lands on Luc, who's standing a few yards from me.

Like twin lodestones, his gray eyes capture me. I can't look away.

Affection, resignation, and grief saturate his gaze. I don't know what he sees in my expression, but it seems to light a fire in him. Passion ignites in his eyes, burning hot and bright.

It takes my breath away.

I'm aware of nothing else but Luc, the gardener-prince I love. The male who wooed me without trying, who accepted me unconditionally. I want him so badly, my chest feels as though it will break apart.

The beautiful, terrible moment is broken by a voice.

"Brother?" Fabien says.

And I know, from the dangerous undercurrent in his tone, he saw everything that just passed between Luc and me.

Fabien is no longer issuing orders. His attention is fixed solely on Luc, and it's the type of attention anyone with a sound mind would avoid. The crown prince is tall and broad, with muscles that his black tunic and trousers do little to hide. There's a rosy tinge to his pewter skin, evidence of the anger overtaking him.

He takes to the air, a weapon in Fae form, an arrow forged of flesh, blood, and anger. And he's targeting his brother.

I gasp and dash toward them, though I know I won't make it in time. If Fabien swings those strong fists at Luc, he could kill him.

I scream.

Fabien is about to slam into Luc when he jolts to a stop, hovering in the air. A quick glance at me, and then he grabs Luc's shoulders and hisses, "That kiss I saw you two share, it meant something. You love her."

To his credit, Luc doesn't pull away. He meets his brother's gaze, nods, and says, "I do. But Aeryn is free to make her own choice, and she's chosen you. I won't stand in her way."

Why does he have to be so kind? Does he realize how hard it's going to be to get over him? I shake my head and quietly mutter, "Damn it, Luc."

Or maybe I wasn't so quiet, because both brothers turn inquisitive gazes my way.

"Never mind," I mumble.

Fabien releases his brother's shoulders and lands on the grass, folding his wings against his back. "And you?" he asks me. "Do you love him?"

If he saw the truth in Luc's eyes, he must have seen it in mine too. I suspect he hopes I'll answer with a polite lie. I can't do that, though. Not if I want to stay true to myself.

I give Fabien a sad smile and whisper, "I do."

He stalks toward me, the muscles in his jaw flexing. At last, he stops in front of me and says, "I know I can give you the life you want. If you're truly willing to try to love me, I—"

Suddenly, there's an angry pixie between us. Jackie flew here so quickly, I didn't notice her until she arrived. Her purple wings are fluttering madly, and her hair is brighter and more flamelike than ever. Her back is to me, so I can't see her expression, but I hear the deep disappointment in the single word she speaks: "Fabien."

"Jackie?" he replies warily.

"I'm going to say something I should've said when you were a little boy. In fact, I should've said it a hundred times since then." She pulls in a deep breath. "You're vain, Fabien."

I can't see much of him beyond her wings, but I can tell he's crossing his arms. "You're the second female to tell me that today."

"I hoped a decade as a beast would've changed you," Jackie says. "It didn't, did it? Not enough, anyway. You're willing to take a woman away from the male she loves, because you're so certain anyone would be lucky to marry you."

"I—I'm going to help her family!" he sputters, sounding a bit like an insolent teenager. "I'm returning Felia's family's land—valuable land that I won fairly, I might add!"

Jackie's voice softens. "Those are both good things for you to do. They're good, important steps you can take whether or not she marries you." For several long moments, she examines him before whispering, "What kind of person do you want to be, Fabien?"

She flies away, leaving the raven-winged prince and me to stare at each other.

He steps closer and cups my cheeks in his warm hands. There's a yearning in his gaze, and somehow, I know it's not really for me. Fabien simply wants a partner. He wants to be cared for. He desires beauty and consistency and passion and all the other benefits of a good marriage.

For the first time, I'm seeing a deep part of his soul. Just a bit, a sliver of who he always was and still is, beneath the beastly body and the winged one. Beneath the wealth and power that are his birthright.

Fabien wants love, like all of us do. But I can't stop thinking about the question Jackie asked him: what kind of person does he want to be?

He opens his mouth to speak.

52

EVERY DAY OF YOUR LIFE

"I want to marry you," Fabien says in a low voice. "I *want* to, Aeryn." He sighs and drops his hands from my face. "But I can't. Not after seeing you kiss my brother. I can't go into a marriage with that memory fresh in my mind."

My jaw drops, and before I can stop myself, I'm shouting at him. "*That's* why you can't marry me? Because you don't want to think about me kissing someone else?" I advance on him. He steps back. I throw his ring at him, sneering when he catches it easily, and continue my tirade. "How many females did you kiss during this competition, *Tor*? For that matter, how many did you sleep with? I saw Rochelle leaving your room one morning!"

Fabien doesn't deny my accusation. He merely stares at me, his mouth formed into an O. The entire garden is quiet. I think even the birds have traded their twittering for eavesdropping.

Since no one else seems inclined to speak, I continue, "In what world is it right for a male to date ten females at once, while expecting all of them to be true to him? And if the answer is, *in the world of Faerie*, then please let me leave right now."

I wait for a response. When none comes, I snap, "Answer me! Are

338

females in Faerie expected to be faithful while males sow their wild oats?"

Fabien shakes his head. "No." He's so quiet, I can barely hear him. "It's not like that in Faerie."

A humorless laugh bursts from my mouth. "So it's only like that with you?"

His head drops for several seconds, and when his gaze returns to mine, there's fire in it. "Yes!" he roars.

I flinch but stand my ground.

Luc is at his brother's side in an instant, grabbing his arm. "Fabien! Enough!"

Fabien shakes him off, though his eyes remain locked on me. "I'm not going to hurt her, Luc. And I meant it when I said I can't marry her. But . . . I lied about why. Pardon me for trying to save face by pinning it on the relationship between the two of you. I wasn't ready to tell her—" He stops talking, pressing his lips together. There's a rosy tint to his pewter-colored skin. As unlikely as it seems, I think he's blushing.

"Tell me what?" I ask softly.

He swallows hard. "I can't marry you because everything you said about me is true, and everything Jackie and Cerise said about me is true, and, Aeryn . . . you deserve better."

All I can do is stare at him and think, *That's the kindest thing he's ever said to me.* A new feeling for him swells in my heart. I might even call it love, though not the romantic type. It's deeper affection than I've ever felt for him. And the change in his appearance has nothing to do with it. It's all about the softening of his heart.

"Will you still care for her family? And Felia's family?" Jackie demands.

Fabien's eyes remain on me. "My commitments to both families stand. They are not contingent on marriage to you, Aeryn."

All my breath exits my lungs in a long sigh, carrying with it years' worth of anxiety. My fears for my family dissipate into the cool air of Faerie.

"Say something," Fabien whispers.

I see the hope in his eyes. He knows releasing me from my commitment is the right thing to do, but part of him hopes I'll talk him out of it. I can't do that—to either of us. We both deserve better than a marriage between two people who aren't truly in love. So I give him a sad smile and say, "Thank you, Fabien."

He sighs, nods, and holds out a hand. Cocking my head curiously, I take it. He turns to his brother, who's still standing beside us, and places my hand in his.

I lace my fingers between Luc's and give Fabien a grateful smile.

"It's time for the servants and me to return to the castle," Fabien says. "The two of you are welcome to stay out here as long as you'd like."

As Jackie flutters by, she winks at me. Other than that, I'm mostly unaware of the faeries exiting the garden. My eyes are locked on Luc.

He doesn't speak, but his gaze is so eloquent, it surely qualifies as a poem. His expressive eyes, his curving lips, his arched brows—they come together to create whole stanzas full of hope and wonder.

I want to lift my chin and offer him my lips. I want to lose myself in him. But I can't, because . . .

"We have so much to discuss," I hear myself say.

"Let's sit," Luc says. When I nod, he leads me through the garden.

"It looks so strange without the statues," I murmur. "I suppose it's how you remember it—" My speech falters as I realize where he's leading me. "This is the bench where you first kissed me," I say as we sit.

"Not quite. Wyatt kissed you here."

I laugh. "It was always you, Luc. I just didn't know it yet."

He shakes his head, looking off into the distance. One of his hands is on my knee, his thumb idly rubbing across the fabric covering my skin. It feels way too good. Finally, he meets my gaze. His brows are pulled together.

"What is it?" I ask.

"Wyatt was a simple gardener who'd learned to be content with very little," Luc says softly. "He couldn't tell you much about who he was. Yes, he was me . . . but not all of me. When we stood in that hallway listening to Cerise and Tor, you heard the truth. She told you exactly who I am."

My gut twists as I recall her words. "She said you were selfish and power hungry."

A tiny smile tugs at his lips. "It's so kind of you not to remember her last descriptor: 'a real ass.' "

I allow myself to smile too. "Yes, there was that." I grab the hand on my knee and hold it tightly. "I also seem to remember Cerise saying that, after she cursed you, you'd probably 'found humility rather than humiliation.' And she was right. You're Luc, but you're not the male you were ten years ago. Wyatt took over your heart."

He yanks his hand away and runs it through his wavy brown hair. "Sure, that's what you've seen in me. But what will happen now that I'm back to my princely life? You didn't know me back then. I hated being the younger son, so I was determined to show everyone I was the stronger one, the one capable of building fortunes for our family and myself. I was working to become a powerful merchant, and I didn't care who I hurt along the way. Cerise's description of me was generous, Aeryn. In reality, I was worse. I'm only glad she cursed me when she did, before I was old enough to do much real harm. And part of me . . ." He trails off.

"What?" I whisper.

"Part of me was glad when she said that even if I won the challenge, I would remain in my cursed form. Because I'd learned to trust myself as Wyatt. I can't trust myself as Luc." He stands and turns his back to me, but his words are as clear as the cerulean sky above us. "You deserve someone better than a cruel, selfish prince."

Several seconds pass before I say, "You're right."

His shoulders tighten.

I rise and cross to him. Standing directly in front of him, I remain silent until his stubborn, tortured gaze meets mine.

"You're right," I repeat softly. "I want someone better than the Luc who was cursed ten years ago. I'm looking for a partner who's learned from his mistakes. Someone who chooses to be selfless and loving, even when it's hard."

He opens his mouth, but my glare must be potent, because he doesn't speak a word.

"I want *you*," I say. "The Luc who learned from his curse, who developed a generous heart. That's who you are today. Money and power won't change that."

"You can't be sure," he says in a tight, low voice.

"I can't be sure the sun won't burn out either. But I choose to trust it, just as I choose to trust you."

"Why?"

"Because you've shown me who you are. I trust you because you're caring and respectful, Luc. Because you're a protector."

He blinks but doesn't say a word.

"Because I love you," I add. My voice is strong, almost defiant. I stare into his eyes, unblinking, daring him to convince me otherwise.

Luc reaches out, grabs my waist, and pulls me tightly to him. Then his mouth is on mine, warm and urgent.

As I kiss him back, my lips part to release a sigh. His tongue slips into my mouth, accompanied by a low groan that nearly makes my knees buckle. As his full lips move against mine, I know I'll never get enough of them. He kisses like the gardener I fell for, but he tastes different—like the sea and the wind, flavors full of adventure and life. I can't stop devouring him, inhaling his breath into my lungs, moaning into his mouth.

His lips brush along my jaw, then find my ear, where he whispers two words.

"Marry me."

I gasp, meet his gaze, and say the only thing I can think of. "Are you sure you love me?" He said he did before my fight with Cerise, but I need to hear it now, when he's clear-headed and isn't afraid I'm about to die.

Luc laughs. The rumble of it against my breasts almost makes me not care what his response is. *Almost.*

"Aeryn." He places kisses on my eyes, my cheeks, my chin. "I love"—more kisses, to my neck and nose and collarbone—"all the parts of you I know." A kiss to the back of my hand and a softer, slower one to my palm. "All the parts of you I've touched." He takes both my hands, steps back, and lets his gray eyes wander over me.

The skin beneath my clothing comes alive in the path of his gaze. He smiles, like he knows just what he's doing to me, and says, "And I love all the parts of you I don't know yet. Please let me spend every day of your life knowing you more and loving you better."

I would say yes—I'd shout my acceptance joyfully—if it weren't for two short words he spoke that pierced my mind, lodging there like thorns.

Your life.

He said he'll love me every day of *my* life, not *his* life. Because even if I'm part Fae, I'm still mortal. I'll die thousands of years before Luc transitions into his eternal form.

At some point, as I considered marrying Tor, I pushed thoughts of my mortality to the back of my mind. I could do such a thing, because I didn't truly love him.

But Luc? The male I love? Well, I'm standing mere inches away from him, but I don't see him. My mind is too full of the image I saw in a book weeks ago, of a strong, virile faerie sitting at the bedside of his elderly mortal wife.

That image felt terribly real the first time I saw it. It's even more real now, with Luc's proposal hovering between us. The male in the picture was utterly heartbroken. And I'm suddenly certain of one thing: I can't put someone I love in that position.

"Oh, Luc," is all I get out before I release his hands and sprint away from him.

I run straight for the castle, because when I'm this upset, all I want is to throw myself on a comfortable bed and have a good cry. But as soon as I burst inside, I nearly run into a smiling, purple-winged pixie hovering in the hallway.

"Oh good, I was hoping you'd come in soon!" Jackie chirps. Her cheerfulness shouldn't make me angry, not after all she's done for me, but, well . . . I kind of want to punch her.

I snap, "It's not a good time." To my horror, my firm statement ends with a sob.

She purses her tiny lips and gives me her best *governess glare.* "Good time or not, dear, you and I are going to speak. I need to tell you who you are."

53

A MARVELOUS VARIETY OF HAIRDOS

When I hear Jackie's words, I go still, except for the heaving of my chest as I recover from my sprint. There are no more sobs; I'm too shocked for that.

The door opens behind me. "Whoa!" Luc says as he halts, bumping lightly into me. "Sorry."

I don't reply. My focus is locked on Jackie. "Who am I?" I demand.

"Would you like to go somewhere private, sweetie?"

"No." I don't even have to consider it. No matter what my future holds with Luc, I trust him with whatever information Jackie's about to share.

"Well, then." The pixie gives me a hesitant smile. "You are Aeryn, the daughter of two humans."

"But I have magic! When we first met, you told me I wouldn't have even seen you in the mirror if I didn't have Fae blood. One of my parents must be part Fae."

"And yet they aren't."

"How do you know?"

Bits and pieces of my own dreams flash through my mind. A faerie with raven wings. Another with bronze skin. Dancing and kissing and more. I shake my head to dislodge the memories. *Focus, Aeryn.*

"Magical dreams?" I ask.

"Yes. I'm too young for dream magic, and I doubt I'll continue to experience it now that I've returned to my true form. As a serpent, I lost most of my other powers, but I began having vivid, magical dreams every single night. Nearly all of them were about you."

I'm suddenly very aware of Luc's warm body behind me, and I'm filled with the same despair that sent me running away from him in the garden. If I'm entirely human, I'll be lucky to live eighty years. That's little more than the blink of an eye to an immortal like Luc.

Jackie's tiny hands grip my shoulders. She shakes me harder than I'd have thought her capable of, considering her size. "Stay with me, Aeryn," she commands. "Don't lose hope. Yes, in my dreams, I saw your past, or, more specifically, your family's past. I observed dozens of generations of your ancestors. They were all human, no Fae to be seen. But I also saw your future."

Again, the image from the book imprints itself on my mind. *Old, dying woman. Young, heartbroken Fae male.* That's the only future I could look forward to if I married Luc. I squeeze my eyes shut and almost miss Jackie's next words:

"Thousands of years of your future, in fact."

My eyes pop open. "You mean my descendants?"

Her hands give my shoulders a little squeeze. "No, my dear. I mean *you.* I saw you living for thousands of years, looking just as you do now, though you had a marvelous variety of hairdos over the eons."

When I smile tentatively, she continues, "I watched you do magical feats, and I saw—" Her eyes flit behind me, and she releases a delighted laugh. "I saw a great number of wonderful things, but I won't share them. Your life should be lived, not anticipated."

I laugh too, though mine sounds almost hysterical. This is so much to take in.

Jackie releases my shoulders. Her expression turns somber. "I saw difficult times as well, for life always includes both. But there was more joy than grief." She smiles again. "Breathe deeply, Aeryn. You'll make yourself faint."

What she's telling me should be enough, but I've always craved knowledge. That doesn't change now that it's knowledge about myself. After I've followed her advice and calmed my breaths, I ask, "And at the end of those thousands of years?"

"Transition," she says.

"Like the Fae?"

"Precisely. You'll go to the very same spirit realm."

My mind is so full, all I can do is stare at the flame-haired pixie. I'm unspeakably relieved when Luc steps up beside me and asks, "So . . . what is she?"

Jackie draws in a deep breath as she looks thoughtfully to the ceiling. Then she turns back to us. "I had one recurring dream that wasn't about Aeryn. I saw a distant past on Earth, so long ago that the humans were of an earlier form, more primitive than the people now on Earth. I watched as children were born to a dozen mothers, all within the same generation. These children had pointed ears and magical abilities."

Luc says quietly, "You used to tell me legends about the Fae race being an offshoot of the human race. You're saying those stories are true?"

She nods. "I saw these children grow up and find each other. They used their combined magic to access the hidden reality that we now refer to as 'the middle region of air.' They created the land of Faerie, where we are now. From these twelve magical beings, the entire Fae race was born."

"Are you saying I'm Fae?" I ask.

"I'm saying I'm not entirely sure what you are, child. You have no pointed ears. You developed dream magic at a young age, which doesn't generally happen. Also, you've shown an affinity for all types of magic, rather than just one. And the magical shield you created? Well, I've never seen its like.

"I wouldn't call you Fae, though you are similar enough that when we met, I genuinely believed you had Fae blood. You are an immortal, magical being born of two humans, just as the first faeries were. As far as I know, you're one of a kind, though you may discover more individuals who are like you. One day, perhaps you'll settle on a descriptor that suits you, just as the first generation of faeries did."

I almost ask her how much magic I have, but I swallow the question. She wouldn't answer it. She wants me to discover my own future.

The other reason I don't ask is because *it doesn't matter*. Yes, I'll enjoy exploring my magic. But I realized when I faced Cerise that it's not my magic that makes me who I am. It's my mind. And something tells me that in the decades—and centuries and millennia—to come, I'll depend more on my trusty mind than on any magic.

I must, however, ask Jackie something far more important. A question I need an answer to, though I'm not sure I want it.

"If I'm the only—the only *whatever* I am, does that mean I shouldn't marry?"

I hold my breath and studiously avoid looking at Luc as I await Jackie's response.

Her green eyes twinkle. "My dear, marry the one you love. My dreams tell me such a path will not steer you wrong." She flies right up to me, cups her hands around my ear, and whispers so only I can hear, "And yes, you can mate successfully with a faerie. In case you were wondering."

Heat blooms in my cheeks and neck. I *was* wondering, but I wasn't sure how to ask. I glance at Luc. His raised eyebrow and tiny smirk tell me my blush hasn't gone unnoticed.

I return my attention to Jackie—but she's at the end of the hallway, flying away from us. She rounds a corner without a backward glance.

"Aeryn," Luc says.

I turn to find him kneeling next to me.

"We can spend our entire lives together," he says. "We can spend *eternity* together. So I'd like to ask you the question I asked before. Will you—"

I throw myself at him. My speed is no match for his Fae reflexes. He catches me and, in a single graceful move, sits on the marble floor, pulling me onto his lap. I kiss him, burying my hands in his wavy hair.

He breaks the kiss to ask, "Was that an answer?"

I laugh. "It was a *yes*. An enthusiastic one."

He gazes into my eyes for a long moment before saying, "You know, I spent ten years learning to be patient, and I don't think I'll lose that quality. But I couldn't be more certain that I want to spend my life with you—my entire life. And, Aeryn, I don't want to wait."

I blink. "What are you saying?"

A hint of mischief colors his grin. "If you don't have any other plans, would you like to get married today?"

54

NOW AND FOREVER

"You want to marry me today?" I croak.

"Or later . . . or not at all, if you've changed your mind."

I can see how the words pain him. "I won't change my mind!" I assure him. "But my family, Luc. I can't imagine them not being here to witness it." It occurs to me, I didn't even consider my family when I agreed to immediately marry Tor. Love makes all the difference, in so many ways.

"Of course! We'll wait until we can bring them here." Luc's immediate consideration for my needs sends warmth into my chest. He arches an eyebrow. "Now, as comfortable as this floor is"—we both laugh at that—"would you like to see my chambers?"

"Of course." I tilt my head. "Where *do* you live, anyway?"

"I'm going to take you to my rooms here in this castle, but I haven't been inside them in ten years. I've been living in the same hidden house where the eliminated contestants stayed."

"Why?"

"Fabien and I were both . . . unhappy after the curse. He was angry, and I was filled with despair. I thought if we both had time alone, we might settle into our new forms and learn to make the most of our cursed lives. So I moved out.

"Occasionally, we spoke. I always encouraged him to embrace his new existence, and he never took that well. We eventually reached the point where we hardly saw each other at all.

"As the years passed, the castle grew quiet. Fabien was no longer roaring in anger. I hoped that meant he'd become more content, as I had. But by then, our relationship didn't seem salvageable." Luc gives me a sad smile. "Now that the curse is broken, I'm ready for a new start. I hope Fabien feels the same. Regardless, it's time to reclaim my chambers."

We both stand, then walk hand in hand through the castle. When we encounter Jackie, Luc tells her we'll be getting married as soon as we can bring my family to Faerie to witness it. Her squeal of delight is so shrill and loud, I'm certain everyone in the castle hears it.

When Luc opens the plain wooden door of his chambers, we see two servants inside. They've dusted and are just finishing changing the linens on his bed. Luc thanks them for anticipating his needs, and we wait in the hallway until they finish.

When they're gone, we enter his sitting room. It's nothing like any house I've lived in, yet somehow, I feel perfectly at home. Translucent drapes over a large window filter the sunlight. Framed botanical drawings bring brightness to the cream-colored walls. The room's dark wooden trim matches the wood of the bed and dresser. Even the floor is warm wood, instead of the marble that covers most of the castle's floors.

Two deep-green upholstered chairs sit before a roaring fireplace, and there's another cozy sitting area beside the window. I spy Luc's bedroom through one doorway. Linens in various ocean hues cover his bed. Another doorway leads to an inviting bathroom with pale blue walls.

A contented sigh exits my mouth.

"Do you like it?" Luc asks.

"I love it," I reply, turning to him. "I could cozy up in one of those chairs by the fire with a cup of tea and a book, and I wouldn't want to move for a full week." A step brings me close enough to feel his warmth. "Or, even better, cozy up in that bed with you. Problem is, even a week won't be long enough there. I'll never want to leave." It's a bold thing to say, but this time, I don't blush.

He kisses me, slow and sweet. Then we sit in the chairs before the fire. He does most of the talking, telling me stories he wasn't free to share before, all about his life before the curse. He doesn't shy away from describing how he became more and more selfish as he grew up. I point out the hints of goodness he held onto, even then—the seeds of the character he chose to cultivate over the last decade.

At some point, Luc goes to the kitchen and returns with a picnic, which we eat on a rug on the floor. We hold hands and cuddle, and we share a few kisses, though mostly, we continue conversing. We can't get enough of each other's words. But I see his gaze flit to the bedroom when he thinks I'm not looking, and I'm pretty sure he catches me doing the same.

Will I stay here tonight?

Dusk falls, and with a word and a gesture, Luc creates dancing amber flames in sconces throughout the room. He's leaning in to kiss me when someone knocks on the door. Luc rises to answer it.

"You must be the faerie who won my daughter's heart," a man says as soon as the door swings open.

"Daddy!" I cry, leaping to my feet. A moment later, I'm in his arms. His grip on me is tight enough to steal my breath, but I'm not complaining.

"That purple-winged pixie brought us here," he murmurs against my hair. "The one who saved my life."

When he releases me, I see, through tear-filled eyes, that my brother and both my sisters are in the hallway. We greet each other warmly. They all look hale and happy, with new clothes and a bit of meat on their bones. As promised, Jackie ensured they were cared for while I was gone.

Luc invites my family in. My father is limping a bit, but his leg seems to be healing nicely from its break. His cheeks aren't flushed as they would be if he'd been drinking. While I'm not optimistic enough to think he's stopped, I'm grateful he's sober right now.

Luc and I give my family a brief rundown of what's happened over the past forty days, though neither of us mentions my magic nor my immortality. I'm still trying to wrap my mind around what Jackie told me, and I'm not sure how to share it with my human family. When Luc and I speak of our love for one another, I don't know how to read the expression in my father's eyes.

My father insists on speaking with Luc alone. That sends my heartbeat into a gallop, but I try to hide my worries with a smile as I lead my siblings into the hallway.

When we return after an hour-long tour of the castle, I knock on Luc's door, wishing I could hear voices through it—anything to give me a sense of how his conversation with my father might've gone. Luc opens the door. The blank expression on his face tells me nothing.

"May we come in?" I ask softly.

He nods and ushers me and my siblings into the room.

My father is settled in one of the chairs before the fire. I sit in the other. Gaze fixed on the flames, he says quietly, "This man—ahem, male—tells me you're a magical creature. An immortal."

Behind me, my siblings gasp.

"Yes," I say.

"He also told me he wants to marry you."

"What was your response?"

"I told him you have better judgment than anyone else in our family. If you love him . . ." At last, my father turns to me. His eyes are dancing with joy. "Then he must be a good male. You don't need my permission to marry, Aeryn, but you have my blessing."

I throw my arms around him and whisper in his ear, "How do you feel about us getting married tonight?"

His laughter vibrates through me. One more squeeze, then he releases me and stands. His voice booms through the room. "Luc, this daughter of mine tells me she'd like to marry you tonight. It may be the single most spontaneous thing she's ever wanted to do." He turns to me again. "I won't stand in your way."

I turn to find Luc watching me, joyful hope filling his smile.

"Let's have a wedding," I say. "Tonight."

55

BLISS

Magic makes it easy to prepare for a wedding.

We spend the evening setting up in the ballroom. Luc uses nature magic to fill the room with greenery and brightly colored flowers. Many of the blooms add their gentle, luminescent glow to the light cast by magical lanterns and chandeliers. Luc and I combine our magic to create a bower of beautifully braided vines, branches, and stems, all covered in flowers. We'll stand under it when it's time to say our vows.

My father and siblings help us, along with Jackie and the castle servants. Soon, the ballroom is breathtaking. Silky fabrics drape across the walls and hang from the ceiling. Jewels of all sizes and colors hover in the air, held there by a maid's magic. Tables overflow with more food than we'll ever eat.

Fabien is the only one who hasn't joined us, and I can't begrudge him his need for privacy. I certainly wouldn't want to watch my sibling marry someone I'd been courting.

Luc and I are standing in the middle of the room, hands clasped, when I hear a familiar voice call, "Aeryn!"

I turn to see Justyne running toward me, along with Desiree

Felia, and Harmonie. They all hug me at once, and it's not until they've pulled away, chattering excitedly, that I see who brought them here: Fabien. He's standing in the doorway, wearing a wistful smile as he watches our reunion.

I pull away from my friends and whisper something to Luc. He nods and calls to his brother. As Fabien approaches, Luc says, "If you'd like to be part of the ceremony in any way, we'd welcome that."

Fabien swallows hard, then nods. "I'd be happy to perform it."

My eyes widen at that, as do Luc's. Neither of us expected him to play such an active role. Luc smiles and shakes his brother's hand in appreciation.

They've spent ten years cultivating distance in their relationship. I hope they're ready to grow closer, starting today.

"What we need," Desiree says, "is music!"

She and I run off to hunt down the stringed instruments that Rochelle stole from me during the revel challenge. We set them up in a corner, and I bless them with the ability to play on their own. Gorgeous, complex Fae music fills the room. It's at times mysterious, at times celebratory, and always romantic. My brother, who's the musical one in our family, watches the instruments with wide eyes and a slack jaw.

A few minutes later, I slip away, along with Jackie, my contestant friends, and my sisters. In my bedroom, the house's magic creates gowns for all of us. My sisters can't contain their shock. Brigitte says her corset is so comfortable, she may never take it off. And Yvonne cries when she looks down at herself, outfitted in a gorgeous green dress that fits perfectly.

I ask the house for a cream-colored gown. Unlike Brigitte, I've discovered the freedom of not wearing a corset, so I specify that I'd like less restrictive underthings. The dress awaiting me in one of the wardrobes is simple and stunning, made of the softest silk. It has a square neckline, a snug waist, and a skirt that flows like water before ending in a small train. Comfortable slippers in a pale golden fabric ensure I'll be able to dance for hours.

My friends braid small sections of my strawberry-blonde hair, weaving them around my head in gorgeous, intricate designs. The rest of my hair falls down my back in gentle waves.

Jackie flits away, then returns with a bouquet of the fragrant purple roses that she first used to draw me here. Holding them, I approach the mirror that's been facing the wall since shortly after my arrival. I doubt Cerise is spying on me now—and if she is, I don't care. With Felia's help, I turn the mirror around. Standing in front of it, all I can do is beam.

"You're radiant," my sister Brigitte whispers.

I can't deny the truth of it. And it's not due to the dress, flowers, or hairstyle. I'm radiant because I've never been as happy as I am right now.

It's nearly midnight when we return to the ballroom. The doors are closed, so I open them just enough to peek through. Luc is awaiting me under the bower. His suit is the deep brown hue of fine wood. It's beautiful against his bronze skin, as is the dark green shirt beneath his jacket. Anticipation lights up his gray eyes.

Most would say it's Fabien who was blessed with classic handsomeness. But that look in Luc's eyes, the way his lips are parted as he waits for me . . . he's luminous. Perfect. It's like he was made for me.

My friends and sisters enter the ballroom to sit with the other guests—my brother, my father, and the servants.

I considered asking my father to give me away. But when I mentioned it to Luc earlier today, he stared at me, true confusion in his eyes. "I've never heard of that human tradition. You want your father to give you to me? He doesn't own you. You belong to yourself, both now and after the wedding."

As I stand at the ballroom doors, I'm glad I'm doing this the Fae way. For two years, my entire identity was wrapped up in who I was to my family. Forager. Hunter. Provider. More often than not, we went hungry, and I felt like a failure.

Now, my life is my own again. Yes, I'm a daughter and a sibling, and soon, I'll be a wife. But most importantly, I'm *me*.

Luc was right. No one owns me. No one needs to give me away.

I draw in a calming breath as I step back from the doors. I'm in the mood for a dramatic entrance. "House," I whisper, "want to open those doors for me?"

As the doors swing smoothly open to reveal me to the room, the collective gasp makes me laugh with joy. I begin my walk down the aisle. My gaze finds Luc, and I can't take my eyes off his smiling lips. When I arrive at his side and see the glaze of tears in his eyes, I have to blink away a few of my own.

Fabien leads us through our vows. It turns out Fae marriage ceremonies aren't all that different from human ones. But I treasure a couple of promises I'd never be prompted to say at a human wedding:

"I shall be true to you for all eternity, in any and every realm."

"I choose to join myself with you. My body. My soul. My magic."

The words feel right on my tongue, and when Luc speaks them, they settle deep inside my soul.

I didn't think to find or create a wedding ring for Luc, but I'm delighted when he pulls out a gold band. A pale blue, round gemstone is attached to it with delicate prongs. It's exactly what I would've chosen for myself. Luc slips it on, whispering that it matches my eyes.

"As crown prince of this Fae kingdom," Fabien says, "I declare that you, Aeryn and Luc, are married, now and forever."

Luc pulls me close and kisses me. We only cut it short because hoots and hollers fill the room, making us laugh.

We turn to face the small crowd. Flower petals of all colors rain down on us—a lovely spell that someone decided to surprise us with. Justyne, who has nature magic, is wearing a suspiciously wide grin. Luc and I kiss again as petals land in our hair and on our shoulders. One even gets smashed between our noses.

The magical music picks up in volume and tempo, and an exhilarating after-wedding party begins. For hours, we dance, eat, drink, and laugh. There are many toasts and even more calls for the newlyweds to kiss. So much joy fills the room, I honestly believe I can taste its sweetness in the air.

At almost four in the morning, the instruments are playing a slow song. My father and some of the older servants went to bed an hour ago, and many who are left are too tired to dance. Luc and I hold each other close as we sway to the music. We laugh softly when Justyne and Desiree, who danced all night and are now cuddled on a couch together, yawn in unison.

As the song ends, Luc catches my eye. He arches one fine brow and slightly inclines his head toward the door. I nod, and we weave our fingers together and leave the ballroom quietly, without bidding anyone goodnight.

"Our chambers?" he whispers as soon as the ballroom doors close behind us.

A slow smile overtakes my mouth. "*Our* chambers," I confirm.

By the time Luc opens the simple wooden door leading to our rooms, my heart is pounding so hard, I wonder if he can hear it.

He lifts me into his arms, laughing when I squeal. "I've heard this is a human tradition," he says.

I place a hand on his chest. His heart is beating as fervently as mine. "Carry me over the threshold," I whisper.

He does. When he closes the door behind us, he doesn't put me down immediately, choosing instead to lower his head until his lips find mine. The kiss is sweet and full of restrained heat. When I open my mouth, he accepts the invitation, sweeping his tongue in. I don't know how long we're in that position, him holding me, our lips pressed together, tongues twining, tasting each other's desire.

His mouth moves to my neck. Breathlessly, I whisper, "Please don't tell me you want a demure, hesitant bride."

He laughs against my pounding pulse. "Never."

"Oh, good. Because I've never wanted anything as much as I want you."

He puts me down. I almost protest the sudden distance between us, until he spins me around and begins unfastening the buttons on the back of my dress. There are dozens of them, and the minutes pass in sweet torture as his hands travel slowly down my back, his nimble fingers brushing my spine over and over. By the time he finishes, my entire body is tingling with desire so sharp, it's almost painful.

Luc gently nudges the dress off my shoulders. It drops into a silky puddle at my feet. I'm wearing nothing but the lacy underthings the house provided for me. I've never been so exposed before a man or male, but when I turn to face him, I feel no shame. This is who I am, and I know Luc will love every line, every curve.

His gray eyes darken with appreciation as they rove over me.

"Your turn," I say. We're both silent as I help Luc out of his shoes and socks, then his jacket, shirt and pants. He's slender, with sleek muscles that create fascinating shadows across his bronze skin. This male I've married . . . he's nothing short of stunning.

We reach for one another to strip away the last bits of fabric hiding our most secret places. When excitement makes our fingers clumsy, we share a laugh. Soon, we're both bare. We stand there, our gazes roaming freely over each other. All we're doing is looking, but I grow lightheaded as my breaths come quicker than ever.

"Aeryn." It's more a breath than a word, and it's coupled with sudden, urgent movement—Luc's arms reaching for me, his mouth slamming into mine, his hands sliding over my skin. I moan into his mouth, my own hands wandering with as much urgency as his.

Without pausing our exploration of each other, we somehow make our way through the sitting room and into the bedroom. Together, we fall onto the soft blue coverlet.

"So beautiful," Luc breathes before his mouth leaves mine to begin its eager navigation over the curves and planes of my body. The press of his lips, the glide of his tongue, the touch of his fingers—they all draw sounds of wordless appreciation from my throat. When my pleasure at last reaches a glorious peak, he devours my cry with his warm, hungry mouth.

Luc holds himself over me, and at my urging, he joins his body with mine. I'm more than ready for him. There's no real pain, only a bit of discomfort that's quickly swallowed by renewed bliss. We find a beautiful rhythm, and I don't know if I'm giving more or taking more —I just know this feels more *right* than anything I've ever experienced. I nearly cry with joy watching the rapture on Luc's face as he finds his own release.

He settles on the bed and draws me into his side, nudging my head until it's resting on his chest. When my breaths have slowed and my heart has calmed, I trace my fingertips over his skin and whisper, "I dreamed of this, Luc."

He laughs quietly. It's a sound I never want to stop hearing. "I've had such dreams too. I've wanted you since the first time we met, you know—though I tried my best to convince myself otherwise."

I smile, then say, "I know my dreams are prophetic, but the particular one I'm referencing wasn't accurate."

"No?"

I cuddle closer, draping my leg over his. "Reality," I say, "is so much better."

56

IF YOU'RE WILLING

The day after our wedding, it's mid-afternoon by the time Luc and I venture from our chambers. We tried to rise in time for lunch, but when we woke, we ended up distracting each other—in the best of ways.

The moment we enter the hallway, we hear unfamiliar voices downstairs. We descend to the castle's lavish foyer, where groups of faeries are standing around, chatting and laughing.

Luc beckons to a green-haired male wearing servant's livery. The faerie rushes over and speaks before Luc has the chance to. "Your Highness, soon after the estate returned to Faerie, people from the area began attempting to enter the property. Prince Fabien stationed servants on the border to tell all visitors to wait until tomorrow. And, well"—he gestures at the full foyer—"here they are. Your brother has been busy meeting with his subjects in his study since early this morning."

"Has Fabien had a chance to eat?" Luc asks.

The servant's brows furrow. "I don't believe so."

"We'll make sure he does," Luc says.

By the time the conversation is over, several faeries are standing nearby, waiting to speak with Luc. They all have questions about the events of the last ten years. He greets each of them by name, introduces me proudly, and promises they'll have answers soon.

We hurry to the kitchen, where the blue-haired chef is cooking and baking with joyful abandon. He tells us he already fed the servants and guests but confirms that Prince Fabien has taken no breaks. Luc says he'll receive guests for a while so his brother can eat. The chef insists Luc and I eat first, and we quickly comply before navigating through the hallways to a room I've never seen—Fabien's study.

It's spacious, and the décor is similar to that in Fabien's room. His entire desk is gold, and there's gilded trim on the rest of the furniture. Everything is finely crafted . . . yet I silently ponder, once again, how little his tastes suit me.

Fabien's blue eyes are red-rimmed and full of exhausted anxiety as he speaks with two faerie subjects who are sitting before his desk. I can't imagine the pressure he must be under, returning to a kingdom that has been leaderless for a decade. When Luc offers to meet with subjects so Fabien can get some food, Fabien's broad shoulders droop in relief. He quickly exits.

I make my way to a corner of the room, ready to observe my new husband carrying out his princely duties. But instead of sitting behind the desk, Luc brings another chair over, positioning it right next to his brother's empty chair. Smiling, he beckons me to sit.

I'd rather stay where I am. Luc is the leader here, not me. I don't even understand Fae culture. It wouldn't be polite to refuse Luc before his subjects, however, so I sit next to him.

Luc greets the faeries by name, then takes my hand. "This is my wife, Princess Aeryn." The pleasure in his voice warms my heart. And the title—*Princess*—well, I don't know what to think about it, but I like how it sounds coming from his lips.

I see the curiosity in the faeries' eyes, but they jump straight into the topic they came here to talk about—a dispute over a small piece of land they each claim is part of their farm.

Luc patiently gathers information, asking quiet, insightful questions. When the faeries get angry at one another, Luc's demeanor quickly calms them. After an extended conversation, we've heard enough facts that I'm confident I can predict what Luc's response will be.

Instead of announcing his judgment, he turns to me. "What do you think, Your Highness?"

I blink at him in shock, then pull myself together and share my opinion. Luc nods and tells the faeries he agrees with me. They're both dissatisfied with the compromise, but my heart tells me it's fair.

I don't realize until the faeries are leaving that at some point, Fabien returned to the room. He's standing by the door, silently watching. When Luc and I rise so he can return to his position behind the desk, he merely nods before taking his seat.

A servant enters. Luc and I are about to leave, but the servant holds up a hand. "I think you'll want to stay for this, Prince Luc."

"Very well. The princess will stay with me."

The servant nods and ushers in the next visitor. He's a pixie, a little smaller than Jackie. His fluttering wings are made of gray feathers, and his hair and skin are pale green. He lands on a chair in front of the desk, standing on it instead of sitting.

"Your Majesty. Your Highness," he says to Fabien and Luc in a voice that's lower than I'd have expected, "early this morning, word was sent to your parents, informing them that the curse on you and on this estate was broken. When they heard the news, they chose to transition to their spirit forms." He pauses to pull in a deep breath. "Prince Fabien, you will at last be crowned king."

Fabien's mouth drops open. Long seconds pass, and I come to the conclusion that he's not going to speak at all. But finally, he says in a strained voice, "Thank you. You may go. Please instruct the servant outside to send all visitors home. They may return tomorrow."

The pixie nods and flutters away.

When the door closes again, Fabien brings his weary eyes to his brother and me. "Please sit." We do, but Fabien again allows the silence in the room to linger. At last, he speaks to Luc. "You did well with that dispute." His eyes find mine. "As did you."

There's regret in his gaze, and I suspect he's thinking about how different this day would be if I were at his side instead of his brother's. He doesn't say that aloud, though. Instead, he turns back to Luc and says four words that steal my breath:

"I cannot be king."

"Brother," Luc says softly, "you can. In a sense, you *are*—it may be months before the official coronation, but you became prince regent the moment our parents left for the spirit realm. You hold all the authority of a king. You were raised to rule. All you must do is listen to the better parts of yourself. You will become a very good king, if you're willing to."

"I . . ." Fabien looks off to the side, shaking his head. He turns those bright blue eyes back on his brother. "Yes, perhaps I could *become* a good king. But it would take time, and after ten years making do on their own, our people need a good leader *now*." He laughs, but it's self-deprecating, free of any real humor. "If I'd spent that decade improving myself, I'd be ready to lead now. Instead, I wasted my time with anger and arrogance."

I give him a sad smile. I won't argue with his assessment of who he was under the curse, but I hope he realizes how much potential for good his heart holds.

"Luc," Fabien says, "you'll be crowned king in my place. If you're willing."

Luc's throat throbs with a hard swallow. "You're abdicating?"

"If you're willing," Fabien repeats.

Luc opens his mouth as if to argue. Then calm acceptance fills his gray eyes, and his mouth shuts. He turns to me. Words aren't necessary; I know the question he's asking: *Are you willing to be queen?*

I could shake my head *no*, and he'd accept my response without question. He's always encouraged me to be myself. If I don't want to wear an unexpected crown, he'll respect that.

But I know Fabien is right. He's not ready for power. He needs time to learn who he truly is. To become the person he wants to be. Luc, however—the prince who spent ten years protecting servants who were trapped in stone—is ready to lead with wisdom and humility.

And while I know nothing about being a queen, I'm certain I can fulfill my duties with Luc at my side.

I nod once.

My husband turns back to his brother. "We're willing."

EPILOGUE

PURPLE ROSE PETALS

The morning of the coronation, I wake to find dawn light filtering through the drapes. I lay my head on Luc's chest, and he stirs, drawing his arms around me and pressing a kiss to my hair.

It's been four months since our wedding. Waking next to him hasn't lost a bit of its thrill.

"We should get some breakfast," he murmurs. "There's a lot to do before the ceremony."

My hand wanders over his body. "But this is the last chance I'll ever have to bed a prince."

He's wide awake now, and the grin he gives me is more than a little wicked. "I can't rob you of that opportunity," he says, reaching down to tug at the hem of my nightgown.

After hours of assisting with final preparations, we're outside, standing in the same open area of the garden where Cerise cursed Fabien and where, ten years later, I broke that curse.

Hundreds of Fae surround us, spilling out of the garden and onto the lawn. Many of them are our subjects, but others have come from various kingdoms throughout Faerie. It's for their sake that we waited four months for the coronation. Powerful, influential individuals tend to be quite busy.

My father and siblings are present, as are Justyne, Desiree, Felia, and Harmonie. As thrilled as I am to have them here, I'm just as happy about the faces I don't see, specifically Rochelle's, Margot's and Cerise's. Since the day they left, they haven't done a thing to interfere with the running of our kingdom.

The same day Fabien told us he wanted to abdicate, Luc and I were declared the prince regent and princess regent. We've had all the powers of a king and queen, but today, we'll officially be crowned.

Fabien agreed to conduct the coronation ceremony, and our subjects seem relieved to see their former leader in perfect health. Over the last four months, we've heard some truly hilarious rumors about why Fabien abdicated. (My favorite involved him turning into a flesh-eating beast who was threatening to devour his subjects. The story had just enough truth in it—and just enough provocative false-hood—to spread widely.) By crowning his brother, Fabien is proving he's of sound mind and made this decision willingly.

Currently, he's in the middle of a long speech about the history of the kingdom and his hopes for its future. His handsome face and dynamic speaking ability have captured everyone's attention. Well, everyone except me. I can't seem to keep my eyes off my husband, who's resplendent in a tailored blue suit. It's the same shade his skin was when he was Wyatt, the gardener I fell in love with.

Finally, a word from Fabien's mouth catches my attention: *chil-dren.* I fix my gaze on him as he continues, "And if our monarchs are so blessed, I know they will teach their offspring the skills they need to lead this kingdom into greater prosperity in the millennia to come."

If is the operative word. Faeries often find it difficult to conceive. Fabien and Luc's parents were old by the time their sons were born.

But I'm not a faerie. I'm something else—something I still don't have a name for.

And I have a secret I haven't shared with anyone.

Without meaning to, I bring my hand to my abdomen. As soon as I'm aware of the movement, I drop my hand, then lift my gaze to Luc to be sure he didn't notice.

He's watching me with wide eyes that are full of hope and cautious happiness.

I release a small sigh. I had well-laid plans for telling my husband the good news. We'd go to this garden at night, just the two of us. Sitting amongst the luminescent flowers, I'd tell him of our growing family, using words I've practiced a dozen times. The chef and I even discussed what should go into a midnight picnic basket.

But seeing the look on my husband's face, I can't hold back. So I nod as a grin tugs at my mouth.

Luc gives me a smile that's full of thrilled joy, and I know if we weren't surrounded by people, he'd be shouting at the top of his lungs. He takes my hand, sliding my fingers between his. The press of his warm palm against mine sends contentment through my body.

Fabien finishes speaking. He turns to face his brother and me as two servants approach, carrying golden crowns.

Luc and I kneel, hands still clasped. Our knees press into purple rose petals that Jackie scattered here before the ceremony. The air fills with the scent of the flowers that brought me here, a fragrance bursting with love and magic.

I hold my head high, squeeze Luc's hand, and await my crown.

A NOTE FROM BETH

Thank you for reading *Beauty and Deceit*! Reviews make a huge difference to authors and readers. Will you write a short review on Amazon and/or Goodreads? I can't tell you how much I'd appreciate it. (While you're on Amazon, click on my author page and Follow me!)

Straw into Gold is a *free* gender-swapped Rumpelstiltskin retelling, full of romance and adventure! Download it free by visiting carolbethanderson.com and becoming an Email Insider.

ABOUT THE AUTHOR

Carol Beth Anderson is an author and professional audiobook narrator who grew up in Arizona and now lives in Leander, TX, outside Austin. Beth has a husband, two kids, and a miniature schnauzer. Besides writing, she loves baking sourdough bread, knitting, and reading lots and lots of books.

facebook.com/carolbethanderson

twitter.com/CBethAnderson

instagram.com/CBethAnderson

bookbub.com/profile/carol-beth-anderson

goodreads.com/carolbethanderson

amazon.com/author/carolbethanderson

tiktok.com/@cbethanderson